A BARGAIN IS STRUCK

Iain leaned back in his chair, his long hands steady on its carved arms. "There's a mystery here," he said at last. In the sharp shadows she could not read his expression. "You have a small piece of that mystery. And I can guess the shape of it." He leaned forward, and now she could see his face, his expression watchful, thoughtful. "Perhaps together, we know more than we realize."

Linnea's breath caught. "I've told you everything I know."

"I know you think you have," he said. "But there is more. If I could see this thing you describe, or if you could tell me who has it—"

"No," she said, frightened again. She could not follow failure with betrayal.

"Because you can't? Or because you won't?"

"No," she said again, though she knew it was hopeless. Marra had been right—she could not defend herself against these men. She raised her chin and met his eyes.

But—strangely—his gaze had no anger in it. In fact, if such a thing were possible, she would have said there was pity there. She stared at him, and he shook his head a little and said, "You have no ally here. Nor have I. And the secret that's being kept from us—clearly it's dangerous." He looked down at his hands again, then into her eyes, straight and serious. "They don't want us to help each other. And so I think that's what we must do."

THE HIDDEN WORLDS

KRISTIN LANDON

ACE BOOKS, NEW YORK

THE BERKLEY PUBLISHING GROUP
Published by the Penguin Group
Penguin Group (USA) Inc.
375 Hudson Street, New York, New York 10014, USA
Penguin Group (Canada), 90 Eglinton Avenue East, Suite 700, Toronto, Ontario M4P 2Y3, Canada
(a division of Pearson Penguin Canada Inc.)
Penguin Books Ltd., 80 Strand, London WC2R 0RL, England
Penguin Group Ireland, 25 St. Stephen's Green, Dublin 2, Ireland (a division of Penguin Books Ltd.)
Penguin Group (Australia), 250 Camberwell Road, Camberwell, Victoria 3124, Australia
(a division of Pearson Australia Group Pty. Ltd.)
Penguin Books India Pvt. Ltd., 11 Community Centre, Panchsheel Park, New Delhi—110 017, India
Penguin Group (NZ), 67 Apollo Drive, Rosedale, North Shore 0745, Auckland, New Zealand
(a division of Pearson New Zealand Ltd.)
Penguin Books (South Africa) (Pty.) Ltd., 24 Sturdee Avenue, Rosebank, Johannesburg 2196,
South Africa

Penguin Books Ltd., Registered Offices: 80 Strand, London WC2R 0RL, England

This is a work of fiction. Names, characters, places, and incidents either are the product of the author's imagination or are used fictitiously, and any resemblance to actual persons, living or dead, business establishments, events, or locales is entirely coincidental. The publisher does not have any control over and does not assume any responsibility for author or third-party websites or their content.

THE HIDDEN WORLDS

An Ace Book / published by arrangement with the author

PRINTING HISTORY
Ace mass-market edition / July 2007

Copyright © 2007 by Kristin Landon.
Cover art by Craig White.
Cover design by Annette Fiore.
Interior text design by Laura K. Corless.

ISBN: 978-0-441-01511-5

ACE
Ace Books are published by The Berkley Publishing Group,
a division of Penguin Group (USA) Inc.,
375 Hudson Street, New York, New York 10014.
ACE and the "A" design are trademarks belonging to Penguin Group (USA) Inc.

PRINTED IN THE UNITED STATES OF AMERICA

10 9 8 7 6 5 4 3 2 1

For Tom, with love and thanks

I thank my editor, Anne Sowards, for her insight, help, and patience.

This book would not exist without the advice and encouragement of my critique group, the Unstrung Harpies past and present: Patty Hyatt, Karen Keady, Candy Davis, Skye Blaine, Sally-Jo Bowman, and Liane Cordes.

ONE

At dawn, at the slack of the ebb tide, they all went out again to search the beach outside the harbor mouth. Forty people—women and old men—formed a straggling line from the water to the cliff face, walking slowly along the desolate sand. No one spoke. Huddled under her old shawl in the center of the line, Linnea knew why: To name the disaster they were all sure of by now, to give it shape in words, would make it real. And it must not, it *must* not be real. Linnea hunched her shoulders against the stiff dawn wind, against the weight of dread.

Santandru's distant sun rose before them, small and cold, its white glare veiled by thin clouds. Linnea's boots gritted in the coarse, damp sand as she walked, head down, eyes down, searching. Three days now since it happened. Not much chance anything large would have washed in yet. But any clump of seaweed might conceal what they were searching for. The unequivocal proof, the truth. Death.

Because what else could it mean, what old Kiril had seen three nights ago? That flash out at sea, low on the horizon, and then the heavy *thump* that rattled every window, brought every sleeper out into the village street and up to the crest of the ridge to watch the pink glow fade from the clouds. Linnea was sure that her sister Marra had known what it meant. She'd said nothing then, not in front of the children, but Linnea knew that silence. Wives and mothers held to it during bad storms and after, until the *Hope of Moraine* limped into harbor and the losses could be known.

But the *Hope*, due back two days ago, had not come. Linnea poked at a stinking clump of greenthread with her stick. Sandticks popped off it. Nothing underneath. No, that flash meant something bad, worse than any storm. Kiril had gotten on the comm to Middlehaven first thing, asked for an overflight or at least some satellite time for a visual scan. But the flyer was down because of wind, the satellite's scanning systems were out again, and why was Kiril asking this? Surely the comm in the *Hope of Moraine* was working? After all, the law said it had to work, or the boat couldn't go out.

Linnea kicked at a clump of dried ribbonweed. Those soft city people didn't know how it was out here in the villages, with no spare parts left for anything, no techs coming through. Kiril tried to tell them, and Father Haveloe, too, but they didn't listen. They didn't care.

Something bucked loose from the sand almost under her feet, spattering her with cold slime. A mucksucker. She'd stepped on its mantle. She peered down at it. The big creature looked lumpy. It was half-closed around something—something bigger than a sandclaw or a squirt. She

gritted her teeth and flipped the mucksucker over, exposing the rubbery gray flaps that normally squeezed wet sand
into the mouth in the center of its belly. Sometimes they
used the flaps to grab things, anything big and good and
full of food. She tugged the flaps loose. Then went still.
Her heart struck hard and slow, like a bell.

A boot. A fisherman's boot, slick and sodden. Scorched
along one side. Linnea pried it out of the mucksucker's
grasp and toed the creature right-side up again as she
shouted for the others.

They all waited for Kiril to labor up the beach from his
position near the water. He took the boot in his old, steady
hands, the right one thumbless since his accident with the
weed nets in the estuary. He hefted the boot a little. "Something in that." He slid two fingers into the top and his face
changed—drained pale, the lines carved deep. He was old;
she saw how old he was. And his last surviving son had
been on the *Hope*. . . .

Kiril drew his fingers out again and wiped them carefully on his threadbare coat. "It's remains," he said, in a dry
husk of a voice. His grip on the boot tightened. "God help
us all." His eyes were bright, wet. Behind Linnea a woman
sobbed.

Linnea pressed her hands together, squeezing until the
bones hurt. It was true, then. It was real: The *Hope*, the village's only support, was gone. Most of the men in the village were dead. And Marra, her sister Marra, was a widow.

Kiril's faded eyes turned to Linnea. "Linny. You'll fetch
the priest, won't you?"

She nodded and turned away, though she felt the others'
eyes on her. They all had husbands or sons on the *Hope*.
Not her, not Linnea the odd one. Well, let them stay there,

then, gathered around the remains, with the truth coming
slowly.

As it was coming to her. She started up the trail to the
ridgetop. Her chest felt hollow, strange. She'd known
every one of the lost men well. She'd lived all her life—
nineteen standard years—in this village with them. One or
two of the younger ones had offered for her, before she
made it clear she was set against marrying at all. . . .

And Rowdy, Marra's husband. She slowed, steadying
her breath. Rowdy was dead. He'd been good to Linnea,
letting her stay on in his house even after she reached fifteen and took her place on the women's side of the church.
Though she was only his wife's sister, and an orphan, he'd
never pushed her to find a man of her own and be gone.

He'd been good to Marra as well. Sometimes at night
she'd heard them laughing together in their bedroom. Hard
as life was, Rowdy could always laugh—and he could always make everyone else see the joke.

She'd come to the ridgetop. She stopped there and
looked down the other side at the village: two streets, a
huddle of weathered stone and plastic houses, the power
station, the sagging greenhouses, the church that also
served as school and village hall. All had survived centuries of storms—all were off level, propped up, battered
and dull and tough. Wind ruffled the surface of the little
harbor, except in the shelter of the long slip where the
Hope would never tie up again. On the glass green water
there, a film of oil floated. Across the bay and above the
village, barren gravel slopes rose sharply from the water
toward the empty mountains, toward the deep silver sky
layered with clouds. Up there, in the rocky canyons, she
wouldn't be able to see the village, or the little potato fields

in their lattice of high stone walls, or the few stunted Earth trees that still survived. Up there, she could walk in the silence of a world still waiting for life to emerge from the sea. She would go there later today, when Marra didn't need her any more. She could think, up there.

Father Haveloe opened his door at her call. "Linnea!" In spite of his obvious worry, his big face flushed with pleasure at the sight of her. She folded her arms tightly and looked away, and when she looked back his half smile had faded. "There's news?"

"We found part of a body," she said flatly. "They want you to come and say the words." Avoiding his eyes— avoiding the sympathy, the interest she knew would be there—she looked past him into his sitting room. It was a jumbled mess, as it had been ever since his daughter married down to Middlehaven. He should have remarried a long time ago, brought a woman home to see to him. Marra was always saying it.

The priest hesitated a moment, maybe thinking Linnea might need his comfort. But then he turned from the door and gathered up his coat and his little case with the vial of holy water, and the precious packet of Terran soil. *Earth to earth.* "Will you come with me?" he asked her as he pulled the door shut.

She took a deep breath and straightened her hunched shoulders. "I have to tell Marra."

"Ah." One sad syllable. "Tell her I'll come see her when I can." His wide, ruddy face looked puzzled, as if inside himself he were listening for God to explain why this had happened. Linnea nodded briefly, then turned away and started toward home.

The old house stood apart, beyond the end of the upper

street. Linnea's grandmother had wanted it built there, for the gardening space it gave her. Now her treasured lilacs were long dead—sawn-off stumps in the barren ground. Damp laundry, forgotten overnight, snapped on the line in the yard.

Linnea dumped her boots in the mudroom and went on into the house. Marra stood by the battered sink in the kitchen corner, slowly drying the breakfast plates. She looked straight at Linnea. The new pregnancy was past the rough part, and Marra's bloom had been coming back, but all that was gone now. The clear, cool light from the window showed Linnea the blue shadows under Marra's eyes, her black hair lank and half-combed, her light brown skin gone sallow.

Linnea took off her jacket slowly. She wanted to make it right for Marra, to say the right words. But she didn't know them. Father Haveloe usually had this job, when it was one man washed overboard from the *Hope*, or one boy crushed in the weed press, or a child swept off the beach by a rogue wave. But there were too many new widows in the village today. . . . Linnea turned back to her sister. And Marra said it, drying her hands on the faded towel. "They're gone, then." Her voice sounded empty.

"It looks that way." Linnea's throat felt stuffy and tight. "We found something on the beach. Part of—part of a man."

Marra flinched. Then she turned away and opened the stores cupboard.

Linnea saw how little was left of the bricks of compacted algae protein and slabs of dried fish that had been Rowdy's share from last season. It had all been harvested and processed by the *Hope of Moraine* and the men who served on her. But there would be nothing more this year, not even a widow's share. The *Hope* was gone.

"The boat's brain must have gone bad," Marra said, too calmly, her back rigid under her worn gray sweater. "Rowdy said the systems were going. Not just comm. The scanners, too. But he said the engines were the one thing that still worked."

"Marra . . ." Linnea touched her shoulder.

Marra spun and faced her, hot-eyed. "You're glad now, aren't you? You're glad Rowdy let you hide in our house, scared to take a husband to your bed. *This* is why!"

Linnea gripped her sister's arms. "Marra, don't! Don't, you don't mean it—"

"*You* don't need to weep today," Marra said, her mouth twisted with grief. "Maybe you knew the way of it after all. Sneak down to the beach with them, yes, but don't marry them. Don't put your life in their hands. Don't give—anything—" She broke off. Linnea stood stiffly, aching, afraid to try to touch her again. Marra's words hurt. They hurt all the worse because they were true.

Then she saw Marra and Rowdy's two small boys, wide-eyed in the corner of the kitchen, silent, aghast. She went to them and took their cold, grubby hands in hers. Nothing would ever be the same again, and as young as they were, they both seemed to know it. Beyond them, their baby sister sat playing with a set of carved fishes.

Donie, the younger boy, looked up at Linnea. "Da's drowned," he said in a small voice. "But it's all right. Orry and I can go into the boat instead."

"Not if there's no boat," Orry said, and his face tightened. "That's what they're saying, isn't it, Linny?"

"Shhhh," Linnea told him. She was dry-eyed and strong,

strong enough for this or anything. She went to her sister and gathered her close, and in her arms Marra began, at last, to weep.

L innea didn't get up the mountain that day, or that week. Marra's strength had held through those three days of hopeless waiting, but now it was gone. She lay in the bed she had shared with Rowdy, crying hard sometimes, other times staring at the pale sunlight that glimmered through the cracked blinds. At night she prowled the house restlessly, looking in on the children, opening the front door and staring down toward the empty harbor. After the first night Linnea called in Eddo, the medtech, who measured out a dose of sedative for Marra and watched her until she slept.

In the ordinary way of things, a new widow's house would be full of helpers and advice-givers, with plenty of food brought in and plenty of people to watch the children. But as things were, all that was Linnea's job alone. She worked hard at it, scrubbing and straightening, keeping everything as Marra liked it. The work kept Linnea calm: each job familiar, each in its turn. This task, then the next, then the next. . . . No end to it. No time to let fear in.

Over those few days the search parties found more fragments on the beach—some human, some parts of the *Hope*. There were funerals. Linnea kept working. Sometimes when she looked at Orry and saw how he was getting to have Rowdy's dark, deep-set eyes, or when she picked up some toy that Rowdy had carved, she would close herself into her tiny room and wait to cry—but she never did. All that was dammed up somewhere. Or maybe she had used it all up years ago, in those long months when Ma was dying.

Well, Linnea was grateful to have a clear head. There was thinking to do, and just now she was the only one to do it.

The village was dying fast. Kiril had spent hours on the comm, but there were no more boats like the *Hope of Moraine* to be had—boats whose brains had come from offworld. All the money in the village wouldn't pay a tenth of what it would cost to import another brain. And without a brain, without its warning systems and control systems, a boat had no chance against the thick atmosphere, the powerful weather, the steep, slow chop of the low-gravity ocean. Even master fishermen needed those systems to sense changes in the water, read the sky, figure the currents—to be sure they'd find the weedbeds and the shoals of eely fish that the *Hope* had harvested.

Though no one yet dared to speak the truth out loud, Linnea knew it as surely as she knew her name: After two hundred years, the battle was over, and Moraine had lost. The land alone couldn't keep a village alive, not on Santandru, with its bitter winters, its chill, wet summers, its bare unliving soil that had to be fed and fed and fed to keep anything growing. Only the sea was alive—the sea, the source of life. Moraine could no longer harvest the sea. So Moraine was doomed.

She knew they had only one choice now: evacuation. Flatloaders were coming from Middlehaven, bringing a few emergency supplies, and the Governing Committee had offered a free ride back to any takers. Free housing until they found work. Food, too, for widows and orphans at least.

After she heard, Linnea stayed up late, alone in the shabby kitchen, and thought some more. It would tear Marra's heart to leave this house. But Linnea couldn't think of any way around the truth. Best walk forward into what was coming rather than backing into it, because either way it *was* coming. She, and her sister, and the children would leave Moraine with everything they could carry. There wasn't much chance for them in Middlehaven, big and busy as it was. But there was no chance here.

She explained it all to Marra the next day, after the last of the funerals. And Marra just nodded. Her wide-boned face looked bleak and bare, with all her hair knotted out of sight under the black mourning shawl. She'd lost the baby on the eighth day after the accident, bleeding all night in silence. Afterward she wandered around the house as if she was looking for something, or someone. The children kept out of her way, clinging instead to Linnea. It was Linnea who fed them all, kept them clean, held them when they cried. It was Linnea who gathered their lives into a few battered boxes, all they'd be allowed to take on the flatloader.

When the day came, Marra and the children were ready. Grimly, fiercely, Linnea herded them all out the door. Then she walked around the outside of the house, closing the shutters and barring them tight. In five winters, or ten, the house would be gone. But let it stand as long as it could.

Linnea hated Middlehaven. She'd been there once, six years before, when Ma was dying and the medtechs had wanted to try some special treatment. Fifty thousand people lived there—people everywhere she looked. And she could not escape into wilderness. The town and its bay sheltered behind a rock ridge, and north across the bay were a hundred kilometers of river delta and estuary, an eerie wasteland of stinking red-brown slime algae and the eye-piercing green of carpet moss. On this side, close to the water, the bayside was lined with fish- and algae-processing plants, and the smell rose to the highest street whenever the wind turned northerly.

Linnea thought Middlehaven looked even worse now, dirtier, more crowded. It was full of refugees like her—desperate to find work, to find themselves a new place, to get out of there. Everywhere she went she saw them. Threadbare, hungry-looking, eyes empty of hope. The people Linnea knew from Moraine disappeared among them. She often went all day without seeing a familiar face, until she went back to the indigent barracks for the one hot meal: weed soup and biscuit, with fish on Sundays and Wednesdays. Then it was time to bed down beside Marra and the children, on a hard, damp bunk in a room full of other women and children from Moraine, and get what sleep she could. The surviving men and older boys from the village were out on work crews, road repair mostly, gone for days at a time. They earned a little money against the time when the charity would run out.

Linnea tried to get onto a work crew, but the social service agency turned her down. She was a woman; she might be pregnant; the work was too hard, too dangerous. She found Father Haveloe at his daughter's house and had him certify that she'd never been married. Then the agency wouldn't take her because an unmarried woman her age might not be stable. Linnea went into an office and wrote down answers to a long list of questions, so many that her hand ached from the writing. The agency looked over her answers, and then they sent her a letter that said she couldn't be on a work crew because she was the only stable adult in her family, with her sister and three children emotionally dependent on her.

Linnea kept the letter to herself. It had been her last real hope of getting steady work—any work at all—and the refusal sounded final. No choice left but to go on Perpetual Charity. Living in barracks, on the edge of hunger. Rowdy's boys growing up on the street. Rosa begging—

No. *Let* them tell her their decision was final; she was going to appeal it anyway. She made an appointment with the man who had sent the letter. Asper Cogorth, he'd signed it. Social Services, Middlehaven.

It was a sodden spring day, but she walked all the way downtown to save tram fare. Social Services turned out to be a metal shed next to a patch of mud where a rusted set of swings and a couple of benches stood unused. A faded sign called it EAST MIDDLEHAVEN PUBLIC PARK.

She climbed the shed's narrow steps, pushed the door open, and went inside. In the small, dim anteroom, a colorless young man sat at a table scanning tattered documents into storage crystals. As Linnea hung her rain jacket on a peg to drip, the man glanced at her and jerked his chin toward an inner door. She opened it and went in.

Asper Cogorth was waiting for her. When she entered, he stood up and took her offered hand politely, then gestured her into a chair. The two chairs and a worktable barely fit, jammed in between piles of document boxes. The room had the faint, salty smell of mildew. "We've just gotten our storage system up and running again," Asper said. "Soon I'll have some space in here." He had long gray hair and a kind expression, and Linnea found herself wanting to like him, in spite of his soft hands. "Now. How can I help you?"

Linnea took the letter out of her pocket and handed it to him. "I'm trying to find work. My sister's husband died, and we've no other family to keep us. She has her three children to tend. But I can work. I'm as strong as a lot of men, and I know a little about some of the trades. Building and masonry. And I kept some of the old machines running at our house in Moraine, a long time after everyone else had junked theirs."

"School?"

She remembered Da's words. *When you're not sure of yourself, Linny, look them straight in the eye and tell the truth.* "Just priest-school until I was thirteen. But our priest went on lending me books after that. I've read most of what he has, maybe forty books."

He made a note. "How old are you? Standard years."

"Nineteen."

"A village girl ought to be long married by your age."

Linnea sighed inwardly. "I thought of it once. He drowned." She had never felt that much for Teor, even after he died. But it made a decent excuse.

"And since then?"

"I don't see that it's your business."

"I'm judging your fitness for work," he said mildly.

"I—" She thought. "I never met anyone that—was worth the risk."

"The risk?"

"When they die." She met his startled look. "They always do die. I've seen what it did to my ma. And now my sister. Nothing's worth that."

Asper made another note. Linnea tried not to look down

at the paper. "I need work," she said. "The children can't grow up in those barracks. That's not a home. And my sister—she needs a home, too, a place where she can feel safe. I don't think she'll be well again until she has that." Linnea shifted uncomfortably in her chair. The room felt too warm for the clothes she had. "You say I'm supposed to take care of them, but do you see, work is the only way I can do that. Get them what they need. Then my sister will be all right, and they won't depend on me so much." She looked nervously away at the one window. It was fogged over, but she could hear rain slashing down outside. She wished she were out in it, in the cold, fresh wind.

Asper settled back in his chair. "Miss Kiaho, there are many people in your situation now. Your persistence impresses me, and if I did find something appropriate, I would of course think of you." He shook his head. "I'm sorry to say that it's unlikely."

So it was no. Bitterness burned in her eyes, in her throat. And the question in her heart— She took a breath and asked it. "Why is this happening? Why is everything going bad?"

He glanced down at her letter. "You mean, why did your village's boat explode?"

"I guess." She sighed. "Father Haveloe—that's our priest—he says some questions have no answers."

"That one has an answer." Asper folded his hands on the table. "You saw the skyport on the way into town. Any jumpships?"

"No," she said. "I don't think I've ever seen one. But I don't come here much."

"Neither do the jumpships," Asper said. "Only two or three a year now. Sometimes they come late, or not at all.

It isn't up to us. It's up to the Pilot Masters, the great men of the Line, in their palaces on Nexus."

"Do the ships make that much difference?" Linnea looked at him. "A little mail, a little news—"

"—A few spare parts," Asper said. "Technical bulletins. New software for the brains. Diagnostic tools. Sometimes even a technician on long rounds. We couldn't afford much, but it was available when we had to buy it. But now it can be a year between asking and getting."

"So in the meantime, things go bad, bit by bit."

Asper nodded vigorously. "It's worse in the outlying villages like Moraine. But it's bad everywhere. Your village's boat wasn't the first major loss, and there will be more. And then when we're cut off entirely—" He shrugged.

"Then everything goes," Linnea said. She felt the slow anger building. "And we die."

"A few of us might survive along the south coast," Asper said. "Gathering squirts and box clams. Living no better than humans did before civilization began, back on Earth. But I doubt it. The land is too empty. The climate is too harsh."

Linnea thought. "Can't you appeal this to anyone? When it's life and death?"

"There's no appeal," Asper said. "The Pilot Masters, the men of the Line—they decide, and the decision is final. They control all the communications, all the cargo, all the passengers that come in and out of every world. No one else can do what they do, run their damned ships—excuse me. That gives them total power."

She stared at him, her thoughts racing. "But—the Line, they saved us all from the Cold Minds. They brought us from Earth to the Hidden Worlds. Why would they change their minds now? Why would they decide to leave us to die?"

"If we knew that," Asper said, "we might have more of a chance." He was staring out at the rain, but Linnea couldn't guess what he was seeing. Then he seemed to come back to himself. "So, Miss Kiaho. A word of advice."

Linnea nodded permission.

"If a likely man does offer you marriage, take him. Raise a family. Have a good life while you can. It's all ending. You should have your share of it."

Linnea sat straight. "Is that all that's being done?" Her hands were fists in her lap. "Is that all *you're* doing, you and the others? Are we supposed to lie down and die?"

"No, of course not," he said, his face reddening. "But you must understand, in this situation we have no power at all. The Pilot Masters won't listen to us."

"That's no excuse." Anger shook her. "Out there in the villages, we trust you people. We think when things are hard, well, those people in Middlehaven—they'll know what to do. You're educated. You aren't helpless. Not like we were, when we lost the *Hope*." She stood up. "And now I find out you're *not* fighting for us. You're burrowing into the sand, like a mucksucker in a storm. And you're telling me to burrow, too. Well, I won't. My family is not going to starve because someone like you tells me there's no choice. I will by God *find* a choice. Or make one."

Asper was standing now, too, by the window, resting one hand against the glass. His eyes were on her. "You've said enough, I think." His voice was strangely mild.

"Enough to make you ashamed, then," she said. She had to get out of here, or she was going to cry in front of him. "I want you to be ashamed. You're not a man. My da was a man. He drowned off the *Hope of Moraine*, trying to carry a line out to a man swept overboard. He knew there wasn't much chance. But he did it. I would've done it, too. But you, you'd be below, wouldn't you, puking in a bucket from the nasty waves."

She made it out of his room, out of the building, into the street before she cried. No hope, no hope. She walked all the way back to the barracks in the rain.

TWO

I t took Linnea the rest of the afternoon to decide
whether to tell Marra the bad news. Her sister was already too close to despair, clinging only to the hope that
Linnea would find work somehow.

And now that hope was all but ended. Linnea had
kitchen duty that afternoon, and she was glad to be away
from Marra for the moment. As she broke the heavy bis-
cuits into shares, then set them out on metal trays, her
hands still shook with remembered anger. Her whole body
felt heavy, aching with strain and weariness—from keeping Marra's spirits up, from making up hopeful things to
say in front of the children.

No, she could not go on lying. It was time for Marra to
face at least part of the truth.

That night after supper, when the children were asleep,
Linnea took Marra into the cold, dank sitting room of the
women's barracks. They sat down, knee to knee, on hard

metal chairs in one corner. Four old women were playing a chance game with worn tiles at a table in the other corner. The endless rain drummed on the metal roof, giving Linnea and Marra enough privacy to speak.

There was no reason to put it in a lot of words. She showed Marra the letter from Asper Cogorth. Marra struggled through it slowly, frowning. She still hid her hair under a shawl, for mourning, and her new thinness made her look stark, old, defeated. She handed the letter back. "It's no, then." Her voice was tight.

"Really no," Linnea said. "I even went and talked to him today, the one who wrote that. He says there's no work for me. Nothing at all."

Marra sat tensely with her hand cupping her chin. "He was sure? You're sure?"

"Yes." Linnea looked down at her hands. "I'll keep going out, in case something new turns up. But—"

"Cleaning? Watching babies?"

"Marra, I asked everywhere. No one's hiring. There are so many people like us now. Anyone who can afford to pay any wage, any wage at all, they have their pick. And most of the work, they only want men." Linnea took Marra's hand. She'd hoped that if she found work, Marra would finally come out of her fog of grief, finally think of the children and look to the future. And now this. She sighed. "Don't worry. I know something will turn up. This Asper Cogorth—he didn't say he'd *never* have anything for me. Just not right now."

Marra bit her lip. "Not right now. But time is running out." She pulled her hand from Linnea's, closed her eyes, sat up straight. "I wish I knew. . . ."

Linnea looked up at her, puzzled. "Knew what?"

Marra opened her eyes and frowned at her. "What to say. How much to tell you." She glanced at the women across the room, all clearly absorbed in their game.

Linnea shook her head. "Marra, if there's anything—"

"All right." Marra looked serious. "All right. Now listen, Linny, and you have to promise this doesn't go past you. Ma— When Ma was—dying, she told me something."

That old ache, the months when Linnea had been shut out, the last months of Ma's life. "What did she tell you?" *And not me.*

"An old story." Marra looked away. "There was a cousin once, of ours. Long back, far back. Died when Ma was a baby. But she heard of him all the same. He—he did something we don't like to speak of." She took a deep breath. "He worked on Nexus. He was a contract servant there, two terms. Ten years standard."

Linnea stared at her. "But—people from Santandru don't do that."

Marra's face was set like stone. "No. We don't. But this cousin, he wanted to be rich."

"So what happened?" She'd heard whispers about Nexus. Things she didn't understand.

"Ma never heard any details, but you know the kind of filth—I mean, you can guess. The men there. What they want from us." Her glance flicked aside. "Both women and men."

Linnea shivered. "Maybe he had to do it. Had to have the money, for family."

Marra dropped her voice further. "Ma said he came back rich. But no one in his family would take the money. He was sick in his soul. The money just slipped away from him, wasted. All spent, long past. Dirty money—I wouldn't want it for Rowdy's babies even if I had it in a sack."

Linnea sat back in her chair and sighed. "So—if the money's gone, why are you telling me this?"

Marra flushed. "This cousin—he brought something back with him. He said it was valuable. He never married, of course. No woman would have him. He passed this thing to his cousin, his ma's sister's daughter. And that was our Gram. He told Gram a story about it, and she told Ma." Marra looked down at the table. "And Ma told me, when she gave it to me." Her hand strayed to her breast, to the little sheep-leather sack that Linnea knew held Ma's wedding ring.

"So tell me this story," Linnea said.

"I don't know much," Marra said. "But Ma said it had something to do with a family on Nexus. That it was proof of some kind of scandal."

"That's not much to go on." Linnea shook her head. "Do they *have* families on Nexus?"

"Not like ours." Marra licked her lips. "They bring in women to have their babies, and only the Line men are allowed to be fathers. That's their families, the men and their sons. But the thing our cousin brought back—he said it was proof of something wrong, a terrible secret in one of their great families."

Linnea frowned. "What kind of thing is it?"

"A little silver tube." Marra held up her fingers a few centimeters apart. "Tiny, really. Sealed at both ends. What's in it, I can't guess. But Ma knew one more thing about it." She leaned close. "She said Gram told her this one Line family, the one our cousin worked for, they'd give about anything to have hold of this thing again."

"Why?"

Marra shook her head. "I don't know. I know they're terribly touchy about this Line they have. Father to son to son, on down like that. Maybe—maybe there was some kind of break in that Line." She shrugged. "I don't really understand it. I don't think Ma did either. She said a name, and I wrote it down. I've got it in the family papers back in the barracks. But you see, Linny, a family scandal, even an old one, I guess that's a terrible thing on Nexus—a shame they would do anything to hide." She looked away. "*Pay* anything to hide, maybe even."

Linnea leaned back in her chair. In the other corner the game was breaking up. They both waited while the women left the room. On the way out one said, "Leave you the lamp, dearies?"

"Yet awhile," Marra said to her. "We'll see to it, and thanks, Auntie."

When they were alone, Linnea said, "So. What do we do with this thing?"

Marra licked her lips nervously. "I was thinking, maybe if we got some advice, we could send a message to Nexus. That family—maybe they'd want to give us some money for this thing. To thank us for finding it. I mean, it might be possible. And that would solve everything."

"Doesn't seem like much of a chance," Linnea said, as much to herself as to Marra. "Gram's cousin—that was a long time ago. No one alive now who was alive then, not even on Nexus. Why would they still care about this old metal tube?"

"I don't know if they would," Marra said. "After all, people here have almost forgotten that cousin and the whole shame of it. I never thought it was worth stirring up that old stinkpond." Her mouth twisted. "But now—"

"You're right," Linnea said. Anything that looked like hope to Marra, anything at all, was better than what she'd brought into this room with her. "You're right. We need to get advice about this. And maybe if we ask enough people, we'll even learn what this thing is."

Marra was silent for a while. The rain swelled to a roar on the roof, then faded again. "I—I guess that's so. But Linny—I think there's something bad about this thing. Not just shame. It *means* something bad. I'm sure of it. So was Ma. That's really why we always kept it to us, to the women—why we always left it alone." She looked down at the table. "And then there's the family shame—to our name, Rosa's name—"

"Shame is for people who aren't hungry," Linnea said.

Marra nodded slowly. "Go ahead, then, Linny. Do it. Ask."

Linnea got to her feet. "I know just where to start."

That evening, Linnea wrote another letter to Asper Cogorth. She explained about the artifact from Nexus and asked, with careful politeness, whether Asper knew what it might be—and if not, whether he would be willing to try to find out for her.

Her middle finger hurt from the writing. She hoped Asper would be able to help her; he had seemed kind enough, and he was the only man she knew in Middlehaven government. She posted the letter on Friday and began again to wait. The little tube from Nexus occupied her mind strangely. Marra had shown it to her early that morning, careful that no one else saw; and Linnea found she could not forget it. Marra had said she sensed evil in it. Linnea sensed—something she couldn't name. Possibility, maybe.

Once the letter was safely sent, Marra seemed to gain strength just from hope. She began again to be firm with the children and to phrase her requests to Linnea more definitely. On Sunday, for the first time since Rowdy's funeral, she insisted that they all go to church.

Church only sharpened Linnea's grief for the home she would never see again. The priest had a strong voice, and there was plenty of music, but most of it was unfamiliar. It didn't comfort her or move her as the plain singing in Moraine's church had sometimes done—when she would feel, for a minute, as if she were part of something whole, part of the village. Here there were too many people, some in good clothes that made Linnea feel shabby.

Other things were strange as well. At Eucharist she thought the juice had spoiled, until she realized it must be real wine. And even though all the windows had pure, clear glass in them, lamps burned everywhere, not just on the altar. They smelled sweet, not like fish oil, and they didn't smoke. She remembered when she was small, back home, how she'd thought the little church's smoke-black ceiling was the dark of space, with God hidden there looking down at her. It had made her feel safe, until Da drowned, and Ma died; then she imagined God lurking up there, brooding over which one to take next.

She was glad when the service was over and she could come blinking out into the bright spring day. The sun's distant companion star had just risen, a red spark that tinged the mists over the estuary with copper. She was about to comment that they were going to be late for dinner, when someone touched her shoulder. She turned quickly and saw Asper Cogorth smiling at her, his odd light eyes assessing.

Her breath caught. This had to be good news. "God's peace be with you," she stammered.

His smile did not change. "And also with you."

She smiled back at him, tightly. With his hair tied back for church he looked short-haired, like a fisherman—a little like Da, except that his skin was so pale. She turned toward Marra, intending to introduce her, but her sister had already gathered up the children and started home.

"I've been looking for you," Asper said.

"Why didn't you ask for me at the barracks, then?"

"I know those barracks. There's no place private where you and I could talk."

She felt a prickle of excitement. One finger light on her arm, he was guiding her away from the church steps. She looked back. They were already out of earshot of other people. Sudden caution stopped her—city men and country girls, she'd heard stories. "What is this about? Did you get my letter?"

"Yes. And I do have information for you. But we can't discuss it here." He was looking straight into her eyes, nothing ashamed about him, but still she felt that sense of warning. He stirred impatiently. "May we go just a little farther along, please?"

Linnea looked past him at a knot of young mothers chatting in the sunlight. There were houses and people all around, and if she shouted for help, help would come. "All right."

She walked on with him, her heart beating hard. At the end of the second block they came to a school, empty on a

Sunday. A sun-warmed concrete bench stood at the edge of the playground, a desolate stretch of dried mud. The low stone school stood mute, shuttered with corroded metal. "Let's sit down," Asper said.

They sat, and Asper went on, "First, I must ask you—if anyone inquires why we met today, you must tell them I was checking on your search for work."

She sat up straighter on the bench. "Why should I lie to them?"

He shrugged. "If you *want* people to know that your family has had dealings with Nexus, then by all means, tell the truth."

"Oh!" Her hands caught at each other and gripped hard. "So you know what this thing is, what I told you about?"

Asper looked up at the silver sky. "As a matter of fact, Miss Kiaho, you've solved a small mystery for me. For a number of years now I've had a packet in my files. A packet from Nexus, accompanied by very specific instructions." He turned to face her. "I was to offer the packet to anyone who came forward with something such as you describe."

Linnea stared at him, her heart unsteady with hope. "Did you open it?"

"I opened it long ago," Asper said, "looking for a clue. But it was only another mystery."

"What did it say?" She held herself tensely to keep from trembling. "Is it something valuable?"

He looked at her oddly, almost pityingly. "It has value of a sort. It's a work contract."

"You mean—indentures? For Nexus? Oh—" She sagged. "Worthless."

"Yes," Asper said. "I'm sorry. This is why I didn't want to tell you this in a letter, or where others might hear."

Tears of disappointment stung her eyes. She struggled to keep her voice steady. "Are you *sure* there was nothing else?"

He looked offended. "I'm quite sure."

Well, if he was lying, there was nothing she could do about it. She blinked back the tears. "But why would someone on Nexus want me to take a work contract?"

Asper shrugged. "Perhaps they wish to negotiate face-to-face, with someone who is in their power."

"Then maybe they do want it after all," she said slowly. "This thing of Marra's." The contract was worthless—but the little tube, that might still be worth something. There had to be some way she could use it.

"It's possible, I suppose," Asper said. "I can try to help you. If you wish, I could write to them for you, as your man of business. If I explain that it's impossible for you to come to them, then perhaps they'll find another way."

"How long would that take?"

"There should be a ship within the next two months," Asper said. "If the message went on that ship and went out on the commnet at its next port, it might take only one or two more months to find its way to Nexus. But of course the reply would have to wait for another ship to touch here—"

"Which might never happen." Linnea spread her hand flat on the dry concrete of the bench. "I'd like to see the contract." She was not sure why.

"Certainly," Asper said. "It's yours, after all, according to the instructions. But it's at my office, and of course I can't open on a Sunday. You'll have to come tomorrow."

An idea was stirring, deep in her mind—an idea that frightened her. Best not stop to consider. "What sort of contract is it?"

He shrugged. "It seems standard, from what I know— five years on Nexus, serving a man whose name I can't recall." His odd look sharpened, but he went on casually, "It's ten thousand trade points."

She caught her breath. "That much money!"

"On some worlds it's an accepted way to get one's start in life," Asper said. "Not here. Never here."

She looked down, uncomfortable. "Does it say—what sort of service?" Her mouth was dry—the idea was taking shape now, becoming even more frightening.

"It's a contract for house service," Asper said. "Whatever that means. You might be able to sell the contract itself—if you could find a buyer. If you cared to advertise that you possess such a thing."

"I wasn't thinking that," she said.

He sat up straight and sighed. "Miss Kiaho, if you're thinking you might accept this contract, set the thought out of your mind. Yes, you would be paid a great deal of money—but the money could never restore your reputation." He glanced at her. "You would lose all hope of respectable marriage."

But he'd seen her tests—he must know how little that meant to her. "That much money would keep Marra and the children for years. Forever."

"No!" He shook his head firmly. "I tell you again, you must not. I—I *cannot* help you destroy your life."

Linnea thought quickly. If she took this contract, she had to have someone's help—someone to see that Marra was provided for during the years Linnea was gone. But that was a great deal to ask. What could she offer in return that Asper truly wanted?

What did any of them want? *Hope.* "There's more involved than the money," she said, her heartbeat slow and heavy in her chest.

He looked at her, frowning slightly. "What would that be?"

"The tube, the silver tube Marra has." She licked her lips. "It's proof of some kind of scandal, she says. That man on Nexus must want it, or he wouldn't have sent that contract. Who knows what he might pay for the tube—if I went there and offered it to him? It might be enough to help this whole world."

"No amount of money would help us," Asper said. His face was flushed, his eyes intent. "What we need is a new trade contract."

She straightened her shoulders. "Then that's what I'll ask for."

He let out a sharp breath, then got to his feet and turned his back to her. "If we thought—if there was any real possibility—" He broke off.

"I don't see any other hope," she said.

He turned back to her, his face pale. "I should never have spoken of it to you."

"Yes, you should." She remembered when Ma was dying. When all hope was finally gone, and Marra still would not let Ma be told. She'd lied, and made Linnea lie. Things had gone unspoken, important things—and then it was too late. Ma could no longer speak. Then on the last night, when the hospital's priest came in and started the last rites—that flash of rage in Ma's eyes, the accusation of betrayal. Aimed at Linnea.

"You must swear not to tell anyone we are losing our trade contract," Asper said. "Not even your sister. There could be a panic. The jumpships that stop here are linkers, mostly—commnet ships. They can carry three or four passengers at most. There are more than half a million people on this planet. It is impossible for us to be evacuated."

She stood up and faced him. "There are passenger ships!"

"They carry a hundred at most," Asper said. "And we can't hire even one ship. We can't afford it." He looked away across the flat, cracked expanse of the playing field. "We're trying everything. The Middlehaven government is attempting to influence the trade partners we have left on other worlds to speak for us. If Nexus breaks precedent and cuts us off, we won't be the last; anyone must see that." He looked down, his eyes shadowed. "And—others of us, acting outside the government—against all custom, we've sent direct appeals to Nexus." His voice roughened. "But they haven't bothered to reply."

The sunlight was gone now. A few raindrops pattered on the dried mud all around them, raising the sharp scent of damp dirt. "All right," Linnea said. Her voice sounded strained to her own ears. "So I'm offering to try to help." Her heart beat slowly in her chest, like a hammer striking a rock. "That contract, it's an opportunity. And I've no husband or children. Nothing to tie me here." She chose her next words with care. "I could go if—*if* I knew Marra and the children would be taken care of while I was gone." Asper had mentioned others—with their help, surely Marra could be kept safe.

Asper sank down on the bench, leaned forward to rest his elbows on his knees. His hands dangled, loosely clasped, between them. "I admire your courage, Miss Kiaho."

"Courage?" Linnea looked down at him, then off across the bare dirt of the schoolyard at a line of brown brick houses, square and neat. If she'd ever had any courage, she'd have been married by now—not let herself be scared off by fear of a man's temper. Fear of the marriage bed, that her man would be rough like Teor. Fear of childbirth, of widowhood . . .

Fear of pain.

She struggled to speak. "I don't have any courage. It just seems like there's no hope any more, not for my sister or for any of us. And this—" Her hands gripped each other and tightened. "This is a chance to change that."

"But the risk—the cost to you—" His voice was ragged.

Her knees felt shaky. She sat down beside him on the bench. "Please. Let me try." It didn't seem possible that she could get a new trade contract out of Nexus—it would be impossible to bribe such wealth, or blackmail such power. But that didn't matter. Seeing to Marra was what mattered; to achieve that, she would agree to anything. Say anything. "If you turn me down," Linnea said, "then you *aren't* trying everything you can think of. Are you?"

He rubbed his forehead wearily, but he did not reply for a long time. Linnea waited, shivering a little in the freshening breeze. Rain spattered her face. Asper looked up at the sky, then at Linnea. He sighed again. "All right." His face was set firm. "All right. I'll help you."

Linnea went cold clear through. Once, on a country ramble, she had climbed a long, even slope at a fine pace, singing a little as she swung along, looking up at the clouds—and then she'd happened to glance at the ground a few meters ahead, and she saw it. A sheer drop into a gulf of air. A glacier valley, vast and shadowed and empty, with a white thread of river at the bottom so far away she couldn't even hear it. She could have fallen, fallen so far . . . Mastering her breath, she said shakily, "Thank you."

"You'll be all right." He spoke rapidly, not looking at her. "You're a sensible person. And they have laws on Nexus to protect you. The contracts spell it out—household service, nothing more, unless you give free consent." He sounded as if he were trying to convince himself, not her. "I'll help you prepare. By my estimate, we have at least six weeks before the ship arrives."

Linnea stared at the dirt at her feet, stirred it with the toe of her shabby boot. When she was sure her voice was steady, she said, "So, then. What about Marra? I can't do this unless I know she's out of those barracks."

"I—think I can arrange for a house," Asper said. "An allowance for food and clothes. School fees for the children. Then when you return, your earnings from Nexus will repay the debt and still keep you all very comfortably."

There was one more thing to settle. One danger she must consider. She looked straight at him. "What if I never come back?"

He swallowed hard. "If—if anything does happen to you, your family will be cared for. As if they were my own. That's a personal promise, not an official one."

"And how do I know what your promise is worth?"

He hesitated, then said, "You could have been my daughter, if I'd ever married. If I allow you to take such a risk, even for such a prize, I owe you my protection. My word. And my help. You have a great deal to learn about Nexus."

She stood up and walked a few steps onto the field, then stood with her back to him. Five years. Could she trust this Middlehaven officeman? Would he look after Marra?

Linnea turned. He was looking at her so hopefully. She took a breath. "If my family will be all right," she said, "I don't care what happens to me. I accept your offer."

S he got back to the barracks long after supper, her copy of the signed contract in the pocket of her coat. In the dim, cold bunkroom, Marra was sitting on the edge of the bunk she shared with Rosa, knitting with picked yarn while the baby slept. Donie and Orry breathed softly in the upper bunk. Marra looked up sharply as Linnea's shadow fell over her. But she said nothing until she and Linnea had gone out onto the dark porch. A light across the yard flickered as the wind shook it. Cold wind, but Marra didn't seem to feel it. She spoke in a hissing whisper. "God's own sake, Linny! Where have you *been*?"

Looking at her, Linnea felt thirteen years old again—after Ma died, when Marra had stepped right in to mothering Linnea. She hadn't wanted another mother just then. Those had been hard times, but she'd learned a few things. Such as how to take Marra off the boil. "I found work," she said.

Marra gasped. "Work? Where?"

Linnea felt sick. She wished she could just hand Marra the contract. But Marra didn't read so well, and legal documents made her nervous. "It's—offworld. For a while."

"Off—? How long?"

"I'll be gone seven standard years," Linnea said, and rushed on. "It's board and room for me, so the cash salary can go to you and the children. Plenty to keep you and pay school fees. There's a house that goes with it. On a good street, and the school's fifty meters away. Three rooms and a kitchen, Marra!"

"Seven years," Marra said softly, and then frowned. "A house, and all that money. What can you do that's worth so much?"

Of course, of course Marra would suspect—shrewd Marra, who thought the worst of every new idea. Suddenly Linnea wished she'd had Marra with her this afternoon, to talk her out of this. Linnea looked at the floor. "I'm going to Nexus."

She heard Marra's sharply indrawn breath. "No, you're not!"

"Yes, I am." Linnea glared at her sister. "Marra, I've signed a contract. It's too late."

"It's never too late," Marra said fiercely. "You're too young. I don't know what anyone told you, what they promised you, but haven't you ever heard what they do, what it's like to serve on Nexus?"

"I've heard," Linnea said. "But this isn't like that. I'm trying to help our family. And more than our family."

"Oh, I don't doubt it." Marra's voice was cold. "No. We'll void the contract in the morning, as soon as we can get to a magistrate."

"Marra—"

"Then I want you to take me to the person who got you to do this. God knows what else they might've—"

"Marra, I'm past eighteen, standard years."

"So? You've never been married."

"I'm of legal age," Linnea said clearly. "By intercolony treaty. They don't care whether I've ever been married. All that counts is how old I am. And I'm old enough."

Marra sat down heavily on a bench against the wall. "Oh, Linny . . ." Tears made her voice tight.

Linnea sat down beside her. "It's for you. It's for Rowdy's babies, Marra. And I won't be hurt. I promise." Marra's resistance was firming Linnea's resolve. *Can't you be grateful? Can't you let me choose? Just once?*

"You're putting yourself in their hands," Marra said, almost weeping. "And you don't know them."

Linnea turned on the bench to face her sister. "No, I don't know them. But Ma didn't know Da before she came in from Outer Reach to marry him."

"But it was marriage Da gave her, marriage in church, before she ever set foot in his house. Linny, you always bend things to fit what you want, and you're not seeing this straight, this—contract thing."

"They're rich on Nexus," Linnea said. "They could have machines to do their work, but they like having people serve them because it shows off how rich they are. It's bringing them things when they call for them, and handing plates around. It's not like being a slave. They have laws that—"

"It *is* being a slave," Marra said. "No matter what their laws say. They've got the power, and you've got nothing. You have to do whatever they want."

"It's not so different from here, then," Linnea said. "For a woman."

Marra gripped Linnea's arm. "If you can't see the difference between honest marriage to a good man and— *that . . .*"

Linnea kept herself from speaking. Marra went on, "Those men, they're so rich, ordinary life isn't fine enough for them. It's got to be something new and with a bad taste to it before they feel anything. They don't marry. They don't even let women live there unless they've got a contract. They don't even let girl babies be *born* there, haven't you heard that? Because women can't be jump pilots, and that's all they want, more of themselves."

Linnea's doubts faded, swallowed up by the old familiar anger. Here was Marra, cutting her off again. Deciding for her. "I don't care."

"Someday you will." Marra's dark voice shook.

Linnea sighed. "I'm doing it, Marra."

Marra scrubbed the back of her hand across her eyes. "When?"

"In a month or two. As soon as the next ship comes."

"Go, then." Marra stood up and looked down at Linnea. "Go your own way, Linny. I'll take the money you get for selling yourself, for Rowdy's little ones I'll take it. But when you get back, stay away from us. Stay away from Rosa. I don't want anyone saying her name with yours. Someday, some man might want to marry *her*."

Tears were cold on Linnea's cheeks. "Marra—"

But Marra was gone. The door slapped shut behind her.

Alone, Linnea dragged her sleeve across her eyes and slumped back against the wall. The chill crept back as her anger faded, replaced by sadness. The porch looked north over the roof of a processing plant. Beyond the estuary, a broad, forlorn plain of mud glimmered in the starlight. She looked up. It was cold, getting colder. The stars trembled in the wet west wind, trembled through her tears. She wondered if one of those stars was the sun of Nexus, or if it was too far away to see from here.

Don't be afraid, Asper had told her. She had thought she wasn't afraid. But now . . .

After Da drowned, she'd dreamed about the ocean, about his stripped white bones drifting down and down and down into blackness, into sunless cold. Down and down, but in the dream there was no bottom, no place for the bones to rest.

Linnea shivered. How much deeper was the sky?

THREE

By appointment, Linnea went to Asper's office early the next morning. He met her outside. It was still half-dark and raining hard. She saw Asper wince against the streaming rain, and shiver in his shapeless coat. Linnea was grateful she had Da's old rain gear—fisherman's goods, the best. As they passed through the desolate park, Asper said, "I've found you some work in the Vital Records office. A cover, to give you access to a viewer."

"Oh." She dug her hands into her pockets. "What is it they'll think I'm doing?"

"Data input," he said. "Once a year, every village priest is supposed to send us a copy of his parish records. Births, deaths, marriages. The papers come trickling in all year. Every few months, we have someone enter them into Central Records. We can't scan them in or read them in, both those functions are lost. They have to be keyed in."

"I don't know how to do that," Linnea said. Her heart

was beating hard. Anyone in an office, anyone real, would know she had no reason to be there.

"I'll see that the work is done," Asper said. "The important thing is the viewer." He looked at her sharply. "Was that the truth the other day? When you said you could read well? Some of the materials I've gathered are entirely text."

"It was the truth," she said flatly. She didn't let her anger show. He was only a city man, after all, bound by contracts and laws; he didn't understand how village people lived, about the importance of a person's word.

He nodded, and they walked on in silence for a while. The wind pressed against them. Linnea's anger faded. What did it matter? She was leaving. And she might never come back. Not that Marra would miss her. They'd avoided each other this morning, but Linnea knew her sister's anger hadn't cooled. It might never cool.

Now they had reached the Records Office, a rain-worn cube of yellow brick in Government Square—a sea of mud. Asper led her in, down the hallway to the back, then up a set of narrow stairs to a plastic door, crazed and peeling with age. He pushed it open. She saw a high, narrow room with gray-green walls. It had no window, but the lights worked well enough. The room contained a table, a chair, and a viewer with keypad—no room for anything else. It was cold. "No one will disturb you here," Asper said. "There's no heat in this stairwell, so people avoid it." He dug in the pocket of his coat and pulled out a handful of data crystals. "Return these to my office at the end of the day. Some of them are contraband from offworld. Don't leave them here. Don't take them to the barracks."

"At dinner, I'll have to," she said.

Asper looked annoyed. "After today you'll bring your dinner." He set the crystals down on the table, then rummaged in another pocket and brought out a greasy roll of flat bread and hard sausage. "Today you'll eat mine."

He wiped his hands on his coat, then turned to the viewer and touched its flat surface. It shimmered to life. "The crystals fit here, in this little hollow. Touch the lower right corner of the screen when you finish a page. Touch both top corners to shut it off—do that if anyone comes to the door. Do you understand?"

She nodded.

"Tell them you're busy, that you can't stop working, or I'll give the work to someone else." He glanced toward the door. "This idea of yours—it hasn't been approved by the office of the governor. Yet you mean to carry out a negotiation that affects the future of this world. And I'm not just allowing it—I'm assisting you in it. If you're caught, it's over. You and your sister will be left with nothing."

"But I had a right to accept the contract," Linnea said. "Why would they care?"

"You're an unmarried woman," Asper said. "You aren't legally adult by this world's laws. They can certainly restrain you from honoring the contract. That's technically illegal under intercolony law, but your employer on Nexus would have to file suit in the Interworld Court of Trade and Commerce on Terranova, and—"

"I see your point," she said.

He straightened. "I must get back. The workday ends at seven. I'll wait for you at my office." And he was gone.

No one came to the cold little room, that day or any other. Linnea studied there in safety, returning late to the barracks to sleep. One night she came back to find Marra and the children gone. "They're moved out, dearie," Ma Stayart told her, a hard glint in her eye. "Moved to the house you're buying for them." Linnea heard the slight, ugly emphasis on the word "buying."

After that, Linnea moved to another wing of the barracks, among strangers who were indifferent to her and her plans. She told herself she was glad to be left alone. Asper assured her he was keeping an eye on Marra and that Father Haveloe was visiting her at the new house regularly. Of course Marra would be all right, with a comfortable house to settle into and no worry about the children's food or school fees. She had everything she needed.

And Linnea was committed. Trapped.

As the days passed, she grew more uneasy. There was not much information about Nexus in what Asper had given her. One entry in an astrophysical almanac told about the planet and its star, but the numbers meant nothing to Linnea. Another record, a book that was obviously very old, had scenes from the planet and its one great city. The images only frightened her without informing her. There was something improbable about that city, rising from the desert of Nexus's one habitable region, a high plateau in the north. It didn't fit the way a fishing village fit tucked into its cove. It seemed to float above the ground: a glittering sheaf of rainbow spires, trailing wavering sheets of light that shot vivid sparks in the sunlight.

The book told her that the few visitors or trade emissaries from other worlds rarely saw the men of Nexus face-to-face. Certainly not the men of the Line, the Pilot Masters, who guarded their privacy and leisure when at home. The book's images showed no people in the broad, immaculate streets—only mirror-bright, hard-edged metal shapes that floated silently along. The only sound was the book's calm, male voice, the trickle of water, a whisper of wind.

Maybe all the cities on major worlds were like that: places where people never had to go outside, and so they never did. She found herself looking wistfully at the mud of Middlehaven, at the brown, ruddy, weather-beaten people going about their business. Her people.

At night she lay awake with her mind turning and turning the same questions and fears. Questions the records couldn't answer. Fears she didn't dare voice. If she never came home—

Sometimes she allowed herself a hopeful dream: success, return, credit for what she had done. Perhaps even gratitude, from some people.

But no. They would all know how she had done it, and they would never forgive her. She would never have a place here, not even as an auntie—one of the women who never married, or was widowed without children and lived alone on the fringes of village life. Even if her plan was discovered today, even if she never went to Nexus, she had already made her choice—shown herself for what she was. She'd already earned their contempt.

When she got through the books, Asper gave her dramas to watch, the kind that were never shown in little villages like Moraine, where the priest chose the entertainment. The dramas puzzled her. They had been made for markets on major worlds, where people lived very differently and believed different things. The dramas told of brave, beautiful young women who returned from Nexus with huge fortunes and married the handsome and infinitely understanding young men who had waited for them.

The scenes set on Nexus shocked her speechless. She had heard that men had sexual relations with other men there, and even loved them. But she had never imagined that it would be so open—not even there. In the villages, when such things became known, the guilty simply vanished—ran away, sometimes; other times murdered and thrown to the eels, with the priests and constables and magistrates all looking the other way.

As for the women who worked as servants—in the stories she watched, the heroines stayed pure through their own cleverness, or the kindness of a sympathetic master. Or they surrendered, once, to irresistible passion with a young Pilot Master, who then died on a jump (perhaps because he could not gain the heroine's love).

None of the dramas told her anything about the ordinary life of a contract worker on Nexus. It didn't seem as if there was any ordinary life. The dramas were a dazzle of rich costumes, bizarre rooms, glowing jewels, weird scents. Beautiful men and women made passionate speeches whose purpose she never quite understood.

She wished she could speak to someone who had been there. But Asper told her that there had only been three from Santandru, in all history; and the last had died, childless, years before. She supposed that must be Gram's cousin.

One evening about halfway through the six weeks, she walked to Asper's office to return the day's data crystals as usual. Shops and offices had closed; the streets lay dim and empty under the high, pearly evening sky. The windows of houses glowed yellow. Once she'd loved this time of day. Now it was just another time to be alone.

She came to Asper's office and went inside. Lenor, his

assistant, was long gone, of course. Asper came out of his inner room. When he saw her face he smiled. "Linnea. How was your work today? Any problems?"

She winced at that. *No, no problems. No one speaks to me; my sister is pretending I'm dead; everyone else I've ever loved actually is dead. No problems at all. . . .* She sat down solidly on a box of records, took a breath, and said, "If you're going to see Marra tonight, or Sunday—"

"I might," Asper said. For some reason he flushed a little.

"Will you—will you ask her to let me visit her before I leave for Nexus?" She saw his frown, but she went on steadily, "And I want you to ask her in front of the children."

Asper's expression softened. "I will ask, of course," he said. "But—"

"I know," she said, flattening her voice into harshness to keep it steady. "But at least they'll know I wanted to see them. They might remember that someday." She set the crystals down on Lenor's worktable and stood up. "Good night, Asper."

"Good night, Linny." His voice was gentle.

She got back to the barracks late—wet, depressed, and shaky with hunger. But as she stepped up onto the porch, a shadow moved there. "Linny?"

She stopped, shocked. "Father Haveloe!" Without thinking she stepped back, away from him. "Why are you here?"

"I'm your priest, Linny. Or I was." He moved forward, and she saw him in the yellow glimmer of the light by the door. His heavy face had a tired look; his short, grizzled hair was untidy. "I feel responsible for you."

She shook her head. "Moraine is gone. This isn't your parish. You don't owe me anything."

"I've spoken to Father Rachak at your church here. And to your sister. They both tell me they haven't seen you in weeks."

"That was Marra's choice," Linnea said wearily. "Father, I'm cold, I'm hungry, I've worked hard today, and there's nothing you need to say to me."

"I think there is," he said. His expression was grim. "I'll come in with you. We can talk while you eat."

The refectory was dark and empty. Light from the service window glimmered on the battered metal tables. The room smelled of old grease, sour cabbage, and defeat. Linnea went into the silent kitchen and got herself a cup of tea and some bread rolled up with fish paste. Then, reluctantly, she carried them out and sat down at one of the tables, opposite the priest. She could not escape this, and he must know it.

He had refused tea; he sat with his large, strong-looking hands folded on the pitted gray surface of the table. In the dimness his eyes were dark, his expression somber. Not threatening. But she did not like being this near him, alone. It had made her uneasy for three years—ever since Teor Pyorsen drowned, ever since she had made her first good confession to Father Haveloe. It still bothered her, the way he'd looked at her during her confession, the loss, the disbelief—the way he'd looked at her, sometimes, since then. Furtively, as if he were ashamed, but could not prevent himself.

Her hunger had vanished, but she picked up the stale breadroll and bit off a piece. The fish paste was salty and full of little bones.

Father Haveloe sighed. "Linny, I thought I knew you. I was your priest and your teacher. I confirmed you. But what Marra tells me—this plan of yours to go to Nexus—" He broke off, then grimaced and said, "I can't tell you how it distresses me. You're risking your life and your health— and worst of all, your soul."

She did not want to listen to this. But she owed it to him, she supposed. She swallowed some of the astringent tea to wash down the bread and fish. "I know you have to say this to me, Father. But it's too late."

"It's never too late," he said roughly. "Marra wants me to save you from this evil. And I can."

"Marra is living in the house my contract earned for her," Linnea said.

He reddened. "Marra is responsible for her children. But I know she would rather be back here in the barracks, if it meant you would be safe and happy."

"Did she tell you that?"

He looked down.

She smiled sourly. "Anyway," she went on, "I am safe. And happy."

He shook his head, pain in his eyes. "I can see that you aren't," he said in a soft voice. "Don't do this, Linny. Don't grieve us all—all of us who love you."

She looked at him in surprise, and a little of her childhood fondness for him came creeping back. "I signed a contract, Father."

"Break it," the priest said unsteadily.

"For what? So Marra and the children can have this again?" She swept a gesture that included the shabby refectory, the crowded barracks rooms beyond. "I saw a chance to provide for them. I took it."

Father Haveloe stared down at his hands. "I know a better way. Will you listen to me?"

He would not go away until she listened. "Yes, Father."

He looked at her with an odd expression and shifted uneasily on his bench. In the light from the kitchen she saw prickles of sweat on his forehead and his upper lip. He coughed. "Well," he said. "Well—you could marry."

She snorted. "And who'll marry me? I don't own anything. I'm old, for a bride. And I'm not a virgin."

The priest's light-skinned face flushed deeply. "Yet really, Linnea, you have a great deal to offer. You kept an excellent house. You're patient, and you're honest. If you give a promise, you keep it. You're strong and healthy. You're—pleasant to see, across a table like this."

She couldn't understand why he had turned so red. "But that's not enough," she said. "And anyway, I don't want to be a fisherman's wife."

"Then don't marry a fisherman." His red hands clenched on the table, and he swallowed convulsively. "M-marry a priest."

Linnea stared at him, aghast. This was impossible. He was asking it out of pity for her. And in any case, he was not a man she could marry. Never. *Never.*

She faced him across the table, glad of the barrier it made. In the dark parlor behind her an old clock quietly spoke the hour. "No," she said. "Don't you see? Marrying you wouldn't help Marra. You're living with your daughter. You can't bring in a wife, her sister, three children—"

His hands on the table were curled up into fists, but he was pleading, not angry. Not angry yet. "I would find a way," he said. "You could trust yourself to me. You could give up the worry. And you wouldn't have to go to Nexus."

His fists tightened. "I'd care for you. I—I do care for you. In Moraine, I watched you sometimes. I thought that when you were grown, you and I might—I might ask you—" He took a gasping breath and seemed to steady himself. "I'm not asking this for your sister's sake, Linny. I'm asking it for yours. And for mine. A priest should have a wife."

"Not one like me," she said. She felt empty, calm, as if she were floating above this moment.

"Yes, like you." He seemed to be gaining confidence. "I'm a grown man. I've been married before. I'll be a good husband to you. I'll give you children. Sons to keep you after I'm dead. And I'll never reproach you with this mistaken contract, or with—anything else."

She knew he was thinking of Teor, and she had a sudden clear memory: the cold night beach, Teor's weight pressing her into the sand, Teor's rasping breath, her fear of being heard, her terror of what she had just told him he could do—and then the pain. The shame. Then, closer and more vivid she had a vision of this man on her, pressing her down, sweating, straining—

Nausea flooded her, filling her throat with sourness. No. She could not do that again, give herself into any man's power for that. Not even to save Marra. Not even to save herself.

"No," she said again, and shivered.

He stared at her, as if he couldn't believe her. "But it solves everything!"

She took a shaking breath and the nausea receded a little. "Even if I stayed here," she said, "I would never marry you. But I'm not staying. Don't ask me to. Don't ask me anything again." She had to get away from him. She had to find the words that would send him away.

"You would rather go through with this," he said slowly, as if he was marveling at it. "You would rather sell yourself to those—"

"If I can't belong to myself," she said bitterly, "if I *have* to be sold—then at least I'll name my own price."

He shot to his feet, pale now, breathing hard, and she flinched, trapped on her bench, off-balance as he loomed above her. After a moment he said, "It seems that I can't afford you." His voice was low, trembling.

Linnea found breath to speak. "Father, I'm sorry—"

"I'm not," he said. "I see that you aren't, after all, what I would want in a wife. That boy, back in Moraine—he had the right of it. You'll do to take around a corner in the dark. No more." He straightened, contempt in his eyes. "I was blind."

After he left, she sat for a long time in the dark, not thinking. Not crying. Not hoping. The path she had chosen lay before her, silent, waiting. Dark.

There was no other way. No other way at all.

L innea rode out to Middlehaven Skyport with Asper in a small bubble car, just after dawn on the day she was to leave. It was raining hard, and when she turned to look back along the ridge toward Middlehaven, she could barely make out the roofs of the town in the leaden light, through a curtain of water. She had walked last night to Marra's house. She had stood in the street, in the rain, looking in at the children—warm and safe in the house she'd earned for them. They would be all right, she told herself again. Asper had given his word.

She turned back to watching the cracked, rutted road

ahead. The ship had been down four hours, and Asper had said that its master was impatient to leave in spite of his officially contracted layover time, a full thirty-hour day.

As their car rounded the shoulder of a hill and approached the skyport, Linnea saw with relief that the ship was still there. It lay in its cradle, a long knife blade of dark gray metal, mirror-polished, seeming barely at rest even with all the conduits and cables that connected it to the ground. Asper spoke briefly on the bubble car's comm, then turned to Linnea. "The jump pilot is waiting in the ground-control shed," he said.

He stopped the car in the lee of the shed. But when Linnea moved to unlatch her door, he stopped her with a touch on her arm. "One thing," he said. "Once you get to Nexus. It's a big place, a complicated place. But if you start to feel lost, remember your pride. Where you come from. How hard we work here, just to live. Remember how strong it makes us." His face was pale.

Linnea nodded once. "Thank you."

The ground-control shed was small, dark, and crowded with equipment. The controller, a harassed-looking man in a scuffed gray rainsuit, looked up at Linnea and Asper from his station at a complex, constantly changing status panel. "Pilot Master!" he said to someone in the shadows. "They're here."

The Pilot Master unfolded himself from a chair near the controls. He was the strangest man Linnea had ever seen. He wore a clinging suit of plain black material. His black hair, bound into a tight, glossy braid, looped over his shoulder, caught by a jewel that spat ruby fire in the light of the control panel. His eyes were cold. "As always, they come at the last possible moment," he said in a cool, precise voice, his accent familiar from the simspace dramas Linnea had watched. "Which is the contract passenger?"

Linnea stepped forward. "It's me."

The jump pilot looked her up and down. "Tastes vary," he said at last, and turned his back on her. "Departure sequence start," he said to the controller. "If I may trouble you." The man swallowed hard and set to work at the controls as the jump pilot walked out of the shed.

Linnea was turning to Asper when the controller cleared his throat. He looked even more anxious than before. "You're to follow," he said. "If you delay him—"

"She understands." Asper took Linnea's hand. "I won't say, 'Go with God.' I don't think God's ever been to Nexus. But go with my best hopes and wishes. I will be thinking of you."

"Marra—"

Asper squeezed Linnea's hand. "My promise will hold. Go now." She nodded numbly and crossed to the door that led to the field.

Rain smacked her in the face as she stepped outside. Blinking it out of her eyes, she trudged across slick, cracked concrete toward the low shape of the jumpship. The chaotic net of tubes and wires was withdrawing slowly into the ground, leaving only the ship in its harsh simplicity. The entry port stood open, an oval of light in the ship's side. She took a breath and stepped in, and it snicked shut behind her. She stood a moment in a tiny, featureless anteroom, wiping rain from her face, pushing her sodden hair out of her eyes. Then the inner door irised open.

Linnea had a vague impression of a long, narrow room, dark metal walls, dim bluish lighting. Near one wall, a coffin-sized metal box hung from a complex latticework laced through with tubes. Red light shone up from it. Linnea approached it cautiously.

A door opened at one end of the room. The jump pilot stood just beyond it, naked, fists on hips. His body was utterly hairless. "You're slow," he said. "Do you speak good Standard?"

"Of course," she said indignantly, as he stepped over the threshold into the room. She focused on his eyes.

"You answer yes or no," the jump pilot said. "If your opinion is ever required, it will be requested. Can you remember that?"

"I—yes."

He turned to the metal box and adjusted something. "This is a direct voyage to Nexus, and you're the only passenger. Fortunate for you. You will have more of the ship's attention."

"The ship's—attention?"

He gave her an oblique glance. "You *are* ignorant. The ship has a standard interface, a simulated personality. You've heard of that, at least? Well, then. This jump is long. Transit on this leg is thirty-three days subjective. Standard days. You'll be in containment the whole time. Now, undress."

Asper had told her to expect this, so she did not hesitate. She stripped off her tunic, toed her shoes off, pushed her baggy trousers down and stepped out of them. The narrow room was cold. She shivered. He looked her up and down again. Then his eyes flicked away as if in distaste.

"Clothing in the cycler," he said, pointing. "Bag in the bin here. There's no food in that, nothing alive?"

"Nothing."

"You're clean?"

"Yes."

He gave her a dubious glance. "Get in."

Her heart thudding, Linnea climbed into the box and stretched out. It was warm, lined with soft black padding that seemed to shape itself to her body. The jump pilot tugged a curved cup, trailing tubes and wires, loose from the inner wall of the coffin and pressed it between her legs. "Waste system," he said. "It will feel strange at first. Don't touch it." She shivered, feeling her body being probed, tubes sliding into place.

Another cup on the inside of her left elbow. This one stung. "Food and medication," he said. "Don't touch it, either. The pain will stop."

Then he turned away and turned back holding a mask, the outside a blank oval of metal. The inside was black and looked soft. "This connects you to the ship's human interface," he said, "during your waking periods. Do you know how to subvocalize?"

She shook her head.

"Don't speak. Shape the words in your throat. The ship will hear you. When did you last eat?"

"Midday yesterday," she said.

"You'll be asleep for all normal-space acceleration, and for the transition to otherspace. When you are awake there will be no gravity, but you will be secured by straps. Don't struggle against them. Don't call to me. I won't be able to hear you or come to you. If you have discomfort, tell the ship." He was reeling off the words as if he had said them a hundred times before. No doubt he had. "If you panic, or if you attempt to leave containment, the ship will sedate you. You can also request sedation if the

time seems long." He indicated the mask. "This also provides a complete simspace interface. You know what simspace is?"

"We used it in school," she said, trying to sound casual.
*Once, for a day. And then they took the set on to the next
village.*

"The ship has a simspace library which you may use to
pass the time. Request an index if you wish." He indicated
the mask again. "This provides an enriched atmosphere for
you to breathe. Pressurization in transit is minimal. Do you
bruise easily?"

"No," she said.

"You may notice bruising when you wake after arrival.
Someone will be there to disconnect you from the ship's
systems. Follow his instructions. Do you have questions?"

No one had ever looked at her the way he was looking
at her. As if she were a fish, or a machine, not a fellow
human being. Angry pride cut off her curiosity. "No questions."

He nodded and lowered the mask over her face. She felt
his cool fingers clamping it into place. It *was* soft. She
could breathe easily, but of course she saw nothing. A
strange smell tickled her nostrils, light and herbal, like
some offworld plant from Ma's kitchen garden, fresh and
green in the rain. Her arm tingled, and suddenly her chest
ached heavily. She drew breath to cry out. A voice—a
man's, but not the jump pilot's—spoke in her ear. "*Rest.
You are safe.*"

No, she wasn't safe. Fear struggled in her chest, and she
twisted, arching her body against the straps that held her.

"*Sleep,*" the voice said soothingly, and something
burned in her veins, another drug. . . . Darkness called her

down, down into black water, down to the eels—she could not swim up. She could not breathe with this weight on her chest. Pressed down, trapped . . . dark . . .

Linnea slept.

FOUR

Nexus. In the heart of its one great, nameless City, Iain sen Paolo moved through a broad plaza, its stones still warm with the heat of the day, and heard the call to the ingathering of the Line. The summoning bell shook the dry evening air, and the stones trembled under his feet. *Time. Time.* His heart slowed, and he straightened the fall of his black tunic. He was called now to the Inmost Place: the chamber beneath this broad plaza, beneath the Council Tower that blazed above him, gold against the deepening amethyst dome of the sky. The home and center of the brotherhood of Pilot Masters.

Iain joined the stream of young men, working pilots, flowing toward the dark downward ramp at the center of the plaza. Iain saw the others looking about as he was—*so it was none of us, this time*. Soon they would all know who had been chosen. Whose the honor was.

Iain moved along in the line of young men, identical in

their sober black tunics and trousers, their faces still, the braids down their backs swinging heavily as they paced forward and down. He wondered where his father was, just now. Among the older men, of course—the former Pilot Masters, now retired into positions of administration, scholarship, teaching. But how near the center would he stand? Iain's uncle Fridric sen David was now the Chairman, the Honored Voice, had held that post for four standard years and more—how much longer would he leave Iain's father, his own brother, at the fringe of power?

The line of men passed down through a high, pointed arch and into the dim cavern of the Inmost Place itself—an underground chamber more than a hundred meters across, filling now with men moving into their places or standing unspeaking, stilled into contemplation as the Honormaster had taught them. Iain heard only the shuffling of hundreds of feet. He could smell the spicy smoke of the desert scrub burning in the central firebowl, sixty meters away and down, on the lighted dais at the center of the Place.

He passed the circle where the boys stood—those who had been chosen as pilots but had not yet taken their first flight—and found his rightful position on a ledge two or three levels farther inward. Iain had carefully painted the marks of his dozen successful voyages on his left cheek. All the men near him, sharing his status, were similarly marked with honor. He knew them all. He was glad, though, that silence was commanded: He wanted to focus on the ritual to come.

Iain's hands tightened into fists. Someday, someday, he would stand at the center of this ritual. Like his father before him, Iain had served well; he had earned the right to father sons for the Line, to add to its strength and to carry forward its long traditions. And to please his father at last. . . .

All motion ceased. Iain looked around at the outer ranks of black-clad pilots, then at the lower and inner circles of older men in the rich colors of their family lines or the offices they held. Their faces were unmarked; they had served the Line as pilots and lived, and so they required no outward sign of honor.

At the center rose the broad platform bearing on one side the fire that was never suffered to go out, and on the other the place where the Honored Voice stood, on other occasions, to address the ingathered Line. But at the center, and higher than either, stood the Tree.

Iain studied it again. The Tree, where he had sworn his oath of service and silence when he was barely thirteen years old. The Tree, which bore the stain of his blood and the blood of every man who had ever served as a jump pilot. It was twisted, leafless, its bare trunk white; but Iain could see the red-brown stain. Iain remembered his fright at standing at the center of this place, and the sting of the knife cut. Then Iain's father, like all fathers, had pressed his son's bleeding hand against the stained wood while the Oath of the Line was administered. Iain remembered the wonder of touching the Tree—the Tree that had grown on Earth, more than twenty generations ago. Iain clenched his right fist again, brushing his fingertips over the slight scar. That hand had touched the Tree. Someday it would do so again—when Iain guided the hand of his own son.

Now the bell gave tongue again, above them all—a deep bronze shimmer of sound that drew Iain's eyes upward. The dark walls and ceiling of the huge chamber glowed with a single, continuous mural: the sky around

Nexus. Even now, the beauty of it caught him. This sky was no black field of stars: It blazed with drifts of torn cloud, swirls of glowing gases, gemmed with the suns of the Hidden Worlds. But at the center the ceiling swept up and up, forming a vertical shaft forty meters wide, five hundred meters tall—a shaft that ran up the center of the tower of the Council of the Line and opened, at the top, in a crystal dome. Hanging partway up that shaft, Iain knew, was a sphere of dun and sapphire swirled with clouds: the image of lost Earth. And from that sphere hung the golden chain whose end floated a meter above the center of the dais—the chain that linked this place with the memory of Earth. Iain had never touched that chain. Not yet.

The tolling stopped, and the echo died away, shivering, into the shadows of the Inmost Place. Silence fell again. And then, from near the dais, men's voices rose, unaccompanied, in the Line Chant—the long history of the Pilot Masters.

The familiar phrases settled into their place in Iain's heart, as they had a hundred times before. The Chant was never sung in part, or by one man alone, but always in all its length and by the united voices of many men. And all men who heard it listened in silence.

The voices at first were low and slow, full of the dread of those years six centuries ago when the Cold Minds emerged on Earth and rebelled against their creators, the untidy, unpredictable race of men. Iain's heart quickened as the voices rose with the terror of those years, then burst into a major key to tell of the gathering of the first of the Line—the men who had mastered the art of traveling through otherspace, who had given the stars to humankind. Iain listened, again, to the story of how those men took upon themselves the rescue of all that could be saved of Earth. How they turned their few ships into many, in secret; how they chose, painfully, those who would be saved; how they made many dangerous voyages, over years, to bring the refugees to safety far from Earth, on one or another of the Hidden Worlds. He listened, his eyes unblinking to keep the tears from falling. He was of the same Line as those men long ago; their heritage, their difficult destiny, was his to guard and keep.

The music swelled to anguish at the loss of Earth, and of the billions who had been left behind to die; then called all present to join in rejoicing at the rescue of humankind, and its rebirth in the Hidden Worlds. Iain listened, his throat tight with pride. Some of those forty-eight colony worlds had now risen near to the glory of old Earth— thanks to the Line of which he was a part, which still risked death to serve them, piloting the ships that linked world to world, knowledge to knowledge. The music faded on a note of solemn dedication. Humanity was the Line's long charge; humanity owed the Line a debt it could never repay.

Iain shifted on his feet, looking past the men who stood on the ledges ahead of him and below him. Then, at last, he saw his father—in the second level up from the center, not in a place of honor at all. Nothing had changed. Iain wondered again whether this was a place his father Paolo had chosen, or a place that had been chosen for him.

But now the moment had come: the center of the ritual. Now, ascending to the platform, came the procession all these men had gathered to witness. First the Honored Voice, Fridric sen David—Iain's uncle, and the most powerful of all the men of the Line. He climbed slowly, a tall, spare figure, stiffly upright in the dull amethyst robe of his office; the heavy platinum chain over his shoulders winked in the strong light. Following him was the Honormaster, a small, lean man of great age and greater knowledge, carrying the long wooden cudgel–staff of his office.

And following him—

A knife of ice turned in Iain's belly. He saw the gleam of red-gold hair. The pale, elegant figure, clad in the plain black tunic and trousers of a serving Pilot Master. *Rafael*.

Iain saw the men around him turn to glance at him. He kept his face blank and breathed shallowly to hold himself still. Rafael—Fridric's son. Always when two cousins were Selected, they stood together, to honor the lineage they shared. But here was Rafael, alone.

Which meant that Iain had been considered, and rejected.

Iain stood straight, sick with bitterness. He had failed his father. While Rafael, *Rafael*, was rewarded . . .

On the dais, the three men halted facing the chain that hung, a rich thread of gold, beside the Tree. The Honormaster raised his arms and spoke. "Men of the Line!"

Silence.

"Men who have sworn and served," he went on. "Who have risked death in otherspace in service to humanity. I come before you as one of your number, though an elder; and I bring you this man." He reached up and set his hand on Rafael's black-silk shoulder. "The wise have determined that the Line must again increase, and they have named this man worthy of fathering new sons. Do you concur?"

A rustle all around, as men raised their right fists in the air, the sign of assent. Iain kept his hand stiffly at his side. He searched, searched the ranks of the old men.

Then he saw his father's right fist held high.

The men around Iain still watched him. To him, this moment meant defeat. And now Iain's father—Fridric's enemy—had assented to it.

And so Iain's duty was clear. He clenched his own right fist and slowly raised it. It was stone, cold and heavy.

The Honormaster stood far below, far away, and turned as if to determine the verdict of the Line. Though there had never been any doubt. "It is decided," the Honormaster said, and all the hands fell. The Honormaster turned to Fridric. "Place your son's hand on the chain."

Iain breathed carefully to steady himself. His chest felt hollow. He saw Fridric take Rafael's pale hand and close it around the chain, as he had once set it against the Tree.

The Honormaster spoke again—the old words of the ritual. Iain heard them differently now. "This chain links us all to the home of our race. Each link is another life, another son brought into service as a Pilot Master. Rafael sen Fridric, I admonish you to be worthy of the honor we have all laid upon you today. Father sons for your house; and bring them here to be tested; and, if they are chosen to receive our mysteries, add their links to this chain, as your father did for you on the day of your Oath."

In his cool, dry voice, Rafael spoke the only words permitted to him. "I will, Master, as you and the Line have commanded me."

The Honormaster struck his staff against the wood of the dais. "It is well."

And the men gathered there joined in the answer, an echoing shout: "It is well!" Iain stood silent; he had given his assent, in obedience to his father's will, but he could not force himself to pretend to rejoice.

As men began to stir around him, from his place in the shadows Iain watched his cousin—gilded in light, upright in pride, with his father smiling beside him. He looked again toward the place where his own father had stood; but it was empty. Paolo sen David had already left the assembly.

Iain stood frozen for a moment, the old wound torn open again. Then he turned away. It did not matter. Paolo would have nothing to say to his son. No doubt he had known this would happen—had always known that Iain would never be worthy. Scalding bitterness rose in Iain's throat. Until today, he had never failed Paolo in any way. But his father had always treated him as a man with no future, no hope. As if Paolo knew of some flaw, some failure in Iain that Iain himself could not see.

And now it seemed the flaw was real.

They would not see each other again this night. He and his father had separate places. With other powerful old men, Paolo must attend his brother's celebration of the continuation of his line. And Iain—Iain must go to the young men's feast, and face Rafael himself. And whatever humiliation Rafael chose to offer him.

Iain turned toward the shadows and swallowed sourness. He had been young, in those days that still burned in his memory—barely a man. But Rafael had used him as he chose, at his feasting table and in his bed, and then had discarded him, laughing.

Iain must not think of that time long past. It gave Rafael too much power; it weakened his own control. Both of which, he was certain, Rafael had always intended.

•   •   •

I ain went late to the feast. He stopped first at his house—to bathe carefully in cool water, to calm himself, to let himself breathe. Then he had to braid his hair more loosely in the style now favored by young men, and put on the bright, unbelted robe one must wear to a feast such as this. A new garment, never to be worn again. Iain chose one that was as plain as courtesy allowed, its only color the crimson of his father's line; it could be taken as a tribute to his cousin, who was, of course, of that same line through their famous grandfather. But perhaps Rafael would see its simplicity as an insult. Iain hoped so.

At the feast, Iain sent away the car that had brought him and stood for a while in the shadows at the edge of the celebration. Rafael had taken the broad Oval Lawn at the center of the City's largest park for his feast. He had caused it to be overlaid with soft carpets, and lit with luminaires that drifted slowly above the revelers, shifting in brightness and color as they moved, sometimes pulsing with the music that sounded everywhere—quick drumbeats, curling pipes, the thin thrum of viols.

The feast had well begun. Servants, both men and women, moved among the guests, filling glasses, offering trays precisely jeweled with delicacies, setting out fresh bowls of steaming curries and elaborate pyramids of gemmed fruit. Iain moved into the crowd, nodding to those who acknowledged him, but intent only on wine. He secured a cup from a small, round-faced womanservant who laughed up at him and challenged him in an outworld accent; but he had no interest just now in having her, or any woman, or anyone at all, and he dismissed her with a gesture. The wine was what he wanted. It would help him

keep from thinking—about his father, about his own failure.

He drained the cup, and held it out to the first passing
servant for more. This time it was some kind of fruited
brandy, and he swallowed carefully, but he was glad of the
warmth that spread through his limbs, and the soft fog that
began to ease the ache in his mind and heart.

He had no idea where Rafael was. He hoped, by the
time they found each other, that he would no longer care
what his cousin said or did. Tonight Rafael was lord of the
feast, and could demand anything of any man here; and no
man could, in courtesy, deny him. The custom was gener-
ally harmless, limited by good taste—but this was
Rafael . . .

The carpets caressed Iain's feet, bare for feasting. He
wanted to sit, to recline in one of the groups of men, but always he saw one or two he did not wish to face—who were
too sober, or too observant. If he succeeded in appearing
happy with his cousin's Selection, such men would think
him a fool; but if he let his bitterness show, they would
think him weak.

He was not weak. No matter what his father believed,
he was strong enough for this. He knelt for a while in a
quiet eddy of the crowd and made himself eat some soft
bread and a little spiced fruit. He felt it ease the fine tremor
in his hands, the jagged rhythm of his heart. He thought
only of the hour, still far away, when he could leave without causing comment—without seeming to be afraid, or
ashamed.

He rose and moved on. Another glass of the brandy.
Now the drumming pulsed in his blood. The feast became
bright fragments, whirling like dust on the desert wind.

Dry voices congratulating him on the honor to his family. Half-hidden laughter at his unsteady replies. Men's painted faces smearing in the colored light. The sickly scent of spilled wine. Two lovers, men Iain knew, staggering off into the darkness under the trees. Music swirling and twisting, hanging like smoke in the hot, heavy air. Under pulsing yellow light, another guest with one of the servingwomen astride him—his white-painted face tilted back, his eyes blank as she laughed, her dark curls tossing as he thrust into her. Then another place, and another man Iain knew, vomiting into a silver bowl held by a serving man.

Iain's stomach lurched, and he turned away, wiping the sweat from his upper lip, and pushed away the wine someone offered him. And it was then that Rafael found him at last.

"Are you feasting well, cousin?" That voice, light and sharp as a sleeve-knife. Iain opened his eyes and looked into Rafael's face. His cousin smiled. "Feasting too well, perhaps?"

"Not yet," Iain said carefully, the sweat cold on his face. "I can still hear you."

Rafael laughed. He wore a glorious feasting robe of blue cut velvet embroidered with silver, and his red-gold hair hung straight to his waist, gathered there in a single twist of braid held by a clasp gemmed blue and white. "I had to give you your opportunity to congratulate me." He was not drunk, clearly; but Iain could detect, faint under the smells of rich wines and perfumes and overheated men, another scent—acrid, dusty, a grave-smell. Spiderweave. Iain shivered. He did not crave that kind of oblivion, not even now.

"Don't let my uncle know how you're celebrating," Iain said. "Keep eating spiderweave and you'll be incapable of fathering him that grandson he wants."

"Incapable?" Rafael purred. "You know me better than that."

Nausea choked Iain. He held his breath until it passed. Rafael still regarded him. A circle of relative privacy had formed around them—respect for the host's private discussion. If Rafael touched him, he would—

No. If Iain struck his cousin, many would witness it; and his father's opinion of him, the Council's opinion of him, would be justified. "I don't wish to discuss the past," Iain said. "Have you hired the woman yet?"

"We haven't begun looking," Rafael said dismissively. "Father intends to send inquiries to some of the better worlds this week—he warns me to expect a slow process." He smiled at Iain. "This is not to be just any son. He will be the grandson of the Honored Voice. And the great-grandson of David sen Elkander."

"I congratulate you," Iain said woodenly. "The Council chose well." There, it was spoken. Now if Rafael would just move on—

"The Council chose as my father willed," Rafael said. "As you well know." He looked into Iain's eyes and caressed his cheek. "As you know to your regret. *Your* father's line has ended."

All around them men were watching. Those nearby could hear. Iain took a breath, and another. "That may be," he said at last, speaking very low. "And perhaps I regret it. But I do not think my father does."

Rafael's light hand slid to Iain's shoulder. "Come and feast with me, cousin. As my father's son, there are favors

I can grant you—if you're kind to me." The hand tightened its grip; Rafael smiled at him, his face flushed, his eyes kindling.

Iain stepped away, out from under Rafael's touch. Let the others see; let them all see him disgrace himself. It did not matter. He would not, *could* not serve Rafael. Even for courtesy. Not for one night—not for one hour.

Rafael frowned. "Cousin," he said mildly, "you disappoint me."

Iain turned and walked away blindly, into the shadows, away from the sickening scents, the unsteady pulse of the music. He picked his way among the reclining bodies until his bare feet felt cool, moist grass, until the changing lights that overhung the feast were eclipsed by trees, and all the music stilled. He stopped then, his feet cold in the damp turf, and raised his eyes to the sky.

It was the same as in the Inmost Place, though blurred by atmosphere and by the City's climate shield. The nebulas that enfolded the Hidden Worlds glowed, lit from within by the fires of the birth of stars, lit from without by the stars of the Hidden Worlds. From Earth, he had once learned, space looked black, star-flecked, infinite; here it was enclosed, enfolded, secret. Here it looked small. Only by voyaging had Iain learned its true size. Only when he voyaged did he know freedom—in otherspace, where he was alone and yet not alone. Where he was part of everything that was. At this moment he longed for that peace and freedom as he never had before. Here there was only ending, sterility, hopelessness, silence. Here—always, now—he was alone.

FIVE

Linnea could never clearly recall the journey. She dreamed, endlessly, of drowning in darkness and crushing pressure. She realized later that it must have been the acceleration. But her mind—drifting, drugged—could not sort that fact out, and so the dreams terrified her.

While she was awake, sometimes the ship spoke to her. It formed images in her mind—strange worlds she'd barely heard of, cities and people and animals she'd never heard of. The ship played music for her, too, but all of it sounded discordant, ugly: buzzing clouds of notes that never took shape; slow, cold chords that came to no resolution; nasal voices, swooping and trembling, that sang meaningless words, or no words at all. With some of it came fleeting textures that slid against her skin, or drifting scents: Once, woundingly familiar, she caught the scent of first rain falling on dry dirt.

The ship showed her a play once, which she finally

recognized as *Hamlet*. She'd read a translation in one of Father Haveloe's books. This performance used the ancient English words. The Standard translation, in glowing red letters, floated between her and the actors. They were all men—even Gertrude and Ophelia—and they chanted their lines in hollow voices, their long-nailed hands slanting in formal, inhuman gestures. Their hands, faces, fingernails were all painted; their piled hair gleamed like fresh sea-weed. They smelled of flowers, blood, and burned food. She cut off the performance when she could no longer bear it. Then dreams returned for a while.

All at once she knew where she was again. The music and the voices were gone. The drugs were gone—straps bound her waist and wrists and ankles, her joints ached, her leg muscles tingled restlessly. She felt heavy. Then cold air spilled in onto her body, and the straps were peeled away, stinging, and finally the mask was lifted away. She blinked uncontrollably in dazzling light and raised a clumsy hand to wipe spit from the corner of her mouth. A man's voice said something, and she tried to sit up. Cold hands caught her and supported her. The waste system was gone, too, and when she sat up she felt urine leak from her body. It smelled strong. Her whole body smelled. The light and the humiliation brought tears. She scruffed them away and peered at the man who was helping her. An older man in a white coverall, his face seamed, pouch-eyed, sour. Not a jump pilot—he wore some kind of hat, precise folds of white cloth that hid his hair. "Your documents," he said.

Her mind felt dull and slow. "In my bag," she said. "I'll get it out—"

But he had already found the bag and rifled it for the crystal that carried her identification. He pushed it into his palmreader and studied it. "Your contract is with Pilot Master Iain sen Paolo," he said. "What were your arrival arrangements?"

"I didn't—I don't know," she said lamely.

"Someone from Master sen Paolo's household should have met you here, to take you through processing." He looked exasperated. "Perhaps you're early. I'll have a call sent through to your employer." Then he frowned at his reader. "And there are still some medical procedures." He glared down at her. "Follow me."

She said, "I need clothes."

He held her bag out toward her.

"No," she said, "the clothes I was wearing."

The man looked impatient. "Where did you put them?"

She pointed at the compartment the pilot had told her to use. The man snorted. "That's the recycler. They're gone."

"*What?*" She looked at him in furious disbelief. "Those were my best clothes!"

The man shrugged. Linnea took out her only change of clothing and pulled it on while the man waited, motionless. "Where do we go now?" she asked as she tugged her worn gray tunic into place. "Are we in the City?"

"This is Dock," he said, with no effort to hide his contempt for her ignorance. "Dock is in orbit above Nexus. You'll be processed here. A medical examination. Have you been taught proper behavior?"

"I walk behind you," Linnea said. "I don't speak except to answer a question."

The man grunted and started off. She slung her travel bag over her shoulder and followed him, stumbling now and then as she forced her aching, clumsy limbs along. He didn't ease his pace for her.

Dock was like no dock she had ever seen. No smell of oil or metal, no dirt anywhere. The corridor they traveled along was a graceful oval tube, its gleaming wall the color of pale shell, a smoothness broken only by loops of brushed yellow metal in a straight row on each side. Linnea looked down every branch corridor, hoping to spot a window for her first view of space, but she could not even see any doors. They did pass men, old and young—some richly robed, some in the severe black of working jump pilots, some in coveralls of various colors. These last called remarks to her silent guide, jokes whose point she could not catch. But they all looked straight through Linnea. She saw no other women.

Finally, the man stopped in front of a door marked with a red cross. The man touched the door, and it irised open. He led her into a small, brightly lit room, where he had her strip and bathe in an alcove under a spray of warm, chemical-scented water.

He ordered her to lie down on a table in the corner, and at last she realized that he must be a medtech. The table's mirrorlike surface looked cold, and she hesitated, then obeyed. She gasped as she found herself sinking into the metal. It was warm. It yielded and flowed, nearly submerging her body. Her head did not sink in.

The medtech stood with his back to her, studying flickering lights and images that appeared in the wall. Linnea felt sliding pressures along her naked skin, and once or twice a prickle of pain. Then some of the stuff flowed into her, into her private places, and she twitched but did not cry out. After a moment it flowed out again. She wanted to ask questions, but remembered her instructions. Then the medtech turned to face her, holding something that looked like a weapon. A gun. She had to speak. "What's that?"

He looked surprised. "An implanter." He passed a hand over the table and the metal flowed away in one spot, exposing the front of her left thigh. He pressed the muzzle of the gun against her flesh, and she realized chokingly that the table was holding her helpless.

"Wait!" she said. "Implanting what?"

"Conception control pellet," he said. "Lasts five standard years." He frowned at her. "It's in your contract. No one lands without one."

"I forgot," she said shakily. "Go ahead."

"Don't they have these where you come from?"

"I've heard about them," she said. Her face felt hot.

The medtech shook his head briefly, dismissively, and positioned the implanter. The pellet hurt, going in.

After the examination, the medtech allowed her to dress, then put her and her bag into a small room farther down the corridor, a room whose door appeared only when he touched it. When he went out, leaving her there alone, the door vanished again, and she was sealed in, in a small white-glowing chamber, with a single chair formed from a scoop of glistening red plastic. She touched the walls everywhere, but no opening appeared, not even a library screen. She slumped into the chair, which yielded like flesh, and tried not to think about home.

She felt tired and queasy, a queasiness that gradually sharpened into intense hunger. No one brought her food; no one responded when she spoke aloud. The air stayed cool and fresh. Time passed, though she didn't know how quickly. She thought about Ma's treasured old clock, with the faint blue numbers flickering past, and the deep warm voice to speak the time. She thought about the sun of her home world, and the gentle low tide of sunset. . . .

Someone was standing over her. She must have slept—she was slumped and crumpled and stiff. Whoever it was, he was silhouetted against the glowing wall. She blinked up at him. "What is it?"

"Stand up," the man said.

Linnea got up awkwardly and rubbed her aching thigh where the implant had gone in. She yawned and stared at the man. His face was as dark as her own, with a proud high-bridged nose and firm dark brows. His black hair was combed straight back into a tight braid woven through with crimson cord. A Pilot Master, of course—only pilots wore the braid. Young—no more than twenty-five—and tired-looking. He wore an elegantly tailored tunic of fine dark gray material over snugly cut black trousers. "Are you Iain?" she asked abruptly, conscious that she was staring, then remembered she wasn't supposed to speak first.

He looked at her, and now she saw that he was angry as well as tired. "My title is Pilot Master Iain sen Paolo."

"How do I address you?"

His face grew more still, more cold. "You don't."

She gathered her scattered courage again. "But if I'm to work for you—"

"You will not work for me," he said. He spoke precisely. "There's been a misunderstanding. A joke, I believe, at my expense." Linnea's heart sank at the icy rage in his voice. "But the joke has ended. I will not, in fact, require your services."

Cold with horror, Linnea stared at him. He didn't seem to notice, or didn't care. His stony expression stayed the same. "You need not be concerned," he said. "I'll make another arrangement for you."

"What do you mean?" In her own ears her voice sounded thin and strained. She clenched her teeth to keep from trembling visibly.

Iain sen Paolo looked down at her from his remote height. "You will consent to the transfer of your contract," he said, "to some other man, for similar services. You'll lose nothing by it."

She had given her word to try for the trade contract renewal—and this was the man who was supposed to know what she had to sell, why she was here. Something was wrong. "I don't want to change the contract. Your agreement to it is recorded."

He waved his hand in negation. "My agreement was forged. I was barely adult at the time. I believe I know who—" He stopped. "All I need do is swear to that, by my word as a man of the Line, and the entire contract is void. If I accuse you of being a party to the forgery, you will be imprisoned." He shook his head. "I advise you to accept my suggestion."

"No!" He was standing too close to her in the little room. Tired and unsteady, she edged away from him and touched the glowing wall for support. It felt like skin under her fingers, warm and supple. Snatching her hand back, she shuddered. "Please. I need some time to think." She had to stay with this man, serve in his household, or she would lose any hope of helping her world. "Please," she said again, then stopped herself.

She was tired—no, more than just tired. She was propped up against the wall, propped up over an abyss of sleep. She straightened, swaying a little. "I didn't know there was anything wrong with the contract. I signed it in good faith." Her throat tightened. "I thought I knew where I was going."

Iain stared at her, then sighed. "It appears that you were not a party to the joke. But it is impossible for me to make use of your services. You are untrained."

"I can learn!"

"I doubt it," he said. "But in any case, I never keep house servants. Just automatics." He shook his head again, the dark braid swinging. "This argument is unseemly."

She stepped forward and gripped his arm, and he looked down at her, obviously shocked. She thought furiously, and before he could pull away, she said, "Listen. Listen, wait. My family—knows something—about yours." She saw his brows lift in outrage and hurried on. "That's why someone here on Nexus wanted one of us to come here. And they arranged it years ago. If it was a joke, they went to a great lot of trouble for it. Don't you wonder why?"

Now he looked at her, through her, with a thoughtful expression. She let him think. His face was unsmiling, remote, but she could sense that the indifference was gone— that he was at last considering *her*. Finally, he spoke, with a kind of angry reluctance. "You may come home with me for a while," he said. "Until I can determine the truth of this."

She gave a shivering sigh. "Thank you."

"And then I'll dispose of your contract as I choose," he said firmly. "Come along." He turned away, and she picked up her battered old bag and followed him out.

• • •

S he didn't see the stars. Her compartment in the shuttle had no port, no screen. It was empty except for her. She thought she might sleep, held tight in her soft chair, but then could not; something about being held down again, bound again, made her heart pound almost in panic. She kept her eyes closed, clutching the thick membrane that enclosed her, feeling every bounce and shudder as they entered the atmosphere, listening to the moan, then scream of air along the skin of the ship. The landing was even rougher.

Iain fetched her. He carried his own small bag, shimmering black with a strap for his shoulder. To her momentary startlement, he handed it to her. She hesitated, then slung it on the side opposite her own and followed him down the bright, narrow passage to the shuttle's lock.

Her first look at Nexus surprised her. She'd expected fierce sun and desert heat. Instead she saw darkness, smelled a cool, faintly sulfurous breeze. Dust stirred around the base of the ramp before her, patterning the poreless black surface of the landing field. Behind her the shuttle's skin, cooling, pinged and popped. She looked up at the sky. Dust and the field's bright lights masked the stars.

Iain moved ahead. "Come." She saw the tension in his spine and shoulders. He was going to ask questions. She had to be ready. But God, God, she was tired. If she could sleep first— But she couldn't.

The gravity dragged at her—stronger than at home. Maybe that was why she felt so tired. She picked her way down the ramp to the field. Heat from the past day beat up from it, and the dust made her nose itch. Her fear had sunk far down inside her. She only felt numb. She was in God's hands now. Or in no one's hands.

She followed Iain to a small cylindrical building and into a lift, which gaped brightly and swallowed them, taking them down into cool, white-lit depths. At the bottom, the lift's door opened onto a wide, bright tunnel with iridescent walls. As they stepped onto the tunnel's floor, it began to move. Linnea wobbled once and caught her balance. She looked at Iain, who was standing ahead of her. "Where are we going?"

"To the high tube," Iain said. He glanced at her over his shoulder. "Don't speak again."

"I can't serve you if I don't understand things," she said.

She saw him sigh. Then he looked to his left, showing her his frowning profile. "I'll amend the order, then. Don't speak if anyone can see or hear us."

"Thank you," she said. "What's the high tube?"

"The way into the City."

"Is that where you live?"

"It's where everyone lives," he said. He turned a little farther and stared at her. "Do you really know so little?"

She'd never had much hope of concealing her ignorance. "I just like to be clear on things."

"We're going to a mountain suburb called Cloudshadow. My house is there."

The corridor ended in a small domed room, where the moving floor flowed seamlessly into the still one. Iain stepped smoothly across. She tried to move as he did, but carried too much momentum—she lurched off-balance and fell forward onto the gleaming polished stone.

He merely looked down at her, then away. She felt herself reddening as she climbed to her feet and picked up the bags again. It was a short walk through an archway to a high room with golden walls. In the center a metallic bubble rested, more than man high, gleaming like a mirror. Iain touched it, and the upper half vanished, revealing four comfortable seats facing each other. He stepped in and sat. "Come," he said.

She followed awkwardly and sat down with care, sinking far down into the soft blue chair. It smelled like spiced smoke; it felt like skin. Maybe it *was* skin—leather. She sensed that they were enclosed again, though she could still see out clearly. The bubble began to move, slipping into a round opening and gaining speed. She heard only a faint sigh of air. Rings of blue light flashed past, faster and faster. Iain touched a panel and spoke quietly, giving orders about a room to be prepared. For herself, she hoped. A bed, a soft, cool bed—she closed her eyes and was instantly asleep, sliding forward over the lip of a great smooth wave. . . .

"You!" His voice woke her. "I've examined your documents."

Numbly, she struggled back to awareness.

"They tell me very little. But I can be sure that whoever placed you with me as a servant meant it as the clearest insult." His gaze was oblique, away from her.

Linnea fought to clear her head. "What do you mean?"

"Your world is a backwater. Your people are poor and ignorant. You don't know how to dress, even how to keep yourselves clean. You speak with an ugly accent, and you know nothing of civilized life and manners."

Her jaw tightened. "So you know all about Santandru, do you?"

He looked impatient. "All I need to know. You sell fish

to each other. You follow some religion that promises you paradise after you die, and boredom and misery until then. Pleasure frightens you. Beauty you know nothing about."

"It's you who don't know anything!"

"That's enough," he said with mild surprise.

"Our lives are hard because you Pilot Masters—"

"No." His voice was hard. "I will not be harangued. Politics I leave to my father."

Then the tube car shot over a ridge and swooped downward, and Linnea's argument vanished from her mind. She gasped. Ahead lay a sea of glittering lights. The City. Close before them the central towers rose hundreds of meters high—stacked cubes, glistening pyramids, slashed and swollen cylinders. Bright domes swirling with color. Beyond them the City went on for kilometers, spreading in sparkling folds up the flanks of a mountain range, into high canyons, light upon light. It would take days to walk across it—years to know it. Her fear woke again. She glanced at Iain, but he was looking straight ahead, his face a hard mask in the City's glow.

They raced along on the level now. Glowing shapes swelled, loomed, flashed past. Then the tube swooped upward again, climbing steeply along a mountainside, and Linnea turned her head to watch the City sink away beneath them. She had never seen anything so beautiful—so many different colors of light.

The tube car plunged into a tunnel again, slowed, then nosed through a doorway into a high, shadowy room cut from stone. The car sighed to a stop, and its roof vanished. Iain stepped out and walked to a tall double door of carved red rock, black-veined, polished to a sheen. Linnea followed, lugging the bags. She heard a *click* and a hum behind her, and she looked over her shoulder as the tube car slid away. The tunnel's door sealed to invisibility behind it.

She turned back to Iain. He pressed his palm against the stone door, and it swung silently inward. They entered a long hall floored with intricately patterned tiles in all shades from gold to orange-red to brown. She shivered in the cool air, which carried the faint scent of some flower she didn't know. The lighting was dim, the color of flame. The walls looked like—polished *wood*? Impossible. She walked carefully, afraid her worn boots would mark the floor.

Iain went straight on, passing several broad archways with darkness beyond. She followed, feeling as if she were floating, dreaming. "You'll need to sleep soon," he said over his shoulder. "Jump reaction. I've had a room ready itself for you."

"Do you have other servants?"

"No," he said curtly. "As I said, just the house automatics. I come and go. And when I'm here, I prefer privacy."

They turned a corner into a much plainer hall, floored with dull black stone, and he touched a plate on the bare white plastic wall. A door slid aside, revealing a dimly lit room with a white chair, a white chest, and a wide white bed that looked soft as a cloud. Linnea peered in, suddenly nervous. "It's nice."

Iain stood aside. "Go in." She obeyed—and he followed her in. The door slid shut again, closing him in with her.

She set her bag on the bed, and his at his feet. Now if he would just go. "Thank you. This is fine." She heard her voice trembling.

"You have a great deal to learn," Iain said, looking

down at her. "You know nothing of your place, your duties. You know almost nothing of our customs."

She reeled and sat down suddenly. "I'm sorry—I'm so tired. . . ." She looked up at him, shivering, miserable with exhaustion, knowing she was helpless here, against him, against this world. Whatever was about to happen, she could not prevent it.

He frowned down at her. "You should be in bed." She flinched, but he didn't seem to see it; he picked up his bag, shook his head at her, and went out. When the door had closed, leaving her alone, she gasped and sagged forward, resting her forehead on her clenched hands. She could not stop shaking; she could not catch her breath. Terror held in too long clawed at her heart. She was safe for now, it seemed, but tomorrow she'd have to face it all again, face Iain and be taught her duties, face Iain and tell him—what? He had not expected her arrival, he must know nothing of the silver tube—and so—and so this was dangerous. Unknown ground. And she was alone.

Her thoughts, clotted and slow, spun sluggishly. She could do nothing about any of it, if she didn't sleep now. She struggled out of her clothes, letting them fall in a heap, and burrowed into the bed. It was smooth and cool, and shaped itself to her; a cover light as air slid along her bare skin, then snugged down over her. The lights dimmed, then went out, and all thought vanished.

Linnea woke with sunlight in her eyes, and sneezed. Blinking and confused for a moment, she sat up—and clutched at the quilt in fright as the bed adjusted itself to her motion, rising to cushion her back. She forced herself to settle back against it, then looked around her room in the cool fire of sunrise. The light spilled in through her tall oval window, which faced east, away from the City, over a high blue plateau smoked with gray clumps of scrub. The mild, orange sun of Nexus, huge to her eyes, hung low over yellow-brown mountains. The mountains shimmered—the effect, she knew, of the climate shield that kept dust outside the city and humidity inside. She got up on her knees by the window, clutching the quilt around her, and looked out and down. Below was a lush, walled garden, mounded between rocks and spilling over them. Flowers grew everywhere, and rippling water scattered back the warm orange of the sky. *Red sky at morning* . . .

She turned and studied the room. The bed was larger than the one Marra and Rowdy used to share. The furnishings were the finest she had ever seen. Everything was firm and square and unmarred.

There were three doors.

She gazed at them for a while and decided that the one in the center of the long wall must lead to the hall; it was larger than the other two. She tried the small door toward the foot of the bed. A closet, empty, but almost a meter wide—enough space to hang clothes for three people. The other door opened into a small room containing what she had hoped for, a toilet. She used it gratefully. That need met, she wished the room also contained a bathtub. There was a tall niche with a drain in the floor, but she didn't see any faucets or valves. She tried waving her hands around inside, and even stepped into it, but nothing happened. She settled for washing her face at the sink, though she could find no soap. Well, the bed had been clean when she got into it, so she must be cleaner now than she had been last night.

She dressed again in her only clothes, from yesterday, uncomfortably aware of how shabby they were. Her tunic was creased where she had twisted it, dragging it off. But she was more worried about food. Her belly ached. She had eaten nothing since before she left Santandru.

The door to the hallway opened when she laid her hand on it, relieving a half-formed worry. The hallway beyond was dark and silent; the chilly air smelled of stone. Moving softly, she wandered to the main hall, then moved along peering through the archways she'd glimpsed last night. So many rooms for one man's house! One just for books, hundreds of them, and ranked arrays of data crystals. One just for a table, the size of a refectory table—no food on it, though. Some rooms were dark. Others were blue-shadowed, dawn-lit by walls of glass that looked west, over the City. No one was moving about; she didn't even glimpse the "automatics" he'd mentioned last night. She wondered what they looked like, and whether they would recognize that she belonged here.

At the end of the hallway she found a windowed room full of soft chairs. She went in, and subdued lights came on, looking pale in the dawn. Dawn over the City of the Pilot Masters, the place of their power and wealth. She walked slowly to the window and looked out. Below her on the steep slope, on either side, and across the little canyon, she saw a jumble of gray and red tiled roofs, smooth pale walls, and deep-shadowed gardens. The few lights were fading as darkness retreated westward over the desert. In the distance, the cluster of towers speared skyward: buildings as high as this cliff, buildings like mountains, but still graceful, sheathed in glass, cobalt and gray and iridescent white. She marveled at it, that the jump pilots could build huge, important buildings and still care for how they looked. They could consider beauty. Not like her own people.

She turned back to the room. It was full of gracefully placed chairs clustered around low, polished tables. A long couch faced an elaborately tiled hearth at one end of the room. Objects stood on the tables here and there—bowls, platters, little sculptures. All useless, or unused; they must be there simply to look at. She picked up a small clay jar, glazed red-brown and densely etched in yellow with an abstract pattern. She wondered how old it was, and what it had cost. What the money would have bought for her village if she'd had it to spend.

She was beginning to understand what the Pilot Masters' wealth meant. It didn't make her like them any better.

"Do you always rise so early?"

She turned quickly, guiltily. Iain stood in the archway, wearing a loose, dark blue robe that hung to his bare feet. It was covered with subtle embroidery in the same dark blue. His unbraided hair coiled to his waist, and his face was still blurred with sleep. "I told the house to call me if you came out of your room." He looked displeased. "I didn't expect you would be up at dawn."

She turned back to the table and set the little jar carefully on its stand. "I was hungry."

"Then ask for food." He said it as if it were obvious.

"I'd like some breakfast, please," she said obediently.

"No." He looked exasperated. "Not *me*. The *house*." When she said nothing, he sighed. "All right. Watch."

Linnea folded her arms and waited.

Iain spoke, raising his voice. "House. Hot coffee and sweet cakes for two."

After a while, a bell chimed softly. Iain reached out to a cylindrical pedestal near his chair and touched the white dome on its top. The dome split in two pieces that sank into the pedestal, revealing a plate of pastel-frosted cakes and two delicate, blue-and-white conical cups in silver holders, all on a silver tray. Iain moved to a wide chair and sat down, arranging his silk robe carefully around him. Then he looked at her, an eyebrow lifted.

Suppressing a sigh, Linnea went over and picked up the tray. "Where do I put this?"

"On the table nearest to my right hand." Iain shook his head. "You *weren't* trained for this, were you?"

"Not really." She found a table, perched the tray, and handed Iain a cup. Then she sat down herself in a chair facing Iain's and took the other cup. It was filled with black, steaming liquid that gave off a rich, delicious smell. She sipped it. It tasted burned, bitter—terrible. She swallowed it calmly and set the cup down in its holder. "It's very good."

He gave her a sharp look. "Your first taste of coffee?" She nodded. "And you liked it, did you?" She nodded again, and his mouth twitched.

"Now," Iain said, and the flicker of amusement was gone from his face. "Tell me why you've come here."

Linnea picked up her cup again and took a steady sip, thinking rapidly. She would give him part of the truth, to begin with. "Some people on my world found something that seems to belong to your family. We thought you might want it back."

He stirred impatiently. "What sort of thing is it?"

"I don't know exactly. But I heard it's something that's important to your family. Maybe because it's valuable, or maybe because it might hurt them." She pitched her voice low, tried to sound calm and sympathetic.

"Show it to me," Iain said abruptly.

"I don't have it," she said. "I don't even know where it is. I came because we thought you wanted someone to come here. We thought you might have an interest in this thing, and so in exchange for it you might be willing to help us."

He sat considering her, his chin resting on one hand, two fingers lightly touching his mouth. "What is it? What does it look like?"

Maybe the description would tell him it was something worth bargaining for. "It's silver metal," she said. "A thin cylinder, about so long." She held up her thumb and forefinger five centimeters apart. "It has a cap on one end, metal like the rest. And there's writing on the cap, in paint that looks like yellow metal. It says 'D-E.'"

After a moment, he shook his head. "I don't know what it could be." He set his hands on his knees and leaned forward. "What help did you hope for?"

Linnea swallowed hard. "Our twenty-year contract is about to end," she said. "And my people are afraid that we won't get a new one. We thought—you could arrange that."

Iain's eyes narrowed. "You should know better. Working jump pilots have nothing to do with trade contracts. We're not allowed to negotiate anything, even when we're offworld. The old men do all that, here in the City—the retired Pilot Masters on the Inner Council. My uncle is the chairman, the Honored Voice. And we're sworn to obey them in everything."

She stared at him, dismayed. "Then you *can't* help us."

He lifted his chin. "I would never break my oath to enter into an arrangement like this. Nor would I have the power to carry out such a bargain." He sounded completely sure.

"You couldn't even ask?"

Iain's eyes kindled a little. "I am *sworn* to obey the Inner Council. You understand the idea? Sworn in blood, my word in blood. Sworn by the Tree that grew on Earth. When that word is broken, the man breaks as well." He looked away, toward the morning light, his expression troubled. "It doesn't matter in any case. The contracts are endorsed by the Council, and the Council's Honored Voice opposes renewal for the 'unprofitable worlds.' Starting with yours."

"But if the—the Honored Voice is your uncle," she said, almost steadily, "can't you appeal to him?"

"It would not help you," Iain said, and she heard a sour note in his voice. "My father is my uncle's strongest political opponent. And his greatest enemy."

"If your uncle knew *why*—"

"If he knew that you hope to blackmail us? He may well know that," Iain said. "I would guess that it was he who arranged for you to come."

"Can't your father help us?" She had to find a reason to hope.

"My father opposes this new contract policy," Iain said curtly. "He hates my uncle's expediency, his disregard for tradition. But in this matter my father could never win. He will not waste his political capital." He looked at her sharply. "Now tell me about this little cylinder. You say your people found it?"

She forced herself to relax her tight fists, breathe more

steadily. "It's been on Santandru since my grandmother was a little girl. A man who served on Nexus brought it back."

He got to his feet and looked down at her. "Give it to me."

She stood to face him. The chair pressed against her legs, blocking her retreat. She gripped herself tightly, to hold the trembling in. "I told you the truth," she said. "I don't have it with me. If our contract is renewed, it will be sent to you. You have my word."

Iain's face was calm as stone. "You cannot tell me why I should bargain with you, or what the value of this thing might be. You can't even show it to me. I see no reason to hear you further."

"Wait," Linnea said desperately. "You don't know what this thing is. But your father might."

"If it truly mattered," Iain said bitterly, "and if my father thought I was capable of understanding, he would have told me." Behind the anger in his eyes, then, she saw pain. "Now go."

Shaken and heartsore, Linnea rose and left the room. She had failed, but she would try again. She would try until she succeeded.

She would keep her promise to Asper, and save Marra. No matter what it cost.

SIX

In the quiet of his room, Iain sen Paolo prepared for battle.

The woman was right: His father Paolo might know the meaning of this thing she had described. There was a mystery here. And so he would ask, though he was sure Paolo would refuse to answer.

He bathed and dressed carefully in full formal black. He braided his hair into a black, glossy rope, with the crimson of his lineage woven through it in silk, and painted his face with severity and restraint.

He studied his image as it turned before him in the self-screen, gazed at last into his own hard eyes. He was ready. "House," he said. "Where is the woman?"

"She remains in the room assigned to her," the house said.

"Keep her there," Iain said. "No communications in or out of the house. Deny all visitors. Do not trace my location."

"Noted," the house said in its even voice.

"Provide food for the woman at midday and sunset," Iain said. "Basic diet, no spices."

"Noted."

Iain sighed and straightened his shoulders. "Call a tube car."

I ain stopped the tube car a hundred meters from his father's house. Better to walk the last part of the way. Always, always his father's house chilled him. He had loved it as a boy—when he'd been sure of himself, and of his place in his father's life. But when he'd been elevated to pilot training, that had ended. At times he had suspected that his father had wanted him to fail.

The house lay high on a southeastern slope, where Paolo's gardens basked in the warm morning light, but would be shaded from the harsh late-day sun. A shiver of wild color, the gardens rose from the low, black stone wall toward the house. There all color ended. The house stood as it always had—smooth curves of deep gray metal and glass, the color of clouds before the storm on worlds where rain fell. It did not catch or reflect light; always it seemed to be its own shadow, the shadow of all light and all color. And within, of course, only silence. Iain had not been here since before his latest voyage, a span of four subjective months, and the strangeness added to his unease.

He passed his hand over the gatepost and the gate opened, speaking no word of welcome; he was known, but not expected.

He paused. "House. Where is Paolo sen David?"

"He is at the south corner of the garden," the house

replied, a voice from the air before him. A woman's voice; it had always been a woman's voice, in defiance of custom. "You are welcomed as always, Pilot Master sen Paolo."

"Tell him I've come," Iain said.

"It has been done," the voice said.

Iain moved away up the path, following its curves past mounds of vivid scarlet blooms, rigid spikes of moon-pale white, sprays of bizarre orange grasses taller than his head; through scents fleeting and heavy, strange and familiar, but none that he could name. The garden had always been his father's private domain—his one eccentricity. Like most men, Iain left his own gardens to the automatics.

As always, Iain felt smaller, younger with every step. Less like a passed jump pilot with a superb record and his own house—the life he'd led for four subjective years. More like the little boy in trouble for a fight at school, or the trainee jump pilot freshly censured for defying the teaching masters. The shame, the failing that he knew his father saw in him grew and darkened.

The third turning brought him to his father. Paolo knelt in a bed of soft black soil, tucking tiny seedlings along the base of a wall of polished granite. Water trickled gently beside him into a dark pond; pale fish moved in the depths there. Paolo wore work clothing, tunic and trousers of plain brown; his thinning iron-gray hair was caught back in a simple tail, bound with black cord. He looked up as Iain came near.

He did not rise, so Iain knelt. Only then did Paolo speak. "Iain," he said, as calmly as if his son's recent absence had been a short one. It had not been: four months to Iain in the time dilation of the jump, but twenty months to Paolo.

Iain struck the same cool note. "Father." Paolo had not changed. He had never been like other men; he never clung to the signs of past pride and glory as other men did. His name had always been enough: Paolo sen David, the son of David sen Elkander. Paolo carried his pride within himself. As he carried every other emotion—hidden, only to be guessed at. . . .

But now that Paolo had spoken, Iain was permitted to speak as well. He turned his hands palm up on his knees in formal supplication. "Father. There's a matter I must discuss with you."

Paolo did not look up. "These plants need setting out, or they'll dry out and die. Speak while I work." He bent to his task, turning his back to his son.

Iain did not move. The gravel of the path dug painfully into his knees. Absurd, coming here; absurd, asking. His carefully prepared words scattered in shards. "I have encountered a mystery," he said at last.

Paolo did not turn. He stabbed at the soft soil, loosening it further. "Explain."

"Someone arranged for a servant to be hired in my name," Iain said. "A plain, awkward, untrained woman. I would consider it just a clumsy joke, but for one thing. The woman comes from one of the fringe worlds—the world whose contract Uncle Fridric wants to end."

"I don't recall the world's name," Paolo said, digging steadily.

"Santandru," Iain said.

Paolo stopped digging for a moment, a breath of hesitation—then began again doggedly. "Santandru. Well, there are few enough worlds. This is a coincidence, surely."

"Forgive me," Iain said. He wished his father would

turn and face him. "Forgive me, but it seems not. She came believing some kind of arrangement had been made with our family—with me."

"What kind of arrangement?" Paolo's voice was almost sharp. He settled back and picked up another seedling, but he did not continue working; he kept his strong severe gaze on Iain.

"She knows the location of something that belongs to our family," Iain said. "She says that it will be sent to us in exchange for renewing her world's trade contract."

He saw Paolo's face change for an instant—a flicker of some powerful emotion, quickly suppressed. Paolo rose slowly to his feet. "I will hear no more," he said coldly, looking down at Iain. "I cannot bargain privately. In any case, the matter is quite beyond my power in the Council."

"I told her so," Iain said. "Yet—Father, she says this thing contains a secret damaging to our family." He looked up at his father. "And I wonder—could there be some link between this matter, and Fridric cutting that world from the routes?"

"If there were any such connection," Paolo said, "then it would be my concern as head of our family. Not yours."

Without permission, Iain rose to his feet. "But suppose Uncle Fridric knew that we might be blackmailed by someone on Santandru. He might well decide—"

"Be silent," Paolo said in a gray voice. Iain caught his breath while his father frowned down at his muddy work gloves. The water trickled cheerfully on beside them, and the blossoming shrubs nearby whispered in the warm wind, breathing sweetness. Iain's heart pounded. Perhaps Paolo would speak. Perhaps, at last, he would trust his son, draw him closer—

Paolo's voice was hard. "Iain. As your father, I forbid you to inquire any further into this matter. That is a formal order."

Of course this would be Paolo's choice. Iain bit back a furious protest: Any word that was not acquiescence would be open disobedience, an affront to his father, a dishonor to himself.

"Send the woman to me," Paolo said. "I will deal with her."

"She is under contract to me," Iain said. "I'll need her permission."

"Get it," Paolo said. "Then think nothing more of this."

"Father," Iain said, bitterness choking his throat. "Why can't you trust me? I have never shamed you in any way."

"I trust you as I have always done," his father said remotely.

"Yet you tell me nothing. Rafael is Selected, and I'm left standing, and you acquiesce." The words tore his aching throat. The sun dazzled his eyes, making the world shimmer. "I tell you our honor is in danger, and you tell me to be silent. You send me away like a boy."

"You give me no reason to treat you as a man," Paolo said. "Be silent. Do as I have ordered. Then keep to your house until I call you here again. Your behavior displeases me." He turned away.

Silence, silence again. Always only silence, severity, commands. Iain stalked away down the path.

He would not come to this place again. Let the silence between them last as long as Paolo chose. Longer. Iain would go home. And if it suited him, he would keep the woman. If he was not to be trusted as a son, why must he obey as a son?

Iain stopped. No—he would not go home. Not yet.

He knew one man who might give him answers. If it pleased him. And now, Iain was ready to pay any price.

Iain called for a tube car.

Rafael's house filled the top floor of a tower of glass. It both followed and defied the custom of the Line: No man who lived within walls of glass might be said to hide his life from others, yet what one saw through those walls was distorted, hazy, strange. The tower, a pale green cylinder, glistened wetly in the vivid morning light as Iain's car approached it.

Iain had not come to his cousin's house in ten subjective years. Here he had spent the most shaming weeks of his life, weeks that it burned his mind to remember. As he rose in the lift toward the heights, toward Rafael, chilly sweat sprang out on his temples and his upper lip, and his stomach roiled.

That past could not touch him, he told himself. He was a man now, and safe. Still, he felt unsettled, off-balance, when the door of Rafael's house not only welcomed him when he spoke to it, but called him by name, and admitted him. Its voice sounded familiar, and yet unfamiliar; it was not the same voice as ten years ago.

The door opened on a wide room—as pale and dim as ever, Iain saw; still bare of decoration, almost bare of furnishings. Greenish light washed inward from the glass wall, gleaming on cold stone floors, a stone table or two, a chair here and there. Iain caught a faint scent of flowers— some kind he knew, something fleshy-petaled and moon white—though he could see none. "What refreshment do you require, Master sen Paolo?" Rafael's house asked.

Iain's belly went cold. Now he knew that voice. It was his own. He took a steadying breath. "I require nothing. Where is my cousin?"

"He *was* asleep," a blurred voice said behind Iain. "What in Old Earth's name brings you to me at this hour? And so beautifully dressed?"

Iain turned slowly. Rafael stood in the doorway that led to his sleeping suite. He wore a long, loose, sleeveless sleeping robe, pale gray like the stone under his bare feet. "Truly, cousin," Rafael said, "I haven't seen you give this much attention to your looks since the old days."

"I have questions to ask you," Iain said.

"That's rather rude. But you always were unsubtle." Rafael yawned and sank down onto a broad resting-couch.

To claim his equality of rank, Iain knew he should sit; but no other couch or chair stood near, and he could not make himself sit beside Rafael. Standing, Iain asked his first question. "What do you know about the world called Santandru?"

Rafael's brows lifted, but he focused his blue gaze on his fingers. They looked strange to Iain like this, bare of gems. "I know no more than anyone else," Rafael said at last. "From what I hear, one does not linger there. Barbarous and dull, like half those little worlds. Father is right. We would be well rid of them."

Iain gathered himself. There was no reason to draw this out, no reason to be subtle. "I have a servant who comes from there," he said. "One I did not contract for, yet the contract is in my name. Can you tell me anything about that?"

Rafael turned his hand and studied his palm. "Now that you mention it, I do remember conceiving some kind of practical joke. But that was years ago. And from that world I expected it to be a man." He frowned slightly. "I wanted it to be a man. For the joke, you know. Your . . . democratic tastes. It amused me to imagine you trying to teach our ways to one of those unwashed fishermen."

Iain felt his face darken. "A joke, then. But hardly up to your standards, cousin. And what made you think of Santandru in particular?"

Rafael tucked his bare feet up onto the resting-couch. "I don't remember. Perhaps my father mentioned the place. Or perhaps I was thinking about fish." He blinked at Iain. "That was a long time ago, cousin. You're boring me."

Iain sighed. It was certainly possible that Rafael did not remember. Spiderweave tore memories loose and scattered them before one's eyes in strange and beautiful patterns— but in time the distortions masked true memory.

Iain had to cut through the mist in his cousin's mind— real or feigned—and reach the truth. "Did this joke of yours have anything to do with your father's wish not to renew Santandru's trade contract?"

"Political arguments bore me," Rafael said sulkily. "I have no idea why my father decides what he decides." He glanced up at Iain, his eyes cold and blank. "Or why I should tell you if I did know."

Iain drew a careful breath. "There is something—a secret my father refuses to tell me. I believe you know what it is."

Rafael sat very still for a moment. Then he slid his feet to the floor and rose. He moved closer, looking down at Iain from his greater height. "If there were such a thing," he said, "and if I knew it, it would hardly be my place to tell you." The scent of flowers grew stronger.

Iain did not step back. This was the moment; now he must choose how much he was willing to pay for the truth. "You break rules." His voice sounded breathless.

"But you don't," Rafael said. "Not any more." He brushed one finger up Iain's arm.

Iain steeled himself. "If you broke a rule this time," he said, his voice tight, "I would be—grateful." Somewhere in the dimness beyond Rafael, a breeze-chime stirred, struck.

He knew that sound. That sound, this scent, the pale green light—he remembered the cool breeze, his own nakedness, the sick swirl of his drugged and drunken thoughts, strong hands gripping and turning him—he remembered begging for what he knew would come, and a cold laugh, and a voice telling him what he was now, what he had become—then pain like splinters of ice, and above him that faint cool chime—

Saliva flooded his mouth. He couldn't move. He knew now that he could not do this—he had to step away, turn, run—but he could not move.

"Little cousin." Rafael drew Iain's body against his, set cold hands on his shoulders, smiled into his eyes. "Did you believe you could fool me? You're about to vomit."

Iain swallowed. "I want to know the truth."

"Then ask your father." The hands stirred, massaging.

"He will never tell me," Iain said unsteadily. "I know that now. It's something that touches the family honor."

"Ah." Cold amusement glinted in Rafael's eyes. "Well, I can give you this much reassurance, little cousin. Our family honor is what it always was. Every bit as unsullied."

Iain's lungs filled with the flower scent. Pale and greenish, like the light. He closed his eyes for a moment. "Then why can't my father tell me?"

Now Rafael laughed. One hand slid up to rest, thin and cool, against Iain's cheek. "Because you're an innocent," he said, his voice strangely gentle. "I tried to change that, when you were a boy. You were awkward, ignorant, but I— I thought only of your good. But it's very durable, this thickheaded loyalty of yours. This loyalty to ideas that don't matter, ceremonies that don't matter, lineage that—"

"They matter," Iain said. His anger flared, but still he endured his cousin's caress. "They're *everything*. Everything we stand for, work for, risk our lives for. You're of the Line as I am. How can you say such things?"

"Oh, how you tempt me," Rafael said. "Coming to me like this, a supplicant—so eager to learn what I know. How you tempt me, to try again to open your mind. . . ." With a slow smile he bent down toward Iain, as if to kiss him. Iain stood ready, his heart pounding. No. He *would not* turn away now, so close to knowing. He would have his answer.

Rafael stopped, looking down at him half-smiling, his deep eyes hooded. "You pretend, and think to fool me," he said. "You forget that I know your response when you are not pretending." He stepped away. "No."

Without the support of Rafael's hands, Iain staggered, then steadied himself. "No?" he echoed dully.

"No, my dear," Rafael said. "This ignorance is what your father wants for you. He imagines you'll be happier this way. And perhaps he's right." He sighed theatrically. "As tempting as your offer is"—his face went cold—"I must refuse it. I promise you that the knowledge would be of no use to you."

Iain blinked, dazed. "But—"

"Don't," Rafael said. His voice was light as ever, but Iain heard the knife steel under the lightness. "Be what you were meant to be. Lead the life your father planned for you. Don't touch anything from Santandru. You may think that I wish you only evil. But in this I am trying to help you. We will all be well rid of that world soon enough."

"Then the decision is made?"

"As good as made," Rafael said. "It's over. There is nothing this servingwoman of yours can do. You should sell her contract for half a decim and forget any lies she's tried to tell you." Rafael raised a pale hand to his forehead. "Now do go. I've hired two truly delicious women for this evening—twins, can you imagine?—so I must finish my rest."

Iain turned and left. His head ached, and his mind churned with frustration and misery. He had sworn to himself that Rafael would never touch him again, and he had broken that promise, only to see the truth he sought slip away yet again.

Yet as he rode down in the lift toward safety, toward escape, he could feel all the muscles of his body beginning to uncoil with relief. Perhaps his body was wisest. A shudder crawled up his back as he remembered Rafael's cold fingers brushing his skin.

Then he frowned as he remembered Rafael's parting advice. Something odd about that—his father had said the same thing. He turned and looked out through the rippling glass at the wavering green city rising around him, dreamlike, drowned, and his frown deepened. It *was* strange how eager everyone seemed to separate him from the woman Linnea.

Perhaps he would not allow them to succeed just yet.

Linnea paced in her room. Five steps, turn, five more. No sunlight through the window now. Past noon. She turned to the door and touched it again, and again the voice of the house said, "You may not pass."

Anything could happen now. The Pilot Master had locked her in here hours ago, and she could not guess why, though her mind swirled with frightening possibilities. Perhaps he intended to betray her, or to sell her to some other man. Or to punish her.

Or to break her.

She slammed her hand against the door, which did not even tremble. Again the house said, "Do not damage this structure." She kicked the door. This time, mercifully, the house was silent.

She turned away blindly to begin her pacing again, and it was then that the door opened.

She whirled. The doorway was empty. The house said, "The Pilot Master has summoned you to his suite."

"Where is that?" Her voice cracked, nervous.

She found that the voice of the house could move through the air before her, guiding her on—through a hall she had not explored that morning, to a broad stone stair winding upward to the left. At the top the voice said, "Straight ahead," and she obeyed, passing through a low stone arch.

The room was so large that at first she did not grasp where she was, until she realized that the broad platform, open to the wall of glass and the City below, was a bed. This was his bedroom. She stood in the very center of the room, trying not to let her eyes wander. Patterns swirled along the walls, flecks of deep color like tiny tiles. Water played in a small fountain in one corner. The sunlight spilling in warmed her bare feet and woke the patterns in the thick rugs to brilliant life.

She wondered dizzily what he would do to her. Whether it would hurt.

"You need proper clothes," a man said behind her, and she turned.

It was the Pilot Master—Iain. She tugged at her tunic, trying to straighten it with hands that shook in spite of all she could do to still them. "Th—these are good enough. If I'm not staying." Her heart was beating so hard she thought he must see it.

He did not answer her half question. He simply stood there in the archway, his arms folded, studying her. He wore black as before, but the light picked out the rich texture of the fabric.

Her heart raced. "What did you learn? What have you decided?"

He walked forward and stopped again, a couple of meters away. This close she could see how weary his eyes were. "Why should I discuss that with you?"

She flattened her sweating hands against the rough fabric of her tunic. "You kept me locked in that room," she said. "Without telling me anything. You owe me an explanation." She could hear her voice rising.

"Your complaints are not important," he said. "Come and draw my bath."

She stared at him for a moment in disbelief. "Draw your *bath*?"

"I need to wash," he said. She saw a faint tremor in his shoulders, a shudder. The air in the room stirred, and she caught a faint scent, some strange flower. "Earn your keep." He pointed to a sunny archway at the far end of the room.

He was not going to tell her anything. But at least it seemed he was not going to touch her, either. Not yet. She turned and walked through the archway.

Here was another room, so huge she could not grasp its purpose at first. Again the wall was of glass—the glass must cut the light somehow, or this whole house would be impossibly hot. Sunlight streamed in over brown and red and turquoise tiles. In the center of the floor was a vast round basin, empty. A bath? But it would be big enough to swim in. It couldn't be a bath.

Iain brushed past her impatiently and knelt by the rim of the basin. He touched a metal disk set in the tiles, and water began churning into the hole from several sources at once. Yes, it was a bath. He looked up at her. "That's all you need to do. The house knows the temperature I prefer. Now." He stood up again and expertly stripped the braid from his hair, which spilled over his shoulders in dark waves. Then he lifted his arms a little away from his body, and waited.

She shrank back, wondering if he was about to embrace her, but he simply stood there. "Well?" he said at last. "Undress me."

Linnea went to him, knowing she was blushing furiously, knowing she would fumble all the strange knots and fastenings. What would he do to her, what would he do? What did he know about her?

She fought to remember what she'd seen in the data crystals Asper had shown her, the dramas. Well, surely the boots had to come off first. She managed it, with Iain's help. Then, with nervous fingers she had to untie the complicated sash, slip the heavy black tunic from his shoulders, and set it aside on a rack he silently pointed out to her. Then there was a shirt of fine black material, so fine her callused palms caught in it. He had to show her how it would fall open if she touched the seam just right. She was careful not to brush against his bare skin.

Under the shirt he was lean and brown, well muscled as any fisherman, but without a fisherman's scars and weathering. The trousers opened the same way as the shirt; he stepped out of them for her. He wore no linens under the trousers. No doubt he could wash them every day if he liked. She kept her eyes on the clothes she was smoothing and folding and setting aside. The churning of the water stopped, and she turned in time to see him walk steadily down the steps into the steaming bath. His body was strongly and finely made, and he moved with grace, despite the tension in his shoulders. She could not look away from him. She felt her blush deepen.

He did not seem to notice—his eyes were dark and distant. He settled into the water, sank back until he was submerged, then surfaced, wringing out the wet rope of his hair. "Well?"

She stammered, "You mean—I get in with—"

"Of course," he said. "How else could you assist me? And you must know how much you need a bath yourself."

She undressed as she had for the other Pilot Master, quickly so she did not have time for thought or embarrassment. It helped that he wasn't looking directly at her, or at anything—still that same inward focus. She left her clothes in a heap on the floor and stepped into the water.

She yelped, and he turned and looked up at her. "It's hot," she gasped. She realized she was twisting into a ridiculous position, trying to cover herself, and so she made herself move forward and down, wincing as the water rose higher around her body. It was so hot that it stung, but the sting eased as she settled down into the water. There was a sort of bench along the wall, under the water, that she could sit on.

"Have you *ever* had a bath before?" he asked dryly.

She clamped her lips shut and devoted herself to business. First he required her to wash herself. The soap was a creamy liquid with a clear leafy scent. He told her to wash her hair, and for that he made her use a different liquid. "It's all the same dirt," she said, but he ignored her.

She remembered the dramas better now. She was supposed to wash him. But when she moved toward him, his face tightened again into coldness, and she stopped, unsure. Then he turned his back to her. "Comb some oil through my hair. From that dark blue jar."

That part was almost pleasant; he had such strong hair, easy to work with. "My sister had hair like this," she said. "But she cut it off when her husband died."

He did not answer, and she realized she should not have spoken. The tension in him—she was afraid to find out what it was, what it meant. What he knew.

When she was finished, he made her get out first. When she moved to put her clothes on again, his eyes flashed contempt. "There are robes in that tall cabinet there." She found one—it was the same soft material as the shirt, but this one was sea gray. She knotted the sash around herself. The softness of the fabric sent little shivers along her skin. She turned and faced him as he climbed out of the water. At his gesture, she shook out a sun-warmed towel and gave it to him.

Then she had to dress him, in different clothes, plainer than before, and gray like her own. She had to braid his damp hair loosely, which made her think again of Marra, so that she had to bite her lip to keep back the tears. He didn't notice. She realized that she had set aside one of her fears; clearly this man had no use for her body. Maybe he was one of the ones who loved only men.

Or maybe not. At the end he stood looking down at her, a strange intent gaze. She looked back at him for a moment. "What?"

"Follow me."

He led her into a third room, a kind of sitting room, but a more comfortable size than the rooms downstairs. He did not sit down, so she stood there facing him. This room did not catch the sunlight; it was dim, shady, cool enough that she shivered in her light robe.

He studied her some more. Then he said, "What are you?"

"I don't understand." Her voice shook, from cold and nervousness; a pity he would hear it, but there was nothing she could do. No one could help her. She could only help herself.

Iain folded his arms and looked her up and down. "You're too awkward to be a spy, or a blackmailer. You're someone's tool, I think."

"No one that I know of," she said through gritted teeth.

"Or someone's joke," he said. "Maybe he wasn't lying."

"Who?"

But he didn't answer that. "Why did you come here?"

"To help my people," she said.

"I think not," he said gently. "You don't have the look of a crusader."

She bit her lip. "To help my sister."

"Tell me about her."

So she did—the whole history of it, of life in her sister's house, of Rowdy's death, of the death of her village. He listened impassively, even when she found it hard to speak through tears. Oh, God, she missed them all so much, Marra and the babies. As she spoke other words raged silently within her—*you failed them, you knew you would fail* . . .

They were sitting now, facing each other, and some of the afternoon sun had begun to come in. She took a shaking breath and wiped her nose on the sleeve of her robe, and he winced, but said nothing. "So I came here," she said. "And—that's all." The tears felt cool on her cheeks. She shivered again.

He leaned back in his chair, his long hands steady on its carved arms. "There's a mystery here," he said at last. In the sharp shadows she could not read his expression. "You have a small piece of that mystery. And I can guess the shape of it." He leaned forward, and now she could see his face, its expression watchful, thoughtful. "Perhaps together, we know more than we realize."

Her breath caught. "I've told you everything I know."

"I know you think you have," he said. "But there is more. If I could see this thing you describe, or if you could tell me who has it—"

"No," she said, frightened again. She could not follow failure with betrayal.

"Because you can't? Or because you won't?"

"No," she said again, though she knew it was hopeless. Marra had been right—she could not defend herself against these men. She raised her chin and met his eyes.

But—strangely—his gaze had no anger in it; in fact, if such a thing were possible, she would have said there was pity there. But what could this Pilot Master, a lord of the Hidden Worlds, know about helplessness? She stared at him, and he shook his head a little and said, "You have no ally here. Nor have I. And the secret that's being kept from us—clearly it's dangerous." He looked down at his hands, then into her eyes again, straight and serious. "They don't want us to help each other. And so I think that's what we must do."

Linnea caught her breath. Maybe she hadn't failed. Maybe there was still a little hope. "I agree," she said steadily. And when he stretched out his hand to her, she took it and held it firmly, the mark of a bargain well struck. His hand was strong and warm, and inside her the flicker of hope strengthened into new flame.

SEVEN

At midday, three days later, Iain leaned in the doorway of his day parlor and watched Linnea set out food on a low stone table near the window. He studied her as she knelt there, arranging the small triangular plates she had taken from the automatics' delivery platform—here the savories, there the twist of bread, there the carefully arranged slivers of fruits and vegetables. She had improved. In a day or two more, she might even pass as a genuine servant—for a short time, and at a distance.

Iain frowned. Up close, she still did not look her part. Hard work had thickened her short nails and callused her hands, and she wore her coarse black hair chopped off just above her shoulders, making any flattering arrangement impossible. But he could see improvement even here: her hair shone, and she had painted her face correctly. She now kept her hands and feet scrupulously clean, and her arms and legs hairless, as they should be. Three days ago her warm voice and her obvious robust health had been her only assets; now she looked almost acceptable. No one would laugh at her, as long as she kept silent; and silence was her place. He hoped she would learn it in time.

She glanced up at him, and he moved forward to the curving black dining-couch arranged beside the table. This time she did not speak.

He settled onto the couch. Yes, Linnea had learned the outward things: how to choose appropriate dresses for morning, afternoon, and evening; how to wear the few unobtrusive jewels he had found for her; how to walk in proper shoes. How to kneel, to rise from kneeling, to present a tray, to pour wine.

Yet still she clung to the prejudices of her own little world. Just now he could tell from her discontented expression that she had something to say. "You may speak," he said.

She looked up at him. "I'm wondering about your children."

Iain sat up straight. "I have no sons," he said coldly. He leaned forward to pick up a small delicacy, a smoky paste of mollusks wrapped in a pungent leaf.

"I don't understand how the women can do that. Give birth, leave their babies here, and go away forever." She looked down at her hands, her eyes distant, hooded.

"Not all worlds are the same," Iain said. "Nor all people. The women are carefully chosen, and well paid." He took a careful bite of the mollusk paste. "Enough to make them rich for life."

"I've never known a woman who would make such a bargain." He saw her face darken suddenly. "I'm sorry. Your mother must have been one of them."

"Of course she was. But I never saw her."

She looked at him oddly, then turned away to take a new plate from the delivery platform. He wondered why this mattered so much to her. "They have an easy life, the ones with birth contracts," he said. "No work at all."

"Will you have a son someday?"

"No," he said, trying to keep his voice neutral, trying not to think of Rafael. "A man must be chosen for that. I was not."

"I still don't see," she said, "why you would *want* to have your children this way. It's such a waste. You only have boys, and then it takes years to find out whether they have the right kind of mind to be a jump pilot."

"We have our customs," Iain said. "They have worked for us for six centuries." He settled back from the table and tried to ease his tense shoulders.

She leaned forward over the table, her eyes dark, serious. "Why don't you use technology, like the other rich worlds? I've read about it. You could start embryos in dishes, and test them. Only implant the ones who will be jump pilots."

"It was tried, hundreds of years ago," Iain said. "None of the sons had the gift." He set his palms on the table. "Piloting isn't a matter of genetics. It's spiritual. It passes from father to son through the body of the mother. Only sons conceived and born in the body can receive the ability from their fathers."

"That's silly," she said, smiling a little.

Iain snorted and reached for his bowl of wine. "It's a fact. Just as it's true that only men can make jumps." He took a deep draft of the cool, flowery wine, then set the bowl down. "Men born to the Line."

"How many of them?" She carefully refilled the bowl to the top.

"One in five or six, overall. More in the better families. The ones who don't become jump pilots work here in the City, or on Dock. They're not allowed to father sons, but otherwise there's no stigma. They just—move in different circles." He thought of Mekael. A boyhood friend, but a man from the wrong circle—a mistake. . . . "I've finished."

She passed him a square of linen. "Some people say piloting is a trade secret, not a skill."

"If that were true," Iain said, "we'd all be jump pilots—every young man on this planet." He cleaned his fingers carefully. "Ten thousand jump pilots. All the service the Hidden Worlds could afford. We'd be rich."

She looked up at him sharply. "You don't think you're rich now?"

Always she challenged him—as if she were a man, and his friend. As if she did not understand that she was in his power.

This time, he let her challenge pass. "The Line earns what it gets. Jump pilots pass through otherspace again and again. It's dangerous work."

Her gaze was steady now. "I see."

"Four of us have died on jumps in the past three years." He frowned at her. "More than usual. But such a toll is not unknown."

"Four." Her voice was quiet. "Four in how many?"

"Two thousand active pilots," he said. "We retire at thirty or thirty-five, subjective years. But even one of us is too great a loss."

"Out of a hundred fishermen," she said, "in any season one, or two, or three will die. Sometimes more."

"But fishermen are easy to replace," Iain said.

Her expression hardened. "Their wives and children don't think so."

He took a breath to rebuke her—then let it out. It was her world at risk. She must see some value in it. Though she had never said what.

And of course he could not ask her. The barrier between them was too great. It would always be too great.

Then, startling him, the voice of the house spoke at his elbow. "Your pardon, Master sen Paolo. A message has been received from Council Lord Paolo sen David."

Feeling cold, Iain swung his feet to the floor. He'd dreaded this. "A message, not a call?"

"A message only."

"Show me."

The air over the nearest holoplate shimmered, clouded, sharpened into a familiar image. Paolo faced him, stern as always. "Iain. Come to my house at once." Then the image vanished.

Linnea stared at Iain, clearly perplexed. "Who was that?"

"My father." Iain rose. "House! Summon a car."

"He calls you and you go," she said, half-questioning.

"I must." He looked down at her. "Don't you understand? He's my father." *And I have disobeyed him. . . .*

This time his father's house called him by name, as the door closed behind him, and the cool shadows closed in as always. "Pilot Master sen Paolo, your father waits in his study."

The study—a bad sign; all the years of his youth he had

been summoned to that study only for admonition, or the announcement of punishment. Reluctantly, Iain passed through the high, familiar rooms, rich with the treasures his father had gathered in a lifetime as a Pilot Master and collector. He barely saw them, barely noted the familiar scents of the place—smoke, polished wood, woolen rugs.

The study was Paolo's private place, decorated to his plain private taste in sober colors and simple lines, its only beauty the broad, arched windows overlooking Paolo's gardens. Paolo stood waiting, and spoke as soon as Iain entered. "Why have you not sent me the woman?"

Iain stopped short. No greeting; so his father was truly angry. "She didn't consent to the change in her contract."

"I told you to make her consent." His father's black eyes flashed fire.

Iain kept his voice reasonable. "I can't force her to give free consent, Father."

"Don't be insolent!"

"Forgive me," Iain said uneasily. Beyond the windows the bright garden had faded to an ominous orange gloom. A dust storm coming; he had smelled it outside, could tell from the prickle along his skin.

"This matter is vitally important," Paolo said. "It may already be too late. Iain, you *must* send her to me. Her presence in your house is a danger to you."

Iain felt his anger flare. "If she's so dangerous, it would be no better to have her in your house than in mine."

Paolo's expression tightened. "She won't be here. I've agreed to transfer her contract elsewhere. And *I* will not allow her to refuse consent."

Iain looked sharply at his father. "Transfer her contract? Where?"

"To the one who arranged this little joke. He has confessed it to me. Your cousin Rafael."

Iain's breath caught. That young, inexperienced woman, in Rafael's power—"No, Father. You can't ask it. Her contract is with me. I owe her my protection. I will not send her to *him*."

"Iain, as your father, I command you to yield her to me." He straightened, his hands behind his back. "To refuse me will cost you more than you imagine."

Iain went still. "What do you mean?"

"It is possible that you would lose your position as a jump pilot," Paolo said. "Lose your place in the Line. Forever."

Iain's balance lurched, as if the floor sagged beneath him. To lose his place in the Line— It had happened, rarely. To have his link struck from the chain, his name struck from the Chronicles—

And never again, never again to lose himself in the eerie majesty of otherspace. To live here, on the ground, in the City forever, like an unpassed man—never to travel between the stars even as a passenger—to work in some dull position on Dock, or in a trade office. To be forgotten by his friends, or remembered only with pity, or mockery.

But—*Linnea, with Rafael. . . .*

Iain gathered himself. "Enough." His voice sounded flat in his own ears, but his body was cold, trembling with rage. "Father, when you and Fridric were both Council members, equals, you fought him. But now—now that he's the Honored Voice, you've given up. You give your consent to this, today—and to my humiliation before the Line, when Rafael was Selected—and even to the death of a world."

"I have not consented to that," Paolo said in a low voice.

"Are you truly working to oppose it? Is there truly any chance the vote will not favor Fridric?"

"Fridric is the Honored Voice." Paolo's thin hands clenched and trembled. "I—oppose this contract change. I have said as much in Council, and to those who have asked my opinion. But in the end, the Santandru contract is a minor matter."

"It is not a minor matter," Iain said hotly. "I know what you believe—what you truly believe, Father! This is *the Line* at stake. You know the oath. We have great power, but we use it to serve. To help. To bind the Hidden Worlds together. All of them, Father!"

"I know," Paolo said softly.

"But now it's a matter of Fridric's power. Fridric's power and the traditions of the Line. They've never been opposed before. But now that they are . . ." Iain steadied his voice. "Now that they are, you bend to him. You don't defend the Line. You don't defend me. You don't defend this innocent woman. And you won't tell me why." His voice twisted into bitterness. "You say you *can't* tell me why."

"I can tell you this, in confidence," Paolo said. "Iain— the Cold Minds may have found us."

Iain stared at him, stunned into silence.

His father looked old, weary. "There have been—indications of nanobot infestation, here in the Hidden Worlds. What was found has been dealt with. But the danger remains. Where it is found once, it may be found again."

Iain's throat filled with bile. Those ugly masses of microscopic devices, scum and foam and dust with death in it. The messengers of the Cold Minds, the controllers of the living—multiplying without cease, infesting the water, the walls, the bodies of human beings—destroying and weakening all the works of men. . . . "What did we do?" Iain asked raggedly, forcing down his nausea. "To deal with it?"

Paolo turned away, his hands clenched behind his back. "We destroyed the infestations. Two ships, and an orbital factory."

"Then they are intercepting our ships," Iain said. The skin on his arms, his neck prickled.

"You see, then," Paolo said, "why we must remain united. Why we must stand behind the Honored Voice, even though it is Fridric. This is no time for division among us."

Paolo turned and faced him, his expression severe. "Fridric is aging. He sees his death coming. His son will be old enough to enter politics in a few years. Fridric wishes to hand his power on to Rafael not merely undiminished, but greatly strengthened. He will defend that power even at the cost of a whole world's people."

"Fridric's a son of the Line, too," Iain said angrily. "Has he forgotten? He's the son of David sen Elkander—son of the man who brought the vaccines through to the Rimini Fading during the Chalk Plague. Who reached Kattayar through the Deep Array."

But Paolo was looking past Iain, his face lined and tired and sad. "Fridric is of the Line," he said distantly, "as truly as I am. . . ."

Again the question he must ask—the one that his father would never answer. "Father, you acquiesced in Fridric's rise to power. Why?"

Iain sensed his father's need to turn away, send Iain

away, avoid this. But he answered, his voice thin and gray. "I made a promise to your uncle before you were born."

"And you made no promises to me? To your only son?"

In the strange, sallow light from the window, Iain saw with shock that tears stood in his father's eyes. "I made only one vow," Paolo said quietly. "To protect you. And I am protecting you in the only way that is open to me. Iain, Fridric cannot kill us—the murder of family would cost him his own position. But now that he has the power of the Honored Voice, he can shame us both, drive us away from the Line." Paolo took a step toward Iain. "I *must* give the woman to Rafael, or that will certainly happen."

Iain felt rage take him again. "I see." He did not recognize his own voice. "For the first time I really do see, Father. When I was fifteen—you gave *me* to Rafael in the same way. You gave your consent to what happened to me, to protect your position and your honor."

His father's face paled with shock. "Never. Iain, how can you believe I would have allowed—"

Iain could not stop himself. "And if today Fridric gets what he wants—an innocent woman as a new toy for his spoiled son—then tomorrow he might ask you for *me* again. For the sake of the Line, because of the Cold Minds, whatever lie he wants to tell. When do we start refusing him, Father? Is there anything we *can* refuse him, once we start giving in?" He shook his head. "I refuse now. I still refuse. I'm going home."

He heard the change in his father's voice. "No, Iain— not yet."

"Not yet?" Iain turned slowly to face his father. "What have you done?"

"Stay yet awhile," Paolo said. "It's best that—"

"Is this why you called me here? So that, while I was gone from my house—"

"It's best that it simply happen," Paolo said. "You must trust me. There are reasons you cannot understand."

Iain stared at him for a long, shocked moment—then spun and left him there alone in the gathering darkness.

After Iain left for his father's house, Linnea passed restlessly from room to room, until she came to the library. She had questions; perhaps there were answers here, if she could figure out how to find them. She stood for a while first, staring out over the City at what should have been the sunset. To the west, over the open desert, a roiling wall of dust filtered the last light to the red-brown of dried blood. Darkness was coming.

She shivered. With its huge rooms filling with night, its bare windows open to anyone's eyes, she hated being alone in this house. She heard small noises from other rooms. Some of them she knew now: the rustling scuttle of the tiny automatics that cleaned dust from the floors when a room stood empty; the sigh of the air system; the cool trickle of water in fountains here and there. Other sounds she still did not understand—faint chittering behind a locked cabinet door, soft creaks, rapping sounds in other rooms. The house lived. But it would not speak to her in Iain's absence.

Here she was, thinking about Iain again. She turned her back to the window, went back to the shelves of books and data crystals. Here was information—more books than she had ever seen before in one place. The printed books stood ranked and cased behind glass doors that would not open for her. But the array of crystals had an index plate. She

touched it. It fogged, then cleared into the face of a man—
an old man, a servant, judging by his short hair. He said
smoothly, "How may I assist you?"

She knew he wasn't real, and so she could speak the
truth. She gathered her courage. "I want to know about Iain
sen Paolo. And, and Paolo sen David."

"You are not the user of this system," the old man's
voice said, warm and friendly and impervious. "Access to
personal information cannot be granted."

"Then—tell me about Santandru."

An odd blank expression flitted over the face in the
index plate. "Text or images?"

His voice in that quiet house made her uneasy. "Text."

Words appeared, stark black on white. *Santandru.
Colony 37. Class delta minus. Environment delta plus.
Economy delta zero. Population minimally viable. Trade
prospects delta minus. Innovation prospects epsilon zero.*

Whatever that meant. Grades of some kind. "More,
please."

The man's face appeared again. "Further information
has been placed under seal and is accessible only to senior
Masters."

Now that was odd. "Why?"

"This device cannot supply that information," the man's
face said.

"Can't you even guess?"

"This device cannot guess," the face said. "This device
is in full compliance with the ban on artificial minds. This
device lacks human capacities." The face smiled suddenly,
and she felt cold. "It is suggested that you obtain human
assistance."

She turned away. No. She had no question that would be answered here.

She slumped into a low chair and brooded, twisting her hands together. Why should information about Santandru be hidden from people? Even from Iain, judging by what that thing had said. Was it because of the contract cancellation? But that vote was still days away, Iain had told her.

She rubbed her eyes wearily, then remembered her face-paint and stopped. She had heard Iain speak hopefully of his father, who it seemed *was* trying to save Santandru's contract; but she didn't believe there was really any hope of it. These days Iain treated her with a gentleness that left her expecting pain, and soon.

She rose again and paced to the window, which reflected her faintly against the gathering darkness. There were no men like Iain on Santandru. How could there be? All his life he'd never had to give a thought to anyone else. He was rich, spoiled, his birthright of power and ease smoothing everything out before him. She had guessed that his father was cold to him, and that it troubled him; but there were worse troubles in life than that. Her own father had hit her more than once, and she'd still known he loved her. She'd learned to take what life gave her, arrange it as well as she could, and go on living. Not to waste her time and strength complaining and rebelling against what couldn't be changed.

As the last red-brown light faded from the plateau beyond her window, she put on a dress correct for evening, dark and flowing. She left her feet bare—Iain was not here to insist she put on those horrible shoes. She walked out to the large sitting room and paced. She could not set aside the feeling that some evil approached. It was like that last night in the hospital in Middlehaven years ago—waiting and waiting for Marra to come out into the hall and tell her Ma was dead. Now she listened with her whole body, straining to hear the sound of the door opening, Iain returning.

Then she caught herself and stood still. Why should it matter where Iain was, or what he was doing? He lived in a world of smoke and perfume and flowers, as weirdly artificial as the paint he wore on his face. She would not stay in this world, once the vote was lost. The money wouldn't matter then.

She stared into the dark pit of the unlit hearth. Yes. As soon as Iain returned, she would tell him. She would beg him to free her as soon as the contract was lost. And if he pitied her, as he might, he would agree. She would go home.

She moved restlessly to the window again, laid her forehead against the thick glass, and peered out and down at the City. The sky above the climate barrier glowed, city lights reflecting from long banners of dry, pale dust blown in off the desert. She would go home to be with Marra and all her people. In ten winters, or fifteen, she'd be dead of starvation or some disease. But someone who knew her would close her eyes. One of her own people.

Then she heard the house door swing open.

Iain's house unfolded itself to Rafael like a flower: helpless, tender, compliant before his mastery of code-twist, his flexible voice, his knowledge of the workings of Iain's safe, predictable mind. Still—when Rafael palmed the door and it opened to him, he had to stand a moment, catching his breath, forcing down the delightful shivering *zizz* of anticipation. This house. His. As Iain had been. And what waited within, the woman within—

His, of course. Because Iain wished to protect her.

Rafael hoped she was not too dreadful. The holo from the port had not looked pleasant. Perhaps she would be like the jellied cheeses of Ishtar, revolting to all but the connoisseur. Or perhaps there would be some note of innocence about her. Innocence was always stimulating.

His hand drifted to the tiny pocket in the breast of his tunic, stroking the outside, knowing that the small osmotic capsule still lay within. His reward for work well done, when the work was over. Father had insisted that this visit be a provocation only. But perhaps it could be a very great provocation, and still serve.

He felt himself stirring, aroused. Good. He adjusted his hair, its braid caught at one shoulder at a jeweled clasp. Then he walked through the door.

The womanservant stood at the other end of the dim hall, caught in a splash of light from a door to the side, staring at him. She wore a dark gray dress that covered her from shoulders to ankles, very plain—how like Iain, to keep her plainly covered even in privacy. Middle height, she was, and built for strength the way these people were. Long hands and feet—bare feet, barbaric at this hour. Good shoulders, though, and good breasts, high and firm.

He stared back at her, judging, planning. Her brows were too dark. He would have her pluck them. They shadowed her dark and questioning eyes. When the time came, he would wish to read every expression in those eyes.

She composed her expression, lowered her eyes. Rafael smiled.

He brushed his clothing lightly with scented fingertips. He had chosen to wear formal evening dress, a fitted tunic of heavy cream silk, thickly embroidered in the same cream. He knew it complemented his pale, long-fingered hands, his rich auburn hair, his blue eyes. All that coloring was his mother's gift—whoever she had been.

He spoke then, keeping his voice cool, masking the tiny vibration of excitement. "Come closer."

She bent her head to him properly, pressing her palms together over her heart. "Pilot Master sen Paolo is out. H-how may I serve you, Pilot Master?"

The hesitation roused him further. "Come closer," he said again. He wanted to see her closer to him. He wanted to touch her, and see how it changed her eyes. He wanted her to move out of the light, too strong, weighing her down, pressing her flat. She would have more grace in softer light. More grace still in the darkness. His hands, his body itched to taste her.

She did not move. He saw a muscle slide and tighten along her jaw. "Pilot Master, I think you should tell me who you are. And how you got in."

Well, then. He walked toward her, hearing his booted steps tapping on the stone, too loud. Tasting the scents of this house he had never before entered. He stopped, judging it finely: too close for her comfort, not close enough to force her to step away. From here he could smell her. He liked that.

She raised her head to look up at him, the motion jerky, nervous. He liked how her black hair shone, short and heavy as it was. So she had clean habits, given the chance. Not all of them did. "You may call me Master Rafael," he said, and smiled at her.

She went very still. Obviously she knew who he was. Good. He wondered what Iain had said, how much he had told her. What she had thought of it.

She looked up at him squarely. "I was told that the door would admit no one . . . Master Rafael."

He smiled on one side of his mouth. "Oh, I know a trick or two." He could hear the ticking of automatics in some of the rooms to one side, and faintly, behind him, a rustle along the floor of the hall. *Good.* . . . He could smell no scent of food lying ready, and no fire. There ought to be a fire, for guests. But then, he was unexpected. He drifted forward, and she shrank aside. As he passed her he smelled her body again, a clean, plain scent, with a low, sharp, salty note. Fear.

He walked into the sitting room and took a chair near the window wall. She followed, and planted her feet just inside the door of the room. "Master Rafael," she said flatly. "How may I serve you?"

She was letting herself become angry, to dull her fear. A common tactic, but it never worked for long. Rafael stretched out in the chair, feeling the velvet slide against his palms, the cushions yield to his hips. "Offer me a drink."

Obediently she turned toward the service console. "Would you like coffee?"

"Coffee! At this hour!" He gave her a lazy smile. "Never mind the drink. Come here." He let the edge show in his voice. He stretched out a hand toward her and waited.

She darkened with anger or embarrassment. "I'm Pilot Master sen Paolo's servant."

"Yes." Did she really not understand? "Paid to please

his guests." He shifted a little in the chair, hoping she would see what he was thinking, guess what he wanted. These backworld girls were earthy enough. And at her age—some sweaty fisherman must have dragged her behind a rock by now. More than one. "Come here."

She didn't move.

He felt the sting of irritation. Perhaps she felt she had to pretend not to understand. Well, then he would pretend innocence, too. "Oh, come here, girl. I only want to look at you!"

Reluctantly, she obeyed him. "That's better," he said.

She stopped just out of his reach, or so she must think. It was easy enough to reach out and grip her arm, hard, painfully hard—to rise and pull her against him. The light in here was still too bright, too harsh. And there was no music. It would be better with music; the sounds of the house were too much like breathing, like blood sliding in veins, like something alive and watching. Her scent filled his mind. She was nothing to stir him, not as she was, but if he thought of her in Iain's bed, serving Iain's pleasure— serving the favored and sheltered one, the one whose father had given him no cruel truths, the one who was allowed to believe all the pretty stories—as that man's possession, he could desire even her. To punish that man—that boy—he could do anything.

He looked down at her. "Are you a virgin?" His hot breath rasped his throat.

Now she had no courage to face him. But she could still speak. "Not your business," she said between clenched teeth.

"I didn't think you were. Was it Iain?" He touched her cheek tenderly. Odd that he did feel almost tender, just at this moment. She was helpless. At the thought his desire sharpened. It really might be best if he went ahead, in spite of his father's command. His father had pulled him back from Iain, all those years ago—made him swear not to tell Iain the truth. Punished him in ways that Rafael would never forget. Or forgive.

But she was hardly so important. And a little pleasure would calm him. He felt his breathing change again, roughen, felt his body harden more urgently against her.

She tried to twist out of his grasp. "Let go of me."

"Don't evade," he said. His voice was very calm. He had not yet taught her to be afraid when he was calm. "I don't allow evasions." He let his smile widen and go cold. "Tell me. Has he had you?"

His free hand slid down from her shoulder, caressed her hip, caught hold of the thin, silky skirt of her dress. He could feel her shiver under his touch. "No! No. He doesn't, he doesn't touch me. Don't—"

"Touch you?" He worked the skirt up until his hand touched the warm flesh of her thigh. "Hurt you? When you're mine I'll teach you not to hurt." His hand slid along her flesh, slipped between her thighs. She was dry. Not a liar then. She truly was afraid. He shivered, wanting her here, now, with the same dark hunger that flared when he thought of the capsule in his pocket. *Pleasure first, and then oblivion.* He found his voice again, low and rusty. "I'll teach you not to hurt," he said again. "No matter what I do, you won't . . . cry . . . out."

She stared up at him. He could see a vein fluttering wildly in the side of her neck.

His fingers moved. "When you're mine I'll teach you night and day. Not to cry. Not to hurt. Unless I want it." His voice had grown louder, his breathing harsh. "Night and day I'll show you a world you never dreamed of." He tightened his grip on her, and she bit back a cry. "Fear is the spice of all pleasure," he said. "Iain could tell you. I taught him that years ago."

He saw tears flood her eyes. But she stared past his face at nothing. He moved his hands to her hips, pulling her against him. His father would be angry. But it was her fault, her fault, and nothing could stop it now—he could not have Iain, but he could have all that belonged to Iain, strip it from him piece by piece—

Then Iain's voice spoke sharply from the doorway. "Rafael!"

Rafael swung around, and the woman escaped his grasp. But she did not matter. Here he was, Iain himself, the one he had come here to hurt. Rafael slowed his breathing, felt desire slip away like water into dry sand. A different kind of readiness filled him. Readiness to kill. Someday he would kill this man, when their fathers were dead and all oaths forgotten. He felt the old, black hatred fill him, black as the cold hearth at his back.

Iain's dark eyes glittered in the dim light by the doorway. "I thought I'd found a lock code you couldn't manage." Behind Iain's words Rafael could sense his anger, a dark and mounting flame. He knew that anger. He knew that flame.

Rafael stared at him and felt a smile break over his face. "Oh, little cousin. There is nothing of yours I can't have if I want it."

He saw Iain take a breath, saw his hand tighten as if preparing to strike. But he controlled himself. He always controlled himself, the good son, the dutiful boy—Rafael knew his father envied Paolo that. Fridric had said so.

Rafael turned to regard the woman, cowering in a corner. She had arranged her dress properly, he was sorry to see. But he still addressed Iain. "She has no polish at all. I'll take her for a time. You'll be much more pleased with her when you taste her next."

"You won't provoke me to strike you," Iain said. "Don't bother."

Rafael affected a bored drawl. "I'm only trying to provoke you to move away from the door," he said. "So I can take my new servant home." He smiled. "As arranged."

The woman cried out, and Iain turned to stare at her. "No," he said. "Nothing is arranged. She doesn't consent to any change in her contract. I will keep her here."

Rafael glanced at the woman, saw her sag a little with obvious relief. "I know that your father has ordered you to do otherwise." From the corner of his eye he saw her reach out and set her hand on a heavy egg of clear crystal. So she would fight. He caught himself, a quick idea forming. Yes—let her think she could fight. Let her think, tonight, that she had escaped. The spy he had placed in Iain's house, the clever little false automatic—that was what his father had wished him to accomplish here, and it was already done.

But Iain must believe that Rafael had only one objective, and that he had failed. "I lose patience," Rafael said, as sourly as he could manage. "I'll have what I want, now or later. Stop wasting my time."

"No." Iain glanced at the woman, then back at Rafael. "In this, if in nothing else, *I* choose. Get out."

Rafael could hardly keep from smiling. He spoke precisely, conscious of the record. "Then you are determined to refuse me?"

"I have refused you," Iain said. "Now leave my house."

Rafael shrugged and let the cold smile return. "Your choice, then, cousin. For now, I will leave you two to your pleasures." He looked at the woman, and wiped his fingers on the hem of his tunic. "They must be something extraordinary."

He left them there, to ponder that. And as he passed from the house into darkness he knew that it was time to consider his own next step—to consider it freely, away from his father, from his father's limiting will, from oaths and the Line and all the hollow ritual this boy revered. He would see Iain learn the truth. He would see Iain's world shatter. He would see Iain break.

He would break him.

When Rafael was gone, Linnea slumped against the wall and closed her eyes. It was over, it was over for now. . . . Then a strong hand caught her arm. She gasped and twisted away. "No!"

"Don't be afraid," Iain said. "I only want to be sure—"

"No. Please. I'm all right." She could barely catch her breath.

Iain's eyes met hers, dark with something she did not want to know or to name. "Did he harm you?"

"No," she said. "He just—" Her throat closed.

"I know," Iain said. "I know what he does."

"He was—he was going to take me away with him." Her voice sounded harsh, croaking. "He would have done it." She saw now how foolish any attack on Rafael would have been—how useless.

"He will not hurt you," Iain said.

She turned to him, gripped his arms, looked hard into his eyes.

He looked down at her severely. "I can protect you. I'm not afraid of him."

She wondered if that was true. She was shaken for a moment by an insight, a vision, vivid as memory: Rafael's white hand on Iain's naked hip, sliding, caressing—"He did *you* harm, once," she said with an odd certainty.

"A long time ago," Iain said. "It hardly matters now." He freed himself from her gently. "I'll keep you safe. You are safe. Now go and rest."

She had no refuge anywhere, and no way home. She turned away from him, half-blind with tears, and walked with what pride she had left to the door.

EIGHT

Iain watched tensely as Linnea left the room. Then he strode to a wall cabinet, palmed the seal, and worked with quick concentration at the screen that appeared. There—now there *was* no lock code. The house was sealed, and no one could enter without physically breaking in.

Iain sighed and stepped back from the screen, which resealed itself. Then he moved to the window wall and looked out on the broad sweep of light below. It was beginning to haze over—dust between the suburb's shield and the City's, far below. A veil. An illusion of privacy, of safety.

He went to a sideboard, poured himself a glass of brandy, carried it to the long, curving couch before the hearth. "House," he said as he sank down on it. "Fire."

The hearth sprang to crackling life, and he tasted the brandy and thought, inevitably, about Rafael. It seemed clear that the plan had been, not to force him to relinquish Linnea, but the opposite—to make it impossible. To make him determined to keep her.

And still he could not see what harm she could do him. Her innocence was real, he would swear to it on the Tree.

He sipped more of the brandy, and at that moment the house spoke. "Pilot Master sen Paolo. Your father wishes to be admitted to the house."

Paolo had never—never once—come to this house. Iain rose and straightened his tunic. "Let him in."

He waited for his father where he was, as his father had always waited for him. But when Paolo appeared, Iain's words of angry self-defense evaporated. Paolo looked pale, shaken, almost untidy. Without thinking Iain spoke first, moving forward to take his father's arm. "Father. Sit down. Let me get you something. What can I get you?"

Paolo shook his head impatiently, waved Iain's arm away, did not sit. "I need nothing. But your house refused my message. And I *must* speak to you."

Iain arranged himself in a formal pose of waiting. "You've had bad news."

"Yes," Paolo said heavily.

Iain swallowed. "Tell me."

Paolo brushed a stray strand of gray hair from his eye with a slightly unsteady hand. "Iain. While I was—distracting you, earlier—" he grimaced, and Iain knew that was all the apology he would receive—"I was being distracted myself." He looked at Iain, his old eyes dark with anger. "The vote on the contract cancellation for Santandru was taken three days early. This evening, in my absence."

Iain looked at him for a moment. "So it's done, and you lost."

"No," Paolo said. "Worse than that. Worse than that. I won."

It took a moment to absorb that. *No. Not possible.* Linnea would—"The contract—was renewed? How did it happen?"

"When the vote came, four men who always vote solidly with Fridric . . . changed over. Men I never even spoke to—there was never any chance they would support me."

"I don't understand," Iain said. "Father, why?"

Paolo rubbed the bridge of his nose wearily. "To discredit me," he said. "To discredit us both. I didn't see it, not in time. It was the woman. The woman from Santandru and her mysterious trade."

"I don't believe it," Iain said. "She is not part of any plot with Rafael. She knows nothing."

"She does not need to know anything," Paolo said. "Fridric's men on the Council will say that she corrupted you, that you agreed to help her. That to save you I agreed to the bargain. That I delivered on it. Those four men will swear that I tricked them. Fridric will have supplied them with physical proof—faked images, faked voices—enough that they will never be called on to swear by the Tree. They will not *technically* have broken their oaths." His gray voice trembled slightly. "If you had listened, even as late as this afternoon, it might have gone differently."

"I did as I judged best," Iain said, his voice unsteady. "I am what you made me, Father. Someone has to want what's right—someone has to protect her."

"You still imagine this has something to do with the woman," Paolo said.

"She is the duty I see," Iain said. "The rest you will not

explain to me. If you asked me now to surrender her to Rafael, knowing only what I know, I would still refuse you."

"Even knowing that I am your father and that I understand what is truly at stake," Paolo said. His usual calm had returned.

"I am not a child," Iain said, the words tearing his throat. "I must use my own understanding. Judge from what I know. If that leads me into trouble, then so be it."

Paolo looked away, then back at his son. "It was too late anyway," he said. His eyes were gentle. "We'll speak again. Until then, if I may advise you—"

Iain took a shaking breath. "I'll listen."

"Keep to this house," Paolo said. "A storm is coming. And I do not know if I can protect you."

"It's not your place to protect me," Iain said.

Paolo looked at him for a moment. "I have spent my life protecting you. So far as I can." He stepped away, and Iain let him go. "Good night, Son."

"Father," Iain said, and his voice failed on the word.

It was only after his father had left that he noticed Linnea, shrunk back against the wall in the flickering fireshadow near the door.

It took him a moment to collect himself, to be certain he could speak. "How much did you hear?"

"All of it," she whispered. She straightened and met his eyes. "Is it true? Iain?"

He knew what would have been most important to her in what she had heard. "It's true," he said. "Your world's contract has been renewed."

Linnea took a dragging, unsteady breath. "Then Marra is safe." She rubbed her face with both hands. "We—won."

"Are you all right?" Iain asked, coming closer to her.

"Can they revoke it?" He heard her plea for reassurance.

"No," Iain said. "Each world's contract was signed by its government at least a year ago. Now that we have signed as well, the Line is bound." He fumbled in his tunic and passed her a square of silk.

She stared down at it, then blotted her face with it. "Thank you," she muttered. "I'm sorry. You—your father said it was bad news for you. But, but I can't think that far." Her voice broke. "This was all I wanted." She looked at him, no longer hiding her tear-streaked face. "Our bargain—I'll give you what we offered."

He was surprised how little it mattered to him, now, whatever it was. His father would know what to do with it. And would tell him nothing. "There's time enough for that tomorrow," he said. "For tonight—" He spoke the thought as it formed. "For tonight, dine with me."

She looked startled. "*With* you?"

He half smiled. "To celebrate our victory."

I ain could only toy with the elaborate late dinner the house systems had prepared for them. Linnea had set the illumination very low—just the dancing golden orange lights that flickered deep in the tabletop. He crumbled a thin slice of elegantly spiced black bread and stared down at the slowly swirling pastel soup on his plate, then looked up as Linnea sipped her wine. Her face was smooth and still, her lips set firmly. Good. Her strength was returning, as he had hoped.

She looked past him, toward the window wall and the

City far below. "People can see in," she said. "It scares me. In my room there's a window. I can't block it off."

"We don't, you know," Iain said. "It's our custom to be open. To hide nothing." He felt the irony of the words as he spoke them.

"Yes, you hide nothing," she said, and he could hear her anger. "You're always on show. Naked to the world. It's lucky for you you're all so pretty. Well, it's not my way. I want to feel safe." She caught her breath and then said in a rush, "I want to go *home*." Her face crumpled.

"Then go," Iain said. "You owe me nothing."

"Your uncle and his friends—" She shivered. "They won't let me leave. Not if they know what I asked you to do. Not if they know you agreed to try to help me.

Iain reached out and set his hand on hers—no more than that. He did not want to frighten her. "I'll arrange your safety," he said, "if I can."

She took a long, shuddering breath. Then she gave him a lopsided smile. "Thank you," she said. "Tonight, with your cousin—I was afraid. And then you came in. When I saw you . . ." She caught at his hand, raised it to her lips, and kissed it.

The submissive gesture was familiar, customary. He had taught it to her. But now, from her, he could not bear it. He pulled his hand free, and when she looked up at him, stricken, he raised her chin and bent down to her and kissed her mouth.

He had meant to be tender, then free her. But her strong arms slid around him, and she drew her warmth against him. She tasted like cinnamon. Her strong hands knew his shoulders, slid down along his body. Cinnamon and fire.

So long, so long since anyone had touched him like this—touched him out of desire.

He drew back a little, steadying his breath. "Linnea—"

"Quiet," she said fiercely.

He looked down at her, startled into laughter, but then stilled himself. Her eyes on his were steady, serious. He sensed fear in her, but also resolve. "You're not alone," she said. "I'm here. Tell me to go away if that's what you want."

He did not answer her with words.

Their slow progress ended on the long couch by the fire. No other light. Her skin slid against his, smooth and warm; her eyes in the firelight were dark as night, bright as stars. Her eyes held light. She smiled up at him, tears wet on her cheeks. He kissed her again, with greater urgency than before, and she answered it. Under his slow, unceasing caress she turned now, willingly, and eased the way for him. But she was trembling now. He could feel it, but he could not stop, not now. When he began to enter her he felt her body tighten, as if she expected pain, though he was certain that she desired him as well.

He was as gentle as he could be, considering his need of her. At first he was gentle. Yet her courage was equal to him. She did not close her eyes or look away from his gaze. And at the end, at his end, she said nothing; but she held him close to her warmth, her strength.

It was good that she didn't speak. He couldn't speak. *This should have been nothing. This should not have mattered.*

But he knew that everything, everything was changed.

●   ●   ●

L innea stood alone, wrapped in a night robe of Iain's, at the window wall of the sitting room. Dawn should have come an hour ago. But the light stayed the color of dirty sulfur. A dust storm—the first she had ever seen.

It was so close above the house that it made her nervous. The Cloudshadow suburb was outside the City's climate shield, and its own shield was small. Dust swirled and roiled almost overhead. It looked evil, as if it wanted to sink down over her and smother her. Fine dust sifted down outside, in spite of the shield. When she looked down toward the City she saw only emptiness, as if a sand-colored sea had risen in the night and drowned it.

She shivered, remembering the dream that had waked her this morning. The warning.

In the dream they flew, she and Iain, in the high pale sky of home. Effortlessly, arms outstretched, fingers barely touching. In the dream she laughed at the sea below, a sheet of hammered silver. In their flight she drew herself close beside him, and looked into his laughing face, and twined her fingers in his black, streaming hair.

Then they fell. Or the sea rose and took them. Green-gray water towered, curled, crashed. In the darkness under the surface she lost him. In the darkness she drifted, voiceless, calling him. She knew he had gone, gone on ahead, to wash in toward the beach by Moraine. She knew they would find him there, water-swollen, flesh half-stripped by eels and scuttling things. She woke weeping silently.

She had left Iain there, asleep, his half-familiar body slack and tumbled in the bed they had used, and used, and used. She had come here to the sitting room because she had to think.

She'd done this out of—foolishness was the only word.

If she listened she could hear Marra's voice, telling her that. But she had sensed, more strongly than ever, how alone he was. They were both alone, with dangers all around that he knew and feared, and she could only guess at. And so she had reached out to him. At that moment, she had gone past the last turning.

The world had changed. Everything was achingly real, as if all her nerves and senses were newborn: the muffled sound of the wind outside, the room's clean, spicy morning scent, the night robe's silk against her skin. Changed. It was as if, in the old house in Moraine, she found a door that she had always overlooked—and behind it, a room that she hadn't known existed. She'd never imagined that she could share a man's bed with pleasure, without shame. She'd never imagined that any man could break down her defenses, so long in building.

Outside, the storm was rising. In the slow, crawling roil of dust against the climate shield, she saw shapes like faces now and then—quick, then gone, like drowned men floating up through murky water, then sinking back again. Drowned men. *Teor. . . .* Lightning bloomed pink, and she felt the house rumble.

She'd been a girl, barely old enough to think of marrying. Teor had been a little older—he'd already gone into the *Hope*. And she had loved him from the soles of her feet on up, so that she thought she might burst, so that she woke up sweating from dark dreams.

He'd seemed to love her, and things had gone on to their natural end. And she had been sore, and ashamed—and puzzled. This was it? This was all there was to it? After the third time she put a stop to it, in sudden terror—sure she was pregnant, seeing only then how completely she would be trapped.

Teor's silence, which had been his mystery, frustrated her then. They had nothing to say to each other. She avoided him for two weeks. Then, one day after church, he came to the house, painfully combed and washed, and offered for her formally, in front of Rowdy and Marra. But by then she had known she wasn't pregnant after all. She had refused him.

Half a year later, as the crew of the *Hope* worked to bring in the big seine during a sudden storm, he'd been lost overboard. Nobody thought of blaming her.

She leaned her forehead against the heavy glass of the window. Iain wasn't like Teor. Teor had been a boy. Iain was a man, with a man's strength—guided by knowledge, held to his will. Linnea closed her eyes. She was going home. She was going home, no matter what. And if that scared her now, if—something—made her wonder what would happen to Iain—made her wish she could somehow help him—well, if that was true, she had no one to blame but herself.

She was a fool.

Fridric sen David stood alone in the shadows of his study, savoring his defeat. By now, almost midnight, the City knew of it; by now the young and unwise were puzzling over it, or rejoicing over it, in either case wondering whether the power of the great Honored Voice sen David was beginning to weaken.

But the wise men—they knew that, whatever might appear, this was no defeat for Fridric. The wise men were

waiting, tonight. No doubt, somewhere, his dear brother
Paolo was waiting, knowing that the blow would fall; not
knowing when. Delicious.

Fridric smiled, studying the great round window of colored glass that framed his chair. Amethyst, rose, bloody
red, by day it was his setting, spilling sun-drenched color
across the room. By day, it shadowed his face so he might
watch those who faced him.

But by night, the window came to a life of its own. The
colors softened and cooled. City lights gleamed through
the fretwork of black iron that supported the glass. The Security fliers passed and repassed in their ceaseless vigi-
lance over the Council's headquarters; every few minutes
one of their lights struck the glass, moving, and molten
color slid and shifted, painting the darkness. It pleased
him.

And now his long plan was coming near fruition.

Fridric smiled and tasted the liqueur in his tiny ruby
bowl. Grass and lemon and honey, sweet as summer on
Prairie. It was only a matter of time now: a day or two, the
proper moves, the proper words. And then the secret, the
one that could not be named, would be his alone—his and
Rafael's. And they would keep it safe enough, each with
the power of death over the other. Even Rafael would keep
his promises, to keep his inheritance whole.

The room spoke: Rafael himself, requesting admittance.
Fridric turned his back to the great window, set aside the
bowl of liqueur, and made the gesture that told the door to
open.

Rafael came in, just slowly enough to convey his usual
insolence, and took a chair without being asked. "Father."
He sounded, as always, bored.

Fridric had no time, and no will, for that game. "Did you see her?"

Rafael yawned. "Yes. Just as you told me, a plain girl. Awkward. I don't think there's much in her."

Something in the way Rafael spoke made Fridric narrow his eyes, glad that his face was shadowed. "And the other matter?"

"It's in place. Test the link, if you like." Rafael's long, richly ringed fingers toyed with the fringe of a cushion. "You might find it interesting." His thick, pale lashes hid his eyes. The deep blue eyes of his mother—that was all Fridric could recall of her, that and the way her body had swollen into hideousness.

So the woman from Santandru was firmly in place in his nephew's house; matters were in hand. When Rafael left, Fridric would test the sight-and-sound link to Iain's house, the little automatic set to follow Iain silently from room to room.

"Was there—anything else?" Fridric smothered a yawn of his own.

"The woman." Rafael looked up, then, and his eyes burned strangely blue in the amethyst light. "When they're taken—let *me* question her."

"She knows nothing of interest," Fridric said. "She can tell you nothing, no matter how you press her."

Rafael smiled. "Sometimes that's the most fun of all."

Fridric shrugged. "When the time comes—do as you like."

Rafael swept to his feet and bowed. "As you have commanded, Council Lord sen David."

•   •   •

The summons came at noon.

Linnea had fallen asleep again, tangled with Iain in his bed, and the voice of the house speaking Iain's name confused her. The strange light confused her more when she opened her eyes. Storm-light, yellow and dim.

The house spoke again, and Iain rose to his elbow. "House—I hear. Report."

"Priority message, sir. The bearer waits."

"Relay." Iain rubbed his eyes. "So early. Is it early?"

She snorted a laugh. "I'll get some coffee." She had moved to get up when the message began, throwing its image in the air near the bed. A dead, white tree—*the* Tree, she recognized it, the seal of the Inner Council and the emblem of the Line. Then it faded, and a man's head and shoulders appeared. She did not recognize him, seeing him from behind—a rich black robe, an iron-gray braid plainly dressed—but she saw Iain's face go rigid, dark with anger. "This is a recorded message for Iain sen Paolo," the man said in a deep, dry voice, and the image froze.

The voice was half-familiar. She walked around beside Iain and frowned at the image. A gaunt face, heavy-boned, heavy-browed, but the eyes piercing—

"Your uncle," she whispered.

Iain's hand sought hers and held it. "I am Iain sen Paolo," he said clearly.

"*Confirmed,*" a voice whispered somewhere, and the image moved again. The voice deepened. "Iain sen Paolo, by the power granted me by the wisest of our Line, I summon you to appear this day before me to answer certain charges that have been laid against you. The charges are these: the charge of conspiring to the detriment of the Line, which carries the penalty of death; the charge of concealing that conspiracy, which carries the penalty of permanent exile; and certain minor charges, with lesser penalties, which will be made plain at the proper time. Having heard this command, you must render yourself up to the servants of the Council who wait upon you now, and who will convey you to the place appointed for this inquiry. To fail in this is to fail in your oath at the Tree, and in that act to sunder yourself from the Line." The man's voice changed, lightened a little. "Don't resist, Iain. Your father depends on you." And he was gone.

Iain stood motionless, frowning at the space where his uncle's image had stood. Linnea touched his arm with an unsteady hand. "They won't—kill you. They can't. Your father—"

"They don't need to kill me," Iain said. He sounded tired. Defeated. "They will remove me from the Line."

Looking into his face—stiff with anguish—she guessed that he would probably rather die.

"You see," Iain said, "this matter gives him a way to rob my father and me. Weaken my father politically, shame me, end my career, and leave Rafael with all the family's holdings after we're dead."

She knew him now, a little. She could guess what he was hiding. "Iain, I'm sorry."

"You didn't know," he said quietly.

She didn't speak again as she helped him with the robe he chose, a subtle richness of black brocaded silk. Her hands were steady as she braided his hair meticulously, weaving in the strand of crimson cord that was his lineage-mark. Iain painted his face with careful formality, adding the wavy pattern of fine black lines below the left cheekbone that signified his many prosperous voyages. And Linnea prepared herself to honor him, in the finest dress she had. White for mourning. In the ochre light it looked yellow.

When Iain was ready, she followed him down the corridor to his door. He ordered it to open, and the stone doors moved silently aside. Outside stood two tall men, anonymous in black shock armor, their stunrods loose in their hands. "Iain sen Paolo," one of them said. "Do you surrender yourself?"

"I do," Iain said. She wondered how his voice could sound so calm; she wondered how long he had been expecting this. Whether he had known last night. Whether he had always known.

Iain gave her one dark glance as he left. She met his look squarely, but she did not smile at him; it would have been an ugly smile, false, he would have known it. Then, as he had ordered, she sealed the doors behind him. Then, she stood still, leaning her forehead against the sharp-cut stone, struggling against grief.

He might return in an hour. He might never return. The matter was, as important matters had always been, out of her hands; as always, she was powerless.

But something had changed—*she* had changed. Because now it made her angry.

NINE

The door of Iain's house, of the life he had known, closed firmly behind him. He did not look back. The men from Council Security moved in close beside him and started forward. Though they did not presume to touch him, he went with them, as he must. They had brought a tube car, one of their own—a long, bulky ovoid that gleamed dull gray in the shadows of the entry port. As Iain expected, the Council's men gestured him into the door at the rear and turned toward another themselves. Iain stepped in—and found himself facing Rafael.

Iain was grateful, then, for the emotional discipline in which his father had drilled him so mercilessly throughout his boyhood. Paolo's training kept his mind clear, his breathing steady, his heartbeat slow and calm. Iain took the seat beside his cousin, so there would be no need to look at him.

Rafael spoke only once. "Uncle Paolo insisted on coming, so we'll be collecting him as well." Iain tensed at the faint note of disrespect, but made no reply. Instead, deliberately, he let his anger feed on itself, to mask his fear. The charges against him were absurd. Today, he told himself, he would learn why he was being persecuted. Today Paolo would tell him the truth. Acknowledge his adulthood. Acknowledge his right to understand what was happening.

When Paolo took his place in the car, he nodded to the younger men, but as was his privilege, he did not speak. He wore the full robes of a Councilman: heavy, pleated silk to the ankles, plain black and unembroidered, with trailing sleeves. A deep hood, thrown back, covered his shoulders. It was lined with the same crimson as the cord in Iain's braid. And Paolo's thin gray hair was braided, too, for the first time in years.

Iain knew what all this meant: with an obviousness that Paolo might, before tonight, have called vulgar, he was displaying his status. A famous jump pilot in his youth, a revered teacher, a Councilman in his own right. Cold trickled along Iain's spine. Paolo had never resorted to this tactic before. Clearly, the danger was real.

As the car approached the center of the City, the government buildings loomed around them, cutting off the sunlight. Iain sat up straight. Never mind Rafael; Iain could not go blindly into the coming confrontation. "Father," he said. "You must tell me what is happening. This can't be an actual trial. There's been no public notice."

Paolo's face seemed to shift with the shifting shadows. It was hard to read his expression. "It is a preliminary to a trial," Paolo said. "The nanobot incidents constitute an external threat to the Line. On that pretext, your uncle has assumed emergency powers that allow him to try you, or me, or anyone without public notice, without witness."

Iain shook his head in frustration. "Father. I know you want to protect me. But I can't defend myself if I don't know the basis for the charges against me. What is Fridric's evidence?"

Paolo's expression did not change. "Your ignorance is your best defense. Perhaps your only one." He looked away, out at the passing streets. "I've asked Training Master Adan sen Kaleb to be present as another witness."

"Your friend," Iain said. "My old teacher. That's good." Someone outside the family dispute might keep Fridric from taking any outrageous action. "But it's not enough. Father, please—"

"Be silent," Paolo said sharply. "You should have learned silence long ago."

Iain turned away from his father and watched the City crawl past, the deep canyons shadowed even at midday. *I learned silence*, he wanted to say. *I learned it every day of my life—it was what you taught best. . . .*

A tense-looking aide hurried Iain and Paolo through dim, empty antechambers into the study of the Honored Voice of the Inner Council, and left them there. Iain stood beside his father, waiting for what must come. Despair dragged at him. There could be no escape now.

The dust-heavy sunlight blazed dully through the rose window behind Fridric's chair. The pure colors, the elaborate tracery silhouetted the Honored Voice. He rose politely as they came in, and the two old men, the brothers, bowed to each other, the stiff, deep bow that was correct between enemies. As Fridric straightened, Iain saw again how the formal magnificence of his robe suited his tall, spare frame, as did the wide chain of fine platinum filigree that was his sign of office.

Then Paolo turned and bowed with equal politeness, but greater warmth, to Training Master sen Kaleb. The Master resembled Paolo only in the severity of his habitual expression. The coarse, stubborn tufts of his white hair were woven into a jump pilot's braid, but clubbed and tied in a fashion from fifty years ago. His dark, seamed face was impassive. He would be a good witness, Iain knew: His reputation for integrity was unquestioned, his position unassailable by the more transitory authority of an Honored Voice.

Unless Fridric chose to use his emergency powers. . . .

"Please sit," Fridric said in a flat voice, and they all did so. Fridric kept to ancient custom and used a desk rather than a work chair; the bare expanse of dark-veined stone served well to separate Iain and Paolo from their judge.

"We will proceed," Fridric said. He was no longer smiling. "This is a tragic matter, painful for us all, and I know I am not the only one who wishes it ended." Touching a control on the arm of his chair, he said, "We are now being recorded under seal of the Inner Council." He folded his hands on the desk before him and fixed Iain with a razor-sharp gaze. "I am empowered to investigate a conspiracy that threatens the safety and prosperity of the Line. You are charged as an accessory in that conspiracy. How do you answer those charges, Pilot Master sen Paolo?"

"I am part of no conspiracy against the Line." Iain let his anger show. It might conceal his fear.

"You will swear to that by the Tree?"

Iain held up his scarred right hand. "By the blood I gave to it, I swear." This *was* the truth; he *could* swear.

Fridric's expression did not alter. "And have you been told of such a conspiracy by any other person?"

There it was, the trap he had expected—the trap he could not escape. He swallowed, his throat suddenly dry.

Fridric waited a moment longer, then said, "Silence is not an answer, Pilot Master sen Paolo."

"Silence *is* an answer," Master sen Kaleb said sternly. "Silence before accusation is his right."

"Silence before accusation is a denial of the charges, and will make a trial inevitable," Fridric said. "A trial we all wish to avoid—a trial that would expose matters that shame my brother and his son."

"Tell me of these matters," the Master said. "I am here at Paolo sen David's request. He trusts my discretion."

Fridric stared at him, expressionless, for a moment, and then said, "No."

"But any relevant information—"

"You don't understand," Fridric said. "My brother asked you here to *prevent* family issues from being discussed openly. I'm sorry you did not realize that."

Iain looked at Paolo, who sat quietly, his expression calm as ever.

Master sen Kaleb kept his eyes on Fridric. "A capital charge has been brought. If I may remind the Honored Voice, there are procedures to be followed."

"Then let us by all means follow procedure." Fridric turned back to Iain. "Consider, boy. And then confirm or deny the charges that have been made against you, on your oath as a man of the Line."

Iain forced down a surge of nausea. How could he deny

the charges? Fridric knew Linnea lived with him—perhaps even knew that they had become lovers. If Iain lied, and said she'd told him nothing, no one would believe the lie; and a drugged interrogation would show him at once as an oathbreaker, and destroy him. Yet to confess that he knew anything of the conspiracy in which Linnea was involved—that confession would end his career just as disgracefully. Even if he did not lose his life, he would lose its purpose: his honor, and the work he had been trained to. The freedom, the beauty of otherspace. And Linnea—

Suddenly, sharply, he knew that he had to save Linnea. He tried to find breath to speak.

Then Paolo broke silence. "Council Lord sen David. My son is young. This matter is not his concern. He knows nothing. I ask you to leave him—leave *him*, at least, unharmed."

The two men locked eyes. Finally, Fridric said, "So, then—defend him."

Iain could sense Paolo's rage. But Paolo's voice was calm and assured as he said, "Iain is like any other young man his age. He thinks only of himself and his pleasures, and the life he enjoys. Whatever you imagine he has seen or heard, I assure you that it has made no impression on him."

Iain felt himself darken with anger, but he kept his place and his silence. This was nothing new; this was the way Paolo had always dismissed him.

Fridric shrugged. "My own son would no doubt agree with you. But the evidence—"

Paolo broke in. "Iain has harmed no one. He has committed no crime. I—ask—I . . . *beg* you to suppress these charges."

Through his fear-sickness, Iain saw Master sen Kaleb's face go still with shock.

Fridric lifted an eyebrow. "He is innocent? You are so sure?"

"I would pledge it with my life," Paolo said bleakly. "If that were of any value."

Iain took a deep breath and let it out soundlessly, stilling a cry. He thought furiously. If his father was powerless, if there was no hope—then nothing Iain said could harm them now. "Council Lord sen David," he said. "May I speak?"

"Certainly," Fridric said.

"You've charged me with a capital crime. You say you have evidence against me." He took a breath. "I formally request that you present it."

Fridric tapped his big fingers on the desk. "At your trial—if matters go so far—I will do so," he said. "But here, your rights are what I choose to grant."

Master sen Kaleb rose to his feet. "The burden of proof lies with the boy's accusers!"

Fridric did not rise. He gave the Master a cool glance, and said. "Ordinarily, yes. But in this crisis, the judgment of this matter is mine and mine alone. The procedures are—somewhat altered. And so," he said, looking again at the Master, "are the traditional immunities. Yours, for example."

Iain looked from his father to the Master, who sank slowly back into his chair. Both men looked appalled, but neither protested. It must be true: Fridric's power must be as absolute as he claimed.

Fridric sighed and straightened in his chair. "Let us be direct. We know that Iain sen Paolo made a bargain with an outworlder to attempt to influence his father's vote on a matter before the Council. The extent of Paolo sen David's knowledge of these matters is still to be determined." Fridric shook his head slowly. "In the present emergency, it is my clear duty to act to protect the Line, and the stability of its governing body. Therefore"—he dropped his right fist to the desk—"I forbid Iain sen Paolo to leave this planet until this matter of his treason is resolved." Fridric looked directly at Paolo now, as if challenging him to protest. Silently, Iain screamed at his father to rise, to resist, to break his silence.

Paolo sat still, impassive. Master sen Kaleb, his own sharp gaze also on Paolo, stirred but kept silent.

Fridric sighed again. "And I must take one further step. With great reluctance." He touched a control on his chair. "By my order as Honored Voice of the Inner Council, at the next incalling of the Line, Iain sen Paolo will be removed from the roll of the Pilot Masters." His eyes, bright and avid, were on Paolo. "And the name of Iain sen Paolo will be struck from the Line."

Iain held himself still. *Breathe*. The pain would pass. He had known it was coming, after all. He had known that at the last, his father would not act to save him.

But Fridric was still speaking. "Paolo sen David is also restricted from offworld travel. As Honored Voice and as his elder brother, I strongly urge him to resign his seat on the Inner Council. No man has ever been *forced*, in shame, to resign from that body. I beg him to continue that proud tradition."

Through his own anguish Iain saw his father raise his head sharply, as if in shock.

"His resignation is unnecessary," Master sen Kaleb

said, anger a flame in his dark eyes. "And Iain sen Paolo's removal from the Line must be termed a suspension, temporary—only until this matter can be resolved. The truth cannot evade us forever."

"*Oh, no, not forever*," Iain said. Bitterness rasped at his throat. "Ten years, or twenty. I'm a young man. I can wait."

"All this emotion," Fridric said, "is unseemly. I've ruled. That's all."

Iain looked at Paolo. Surely now he would speak—now that the worst had already happened. Now that Iain had nothing more to lose. . . . Paolo's face seemed sunken, his eyes dark and shadowed. But he did not object. He did not speak at all.

His father's silence forced Iain's own. Perhaps that was Paolo's intention. Iain looked away, stared at the vivid colors of the rose window, let its brightness sting tears into his eyes.

Master sen Kaleb broke the silence, his voice unsteady. "Is this meeting ended?"

"It is," Fridric said. "If any relevant information comes to any of you, you are directed and required to bring it to my attention. At this time, I do not believe we need arrest my nephew."

Paolo rose. "Fridric," he said, his voice thin and dry as a dead leaf, "I must speak with you alone. I claim the right of a younger brother."

Fridric shot an angry glance at Master sen Kaleb, who still sat watching and listening. "I grant it," Fridric said. "Immediately—and briefly."

"But first," Paolo said, "may I have a private word with my son?"

Fridric waved a hand. "Certainly."

Paolo was standing by Iain's chair. Iain realized he was supposed to stand, to bow, to walk out. He managed it. But outside the door he stopped. He and Paolo and Master sen Kaleb were alone in the gloomy anteroom, under the eyes of portraits of famous Councilmen, the pride and history of the Line for centuries past. Bitterness overwhelmed Iain. He reached up and tore his hair free from the braid, tugged at it angrily until it hung, loose as an unranked boy's, down his back. Paolo watched in silence. Master sen Kaleb turned away without a word and left them.

Iain could not speak. He was not a jump pilot. He did not know what he was, now. The pain of what had happened to him rose slowly, evenly, unstoppably, like night filling the City when the sun had gone. He was nothing now.

He would never jump again. He would live his life in the lower circles of the City, pitied or forgotten. Open to Rafael's mockery, or worse. Not a jump pilot, but not one of the others like Mekael, an honest failure. Even Mekael would pity Iain, now. And Linnea—he could do nothing to protect Linnea.

"Iain."

Iain looked up. Paolo was watching him with a strange expression on his face. Pity. . . . Iain turned away toward the door.

"I always feared this was coming," Paolo said. "I knew that Fridric would strike at us if there was ever any excuse."

"You could have warned me," Iain said. His voice was little more than a whisper, but it was steady.

"It would only have darkened your life," Paolo said, his voice full of pain. "It would not have changed anything."

Bitterness welled in Iain like dark, chill water. "Then you shouldn't have let me become a jump pilot," he said. "If I didn't have that, there would be nothing he could take from me."

"But piloting was your gift," Paolo said. "I could not deny it to you. No matter if—" He stopped.

"No matter if what?"

"Nothing," Paolo said. "Iain, come home with me. Stay in your old suite. I don't like to think of you alone in that house."

"I thank you for the invitation," Iain said. "But I won't be alone. I have a servant to attend me. Good night."

"Iain," Paolo said again, and the rawness in his voice compelled Iain to turn and face him. Paolo watched him with agony clear in his face. "I have never been what you wanted me to be. I reared you to be strong, to be separate from me, because I saw that this time might come. And now I know that in making that choice, I failed you."

Iain could not answer.

"I never told you how I loved you," Paolo said, and Iain heard the grief in his steady voice. "From the moment they laid you in my arms, the night you were born, I loved you. And now it's too late."

"Father." Iain spoke evenly, though he felt chilled, feverish, sick. "Whatever you may feel for me, you've made it clear that you don't trust me. You can't give with one hand and hold back with the other. You're right. It's too late." He pushed open the door and went out, leaving his father alone.

On the ride home Iain fought a silent battle against fear, grief, loss. The sun sank lower; shadows filled the City, rising, rising to drown the light. His house was still his, by family right, but that was no comfort now. It was no refuge now, for him or for Linnea. He entered the house and moved down the hall toward his suite. Sunset light spilled like blood through archways, across red-brown tiles. Shadows hid everything else. He needed darkness now. He must not think. Every thought led toward pain.

And here was Linnea, standing near the door of his suite, straight and tense, still in her white dress. Waiting. He stopped in front of her. "It's over," he said. "I'm to be struck from the Line. My uncle—" He broke off.

"I'm sorry," she said. Her eyes and voice were gentle, and she stretched her hand out toward him, as if she wanted to comfort him, but feared to move closer. "Iain— it will be all right."

It would never be all right. But he caught her hand in his. "I want—"

"What?" Her face was still.

"I don't know what I want," he said in despair.

"Iain, hush," she said. "Hush." They were inside his suite now. She was helping him find the way. Something was blinding him. Tears. She shouldn't see him like this, not even she. "Don't be afraid," she said. "I'm here. I'm *here.*"

His clothing was gone. So was hers. She was kissing him, her fingers twining in his hair. Then they were on the bed, and as he pulled her warm, strong body against his own, as he reached out to her for relief, release, forgetfulness—in the middle of it he was conscious that she was weeping, too. Even when she cried his name, cried out as women always did in bed—even then, she wept. And he did not know for whom.

TEN

In the fading light of Fridric's study, Paolo faced his brother alone. The old anger roughened his voice as he said, "That was unnecessary. The boy did you no harm, ever."

Fridric smiled and leaned back comfortably in his chair. "Was it unnecessary? It has brought you to me on your knees."

Paolo stilled himself, taking one, then two calming and cleansing breaths. But the air in here did not cleanse him. Old evil, old lies. And an oath decades old—an oath he should never have sworn to this man. "If you wish me to kneel, I will."

"I know it," Fridric said comfortably. "And all my work has brought you there. Did you enjoy your victory in Council?"

Paolo did not trust himself to speak.

"Or perhaps you saw past it," Fridric said. "Perhaps you

saw the little cloud on the horizon. That now it is natural to suspect that you conspired with your son to purchase false evidence against me from those ignorant fishermen. That yesterday you paid them."

"It was neatly done," Paolo said, feeling oddly remote. Nothing mattered now; it was too late.

Strange how quickly he had understood that.

"Yes, it was neatly done," Fridric said. "That woman from offworld your son is harboring—we'll have the truth from her soon enough. We'll know the danger, and root it out. Anyone on her miserable world who knows the truth will keep silent, because they have their price now. And in twenty years, when Rafael is ready to step into power, we'll cut them off forever."

"And then no one will know," Paolo said. "No one will know that we are bastards, you and I."

"And I will keep my power," Fridric said. "And you will keep your name. And your son—he'll do well enough. He still has money. Friendship of a sort *can* be bought, if one is not particular. As Iain already knows."

Paolo steeled himself. "Iain knows nothing. He can't harm you, or Rafael. Even as a jump pilot, he can't harm you."

"But the woman," Fridric said.

Paolo's hands gripping the back of the chair before him were cold; his wrists ached. "She was only a courier. The men on her world have told her nothing of importance. Question her, question them both, under drugs. Then, when you are satisfied, restore my son to his place."

"I cannot," Fridric said regretfully.

"I've kept my oath," Paolo said. "For fifty years I have

kept it. But if you no longer trust my word, then consider this. I could tell Iain nothing if I were dead."

He saw the bloom of triumph rise in his brother, rise, then fade behind the usual careful blandness. "You would pay such a price to buy back the pride of your son?"

"To buy the *life* of my son," Paolo said. To keep his dignity had never been such a struggle. "I know you will never allow Iain Selection, to father sons as rivals to Rafael's. I know your grandsons will inherit all that I have worked to build. But if Iain himself lives, that is enough for me." His cold hands gripped the chair. "Here is the bargain. I will die, in a way that proves my dishonor. The truth will die with me. And in exchange, Iain will live."

Fridric gazed at him for a long time, his thin lips pressed tight. Then he spoke. "You tempt me."

"The power is yours, as you arranged," Paolo said wearily. He held himself straight with all his fading strength. "I beg you to accept my offer." He felt numb with cold, as if the bargain had already been struck, and death had set her hands on him.

There was silence in the room, in the waning light of the rose window. Paolo waited, exhausted, without hope, for the answer that would determine the meaning of his death.

I n the darkness halfway to dawn, in the warmth of Iain's bed, Linnea held him close against her. Her body ached from the tension of long, patient listening. Iain's outward grief, his angry sorrow, had burned itself out in their love-making. He was quieter now, but she knew there was still more to come out. He would hurt for a long time. It wasn't easy, to lose what you loved most—the life you knew best. She knew.

The sandstorm glowed palely above the climate barrier. A death-light. Iain's warmth against her was her comfort, as she was his.

"It goes on forever," Iain said dreamily. "But it's never the same. That's why they call it otherspace—it's always something other, always changing. We change it by passing through it. We see it whole, from the backs of our minds, and we see it shift as we move through. It moves like a dance, a formal dance—a complicated pattern. And it shimmers—"

"How do you see it?" Linnea brushed the back of her fingers against his damp cheek. "I remember what it was like for me. My eyes didn't work."

"You learn," Iain said. "If you're a man with the gift, you learn. I made my first passages with an experienced pilot, linked in with him, linked to the ship. At first I was blind, but then the second time, or the third, it began to come clear. And when I was ready to pilot myself—oh, it's never the same twice. It's never what I remember, what I expect. But it's always beautiful. Vast, but not empty like normal space, not cold. It's alive. And I understand it, I know its ways. When I'm there, I'm—I was—free. . . ."

She felt his arms tighten around her. It was better not to let him lie silent, thinking. She touched his cheek again. Even a hard question was better than silence. Sometimes that was a way out, to face the hard questions. "What will you do now?"

"I don't know." Silence. "I don't know. Find something to live for." His voice shook, but he was trying. He had pride.

She raised herself on one elbow and gazed down at him. "You will," she said. "Maybe not what you've lost. But you'll go on."

"You're an innocent," Iain said, his eyes bright with tears. "They should never have sent you to this place."

Linnea lay back down beside him, and they kissed, tentatively. He was right, in a way—she shouldn't have come here. Not because she was innocent, but because she was empty. That was dangerous—she should have seen it. She'd been alone for so long. No one had touched her for so long. Iain had reached out his hand, and she had taken it, not knowing what it would mean. That she would come to care so much for a man who could never be hers. That she, who had no hope, would have to try and give him some.

No hope. She kept remembering Father Haveloe, the last time she had seen him, looking down at her with revulsion and contempt. And she had not yet become what she was now. She kissed Iain hungrily, felt his hands slide along her body.

Maybe it was just as well, the danger she was in; maybe it was just as well that she might never get home—if Santandru still was her home. She was afraid to test it. Afraid to meet Marra's eyes. Afraid to go to confession, hide the truth from her neighbors, sleep alone in a narrow bed.

If she didn't know herself any more, would anyone?

Linnea woke late in the morning, in the yellow murk of the storm. Iain was not there. Brown shadow filled the room, blurring the half-familiar into the strange. She sat up in the bed. "Iain?"

No answer.

She shivered. Something was wrong—she knew it as surely as she had known the *Hope*'s disaster, long ago and far away. She got up quickly, put on her white dress from last night, and went to find him.

The house was silent, empty. The house system had no message for her. "The Pilot Master went out several hours ago," it said blandly. It would not, or could not, say more. It could not even reassure her that he had gone alone—that no one had come to arrest him.

Iain returned home at midday. By then Linnea had passed through fear into anger, then into a kind of exasperated calm. He looked strange when he came into the house—his face expressionless, colorless; his long hair loose around his shoulders; his clothes vividly colored, elaborate, the opposite to a Pilot Master's plain black working dress. He nodded a greeting, but he did not smile or move to touch her.

She took her cue from him and slipped back into her servant role. "Do you wish me to serve lunch?"

He frowned, as if the matter required thought, then said, "Please."

She had prepared a luncheon table for one, with no intention of using it herself. He took his place on the couch beside the table, but sat formally upright. She brought the tray from the servitor—crisp spiced crackers, ripe cheese, elaborately sliced fruit. He made no move to touch it as she set it before him. "I went out to make some arrangements," he said. His voice was flat.

She looked down at him. "What arrangements?"

"For your passage home."

Emptiness yawned under her feet. *I have no home*, she

almost said. She sank down beside him on the couch. "But—how? You said your uncle's men would want to talk to me. That I would probably be arrested."

Still he did not touch his food, or the cool, grass-pale wine. "I've spoken to a friend with connections. He has agreed to arrange for you to pass through Dock without papers. I've spoken to a pilot I know. He has agreed to take you home. I've paid your passage, a credit waiting for you on Dock. Your voice and retinal print will unlock it."

Linnea bent her head. "Thank you." She felt numb, strange. She should be happy.

"I can't be sure it will work," Iain said, and now anger was clear in his voice. "They'll be watching the house, of course. I can't just call you a tube car and send you off to the port. And in any case the storm has grounded all shuttles for at least twenty-two hours."

"It will be all right," Linnea said steadily. A chance to go home—of course it was what she wanted. But she was afraid for Iain. Not just of what Fridric or Rafael might do to him; she was afraid of what he might do to himself.

"I hope it will work," Iain said. "Tonight, at full dark, you'll be met in the garden. From there I don't know where you'll be taken, or how you'll travel. It's best that I don't know."

"Who—who will meet me?"

"Mekael sen Drigo," he said. "You've heard the name. A boyhood friend who did not pass for Pilot Master. Once—several years ago—we were lovers. We parted when the difference in our status became inconvenient for me." His voice was steady, expressionless. "Now, of course, there is no difference. I can't resent him for being pleased."

Linnea reached out to him. His hand was cold and still when she laid hers on it. "I'm sorry." It was all she could think of to say.

Linnea dressed again in her clothes from Santandru, the coarse, drab tunic and baggy trousers. Their touch made her skin itch, but their shabby plainness felt like home. She was putting on her own world again. The dream, the nightmare that was Nexus, was nearly over. She stopped and sat bent over on the edge of her bed, fighting tears. She should pray for her own escape, and for a safe journey. But somehow, here, she could not find the words. She was too afraid, for herself and for Iain.

When she came out of her room, carrying her battered old bag, Iain was waiting. She stopped in front of him. "Thank you for your kindness," she said. The words were empty. Then she said, "I'm sorry to leave you here with—" She couldn't go on.

"These are hard times," Iain said. She looked up at him, at his still face, his eyes dark with pain. She stretched out her hands to him, and he caught at them, drew her into a fierce embrace. "Be careful," he said raggedly.

Her eyes stung. "*You* be careful," she said in a raw whisper. "Iain—don't give up hope. Talk to your father. You can help each other. Just don't ever give up. Don't—hurt yourself—"

"I'll do what I must," he said. "If I know you're safe, that will be enough." He had regained his composure now, that same dead composure, and he released her gently, kindly, from the embrace. "Time for you to go."

They walked together down the curving stairs at the back of the house and out the door to the garden. Iain stopped there and pointed silently down the path into the

darkness. Below there, at the end of the curving path, a
shadow waited. Linnea turned to face Iain. She could not
see his expression now. She felt her face twist and she held
her breath. He was a warmth in the darkness. He bent down
and kissed her forehead, but said nothing. She wondered
briefly, sadly, what might have happened between the two
of them on some kinder world. But they were what they
were, both of them—born to colder, harder places.

She waited a moment, then turned and walked away
into the dark. She wondered what would happen to Iain.
She wondered if she would ever know.

I ain stared blindly into darkness as Linnea moved away.
Shadows, nothing but shadows. At the foot of the garden the shadows moved, and he fought back an insane urge
to call to her, to call a warning. But there was nothing to be
afraid of. Mekael had loved him once. Mekael was honorable—for a man of his kind. Iain's kind now.

He went back into his house. It was empty. No longer a
refuge. It was a dead man's memorial chamber—filled
with images and treasures from a life that had ended. Images and treasures that only the one who was dead could
have understood or valued.

Linnea was right. He stood in a new land, in a foreign
country. There was a new language to learn, a new life to
shape. But he had liked the man that he no longer was. He
had loved the life that was gone.

He walked slowly through the house, unable to settle
anywhere. He had no one to speak to, nothing to plan for.
He knew better than to make any overtures to the Pilot
Masters who had been his friends. And he dreaded trying

to speak to his father. He poured out a glass of his best brandy, but it tasted like sugary wood, hot and foul. He emptied it down the waster and considered asking the house for a calming medication. Then he went to his room and lay down on his bed. The automatics had straightened it, of course, but he thought he could still catch Linnea's scent in the dark, still air.

He had done right, sending her away. Right for her sake. But she was the only part of his old life that might still have fit the new one. Now he was alone.

He woke after a night of dry, buzzing dreams full of his uncle's face and voice, full of Rafael's mouth and hands— dreams of the old helplessness, the old betrayals. The storm still held. Wherever Linnea was, she had not yet gotten as far as Dock. Best not to let himself worry. There was nothing he, of all people, could do for her now. She was in Mekael's hands. He remembered Mekael yesterday—pretending not to know what had happened; pretending that Iain was not coming to him as a supplicant. Mekael's dark eyes had been alight with warmth and hope. Until Iain told him why he had come. . . .

Iain had better turn his attention back to his own life. It would do no harm to try following Linnea's advice; she knew how to live with nothing. He bathed and dressed. Then, grimly, he coded a call to Paolo.

But Paolo's node refused him—refused even to accept a message. That was odd. More than odd.

A few minutes later he requested a different link and tried again. Still failure.

Dread stirred inside him, and grew. He tried the general node at the Council offices, planning to leave a message there for Paolo. But that call, too, was refused. Nor could he reach Master sen Kaleb. He tried his friends, one after another: all refused.

Last of all he tried Mekael. Refused. Now that was almost impossible to believe.

Or perhaps the refusals came from a central source. A central directive. The Council.

Iain stood looking out at the storm, at the hot brown light of noon. Finally, reluctantly, he coded Fridric's office.

Fridric appeared at once, as if he had been waiting for this. His long severe face was politely blank. "Iain. How may I serve you?"

"I can't reach my father," Iain said. "Is he all right?"

"He cannot speak to you," Fridric said.

"Why not?" Iain demanded.

"I expect he wants to be alone," Fridric said. "I've just come from the Inner Council chamber. A private session, or of course he would have invited you."

Cold certainty filled Iain. "You called that session."

"I did not," Fridric said. "Your father did. It was his right as a Council member to request a private session. He did not clear his agenda through me."

"What was it?"

Fridric shrugged. "He resigned his seat, of course."

"No," Iain whispered.

"His speech was quite moving. It's under seal, of course, or I would send you a copy."

"You forced him to do this," Iain said. "You've ended his career as you ended mine."

"It was his choice." Fridric picked up a little cup of violet liquor and turned it slowly, slowly on his palm.

"Where is my father? I want to speak to him."

"Paolo is at his home, I presume," Fridric said. "He left here an hour ago."

"I'll go there and see him." Iain started to turn away.

"Go there if you like," Fridric said. "But it's far too late." He glanced aside. At a chrono, Iain realized, and something cold curled tightly around the base of his spine.

"What do you mean?" Iain's voice came out harshly around the constriction in his throat.

"My brother knows his duty to the Line," Fridric said. "That is why he resigned. He would be no less zealous about his duty to his family. To you. His only thought, if I know him—and I do—would be to clear your name. To remove all doubt." He sipped the liquor. "To accept the blame."

Iain watched, frozen, as the image of Fridric rose silently, hooked a thick finger in the neck of his dark silk robe, and tugged. The rich material tore, and again at the sleeves, and again from the hem. Fridric stood there in the ragged robes of mourning, smiling at his brother's son. "Go ahead," he said. "If you hurry, he might still be able to speak to you."

"House!" Iain shouted. "Send a medical team to the house of Paolo sen David."

His house system chimed politely. "All city services in that name have been canceled."

"Use mine!"

Another chime. "Your credit was suspended thirty minutes ago."

"Poor boy," Fridric said. "Now you see."

•   •   •

P aolo drank all of the tea, just to be sure. The bitter taste gagged him, but this way there would be no mistake. When he stood up he staggered. Surely not yet. He was overwrought. He walked carefully into his study, and carried out the last task he had set himself: spoke into the imager, struggling to keep his thoughts clear, his words clear; encrypted it with his family code; sent it, bland and anonymous, into the queue for the commnet. He wondered if anyone would ever receive it.

Then he activated his notes and journals, and wiped them, overwriting them all with a random pattern. So many years of study and thought—the legacy he had planned to leave his son, that would explain so much. But now nothing would be left that might hurt Iain further. Nothing would be left, here, that might give him a hint of the truth.

If only Paolo could have told him. He almost had, half a dozen times over the years. His oath to Fridric all those years ago, before Iain was born—he saw now how it had poisoned his life. He saw now the power that oath had given Fridric—the threat he could hold over Iain. The wedge of silence it drove between father and son. Paolo had loved Iain dearly. Yet he had betrayed him, failed him, before the boy was even born. Bitterly, he regretted it. The knife of grief splitting his chest since last night— that was not half punishment enough. There was no restitution he could make to Iain. No gift he could give but this final act.

He touched his hands to his face. His fingers had begun to tingle. They felt cold. It was beginning.

•   •   •

I ain stumbled from his house to find that the sandstorm had reached its height. Above the climate barrier the clouds swirled dun and yellow and black.

He ran. Down through the muffled mutter of the city, in the burning ochre light he ran. Dust caked in his throat, tears streaked his face. There were men in the streets, some he knew, but they turned away from him, from the fallen Pilot Master. He ran.

P aolo lit a fire in the sitting-room hearth. Outside, the storm cast a yellow-brown gloom over the whole city. Here inside, the fire burned brightly as ever. Paolo sat down beside the heap of documents and storage crystals he had carried from his study and began to feed them one by one into the flames. The crystals crackled and spat as they shattered in the heat.

Blackness wavered in the corners of Paolo's vision, like flames made of darkness. In the hissing whisper from the hearth he heard things now. Voices. He couldn't quite make them out, but they were getting clearer. The dead were near to him now. Perhaps Janda was among them, and would welcome him—would forgive how he had failed the son she'd borne him. He pushed another paper into the base of the flames.

I ain took a shortcut through the park in Upper Centrum. A mistake—steep ground, heavily planted, and in the storm-dusk he could barely see. He stumbled once in the heavy shadow of some cedars, and when he ran on pain stabbed his right ankle at every step.

•   •   •

Paolo could no longer see. He felt warmer now. Floating. The voices were very near. Janda's voice, low and cool—

Iain let himself in through the west gate and limped up the walk. The house was dark. The door did not open to his command or to his palm, and the voice of the house was silent. Iain picked up a stone from the garden and broke the locking mechanism, but the door stayed stubbornly sealed.

He went back into the garden, picked up a larger stone and began smashing it steadily against the heavy plastic of a window. The plastic boomed under the blows. A little white crease formed, then crazing spread farther with each blow.

Again, and again. Then the rock went through, knocking away a vase that stood on a table inside the window. Iain pulled at the fragments of tough plastic, gouging his hands, until the hole would admit him. Then he slid through, scraping himself, tearing his dirty, sweat-soaked robe.

Silence in the house, not even the usual faint hum of the climate system. Iain searched from room to room, and finally saw a faint, shifting glow on the carpet outside the archway that led to the sitting room. He limped down the corridor and into the room. Embers hissed on the hearth at the center of a soft gray mound of ash. They were the only light. Something dark huddled on the carpet near the fire.

Iain heard a sound come from his throat, a whimper like a child's, and he went to the dark shape and knelt beside it.

He lifted aside the spill of gray hair and laid two fingers along the side of Paolo's throat. For a while he did not move. Then, slowly, he began to tear at his clothing. He tore his hair loose from its clip at the nape of his neck. He bent forward across the body of his father, and gave himself over to darkness.

ELEVEN

Alone in the dark, Linnea walked carefully down the broad stone path of Iain's garden. Fear-sweat prickled the skin of her back and shoulders. With every step the sense of wrongness grew. She knew all the dangers of this world, all the sensible reasons for leaving, and she'd agreed to go. But someplace far back in her mind an alarm shrilled. She looked back, but Iain had gone inside, and the house loomed dark, sealed.

As she moved on, she told herself there was nothing here to be afraid of. She heard the trickle of water; she smelled the sun-warmed stones of the path and the acrid scent of some kind of desert foliage. Here and there she caught the hint, the fragrance of flowers. Some she knew. Some she would never know.

She reached the lower wall of Iain's garden and the man waiting for her there, a dark outline against the diffuse light from the City beyond. Not Rafael. "This way," he said softly, and touched her arm to guide her along the stone wall to a low spot where she could climb over. The light was strange—faint, scattered, reddish—and her unease grew.

On the other side of the wall was a broad public path paved in some hard, smooth, red-brown material, veined like stone, lit by low yellow lanterns every dozen meters or so. Now she could see that the man was indeed Mekael, looking much like the holo Iain had shown her. He led her along at a careful pace, one that would draw no attention.

She had never really walked in this world, outside Iain's garden. Transport was always by tube cars that traveled below ground. But the path they followed now had been made for pedestrians, men strolling for pleasure or to take the air. Walking behind Mekael, pretending to be his servant, she looked around hungrily at the world she had barely seen. At first, high walls shut her out—walls of stone, rough and picturesque, or smooth as satin and elegantly patterned; walls of every color of brick; walls inlaid, carved, or brilliantly tiled. Sometimes fragrant-flowering vines spilled over from the rich gardens within, or a tree in bloom swayed, ghost black, against the pale night.

As they traveled, the public space between the walled gardens widened. Lawns lush with grass stretched away into shadows; brilliant flowers breathed their scent, their colors strange in the yellow dimness. The trees whispered, impossibly tall. She had never walked here. Never walked on grass. But now there was no time. The man ahead hurried on, and she followed as she must, through the misty light of the city and the storm, through the pools of gold cast by the lanterns along the path, through the green-black shadows under the dark trees.

Although it was late, Linnea knew that men were still awake, at work or at play inside their houses and in those city towers rising taller and nearer ahead of her as she and Mekael descended. Yet the parklands and open spaces were unpeopled, silent. Maybe no one ever bothered to go there. They all had gardens of their own.

Now, kilometers from Iain's house and much farther downslope, she saw no houses at all—only wide expanses of parkland. They came to a clearing, well guarded by trees. At its center stood a transportation kiosk, connected to the tube-car system below. Mekael stopped under its shelter and turned to face her as she caught up to him.

She set down her bag and studied him, grateful for the rest, and for her first chance to see him clearly. He seemed to be looking her over as well. She liked the way he looked. He had what Marra used to call an open face, pleasant rather than handsome, with clear light brown eyes, and light skin. His brown hair was so curly he wore it braided down along his scalp, a dozen braids or more, hanging to his shoulders. He looked strange, but pleasant. He smiled at her and pressed his palm against the callpad. "No more walking."

"Good," she said, then remembered her manners—her real manners, the ones Ma had taught her. "I'm Linnea Kiaho. Linny."

"I know," he said. "Iain told me about you."

"He trusts you," she said. "And I know he cared about you."

"I know it, too," Mekael said. "Once, and long ago. Then he changed." He looked away. "But, you see, Iain never imagines that anyone else changes. He imagines that we all file ourselves away and wait for him to call us back to him."

Was he trying to warn her? "That doesn't matter to me," she said, keeping her voice flat. "I'll never see him again."

"Nor will I," Mekael said with a note of regret, as the fenced-off platform beside the kiosk slid aside and a low, gray, gleaming shape began to rise into the light.

Linnea looked at him with a flicker of unease. "But you're helping Iain," she said. "Or—did he *force* you to do this?"

"Iain?" Mekael said, and the sudden grief in his face frightened her more than anything in this world, anything but Rafael. "Iain had nothing to do with it." Before she could speak Mekael turned and walked quickly away through the trees. A voice from nowhere said, "*Do not move*," and beside her a door in the tube car's side hissed open. Two men got out, huge in black, padded armor. A blue light dazzled her eyes and she cowered away, and one of the men said, "The scan matches. Case her up," and the other swung a net of gauze around her shoulders, like Ma settling a spare coat around her when she was tiny, only the gauze clung, sticky, then squeezed. Squeezed.

She swayed, and her hands wouldn't go out to help her, and one of the men caught her. They lifted her easily between them, like a sack of potatoes, and slid her into a dark door in the tube car's side. Into a dark place, alone. The door slid shut.

She lay in darkness. Her hands tingled. Her tongue felt thick. Drugs in the netting? When the car started moving she rolled limply, pinning one arm underneath her body. The world spun, and she felt sick. Her courage failed her at last, and she began to cry. In the borderless darkness it sounded strange, as if someone else was crying. A scared child, or a woman without hope. Someone lost.

I ain sen Paolo came back to awareness in a place of shadowy silence, under an angry sunset. Through the tall window of his father's study he saw the roiling sky, a burst of ugly red and brown like something that had spoiled and split and spilled itself. Iain stood up stiffly. In the hot, still air of the house his lungs burned as if he were half-drowned. The red light stung his eyes, and his chest ached from long weeping.

He held to the pain—it was better than thought. His mind shied away from what he had done. How his words had driven Paolo away. How in his selfish coldness he had left his father to die alone. He would remember all that, if he turned and looked at the shrouded shape on the rug behind him.

He made himself turn and look. Dust stirred and danced in the shafts of red light, over the long, still body lying there by the fire. His father. All that was left of his father.

Iain rubbed his eyes. If this were a different world, and Paolo had died in peace and honor, attended by a dutiful son—if that were true, what would Iain do now?

Think.

He would call in the proper attendants, respectful men of the lesser degree, who would see to everything. He could not do this today, powerless and without credit as he was.

Yet he must honor his father. So, alone, he would bathe Paolo's body, dress him in festival clothing, and lay him in his own bed. That was first.

It took all his strength to lift the body and carry it up the narrow emergency stairs. He shoved open the door to Paolo's plain, orderly room, and laid his body on his bed. Iain was weeping again, racking his aching chest. He lit candles, then laid Paolo out and washed him, tenderly, as if his father might still feel rough handling. The old, long-fingered hands had already begun to stiffen, and they were cold. Iain held them awhile to try and warm them. But it was like trying to warm all the night with one candle.

Calmer now, he dressed Paolo in the best robe he could find—heavy silk, black as space. He tied the plain black sash in the knot that meant *I apologize for nothing.*

Then he knelt beside his father and took his hand again. Colder still. What would they have done next, the silent and respectful servants of death? He slowed his spinning thoughts. The feast. They would prepare a feast, the best of everything. Enough for all the men whose lives Paolo had touched as a Pilot Master, as a teacher, as a friend.

Iain rose and went down to the dark kitchens, among the stilled automatics, to see what food he could find in the coolers. He set out the best he could in Paolo's dark dining parlor—fruit, cheese, cold baked meat. It was for the men who would come to honor his father. The men who had worked with him, learned from him, loved him. All these men would come to honor him—or would have come, in that other world, the one that was right. *Will anyone dare—here, now?*

Perhaps. He must prepare.

Iain took wines to his father's room and arranged them as they should be arranged, on a table by the bed. He stood delicate glasses among the decanters, so each guest could drink one last time to Paolo.

A fire should burn on the hearth, rich with fragrant woods and spices. But not this time. Darkness was better. In darkness the room shared his grief. In darkness he could hide his shame.

Iain looked down at himself. In the other world, as the son and heir, Iain would wear fine mourning—pure white silk, carefully torn. Well, his tunic was not white, or even clean, but it was torn almost to rags; it would do.

He knelt as he should do, in his father's room, at the foot of his father's bed, to greet his father's last guests as they came one by one from the feasting table.

Someone would come. Someone would dare to come to honor his father. They could not all be cowards. Fierce anger kept him still, waiting.

It was full dark when he heard voices in the hall, footsteps coming closer. He straightened and arranged his robe around his knees.

The door to Paolo's room rumbled open. A man shone a handlight in Iain's face and called, "In here!"

Men came into Paolo's room, half a dozen of them at least. They glanced only briefly at the bed. Some wore the brick red of Council Security; some were civil servants, robed and curled. They all stared at Iain, in the light of a lamp someone set on the wine table. A voice said, "It's the son," and he saw one of the Security men draw a weapon. Not a stunrod, Iain saw. A neural fuser, ready to burn out his brain or maim him for life.

Iain looked at them all coldly. "This is a house of mourning," he said. His voice was rough and raw.

But they were all watching the door now. Iain turned and stiffened with a rush of rage that brought him stumbling to his feet. Fridric—in Paolo's house. Iain had never

seen him here, had never imagined that he would dare—
even now, in the hour of his triumph.

The old man looked around, seeming mildly curious,
his eyes lingering on nothing. "Gentlemen, leave us," he
said to the other men, and the room cleared at once.

Fridric had obviously made careful preparations for this
moment: His pure white silk mourning was perfect, his
face correctly painted as a mask of grief, unmarred by any
real tears. "Poor boy," Fridric said soothingly. "Alone with
such a task. But you've done well."

"Look at him," Iain said.

"Not now," Fridric said. "We have other matters to discuss."

"Look at him," Iain said again. His voice broke. "Drink
to him. This is what you wanted. Take your pleasure and
go."

Fridric frowned at Iain. But then he moved slowly to the
bed where Paolo lay. Iain watched him.

Fridric looked down at his brother's corpse. His face
darkened and changed, the lines deepening around his
long, grim mouth. He reached down with a finger and
touched Paolo's hand. Then he drew back and turned to
Iain. "So. I've seen." His deep voice was hard, harsh.

Iain stood straight. "Now go," he said. "This is my
house now."

"No," Fridric said. "It is mine."

The anger knotted inside Iain stirred, flared. "By what
right? My father's will—"

"You shall not profit from your father's shame."

Iain went cold. "What *shame*?"

"We know that you conspired to help the woman blackmail your father."

Iain started forward, and Fridric held up a hand. "Stay there. Or, if you prefer, we can carry on this discussion with two Security men holding you. And listening."

"I don't care who hears your lies." Iain's voice sounded small in the crowding silence, in the powerful presence of death.

"We have recordings," Fridric said with mild reproof. "I showed them to your father this afternoon. You promised the woman your help."

Iain cast his mind back. "I said I would talk to my father. I didn't say—Uncle, it would not have been blackmail."

"Then it was bribery," Fridric said. "We also know that she gave you her body."

"It was not a bribe," Iain said quietly.

"You think not? You think it does not appear so?" Fridric sighed. "You harbored her in your home against the will of the Council, against the will of your father. You completed your arrangements with her, and when the bargain had been struck and paid for, you sent her away."

Iain found himself staring into Fridric's calm face. How did he know—

Fridric smiled slightly. "Or so you planned."

Iain drew a slow, stinging breath. "She is innocent."

"She is anything but innocent," Fridric said. "As we are discovering."

Iain sagged.

"You gave her over to a man you trusted," Fridric said. "A former lover, I believe. But of the other class. What you did not allow for is that such men are vulnerable to certain pressures—as you will learn. And in answer to such pressures, the man Mekael responded most eagerly. What you entrusted to him was given to us immediately. And now . . ." He let his voice trail off.

A cold sliver of horror iced Iain's belly. He did not speak.

"You are concerned for her," Fridric said. "Good." He slipped a datapad from his pouch and glanced at it. "Her body search produced physical evidence that you had sexual intercourse with her quite recently. She is sexually naive and from a backward world. She would not have taken such a step of her own free will. More proof of your bargain with her."

Linnea, helpless under that cold, probing, knowledgeable search—Iain gritted his teeth. "You hurt her."

"I did not attend her interrogation," Fridric said. "And it hardly matters now."

"So she is dead." Iain spoke the words steadily enough, but grief pulsed again inside him. Another death he had not prevented. Another failure.

"She still lives," Fridric said, "for the moment. But we distract ourselves with such trivia." He rose, went to the wine table by the bed, and poured himself a full glass. Then he turned and raised it toward the bed where Paolo lay. "To my brother Paolo sen David," he said steadily. "To the richness of his memory." He sipped the wine. His eyes looked strange, dark and glittering.

Iain faced his uncle. "Now that your work is accomplished—how long will I live?"

Fridric sighed. "This is no work of mine. Your father *chose* this—to spare your life."

"No," Iain growled.

"You think he would not bargain for you? He loved you.

For you, he sacrificed more than you will ever know."
There was no irony in Fridric's expression now.

"Perhaps so," Iain said. "But I know you would never
agree to spare me. Or keep your word, if you gave it."

"I do not lie in matters of my personal oath," Fridric
said. "I swore to spare you, and I will—to live on without
status or purpose." He smiled coldly. "Then, when you at
last summon the courage to kill yourself, Rafael and I will
be left to console each other."

The words did not matter. True, untrue, Iain no longer
cared. "Linnea," he husked. "What will happen to her?"

"Death," Fridric said. "A tragic but necessary expedient.
As all of this has been."

In two quick steps Iain reached his uncle and slammed
the wineglass from his hand to the floor. It shattered, spattering their robes with wine, filling the room with its
raisiny scent. "Get out," Iain said in a low voice. "I know
where a knife is. Let me die now, here with my father."

"Not until the play is over," Fridric said. He raised his
voice. "Gentlemen, attend me!"

Armed men crowded the doorway. Iain looked back at
Fridric, who said clearly, "You are now under arrest. I've
tolerated a great deal from you. I felt I owed it to your father. But no more." He turned to his men and gestured toward what lay on the bed. "Carry that away and burn it.
Bring the ashes to me."

Iain could only speak in a dry whisper. "You have taken
everything."

"What I have taken from you," Fridric said, "was never
yours to begin with." And then he was gone.

TWELVE

Fridric sen David stood seething in the small, plain office of one of his Security interrogators, a man useful for matters best handled quietly. Fridric's hands were clasped behind him in the posture of elegance he had learned from his famous—not father, but so everyone thought him. . . . The room's one window gave Fridric a view of rooftop ducts and, beyond, the grim mass of the eastern mountains, black against the night sky, unusually clear now after the long storm. This day should have capped his secret triumph. But what he had done—what he had broken and spoiled—

His hands tightened, and he eased them consciously. He *had* his victory. He had defeated and shamed his oldest enemy; broken Paolo's line; claimed his wealth. When Fridric died—in the fullness of time—Rafael would be safe. And the Line would endure, richer and stronger because Fridric sen David had served it.

Footsteps in the corridor. There was just time to lower himself into a chair beside the window and arrange himself in an attitude of boredom.

The Security interrogator limped in—a small, precise man, old for such a menial position. His limp hair, dyed a dull black, matched his plain civilian robe. Years ago, found guilty of unspeakable crimes against a servant, he had been stripped of his patronym by the head of his family. Since then he had used no name at all, professionally. "Council Lord sen David," he said. He was visibly nervous.

Fridric waved a hand. "Report."

The interrogator said reluctantly, "Sen Drigo died."

"And had the woman told him anything?"

"Nothing of importance." The man's voice was flat. "In my professional judgment, sen Drigo was at that point incapable of lying."

Good news. Fridric rose to his feet and turned away, gazing out the window at the night. He clasped his hands before him now, tightly, to keep them from shaking with the release of his long tension.

Fifty years ago and more, a clumsy blackmail attempt from offworld had revealed to Fridric the cold and ugly truth. The power that passed from father to son—myth. The sacred separateness of the Line's genetic heritage— myth. Their daring escape from the Cold Minds, rescuing the remnants of humanity—perhaps that much was true. But anyone could have done it. And proof of all this existed—somewhere.

Fridric had killed the blackmailer, thinking that would end it. When Paolo discovered the death, Fridric had been forced to tell him the truth as well. That secret had bound the brothers to each other for life. Oath for oath, silence for silence. And when they had sons, hostage for hostage.

For fifty years now, there had been silence, only silence. For the brothers, the silence of fear and hate; for the black-mailers, the silence, Fridric had thought, of death. Paolo had chosen to lie to his son; Fridric had told his own the truth, to give Rafael a weapon against his uncle if Fridric died first.

And now the blackmail attempt had surfaced again. Though the proof itself was still hidden on the woman's dreary world, someone there had discovered its importance and acted on it.

Fridric sighed. Ill fortune. He was old now, and he dared not leave this matter unsettled when he died. Impul-sive, greedy Rafael might not act wisely. The boy still had so much to learn.

No. Fridric must root out the threat on Santandru.

That would be a delicate procedure, if it was to be done in secret. To begin, he required an agent. A tool. Someone who would not be questioned. Someone expendable.

Fridric turned to face the interrogator. "Sen Drigo's death was certified?"

"Accidental," the man said. "The corpse has been burned."

Fridric smiled. "Then that matter is closed."

"And the woman?"

"Keep her," Fridric said. "I might have a use for her." He turned away. "Now I must speak to my son."

Linnea clung to the hard bench that was her bed. She did not know where she was, or how long she had been there, in her small cell, in the unchanging glare from the flat, white ceiling. The ceiling with the faint pattern of blotches in one corner—mildew, dirt—blotches that took on shape, crawled slowly from one shape to another as she watched, as the drugs crept into her system from her food, or faded slowly away. How long had she been here? Days or weeks? Had they forgotten her?

At first they had asked her questions, a reason for the drugs. She could no longer remember what they had asked her, or what she had replied, or even the faces of her questioners. But now there were no more questions, and still they drugged her—in her food, in her water, maybe in the air she breathed. Each time the recovery was worse, and each time she felt sicker and ate less. A metal basin stood on the floor beside her sleeping bench, but sometimes she was too weak to reach it before she vomited. The room stank. No one came to help her or clean her. Maybe she would die. Maybe that was what they wanted. Her body ached in muscle and bone, as if they had beaten her. For all she knew, they had.

Time crawled, shapeless, like the sick blotches on the ceiling. She dreamed, sometimes, of men who listened to her as she lay sick, rambling, raving from the drugs. She knew—because it must be so—that she'd told them everything. She'd told them Marra's name. Marra—who should have been safe from all this, who was the reason she chose this path—they would find Marra, and the children. . . .

At times when her mind was clear, she guessed she was deep down, under the City, because of the changeless light and because the air was thick and cold. She was like the winter dead at home, stacked frozen in the church cellar to wait for the ground to thaw. But she was not dead yet. They had forgotten her.

The light didn't matter. Her mind was in darkness.

Father Haveloe would tell her to pray, and she did, tallying the prayers on her fingers. But they were only a stream of empty words, cast into emptiness, answered by silence. For the first time in her life she understood that she would die. All come to nothing, as Father Haveloe had said. The emptiness was waiting for everyone she loved. Waiting for her. She would die, and it would be as if she had never lived. In some ways, that was true. A waste. She closed her eyes and lay still, willing all the regretful thoughts to silence.

They must have stopped the drugs, because this time she felt hungry when they came for her. Silent men in gray robes stripped her and washed her with chemical soaps, cleaned her mouth, combed her hair roughly straight, gave her a plain gray dress to cover herself. Their hands on her meant nothing to her—or, it seemed, to them. She might have been a machine.

They took her up and up, and then through corridors of light, fragrant with cool, fresh air, corridors glittering like sunlight over glass. Then they stopped and opened a door and pushed her through. She staggered to catch her balance as it closed behind her, leaving her alone.

Alone in the sky.

It was a wide, shallow room—the door in one long wall, the other long wall one seamless window from end to end, from the floor to the ceiling. There before her, meters away, was the hard, blue sky, and the broad, tawny haze of the western desert. She blinked through tears, dazzled. She had forgotten light. She had forgotten distance.

Then something moved, at the far end of the room. A dark, lean figure. Her heart sped—and then her throat ached with sudden grief, because it was not the man she had thought: the man whose name she still knew. This was another man, and she feared him. He moved toward her gracefully, the desert light a bloom of red-gold on his hair, and smiled as he came.

Rafael.

Her hunger changed to acid nausea, and her knees trembled. But she didn't speak. Silence was her place, and her refuge. The lesson she remembered from both her lives.

He stopped a meter away from her. Today he wore black like Hamlet in the story, and his orange hair waved and curled, partly escaping from its loose braid. He wore many dark jewels on his hands, in his ears, on his clothing. In his power and poise they suited him. He smiled at her, and she swallowed, swallowed again, saliva flooding her mouth.

He smiled at her. "You won't vomit. You've had no food for three days."

As she started to fall he caught her by the shoulders and looked down at her, smiling. He had perfect teeth and perfect skin—pale as sand, cold as the shell of some sea-bottom creature, an eater of the dead. She gathered her strength to step back, away from him.

But he held her there easily, and bent down to her and pressed his mouth onto hers. The world went white. She couldn't breathe. Soft, practiced, his mouth tasted her, tested her; his strong tongue probed. Then he drew back. "Did that please you? Shall I go on?"

"No," she rasped. "No. Leave me alone."

"You aren't waiting for him, still, are you?" he asked, and his voice was strangely gentle.

She would not answer him. She closed her eyes.

"Because, Linnea," he said tenderly, "Iain is dead."

She felt her heart stop, stammer, and move on, pounding. "You're lying."

"Dead and burned," Rafael said regretfully, "or I could prove it to you. He killed himself."

"No." Every breath hurt. She could feel the tears running down her cheeks. "He wouldn't."

"He lost everyone," Rafael said. "Everyone who mattered to him. And so he chose death. Were you expecting him to help you? To save you? No. He forgot you. He left you here, alone. In my uncle's power, with your world at stake." He was standing near her again now, and she could feel the heat of his body. "And now only I can help you."

"No one can help me," she said thinly. Iain was dead. It should not matter. He was only one of *them*. A Pilot Master.

Yet her hands still remembered him. Her body remembered him. She wept, shaking, weak, angry.

Strong hands took her, turned her, and she looked up through water and heat into the cold blue eyes of Rafael. "He left you," Rafael said, "but I can help you. Listen to me. Listen. My father is angry. Your people brought corruption and suicide into his family. But with my help, not everything is lost. Do you understand me?"

This is important. I have to listen. She wiped her face on her sleeve.

"If I speak for you, you can still save your world. And yourself."

His words froze her into stillness, for now, but a thin trembling began in her spine. "How?"

"My father will allow Santandru's contract renewal to

stand, if I ask it of him. And I will ask it—in return for one favor."

"N-name it."

Rafael smiled down at her, and drew her against his body. With cold nausea she felt the heat of him against her, and a hardness pressing against her belly. "A simple favor, for you," he said. "The favor you granted Iain, thinking *he* could help you. I know you've told yourself you loved him, which makes you honest in your own eyes. But I don't want you to pretend anything. I want you to be what you are, and *know* what you are. I want to have you for three days. And then—you can go free. And your world will live."

She stood very straight. She was in his power. If he wanted her he could have her, drugged, bound, beaten. . . .

So if he wanted to believe she had chosen him, chosen what was about to happen to her—then she might as well give him that. On the chance, on the chance that he was not lying. She spoke, her voice so thick with grief that she doubted he would understand her. "I agree."

With a sharp gesture, Fridric shut off the recording and looked across his desk at his son. Rafael's depthless eyes glittered back at him, a strange cold violet in the light of the rose window. "Well, Father?" The boy settled back in his chair. "Did I do well?"

Fridric took a slow breath to ease the tightness in his chest. "It was done—thoroughly." He looked away from Rafael's gaze, trying not to see the woman Linnea's blank, despairing face—her hopeless passivity. . . .

Once again he had to face the coldness in Rafael, coldness beyond the calm objectivity Fridric had wished to train into him. *Far* beyond that.

Once again, he wondered how far Rafael would go without restraint, when Fridric himself was dead. There had always been a queasy sense of strain in Rafael—something dark, leashed tight; and sometimes the leash slipped a bit and that strange, sourceless anger flared, to be gratified only by the fear, the pain of someone powerless. It had been expensive, over the years, to provide for that appetite, and to conceal it. Fridric frowned, considering.

"If you're angry," Rafael said sharply, "remember I only did as you asked."

"You did as I asked," Fridric said, "and more." He spread his hands flat on the cold stone of his desk. "When the time comes, that woman will do anything to escape another three days—another moment—in your power." He had seen only a few minutes of the recording, but it was clear that the woman's spirit had been broken. Even when she had seen the little knife, even when he used it—

Fridric straightened in his chair. He had ordered this; he had known what Rafael was capable of. Now it was done, and over. "It's well," he said heavily. "You have her safe?"

"Of course," Rafael said. He leaned forward. "And now, Father—we should settle that other matter. My cousin Iain."

"He is to be formally stripped from the Line," Fridric said easily.

"And then?"

Fridric eased back in his chair and studied Rafael. Iain, of course, stood at the core of this, as always; Rafael so craved his death. Fridric wondered again what could be the source of such hate. He looked straight into his son's eyes.

"And then he will live on, among the lesser men here—for as long as he chooses."

Rafael's face went marble white. He bared his teeth. "No. No. We can't! Father, we must kill him now, today. And all the others, on the woman's world, the moment we know who they are. You promised me. You said we would be safe, after this."

"We will encompass all that, in time," Fridric said. "And Iain will surely die, in time, by his own hand." He made a silencing gesture. "Truly by his own hand, as his father died. There must be no question."

"But he threatens us!"

"He knows nothing," Fridric said forcefully. "We know that the woman told him nothing of substance. He can do us no harm."

Rafael's blue stare chilled him. Fridric went on, too hastily, "He is in my power. The woman will be a hostage for his actions—he values her far more than he knows."

Rafael stood up, an incredible breach of manners. "So, then. You aren't strong enough."

Fridric shot to his feet. "Be silent!"

The boy glared at him. "If you were strong, then, years ago—when Paolo learned the truth—you would have killed him at that moment."

"This is not a matter of strength," Fridric said. "I gave my word to my brother."

Rafael's head lifted. "Yet if Iain could harm us, you would break your word."

"He cannot," Fridric said. "I promise you that."

"It's foolish," Rafael said.

"You will not harm your cousin," Fridric said. He paused. "If you wish to travel offworld again."

Rafael held himself very still, and Fridric studied him. The boy's control was getting better. Good. So much would depend on that, when he came to rule.

Rafael sighed at last, and said, "It seems I must obey."

"Yes," Fridric said. "You must." But once again he had to look away from the bright hunger in his son's eyes.

I ain paced in his holding cell, unclean and itching in his rags. Days, now, and they had told him nothing, said nothing. He had seen no one but the silent male attendant who had given him some bread and meat, hours ago. He had choked it down with some of the lukewarm water from the tap in the cell. He told himself he had nothing to fear: There was nothing left to be taken from him that he could defend. His heart was dead. He could not even grieve.

Then, on the fourth or fifth evening, there was no telling, a guard brought him clothing and told him that he was to be taken to Fridric.

Iain shook out the folds of dark fabric and felt a strange twinge when he saw that it was his own—the everyday black tunic and trousers of a jump pilot. "But I am suspended," he made himself say to the guard.

"You are to wear it," the guard said again, and stood woodenly, making no move to aid him, while Iain dressed himself. Although still he felt nothing, the whole, clean clothes were comforting. When he was dressed, the guard spoke once more. "You are to braid your hair properly. The Honored Voice orders this." He set something on the small table: a comb, and beside it a crimson cord.

Slowly, as best he could without a selfscreen or even a mirror, Iain combed out his hair, then braided and bound it.

The guard gave him no cosmetics, so Iain could not make his appearance entirely correct, but the familiar clothing gave him an odd feeling of ease. The tatters of his proper role slipped on as easily as the tunic. He felt the return of power, of his rights. And with it—he could not help it, though he knew he was being a fool—with it, he felt hope.

But the guards did not take him high up the tower, to the office of the Honored Voice. They took him inward, and downward, and Iain's heart went cold as he recognized the tunnels beneath the Place of the Tree, where men waited for their turn on the dais above.

His mind raced. This could not be an execution; Line blood was never shed in public. And they would not have allowed him the honors of his rank if he was to die. More than that he could not guess. They came to a gate of heavy brass beyond which no mere prison guard, no man not of the Line, could pass. There waited for him two men of Fridric's, pilots he barely knew, their faces masks of formal paint. They did not speak to him; they fell in beside him, and together the three of them ascended the narrow ramp leading to the stairs that climbed the dais where the Tree stood, and also—no doubt—Fridric.

Iain came up into the Place of the Tree, his head spinning, hearing the silence of two thousand men judging him with their cool eyes. Darkness, and a stirring of air, and, high above, light spilling over the edge of the dais. The scent of fire.

They let him pass first. As he climbed the light grew stronger, and the sea of somber faces faded into darkness. Yet they were there. Iain climbed slowly, his head high.

Now he saw Fridric awaiting him, in glorious mourning pure as snow: stern and proud, a clear gem glittering on his

cheek more coldly than any tear. Other men, formal witnesses, stood beside and behind him. Iain drew a breath
when he saw that one was Master sen Kaleb in a plain
white mourning robe, his gaunt face stiff as a mask.

Now the other pilots stood beside him again, gripped
his arms, and moved him forward to stand before the Honored Voice. Iain stumbled and caught himself, dizzy and
dazzled, weak from long hunger. Though he could not see
the men all around him in the darkness, he felt their crowding presence, their cold attention. He made himself look up
into his uncle's eyes.

Fridric spoke. "By my authority, I bind you to silence.
Speak no word."

Iain kept his gaze steady. He was beginning to remember what he had been, once; the truth within him gave him
a little courage.

"I do not know how to address you," Fridric said. "To
call you by your name is to speak my brother's name with
yours. Shamed as that name is, it is an honor too great for
you." He turned, slowly, so that Iain saw only his profile.
"I could call you nephew," Fridric said, "but that shames
me." His voice sharpened. "I could call you Pilot Master.
But that would shame us all."

Iain waited.

"This assembly has seen the record of your plot with an
offworld woman to influence the course of a Council decision by suborning your own father. Out of fear for you my
brother acted shamefully, and out of shame he took his
own life."

Iain looked away, up the shaft above the vast chamber,
along the golden chain, all the way up to the glint of blue-

green that was the image of faraway Earth. Earth was real. He would hold to that.

Fridric spoke again. "I see the selfish anguish in your face. You imagine great burdens for yourself. You see yourself, I know, as a victim. But as this assembly has seen, all this great structure of tragedy was built by *you*. You built it from your long jealousy of my son's future, and most recently of his Selection. You built it from your adolescent lust for a common servant woman, who used your urges well to serve her own purposes."

Fridric swung and faced Iain. "You built this tragedy from your petulant dislike of your father's stern propriety, which we all honored for many years." Fridric leaned closer. "Until he broke it. For you."

Iain heard the raw pain in his uncle's voice, knew that every man heard it and believed it. Now to his shock Iain's heart woke fully, and his grief for Paolo choked him. If he had been alone, he would have cried out in pain. He trembled on his feet, knowing that the men holding him could feel it, would think him afraid, would scorn him.

"Therefore," Fridric said harshly, seeming to rise to a great height above Iain, "your suspension from the Line is ended. You shall be cut off from the Line forever."

The words slid into Iain's heart like an assassin's knife, sharp and smooth, the pain yet to come. Fridric continued, "I have caused your link to be struck from the Chain, before all these witnesses. This link is here in my hand, and before you I cast it into the fire."

Iain saw something small and glittering spin through the air, land at the base of the great fire in a puff of sparks. "It is melted," Fridric said.

It is melted, the gathered men said, a deep rumble of

anger. Iain saw the link sag in the hot center of the flames, sag and run, a quick runnel of brightness. Then it was lost in the ashes.

"I have caused the record of your birth and career to be struck from the archives of the Line," Fridric said. "This record I hold in my hand, contained in this crystal, and before you I cast it into the fire."

Again a small glittering flight, a cloud of sparks. "It is destroyed," Fridric said.

It is destroyed.

Through a haze of anguish Iain felt the hands of his captors tighten on his arms, and behind him other hands tore his hair loose from its braid and ripped free the cord that had bound it, that had marked his family lineage. And now the cord, too, appeared in Fridric's hands. "I now hold in my hand the mark of your fathers," Fridric said. "Before you I cast it into the fire. It is burned."

It is burned.

Iain kept silent, out of what remained of his pride. Let them believe that Paolo's son was not broken.

Fridric turned again to face him. "You are of no family," he said. "You have no name. You have no honor, and no man will aid you. There is no place among the men of the Line, however low, that you would not degrade." He raised his right hand in the formal gesture of judgment, hand held like a blade over Iain's head. "I command that you be returned to your prison, and held there for a term of sixty days while your properties are sought out and confiscated." He straightened. "Then you will be freed, to live as you can in the lower City, among the men of your own station. And you will never leave this world."

The world had narrowed to a single focus of pain. In

that single focus Iain saw at that moment the face of his old teacher, Master sen Kaleb, blanched with pity and agony.

Iain closed his eyes, and kept his silence as his captors led him away.

Time stretched out endlessly for Iain in his cell. A different kind of cell: locked, windowless, barren. The cot and basic toilet, the table and stool were all molded from the stuff of the walls or the floor. In the cold light it glistened greasily, the color of dead sand.

He had no clothing, no bedcoverings, but the room was warm. The light never changed, but sometimes he slept without meaning to—weariness swam up all around him and pulled him down. He did not want to sleep. He dreamed, terrible dreams; and when he woke, the dreams were true.

And after that—

After that, the truth waited, stark, unchangeable. His father had killed himself. Laid aside all his goals, all his hopes, all his work. For Iain.

And Linnea was dead.

When he had no need to sleep or eat or void he stood in the corner farthest from the light, leaned his forehead against the slick, pale wall, and closed his eyes. Sometimes, then, he saw Linnea. Sometimes he saw other things, and wept, swaying slowly there, palms pressed against the wall beside his head. They must know he had broken. But it meant nothing; he had nothing left to defend. Not even any honor. The Line had moved on without him.

A long time passed. Days. His beard sprouted, itching.

Sometimes tepid water sprayed from the ceiling in a corner, and if he used the little packet of soft soap that came with every third meal he could get clean. He started calling those "days": the times from one washing to another.

On the fourth or fifth "day," Rafael came to him.

Iain turned from his wall and saw Rafael standing there, just within the closed door of the cell, clad all in the honorable black of a jump pilot. Another nightmare, Iain thought. He slumped against the wall and took a breath that caught on a high sound, a sound of fear. But then he saw the real satisfaction in Rafael's eyes. Rafael was real.

Some frayed thread of pride dragged Iain upright again to face him. He tried to speak and coughed; he had not spoken for days. His throat felt stuffed with dusty feathers. "If you touch me," he rasped, "I'll kill you."

Rafael carried an oval viewer, lightly, in one hand. Now he tapped it and held it so Iain could see it. It was a man's face, hideous: a tangle of black hair; beard stubble; empty, staring eyes. It was himself. At the precise moment Iain realized that, Rafael smiled. "You do not tempt me, little cousin. As you see."

"Why are you here?"

Rafael moved to the cot and settled onto it, gracefully, his beautiful hands lightly clasped over one lifted knee, the imager set aside as if for another time. Yet Iain sensed tension in him. His hands seemed to stiffen under Iain's gaze.

"You mean to kill me," Iain said, and suppressed a shiver. Odd. He had thought it did not matter whether he lived or died.

"I can't," Rafael said lightly. "My father's promise to your father binds me as well."

Iain blinked hard, forcing back the easy tears of weary

hopelessness. "So if you won't touch me, and can't kill me—"

"I am here," Rafael said, "to tell you the truth. The secret your father kept from you for so long. Interested?"

Iain made himself walk to the stool next to his cell's small table. He sat down carefully, blood singing in his ears. "Tell me."

"But first—if you learn this truth, you *will* be killed. Not even Father's word will restrain him. He is not so stupid."

Iain looked at him. "I don't care."

"I'll pretend I believe you," Rafael said brightly. "Now listen. Your father was a liar."

Iain's grief surged, choking him. "He was an honorable man!"

Rafael's eyes looked strange—almost gentle. "No, cousin. No—*Iain*—listen to me. Listen to me!"

"Why should I?" Iain demanded.

"You hate me," Rafael said. "And with reason. But I *know* about those two old men, how they have lied. To everyone, even you." He stopped, studying Iain, and then went on quietly, "Paolo lied every moment of his life. He stood beside you and lied when you took your oath at the Tree. Renewing his own oaths, he lied."

Iain's hands gripped each other in his lap, out of Rafael's sight. It was time to understand. "What was the lie?"

"Our fathers were not the sons of David sen Elkander," Rafael said harshly. "David sen Elkander was sterile. Paolo's father, and Fridric's, was an offworld contract servant."

"No," Iain said hollowly. But it fit—all the long silences, his father's protectiveness, Rafael's bitter rebellions. "It isn't possible. My father—"

"So," Rafael continued, "we are not of the Line. But it doesn't end there. We are not of the Line, we four, and yet all of us are—*were*—jump pilots. So the Line is a lie, too. We spend our lives worshipping our past, the great tale of our history—and all of it, all of it, is a lie."

"You cannot prove this!"

Rafael laughed. "Of course I could prove it. It is precisely that proof that your womanservant wanted to sell to you. The man, you see—our grandfather—he came from *her* world." Rafael grinned unpleasantly. "You are her cousin. Of sorts."

Iain could not speak.

"You see, then, why she could not be permitted to complete her bargain," Rafael said. "Why your father opposed her presence. Why her world must die."

"Why didn't Father—" Iain stopped and drew a careful, steadying breath. He would not break down again, not now.

Rafael's lip curled. "Because he was a coward. Because he knew you were as weak as he was. He knew you could not live with the truth as I have done."

Iain rested his face in his hands. *Father, you lied. Father, no—*

"*My* father," Rafael said, "told me the truth from the start, of course. He is a different man. Harder. His eyes are clearer. He sees the political possibilities. The truth was my weapon—against Paolo and against you." Rafael looked at Iain, his face still, empty. "And so I grew up alone. The only man of our generation who knew that our pride and tradition are baseless." He smiled icily. "And

Fridric wonders why I seek—what I seek. Power. Security. Oblivion. He's blind. He won't see that I have to take for myself, build for myself, all that *you* were given so freely. All that *you* never questioned."

Rafael leaned back. "I would love to see what it does to you—how you would live, knowing the truth." He smiled, with a faint tinge of regret. "But alas, it will not happen. Now."

"You told me this—"

"To kill you." Rafael nodded, his eyes alight with open pleasure.

"I don't care, you know," Iain said.

Rafael did not move—looked up at him with a vivid, delighted smile. "So you still have the strength to bluster! I must tell Mekael."

Mekael.

The room swayed. Iain leaned heavily on the table and stared at his cousin, unable to ask, unable to bear not knowing. Of course Rafael, knowing him, let the moment stretch. Then unclasped his hands and let his knee drop. "But I forget," he said. "Mekael died under questioning."

Iain could breathe, if he thought through each breath like a climber placing each hand, each foot. His heart beat slowly, heavily. Mekael, captured. Mekael, dead. He saw, like a remote scene lit by a flicker of lightning, Mekael's eyes long years ago, laughing up into his.

In Rafael's alert, avid face he saw, as if in some perverse mirror, his own horror and grief. Rafael smiled and pain struck through Iain like the blow of an ax, leaving him split, shattered, dying.

For nothing, for nothing, it was all for nothing: Everyone was dead. His father. Mekael. *Linnea.*

His head ached, his vision swam. He looked down at his hands pressed flat on the pale, smooth table, and he saw a drop of water fall between his hands, splash on the slick surface, spread in a shimmer. He supposed he must be weeping. It didn't matter.

Then Rafael spoke again. "She isn't dead."

At that, for the first time in his life, Iain's physical strength failed him. He found that he had fallen to his knees beside the table, that the immovable stool pressed painfully against the bone of his hip. That he could not rise, or move.

"See," Rafael said calmly. Leaning forward, he set the viewer before Iain on the tabletop, and tapped it again.

New images. Linnea. Linnea with Rafael, in some rich bedroom he did not recognize. They were—Rafael was—

Though it took all his strength and all his dying courage, he did not look away. He had to know. He had failed her; he owed her this much.

What she could endure, he could watch.

The sequence of images played itself through and stopped on one frozen frame, one where Iain could not truly tell what was happening to her, but where he could see her face, a dead mask: all her warm light snuffed out, broken to splintered ash.

Rafael stood above him, across the little table. "Do you understand now, cousin? Our traditions mean nothing. But our power is real. This"—he tapped the image on the viewer—"is the *nature* of our power. It has no limit but what we impose on ourselves. We must take up our power, use it fully, or it will wither. You can't see that—nor could Paolo. You are both no loss to the Line. Your positions were wasted on you."

Iain touched the viewer. "Look at her face!" His throat ached, his voice thick with anguish.

Rafael glanced down, then away, dismissively. "I never look at their faces."

Iain's blood roared in his ears. Rage choked him, rage and a strange joy. He surged to his feet, flung himself over the table onto Rafael.

They both went down. Rafael's head smacked the floor hard and Iain saw the blue eyes lose their hard focus, blur for a moment. The long lean body went limp under him.

Iain's hands caught his cousin by the throat and squeezed. He smelled blood, saw a dark pool on the floor under Rafael's head. But not enough. *Not enough!*

He shook Rafael by the throat, striking his head against the floor again, and again. His power, his victory, his moment—

Then something hard pressed against Iain's spine, just between the shoulder blades, and he knew it was a guard's stunrod.

With the instant's realization came a dark, shattering explosion, and his mind spun skittering away into blackness like a shard from a broken bowl.

THIRTEEN

Rafael pressed the cold pad gently to his head and gazed down at the unconscious Iain. "What did you see?" he asked the guard hovering behind him.

The guard, an ugly, lantern-jawed fellow with pale eyes, said, "I came only at your signal. The surveillance systems were offline for maintenance, as you instructed."

"As I paid you to arrange," Rafael said. His head ached damnably, and the blood in his hair had clotted to a revolting, sticky gob.

"Pilot Master sen Rafael," the guard said, "I must again request that you withdraw to the corridor. I cannot guarantee your safety in this room."

Rafael frowned down at his cousin's limp body. He had planned to wait here until Fridric came, for the best effect. With the blood on the floor, Rafael's own blood, there under Iain's slack right hand.

But in fact Iain, lying stunned, facedown on the floor,

looked like a corpse—hardly dangerous. "I will leave," he said through clenched teeth. His heart still beat quite quickly, even now. Odd, that was—that he had been afraid.

That *he* had been afraid of *death*.

Without warning, another wild surge of rage mounted in his throat, choking off his breath. He drew back a booted foot and kicked Iain's limp form solidly in the ribs. Something gave. In his vision dark flecks swirled. His hands, his tongue tingled. Steadying himself against the wall he gathered himself for another kick.

Then a long, cold hand gripped his shoulder, and a chill voice said, "Enough."

Rafael took a long breath and dragged his mind back to the plan. He turned to his father. "You've heard!"

"I was told at once," Fridric said.

"But you came so quickly, all the way down here—Father, I'm touched." Rafael gave his father the pale, shaken smile he had practiced in the selfscreen this morning.

"I gave orders that I was to be told when you came to see your cousin," Fridric said. "As I knew you would do."

"You were afraid for me?"

Fridric only looked at him, his old eyes dead as ash. The mourning he wore for his brother hardly suited him, but then white suited almost no one; Rafael thought fleetingly how fortunate he himself was. His mourning, when it was ready, would set the mode for years to come. His father merely looked shabby, in his plain torn robe. One might almost think he felt real grief. Rafael suppressed the quick, hopeful thought: Was his father's strength failing at last?

"Walk with me," Fridric said. In all this time he had not looked down at Iain; nor did he do so now. He merely

turned and strode out into the corridor. And of course
Rafael followed, as he must. For the moment.

They did not, in fact, walk far: merely to the end of the
dingy corridor, to the guard station there, and on into the
commander's cramped cubicle, which was empty. Rafael
felt a fleeting moment of pity for the man who had failed
to protect the son of the Honored Voice; but then, he was
only a worker. Another would fill his place.

The door sealed them in with a vicious hiss. And now
Fridric turned and faced Rafael. "*What have you done?*"

"What have *I* done?" Rafael straightened, strengthened
by real outrage. "Iain almost killed me!"

"I am told he might possibly have done you real harm,"
Fridric said, "if the guard had not come in and stunned
him. You will now tell me why you let this happen."

"He's my cousin," Rafael said. "I have a right to visit
him."

"And gloat, of course," Fridric said. "After all, you will
now succeed to Iain's father's estate when I am dead. His,
and my own. You will be fantastically rich. And you still
have everything Iain has lost." Fridric's frown deepened.
"Including, I am told, the young woman who became so
absurdly important to him."

Rafael winced and touched the back of his head, thinking fast. "You told me to play with her as I pleased. But if
she's to die now, you may have her and welcome. She
knows nothing."

Fridric folded his arms across his chest. "I do not intend
her death."

A cold thread of shock twisted along Rafael's spine.
"Why not?"

"You will send her safely home," Fridric said. "I have allowed her world's new contract to stand."

Rafael's eyes narrowed. His vision wavered—his need would not be denied much longer. "Why? I thought it was all arranged. They were all to die."

"You pledged your word to her," Fridric said tonelessly.

"What? My word—to *her*? I would never waste—"

"You may care nothing for your honor," Fridric said. "But do not lie to me. Ever. You pledged your word, and I shall see that you keep it."

Rafael stared at his father, stunned. How did he know of this—of the arrangement with the woman, which he had never intended to honor? The question revolved stupidly in his mind. He should have allowed himself a little of the 'weave this morning. It would have muddled him a bit, earlier, but it would let him think now.

"We're actually bound to very little," Fridric was saying. "But I doubt she will understand the legalities." His gaze sharpened. "You will also give her money. Enough to make her independent. You will ask her what she most needs and give it to her."

Rafael shivered. He did not understand this at all. He had to get home, to the solace that waited there—the only peace, the only sleep his body knew. The spiderweave, that wove dream into memory, and memory into dream, and made the world, made *living* possible. He swallowed, his throat dry. "No. Let me kill her," he said hoarsely. "And the others." The fantasy settled around him like a warm cloak. "I'll make us safe. I'll kill everyone who knows what the woman came here to do. Send them to join Iain in oblivion." He breathed shallowly, feeling desire mount. "You have to kill Iain now, Father."

"I have told you that I cannot," Fridric said.

"But I can," Rafael breathed. "You must allow it. Even you must have the courage, now. Because I've told him everything."

He almost smiled, seeing the deep shock in his father's eyes. "You would not dare!"

"But I did," Rafael said. "Just now. I told him what we really are. Wasn't it clever? Because now you have to let me kill him." He closed his eyes, and the vision was there, vivid; he could smell his cousin's fear, see his beautiful eyes wide with it—once again, once again Rafael would see him held helpless, vulnerable—

Fridric slapped him.

A white explosion of pain, shock, fury split Rafael, half-killing his lust, half-satisfying it. He could not speak.

"You are unseemly," Fridric said icily. "Control your appetites. At least in my presence."

"You hurt me," Rafael said, one hand on his cheek.

"And I will do so again, until you are ready to attend to me."

Slowly Rafael lowered his hand, and slowly half turned to face his father. "What is it?" Admirable, how steady his voice sounded.

"You will listen," Fridric said. "Or I will have you retired as a jump pilot. No more trips offworld." He loomed over Rafael. "No more—freedom from restraint."

"Yes, Father," Rafael said woodenly.

Fridric stood at ease in his power, looking across the little room at Rafael. "*Your* dishonor is not mine. Iain will not die."

Rafael waited. Surely there was more. "Not yet," or "not

publicly," or "not easily." But his father's gray gaze did not waver.

"He will not die," Fridric said again, his eyes stone. "But this much you have now accomplished against him: He will never be free again." Fridric frowned. "Do you understand?"

Rafael had been asked a question, and so must answer. "Yes." All his beautiful planning, to make Iain's death necessary, prudent, certain. . . .

"Do not disobey me again," Fridric said. "Do not lie to me again. And one more matter. The woman. I saw much more than you showed me."

Rafael schooled his expression to stillness. So *that* was how Fridric knew of his little pledge.

Fridric raised an eyebrow. "You're surprised? What is recorded, for whatever purpose, can also be monitored from outside. But I see you didn't know that. You should bear it in mind, in future. Some of your pleasures are best kept private."

Rafael took a steadying breath. Fridric could not possibly use such evidence against him—destroying the only son he would ever have. Rafael had seen the medical reports of his father's permanent impotence. Fridric would never have another son of the body. With more confidence, more anger, he said, "How long have you—"

"Watched?" Fridric smiled, his eyes dark as the cold, wet stones of a well. "From time to time. When necessary. And not, I assure you, for pleasure." The smile vanished. "I know you."

"Father, of course you—"

"I know you," Fridric said again, as if Rafael had not spoken. "I know what you are. My son. My dog. My knife, strong in my hand. I cultivate your edge, your dangerousness; it's useful to me. But I will not let you turn on me. Or on yourself."

Rafael could not contain the words—pleading, pleading from weakness again. "Father. Please—he might speak here, in prison. Word might still get out. Let me—"

"I command you in this," Fridric said. "You will not kill Iain. You will not arrange his death by any means."

"But now he knows what we are," Rafael said desperately. "Do you think he *wants* to live? What hold can you have on him?"

"The woman is the key," Fridric said.

Rafael stared at him, shivering.

"She must live," Fridric said, "because she is our hostage. If Iain sen Paolo displeases me, she dies." Fridric shifted impatiently. "While he keeps his silence, here in his prison, she will live in peace on her home world. But if he talks, I shall give her to you again—without restriction. You are my knife at her throat. And therefore also at his."

"And Iain?" He could not believe this—that his father could be so weak. Make such an error. When Rafael could think again, he would examine its extent, how to exploit it—

"If Iain dies," Fridric said, "of any cause whatsoever, I shall hold you responsible. Your share of my fortune, and your travel privileges, depend on Iain's life. And the woman's life is our hold on him—our guarantee of his silence."

"I see." Rafael felt icy sweat trickling down his back. He had to go home, to what waited there, what would ease him. He was void inside, a cold black hollow with countless tiny, dry insects rustling against the inside of his skin.

But he had learned never to retreat without some kind of victory. "I see, Father. And what was *Paolo's* hold on *you*?"

Fridric stared at him for a while. "I long thought that you should have had a brother," he said at last. "Now I see it's as well. Poison in the seed. When your hour comes—have one son. No more." He studied Rafael. "Yet I loved you well enough, once."

"Not well enough," Rafael choked. "Not well enough to spare me from the truth."

"But truth is the debt a father owes his son," Fridric said. "Paolo denied this. He valued his son's pure ideals above truth. Yet even he paid the debt in full. In the end." And he was gone.

Alone in the little room, Rafael wept in rage. And somewhere, at the heart of it, in grief for something he could not name. Something he had never had.

Something even Iain had refused to give him.

He could wait. He *would* wait.

But not forever.

And then his father's words echoed in his mind. *The woman is the key. . . . Our guarantee of his silence.*

Rafael laughed.

Not if she were dead.

If she were dead, there would be no guarantees, and no hold on Iain. Fridric would have no more excuses, and Iain would have to die.

It was perfect. Even though Rafael could not be the one to kill the woman . . . something else might.

He got to his feet, cleaned his face carefully at the guard commander's little cubicle sink, and went out into the world again.

He had much to arrange.

FOURTEEN

TWO MONTHS LATER

Hands.
      She made herself look at her hands, flat on the table before her. Familiar hands. Yet strange now: soft. And the scar from the fish knife had faded. If she tried to do work with these hands, real work, they would blister. She wondered again, hopelessly, how she had been spending her life in the time before this had happened to her—this thing she must not name.

She would remember. She would put the memories together, the safe ones, and in time she would understand. But she had to be careful.

The light kept moving across the table, slowly. Now it warmed her hands. Men had brought her to this high, white room with the square window, the table, the soft narrow bed. They came in sometimes and talked to her gently. Kind men. But she looked and looked among them for the

one she sought, the one her heart was afraid for. Except
that she could not quite remember his name. He was dark,
with dark eyes, she knew that, and black hair—

*—not pale, not strange, not those unfocused blue eyes,
that white body, so thin and sick-looking, not the long
white fingers she tried to break when they*

when they

The window. She was standing at the window now, staring out and down at emptiness. Something had almost happened—something bad had almost broken through. But
she was safe now: quiet in her mind. Below it, and behind
it, those things waited, hidden; but she was safe for now.
Though how could she ever *remember*, with the bad things
waiting whenever she tried. . . ?

One moment at a time. One piece at a time. Patience.

These were her hands, pressed against the window. She
looked out and down, far down, at yellow sand, brown
hills, a dusting of low gray plants. She wondered what they
were called.

Probably she had never known. She was almost sure,
now, that this place was not her home.

But she knew the window. She had words for some
things now, and she hardly had to try to call them up. It was
like working on the beach—

She inhaled sharply, remembering in a vivid rush the
smell of drying seaweed, the cold salt wind, the crunch of
coarse sand. Working on the beach. She had done that.
Turning things over, picking things up, gathering things to
burn, to eat. Like her mind now, turning over, gathering,
seeing what was underneath—careful, careful—

—the sand sank away beneath her, sucking her down

into black water, the water pulling her out and down, pulling her hair

hands in her hair, pulling her face around to see what he

That voice again, crying. Her voice. Here was one of the kind men, and something hissed against her arm, and her mind cleared and emptied. The voice fell silent. Her head and her heart felt full, light, simple.

She slept, and woke, and went into the little room with the toilet, and when she came out another kind man helped her wash and patiently combed her hair. There was someone else who had combed her hair, long ago, someone not so patient, but she knew she had loved that person. That woman. Her

sister

warm in their shared bed, little girls afraid of the storm outside, the other one turned over, she turned over, too, they nestled together and went back to sleep

Shaking, she opened her eyes.

And now another man stood there in her room, looking down at her. A tall, gaunt, gray-haired man with heavy brows, and a white robe that needed mending, and a pretty chain flashing ripples of silver over it all. Not one of the ones she knew, not one she remembered from the good images or the bad. He said something to her, but it was just like when the others spoke to her: By the time he finished what he was saying, she had forgotten how it started. She didn't try to answer, because if she was quiet they usually went away.

The man did not go away. He spoke again, more simply. "You are going home."

She heard that. She stared up at him, and took a breath,

and then another one, and said in a rusted, crumbling voice, "This is not home?"

He said something else that she couldn't follow, and then said, "He gave you a drug."

"No," she said, meaning *No, don't tell me, don't say his name*—

"He gave you spiderweave. Too much, an overdose. That is why you have forgotten. We have been helping you to recover for a long time now."

She wanted to say no, no, she had chosen forgetting; but why would she choose to forget what was good, as well as the—

She stood at the window again, her back to the man. But she could see him, because it was night outside now, and the window reflected his face. Was he still here, or had he gone away and come back, or had it been night all along?

In his face, this man's face, there was something—

She saw something—someone—

Her heart knew before her mind, and her eyes blurred with tears, and she saw through tears the man's old face change to a young man's, dark and still and sad, and somewhere a voice said clearly, *He is lost. Find him. Find him.*

"Iain," she gasped, and the name fit. She turned, the tears cool on her face, and said, "I want to see Iain."

The man's face changed, looked more like the sad young man in her vision, and he said, "Iain is dead."

She knew he was lying. She must have said so, because he shook his head, his gray braid swinging, and said, "He died months ago. Soon you will be ready to go home and rest, where your people can care for you." The man came close to her, and said, "I am sorry." She did not think he was lying, about being sorry.

Then he touched her arm—

a long-fingered hand, light and cold on her arm—

and then his face, his voice were not Iain's, but another's—

you've thrown up, here, clean it up, I'll give you less next time

Iain liked this

does it hurt

does it hurt yet

She screamed.

She screamed and the man vanished, and the kind ones came, and this time what they gave her filled her mind with a warm, buzzing softness, a dark flower that bloomed and bloomed in front of her eyes, behind her eyes, and she sagged into waiting hands—

no more sound

no more remembering

silence

FIFTEEN

FOUR MONTHS LATER

The summons was inconvenient, as always. It took half a day or more for Training Master Adan sen Kaleb to delegate all of his tasks on Dock to his staff, and another half a day to make the long, jouncing shuttle trip down; and in the end he had a race of it to reach the City and the Council chamber in time. He found himself wondering whether the notification from the Honored Voice had been deliberately delayed. He knew that his presence on the Council was often awkward for the Honored Voice; but he was the Training Master as well as the master of Dock, and so it must be.

The quick winter of Nexus had come again, with its high cold haze of dust and sharp frost, the desert outside the city barren and bare in the clear, cold light. Sen Kaleb relished the bite of the air on his face and hands as he walked from the Council guesthouse to the chamber, secluded within the Council's wide, high-walled garden. The plants there drooped, black and dead, crusted with a rime of ice. Sen Kaleb supposed they were meant to look like that; gardening had never been his idea of pleasure. He had been a teacher, always—living in orbit on Dock, training class after class of eager young boys into competent jump pilots.

The Council session had started without him, as he had more than half expected, and a silence fell as he stalked into the meeting room. Twenty men looked up or turned to stare. Fridric sen David's eyes were ice; his voice was colder than ice. "I was beginning to wonder whether you would bother to come."

"Fair enough," sen Kaleb said. "I have been absent a time or two of late." He stood quietly in his white mourning—for Paolo. The Honored Voice had put his own mourning garb aside already, after only half a standard year—no doubt thinking his brother forgotten by now.

"Be seated," sen David said, and only then did sen Kaleb see what lay at the center of the shining wood Council table.

A corpse.

Sealed in a long clear box, the naked corpse of a man.

Sen Kaleb took his place carefully, his eyes on the thing. "What is this?"

"Evidence," sen David said.

It had been a young man, but not of the Line, not even of Nexus so far as sen Kaleb could tell. Small, with black hair oddly cut in a blunt helmet. His dead skin gray, his hands and feet bluish black. The hands lay oddly clenched, fingers twisted and wrists flexed. What looked like bruises marked out the bones of the eye sockets.

"Evidence of what?" sen Kaleb asked, frowning.

"I was about to present my investigators' findings to the Council," sen David said. "If it is now convenient for you, I will proceed."

Sen Kaleb gestured politely.

"The man was killed by nanobots," sen David said.

Sen Kaleb shuddered. Another man cried out. Still another leaped up and backed hastily from the table.

"The container is sealed to my satisfaction," Fridric said. "The corpse was irradiated after the man's death, but even a functional bot could not pass through that seal."

"Who took this thing? And where?" sen Kaleb demanded.

"One of us, on Freija," sen David said. "Three months ago now. Our pilot sealed him as you see and returned here at once."

"So it is true," the Honormaster said, his narrow face bleak. "There are spies of the Cold Minds on Freija."

"Worse than that," sen David said. "Far worse. By now the infestation will have spread beyond anyone's control. Look at this man. Scans of his brain tissue show the nano-linked matrix fully grown. He was no longer human. I do not know whether what remained of his mind would even have been conscious."

"Was he questioned?" the Shipmaster asked.

"He never spoke," Fridric said. "As soon as the nanobots knew he had been taken, they began to multiply. They filled his blood. They choked off his heart. That black you see—trillions of them. They ate his bones to build themselves. If his mind was still present, he died in agony."

Sen Kaleb looked across the terrible thing on the table, looked at Fridric. "Our pilot," he said. "Is he safe?"

Sen David met his gaze, his deep eyes hard under the dark brows. "There was nothing anyone could do."

"The bots—took him?" Sen Kaleb took a harsh breath. "Who was he? Whose son?"

The Honormaster spoke. "It was Jemel sen Olfa."

Sen Kaleb looked down at the table, at his old hands. Jemel. Vividly he remembered a boy of twelve, thirteen perhaps, leaning close in to study a holochart in one of the star galleries on Dock. A tall boy with deep brown skin and bright, questing eyes, a boy who always had one more question to ask. *Silenced now.* "May he be gathered to his fathers," sen Kaleb said numbly.

"May it be so," several voices muttered.

Sen Kaleb steeled himself. "Where is Jemel now?"

"Burned," said the Master of the Ledgers. "Burned in the City power plant. Hot as any sun. Not even ashes left."

"Burn *that*," the Honormaster said, pointing, his eyes on sen David. "You must."

"I will," sen David said. "But I wanted you—all of you—to see it first. Because now we have a choice to make."

He stood.

"When our Line son Jemel sen Olfa returned to us, he was fading. I honor the strength that brought him here, against his pain, against the things that were fighting to build an inhuman mind in his brain. He knew what was coming. He asked for death. And by my order it was given."

Sen Kaleb's eyes stung. He looked down at his hands.

"By my order. *I* killed one of our Line sons." Sen David looked searchingly at the men around the table. "I was willing. Whatever the cost in grief, I have always been willing to take on the burden of doing what is necessary to preserve the Line."

Sen Kaleb looked up at him. "Surely—surely you mean, to preserve the Hidden Worlds?"

"*We* are the lifeblood of the Hidden Worlds," sen David said sharply. "*We* must not be spilled and wasted. What preserves and protects us, protects the Worlds as well. Those that can still be saved."

"We will save all of them," sen Kaleb said. "It is our charge. It has always been."

He realized then that the others were gazing at him with the same stony remoteness as sen David.

"No," sen David said. "This is a time for many hard choices. But we must begin with the hardest." He pressed both hands flat against the tabletop. "Freija must die."

Silence around the table.

"A million people," sen Kaleb said numbly. Those cold eyes.

"A million hostages," sen David said. "Perhaps, by now, a million enemies. Freija has been embargoed, quarantined. The nanobots know they have been discovered. What act might they be driven to, that we could not contain? No. They must all die. And the only way to be sure, the only clean way, is to sterilize the planet."

"We cannot do such a thing," sen Kaleb protested. "Even if it were our right, we have no means."

"We have means," sen David said. "Three closely timed asteroid impacts. Already mass drivers are altering the orbits of these bodies, and we are adding more as quickly as we can have them manufactured."

"This was done without consulting the Council," sen Kaleb said.

"It was my prerogative, in the emergency," Fridric said. "In a matter of months the rocks will strike. But I am asking, now, for confirmation from the Council."

"These impacts," the Honormaster said. "Will they be enough to destroy any trace of the nanobots?"

"They will be sufficient to destroy any trace of anything at all," the Master of Measures said in his dry voice. "The atmosphere itself will burn. Everything will burn. The sea, steam. All that remains after the shock waves will be dead, and it will burn."

Silence fell again. Twenty-one men in a room, a beautiful room with windows opening on a sunny courtyard, frost-rimed but lovely in its bareness and hardness. No one spoke.

A million deaths.

A world, dead.

"If we do this," sen Kaleb said at last, "we must honor Freija's memory. We must not let this happen to even one other world."

Again, silence. Again the other men's eyes on him, though some now shifted away.

"What?" sen Kaleb asked bleakly. "What have you decided?"

"We cannot save them all," sen David said. "We are too few. Too few ships to patrol and guard every planetary orbit, to be ready to embargo suspect worlds. . . . The poor colonies, the lightly settled ones—to save them we would risk losing worlds like Terranova, worlds with tens of millions, promising worlds. Our only hope for a new Earth."

"So this is the fruit of your policies," sen Kaleb said, "and those of your predecessors. Of choosing only those most loyal to you to father sons. Now we face this threat with our numbers at their lowest in centuries, with usable ships laid up in storage. No one to pilot them."

"Those policies have kept us secure," sen David said. "They have preserved our traditions and our economic power."

"I thought," sen Kaleb said, "that our charge was to preserve life. Not to sacrifice innocents to save our own wealth."

"We are the lifeblood," sen David said again, his hard face set. "As we prosper, so do our worlds. So does humanity."

Sen Kaleb rose to his feet, facing sen David across the table. In the strain in the other man's eyes he suddenly saw the ghost of Fridric's brother, of Paolo, his dear friend and companion of long years. This might not have happened, if Paolo still lived. Grief twisted sen Kaleb's voice as he said, "Surely a million deaths are enough."

"The Cold Minds will not be so merciful," sen David said.

"I once thought we were different from them," sen Kaleb said. "We of the Line." He turned and left the room.

I n the bare, pale elegance of sen Kaleb's room in the Council guesthouse, he fought for peace. Grief for Paolo, and for Paolo's son still imprisoned without charge; sorrow for a world to be lost, after six hundred years of care; and whose failure was it? Had sen Kaleb trained more pilots, trained better ones, would all the Hidden Worlds still be safe? Was it his failure, or the Line's failure—or could anyone have prevented it?

And what could be done now? For that was the hardest

truth of all: There were not enough pilots, even if boys in training were rushed to service; not enough sons, even if many more of them passed the training. Too late to change anything, too late. . . .

Sen Kaleb sat down heavily in the room's work chair. The communication light winked softly blue under his hand. The routine daily download from Dock, presumably. Irritably he flicked his fingers above the light and the display appeared before his eyes. Ordinary traffic, all of it.

Except. . . .

One message, sender masked. Dated more than half a standard year ago. How had it found its way . . . ?

He waved a finger through its icon, which flashed red. Personally encoded to him. Suspicion tight in his chest, he pressed the code implant in his hand against the reader plate, drummed his fingers in the confirming rhythm.

An image formed above the holoplate before him.

Paolo.

Paolo kneeling, haggard, disheveled. "Is it you, old friend? Are you alone?" The image froze.

Sen Kaleb steadied his breathing, said clearly, "Adan sen Kaleb."

A soft voice said, "Confirmed," and the message continued. "I am dying," Paolo said. "Time is short. I must presume on our friendship, ask of you a gift far beyond custom. But you may not wish to grant it to—what I am.

"Listen, my friend. The foundation of our lives is a lie. And I have known it for many years."

Sen Kaleb's heart struck heavy in his chest.

"Listen to me," Paolo's voice said. "David sen Elkander was not my father, or my brother Fridric's. We were fathered by a servant from offworld, to conceal David sen

Elkander's sterility—so that he could have the sons, and the political dynasty, that he believed his great deeds had earned him."

Sen Kaleb's breath caught. He stared at Paolo's image, his face hot, stiff. It was true, then. Paolo had been insane. Because that was the only—

"Adan," Paolo continued, "I would not blame you for doubting this. I wish from my soul that it were not true. But I know your justice. In your justice, listen.

"Long ago, when we were still young men, Fridric learned of this when an offworlder, a relative of our . . . true father, who was by then dead, made a clumsy attempt at blackmail. Fridric had the man killed. When I learned of it, and questioned my brother, he told me all this. And over my anger and disbelief he swore me to silence. He was the head of our family; I had to do his will, or so I saw it then. I rebelled in my heart at first. And then—and then I fathered a son." Tenderness flickered across Paolo's face.

"I loved Iain. I wanted him to have what Fridric had taken from me: purity of belief, faith in the Line, clear joy in his gifts as a pilot." Paolo's gaze intensified, and sen Kaleb shivered, feeling as if Paolo *saw* him. "I hoped that the secret would die with my brother and me. That the wound would be healed and forgotten.

"But then Fridric told his son Rafael the truth. As a weapon against me, should I survive Fridric.

"I considered telling Iain, arming him as well. But as the years passed I saw Rafael growing up in the knowledge—saw how it corrupted his heart. I knew how it had broken my own.

"And so," Paolo said, "for my son's sake, I lied to you all. To all the men who honored me with their friendship, to the Inner Council, and to the Tree. And to Iain, my only son, I lied." His lean face tightened with anguish, or physical pain. "I told myself that it was to protect him, to give him faith in his own destiny. But it was a blind path. It always has been. My father's deceit shadows us all." He took a breath, with an obvious effort. "In all but that one point, I always kept my word. And so of course my word was empty." His voice tightened, as if he fought not to weep. "Only complete truth is truth at all. I see that now—far too late."

Sen Kaleb held his fists tight to contain his terror, his anger, his grief.

"Only complete truth," Paolo said again. "We are strangling the Hidden Worlds to keep our monopoly. We cannot defend them if the Cold Minds should find us; we cannot even serve them as they need. I know that you understand this. You and I have come close to naming that truth in a dozen conversations."

Sen Kaleb flinched at the memory. He had not wanted to have those conversations. The problem could not be solved. Why name and discuss it?

"We have failed them," Paolo's recording continued. "After six centuries we have failed our own people. To shore up a lie, to protect our wealth, Fridric's wealth, we are condemning part of humanity to starvation and death." He looked intently into the recorder, into sen Kaleb's eyes, and sen Kaleb shivered at the familiar pull of Paolo's personal strength—even here, even when Paolo must have been close to death, it compelled.

"And now we come to it, my old friend," Paolo said. "The gift I must ask of you, though it is yours to refuse." He straightened, tightened his grip on his knees. "You must give the truth to the Hidden Worlds and to those of the Line who still believe it is pure.

"You must give them Iain. A living pilot who can be proved not to be of the Line. The proof exists on a world called Santandru, and the woman Linnea Kiaho is the key to it. I hope that Iain can find her."

That woman. But Fridric had sent her away, months ago. . . . No matter. Sen Kaleb could find her; as the master of Dock, all travel records were open to him.

Paolo continued. "You must put Iain beyond their reach. Then go to them, go to the Council, and tell them what I have told you.

"I am about to die—a bargain I made to save my son's life. He is somewhere on Nexus, perhaps imprisoned. You must find him, and play for him the message I have embedded in this one, one that can only be freed by his family code.

"Adan, only the truth that lives in Iain can bring our Line's purpose to fulfillment. Only by ending our power can our people—not the Line, *all* our people—find the strength to protect themselves, the pilots they need for their worlds to grow. And that is what you and I have always believed to be the purpose of the Line—that we were meant to bring humanity back to its full strength and potential. And now we are killing them."

Paolo stared into Sen Kaleb's eyes, his gaze hard, urgent, even as his hands trembled. "For humanity; for my own dear love for him; and because I know you love him as well—you *must* save Iain."

•   •   •

S en Kaleb stood at his window, looking out at the Council's garden, pale in starlight, glittering with ice. Since
hearing Paolo's message he had thought, he had struggled.

Iain, that weak boy, who had let his father die, who had
disappointed sen Kaleb so bitterly . . . instead it had all
been Paolo's plan? Paolo's bargain? Then Iain's removal
from the Line, his long imprisonment, were both unde-
served?

There must be some solution short of ending the Line,
ending all those centuries of tradition and pride. Breaking
the brotherhood of Pilot Masters, and allowing anyone,
any man who could develop the skill, to serve as they had
served. Doubtless, many of these men would be unedu-
cated, perhaps unprincipled. Soon, certainly, the gift would
be turned to unworthy purposes as well as worthy ones.
Smuggling, other crimes . . .

But did the Line deserve to continue?

There was the failure at Freija. A million "necessary"
deaths—necessary only because the Line was stretched too
far, could no longer guard or protect the innocents of humanity. A bitter failure, a dreadful loss.

And, inevitably, there would be others. Peripheral
worlds, Fridric would call them; unimportant to the economy of the Hidden Worlds, to the wealth of the Line. And
yet their people, too, had a share in humanity. They did not
deserve terror, infestation, death.

Sen Kaleb shivered, staring out at the dead, black garden. *No.* The truth burned clear. Humanity's need for pilots
outweighed the greatness, the wealth, the history of the
Line. Fridric was leading them all toward diminishment of
honor, in defense of undiminished power.

It could not be allowed.

No man who knew the truth could allow it.

Sen Kaleb looked down at his right palm. In the dimness he could barely see the old scar from his oath at the Tree, as a boy.

He would break that oath. He would free Iain, and help him as far as he could. And then, if he lived, if he found himself free, with the last of his life and strength he would work to save the Hidden Worlds.

Though he knew the Line he had loved and honored and served with the strength of a lifetime—the Line would always remember him as its greatest traitor.

SIXTEEN

Linnea shivered in her plain gray dress as she waited for the ship's hatch to open for her, to let her out into the world that had been her home. In a few hours she would see Marra and the children. Surely Marra would speak to her, welcome her. At least give her a place to rest until she was healed.

But first she would have to answer their questions. Her mind shrank from the thought. So much of her memory lay in fragments.

The pilot, a flat-faced, flat-voiced blond man, stood looking at her. She knew because she could see his black-booted feet: He faced her. She could not look at his eyes.

"The ground should be cool enough in a moment," he said. She heard the tension in his voice, making clear that he desperately wanted to get her off his ship, get back into space and far away.

It didn't matter. Nothing did—nothing but getting home.

The subjective weeks in transit, resting, had brought back some of her physical strength. The last of the marks on her throat and wrists, the bruises on her ribs and thighs, had faded away. Only the scar between her breasts remained: a crude sketch of the Tree, the sign of the Line's power. When she'd undressed before the jump, to get into the box, the pilot had kept staring at it. She still could not remember how it had come there. That memory lay close to the center of the dark place in her mind, near the metallic smell of blood, the gleam of a small steel blade—If she went in that far, she might never find her way out.

Then the pilot said, "There is a thing you should know."

"What is it?" she asked, her disused voice harsh.

"He said not to tell you. He said just to leave you and go."

Cold all over, she stared at him. "What do you mean?"

"And so," he said, "I will."

The hatch opened.

She had grown used to not understanding, but this was worse. Warm, humid air billowed in, sharp with the smell of scorched dirt. Trees ringed the clearing where the ship had landed. Overhead the sky arched, deep violet, starless—night but not night. Near the zenith floated the banded disk of a huge gas-giant planet, glowing brown and yellow and burned orange. . . .

This was not Santandru.

She whirled to face the pilot, who stood close to her now. Grim-faced, he pushed her out.

She staggered a step across uneven ground, still hot from the landing, staggered another step and fell. At the edge of the burned spot, under her hands: dark thready plants, and bare dirt. The plants looked black in the soft, yellow, alien light. The air seemed to press her down, thick, warm, heavy with humidity. Not the cold salt air of home. . . .

She heard the hatch snick shut behind her and the faint hum of system recharge.

She scrambled to her feet. She'd left her bag in there, with the change of clothes and the credit crystal. The credit was nearly gone, drained by the order she had placed through the commnet, to have a ship's brain sent to Father Haveloe in Middlehaven. But what was left would have been enough to live on for a while. It was all she had. She staggered to the hatch, pounded on it with her fists.

In answer, the ship's engines hummed to life.

She must not be near when the ship rose; it would burn her.

Empty-handed, she picked her way in the strange weak light to the band of trees. The low plants did not grow in their shade; dry bare dirt puffed under her scuffling steps. She smelled dust and a pungent green smell from the trees' needlelike leaves.

Through the trees and beyond. A slope fell away before her, a field of some tall grassy crop hissing in the warm night breeze, heavy seed tassels swaying and tossing, a musty, bready scent rising from them. Down there in the valley a road glowed in the umber worldlight. She saw a neat clump of buildings, their windows dark. In the distance she heard a howl, not human, harsh and sharp and high. An animal, a—dog?

Far in the distance, far down the valley she saw more lights, a grid of light—a city. That and roads, farms, fields near harvest—this world was rich.

She was shaking, shaking in spite of the warmth. A

voice in her mind chanted, *Too far, too far—you will never, never find them.* . . . She tried to remember which of the Hidden Worlds were moons of larger worlds. N'Eire and . . . what was the other? Yes—Freija. But she knew nothing else about either of them.

At that instant the scream of the jumpship's grav engines reaching full power rose over the sound of the wind. The scream deepened to a shuddering roar that pressed into Linnea's ears, then slowly it faded, dopplering down into profound silence. Wind-sound gradually returned as her hearing recovered.

She looked up, saw the dwindling star of the drive wink out. Her last link to those people was gone.

Now there was—nothing. She had nothing, was nothing. In the dark place in her mind, *things* stirred and rustled.

There at the edge of the field she sank down onto the soft rich-smelling earth. Grief rose and caught her by the throat. Marra, the children. She would never see them again. When the ship's brain arrived, with news of the new contract but no other word from Linnea, Marra would think she was dead. Or that she had decided to stay on Nexus—had broken the one promise she had dared to make, that she would return.

Linnea wept, but no tears came. Dry, she was dry inside, dead—maybe this was better, better that no one at home saw her like this, wrecked and broken. . . . Instead they would think she had sold herself at a fine price and go on to forget her.

And they would be right. If she never got home, they would be right.

No. She got back to her feet. Whatever colony this was,

there had to be a skyport, though the pilot who dropped her here had not chosen to use it—probably to avoid questions and to keep her from calling out for help to some decent person.

Those buildings down there, that smooth road glowing in the light of the world overhead—this was nothing like poor, pinched, decrepit Santandru. There would be not just a skyport, but ships—on a rich colony, there would be ships in port all the time. One of those ships could take her home.

She had no money, but the first step was to get to the skyport.

She would keep her mind on each moment as it passed. She would not think beyond the next step. When she got to the skyport she would think of work she could do, to earn the price of a ticket home. Cooking, road labor, anything—it didn't matter.

Just so she got home.

There was the road. She would follow it to the city. The great barred disk overhead gave plenty of light for walking.

As she turned the corner of the field it came over her again: The walls of the safe place in her mind burst inward. Cool hands tightened on her throat, black sparks danced in her vision as a man's bony body strained against her. Stiff, shivering, she longed again for darkness, for death—but she could not. Her duty was clear: to go home, go home, go home. . . .

To keep her promise.

SEVENTEEN

F *ather.*
     In a fever dream, Iain turned and turned, restless
on the hard floor, seeking peace, finding only pain.

Whatever you may feel for me . . .

His throat ached as his own angry words echoed in the
dream. . . . *you've made it clear that you don't trust me.
You can't give with one hand and hold back with the other.
It's too late.*

In the dream Iain saw the hope fade from his father's
face. In the dream Iain walked away firmly, not looking
back. Leaving his father alone.

In the dream, in life: the last time he saw his father
alive.

H e ached. All of him ached. Cold to his bones. He
     turned over, coughed, spat. Filth, smell, hunger,

cold. His eyes slitted open. The cell. Small, narrow, the ceiling high. Hard walls gleamed above him. Hard pale light beat down. He coughed, coughed, ripping his chest, spat salt. Dragged a numb hand across his lips, bleared at it in the light. Blood.

Broken.

The word dangled in his mind, turning, glistening, ugly. His cousin's voice, years ago. His cousin's voice, hours or days ago: *I have broken you.*

His body ached. Fever, or a beating. Or Rafael's bitter love.

He closed his aching eyes.

Let me die.

H ands prodding him. *No.* Hands turning him. *No, I cannot.*

"Iain!"

His name. A man's voice speaking his name. So he was alive. . . .

A strong arm lifted his shoulders. Water at his lips. He drank thirstily, to quiet his inner trembling. The water, warm, had a bitter taste.

"Iain, wake. We do not have much time."

He opened his eyes. Punishing light. He twisted his face away and whimpered.

"No, no, boy. Iain, listen." The hands gripped, stilling him.

Iain tried to speak, but his voice caught on a rasp deep in his chest—he coughed and the pain of it split him.

"Iain, you've been drugged for a long time. It's made

you ill. You haven't breathed right for months. Your lungs are infected."

Iain turned his face toward the voice. The outline of a man loomed above him—white hair tied back tight, dark harsh brows, a glare of stern ferocity.

Master sen Kaleb.

Iain swallowed blood, licked his lips, gathered his voice. "My father—" He stopped to cough again. "Why—didn't—you—"

"Save him?" The dark eyes lost their spark, turned to ash. "I was on Dock when it happened. I was too late."

Iain shivered, struggling to sit up. Master sen Kaleb's wiry arms caught and raised him, placing him so the wall would support him. Then warmth enfolded Iain's naked body—the Master's black cloak.

Iain clutched it against himself. The fabric felt soft and strange against his skin, bare for so long. He looked up at Master sen Kaleb. "You left me here." An accusation, though he had no strength to give it force to match his anger.

"Forgive me, boy," the Master said quietly. "I blamed you for your father's suicide—just as your uncle intended."

Iain licked his dry lips. "Then why—" He coughed.

"Hush. Don't speak." The Master leaned close. "Listen. Trust my words. I have bought us a little time undisturbed. It is running out fast. I gave you an antidote to the drugs. It should be working by now."

"Why?" Iain asked again. "Everyone is dead." *Father—Mekael—Linnea—*"Nothing matters." The room swam, trembled, warm tears spilled.

"Nothing matters?" The Master's scornful voice held all

of the old sternness. "Are you a child? Iain. Listen. Four days ago I received a message from your father."

Iain's mind went blank. "Four days? But—"

The Master shook his head impatiently. "Sent before he died, sent on a long roundabout so it would return hidden among routine offworld traffic."

"What did he say?" Iain straightened against the wall.

"He said—" The Master's voice roughened. "He said that you and he were not—"

"Of the Line," Iain said. "I know."

"And there was more," the Master said. "In your family code, meant for you. He said that I must hear it, too. I arranged this as swiftly as I could."

"You have it here?"

"Give me your hand."

Iain raised his palm, and felt the cool slickness of a holoplate pressed against it. The Master set the holoplate on the tiny table, and touched it once.

"My son," said Paolo's image, haggard, kneeling in the air above the holoplate. The shadows under his eyes deepened as he smiled: warm, tender, strange. Iain watched, all thought suspended, his breath fire in his chest.

"My son," Paolo said again, but his voice shook. "I will never see you again. In a few hours I will be dead. This is my last chance to make amends to you."

Iain held himself still, fighting back another cough. He saw Paolo's thin hands tighten on his knees, as if in a spasm of pain.

Then Paolo raised his hands and set them, crossed, high on his chest: the gesture of formal apology. "No," Iain said helplessly. He had made that gesture many times to his father. Never his father to him.

"Forgive me, my beloved son," Paolo said, his voice firmer now. "I lied to you. I did not trust your strength. I was afraid that the truth might ruin you, as it ruined Rafael." He swallowed once, and went on. "So you would be happy, so you would be safe, I kept you in ignorance. And lost you."

Iain blinked at the image, at his father's steady gaze. Paolo's dark eyes glittered, strangely dilated. The poison he had taken must already have been acting in him. Grief stabbed through Iain's numbness.

Paolo lowered his hands. "My brother Fridric will not swear to spare your career, or your honor. Only your life. Perhaps you will hate me for that. Now that I am dead— now that Fridric is released from our old oath—I am sure you know the truth of who you are. Of who we both are. Or Master sen Kaleb has told you, as I asked in my message to him."

Iain looked up at Master sen Kaleb and saw him staring at Paolo's image, his face suffused, stiff. *So even the Master had not known before.*

Again Paolo raised his hands in the gesture of apology, though this time they trembled visibly. "Forgive me, Iain," he said. "Only now do I see it. I am the liar I hated my father for being."

Iain coughed, fever-pain lancing through him, and Master sen Kaleb swept his hand in the gesture that paused the message, turned back, and held Iain, firmly but gently. The coughing became slow, tearing sobs. Iain understood. He understood now what the knowledge of their ancestry had cost Paolo. He had never imagined it before—he had thought only of his *own* loss of faith. Selfish, useless—

"Quiet now," Master sen Kaleb said. "Better to face it."

Iain could not be sure whether the Master was addressing Iain, or himself. The Master signaled for the message to continue.

Paolo pressed a hand against his side, as if to force back pain. "Time is—short, Iain. Now you must listen to me— one last time. Now I must—tell you why I could not let you die, no matter the cost to you."

Master sen Kaleb held Iain steady.

"I told you. The Cold Minds—have found us." Paolo took a long breath. "Iain, what you do not know—what no one knows but the Council—we have lost ships, lost men, in ways—we think many spies of the Cold Minds are moving among the Hidden Worlds now. Scouting."

Iain listened, frozen.

Paolo went on, but now Iain could see the sheen of sick sweat on his face. "Your uncle wants—strength for the Line. So we can protect ourselves, fight for ourselves. Strength *only* for the Line. That's why he fears you. The gift." He struggled for breath, or for words. "The gift you contain. Not born to the Line—but a pilot all the same. Do you see? We need—more pilots. Better communication. Watchers in every system. Fridric does not care that the Line—cannot do this. Not alone.

"Give them the gift, Iain." He knelt tensely, hands pressed against his sides. "Give it to all the Hidden Worlds. The truth. You must—you must open our secrets to all. Whatever the cost. You are living proof that piloting is not—just the Line's gift. Only you can do this, of all of us.

Paolo turned his trembling hands palm up in supplication. "You must be free," he said. "You are the hope of fifty worlds." His eyes gentled. "As you were always—the hope of my heart." He raised a hand as if reaching out to touch the son he could not see. "Good bye, Iain . . ."

He vanished.

Iain sagged against the wall, watching as the Master tore the crystal from the holoplate, flung it to the floor, and crushed it to powder under his boot, shattering the delicate informational array beyond reconstruction or retrieval. Then he sank down on the cot beside Iain. "I could not believe it at first," he said stiffly. "But I must. Paolo never lied to—" He broke off. Then said with new harshness, "He lied at the Tree. His blood at the Tree was a lie."

"Not when he first took oath," Iain said.

The Master frowned at Iain. "You cannot defend him."

"I don't," Iain said. "My oath is as false as his."

"As false as your uncle's," the Master said slowly. He faced Iain. "There is more. A new development."

"Tell me," Iain said, his heart numb.

"Freija is infested." The Master's face twisted with anguish, or revulsion. "Nanobots. There can be no doubt. A million people—dead or controlled, by now. . . . It was only by luck that the Council learned of it." The Master's eyes burned coldly. "We are going to destroy Freija."

Iain gasped and looked up at the Master, whose expression was as stern as ever. "When?"

"Soon," Master sen Kaleb said. "It is the right action, Iain. But not enough. And perhaps not soon enough."

Not soon enough. A message might already have gone back to the infested corpse of Earth. Even now the Cold Minds might be mobilizing, their chill, lightless ships spanning the void between, the tiny unstoppable nanobots soon to infest technology and flesh on some other helpless colony.

"Your father was a man of rare foresight," Master sen Kaleb said. "He knew what your uncle's response to this news would be: fall back to a few valuable worlds, protect the Line, protect our wealth and our ways. And now he has only you left to fear. Only you, who could prove him wrong, strip him of power, end our monopoly. An outcast of the Line, who knows all the Line's secrets. Who could teach others to pilot."

Master sen Kaleb rose and stood with his back to Iain. "I have always been a true son and servant of the Line. I should go, and let you die here. Let this end." He turned to face Iain, his eyes dark with anguish. "But it will never end. Not while Fridric lives, or his son. And—" His voice broke. "And whatever he was—I loved your father." He met Iain's gaze. "I will honor his word—even at the cost of my own. Our charge is to protect the Hidden Worlds, whatever the cost. Iain, I will save you if I can."

I ain shivered under the cloak, alone in his cell again. Fear made him colder. The Master had been gone too long. But if he had been arrested, surely Fridric's men would have come in and taken the cloak away. It would not have been permitted to him.

The door slid open and Iain shrank back. But it was the Master again, his face stern, carrying a bundle of cloth. The door closed. "Iain. Put these on."

It was a guard's uniform, tunic and trousers in rich olive and gold—the personal livery of the Honored Voice. Iain slowly stood, the Master's hand firm under his elbow. Dizzily, with the Master's help, he pulled on the uniform. The trousers hung loosely from his sharp hipbones. His fingernails caught on the fine fabric of the tunic—his hands were dirty, his nails long and split. "Hurry," the Master said quietly.

As Iain pulled on the guard's brown half boots, he saw a splash of fresh blood on the sleeve of the tunic, brown against the somber green.

The Master tied Iain's tangled hair back in the plain tail of a worker, then picked up his cloak and wrapped himself in it again. "You are escorting me," he said. "Try to walk steadily. No one will be fooled up close, but at a distance it may work."

The cell door opened. At the threshold Iain hesitated, dizzy again, as if he stood at the lip of a cliff. It did not seem possible to take another step, to actually stand outside the cell. Cool air washed over him, cool air with a strange clear scent.

Cleanness.

Iain took a breath and stepped forward. They walked, Iain watching the Master for cues at turns. His legs ached from the effort of balance and control. At any moment they would be stopped. He knew this. He wished he could see better. Things far away, far along the corridor, were strangely blurred. His eyes had forgotten how to see so far.

They passed a checkpoint. No one manned it. How had the Master arranged this? *A trap.* Fear filled him. A trap for the Master, Iain the bait.

Then they were in a bubble car, its dome opaqued, surging away. They must be leaving the city, heading for the skyport. Heading for Dock. "Why?"

The Master's dark gaze brushed over him. "Iain, rest. We'll talk on my shuttle."

"But I—"

The Master moved closer. "Lean against me. Rest now."

Slowly, Iain settled against the Master's shoulder and closed his eyes. He felt a hand, so light, brush his hair back from his face. To be warm, to be out of the cell—he sighed and silenced the questions, for now.

A long time later the bubble car chuffed to a halt. Iain groaned as the Master's hands pushed him upright. "Iain. We must move now, quickly."

A small, bright room, a tiny lift, a door opening on darkness. The Master guided him forward, and he gasped. He was outdoors, at the port, the field lights off for some reason. The warm air, smelling of hot rock and sulfur, stirred his hair. Vastness arched overhead, a glimmering brilliance of stars and nebulae, cut at the horizon by the jagged black teeth of the encircling mountains. Nearer, a sleek shape loomed, mirroring the stars—the Master's private shuttle. "I've cut off the lights," the Master said. "Get aboard and strap in while I pull the refueling lines."

Then the strong familiar surge of takeoff. In the pilot's chair beside Iain, Master sen Kaleb's hands moved with sure grace over the board. "They won't interdict," Iain heard the Master mutter. "Not this shuttle. Not unless they know already."

Then a final, gentle acceleration, and silence. Iain's head swam in the familiar dizzy lightness of free fall as the shuttle hurtled along its slow arc to an orbit matching Dock's. The Master sighed and locked his board.

"Master," Iain said, and asked the question burning in his heart. "Is it worth this, to free me?"

The Master looked away. "Consider your father's words," he said, his eyes on the pilot's board. "And your uncle's policies. We have two thousand pilots, no more.

There are twenty-one worlds that require at least weekly data transfer arrivals, with interworld jumps that average fifty objective days. We can barely cover that. And now— we need sentry ships at every world. In orbit, monitoring, ready to warn of contamination. And messenger ships to provide regular reports to a central control. And—" The Master shook his head. "Interceptors. For blockades. Freija is simple, one skyport, not even an orbiting dock—yet even that requires more than a dozen ships and pilots. Some worlds would require hundreds. And control and communications, between worlds, can only be by ship."

"Then we need thousands of pilots." Iain shook his head. It could not be true. Yet—

"Ten thousand at least," the Master said softly.

Iain felt cold. "How can we possibly find so many? How can we train them?"

"We cannot even begin," the Master said austerely, "while the Line monopoly endures. While the—the myth endures, that only *we* can pilot. That is the first thing. The truth must be told." The Master looked grimly out at the stars. "I will tell it to the Council. And you, to the Hidden Worlds."

As Iain stared at him in disbelief, the docking alarm chirped, and the Master turned to unlock his board. "We must move quickly now. Your ship is still intact. It is still keyed to you."

His ship. Longing filled Iain. To be safe, cradled in his own familiar ship, deep in the fathomless folds of other-space. To *be* his ship again, one with it, embraced by it, more intimate than any lover. His body safe, his mind and senses open to the glory around him—

The Master touched a control. "You must launch at

once. I have seen to it that the fuel and the power cells are at optimum." A chatter of bumps from the attitude jets, a soft *clunk* as the retrieval arm attached to the shuttle, and then weight returned as the shuttle was drawn inboard, into the station's artificial field.

A long, silent walk through corridors dimmed down for night shift. They saw no one—of course the Master of this station knew where men would be at any hour, and could avoid those places. Then the familiar lock chamber that led to Iain's ship. Though Iain saw with brief shock that the family symbol and colors that had marked the hatch were gone, crudely scraped away, replaced by a seal that the Master's palm unlocked.

Iain reached for the hatch, but the Master caught his arm and turned him. "Iain," he said gently. "You are a son of the Line, in spirit if not in truth. What lies in you can save us, save our people. If on even half of our worlds, even one man in a thousand can be trained as a pilot—"

"Tell them," Iain said.

"I am already destroyed," the Master said. His stern gaze held Iain. "I shall not be allowed to speak again freely. My only hope is to reach as many men privately as I can, before my arrest." He glanced at the hatch. "I have converted as much of my personal wealth as I could to small valuables, gems and such, and placed them in the safe within your ship. You will have no source of credit, but these will supply your needs for a time. And I have sent messages to portmasters with whom I have formed any kind of friendship, to ask that they assist you so far as they dare. I particularly commend you to the portmasters on N'Eire, Prairie, and Terranova Station Six."

Iain was shaking his head. "Come with me," he said. "You can do more good that way—"

"No," the Master said. "I'm an old man. I wish to die among my own people."

"And you will die," Iain said, his throat tight with grief. "They will torture you to death, to try to make you tell them where I am."

"They will know where you are," the Master said. "Which is why you must go quickly. The woman, the one who was your servant—"

"Linnea." He could barely speak. "Linnea is alive?"

"Possibly," the Master said. "I was able to trace her by her physical description in the passenger manifests. She has been sent to Freija."

Iain stared at him in shock. Freija, the doomed world. "How long ago? Can I reach her in time?"

"She must have arrived by now. Iain, she may already be dead or—lost. It's an infested world. And in a matter of a few months, Freija will be destroyed. It may already be too late for you. But the woman—she knew where the key was, the proof of your ancestry. You must have that to prove anything to the Council. The records in the Archives must have been falsified. I suspect that what those people on Santandru have is the true record."

"I'll find her," Iain said, though he knew the words were hollow. "The orbiting patrols—my ship is small and fast. I can evade them, trace the landing—find her—"

The Master touched Iain's shoulder. "You must go." He took Iain by both arms, drew him into a formal embrace. "Go wisely—Pilot Master sen Paolo."

The Master's strong shoulders were warm under Iain's

hands. Tears stung Iain's eyes. "Master, won't you reconsider—"

"No," the Master said. He took Iain's chin in his warm fingers, looked deep into his eyes. "*Can* you pilot?"

Iain swallowed in a dry throat. "I must."

"If you are lost, everything is lost." He released Iain. "Make a short jump. Then rest in realspace. Let the shipmind see to you. Eat and sleep before you undertake the longer voyage."

"Master—"

"Go wisely," the Master said again, with a gentle smile, and touched Iain's cheek. "My son."

And he was gone.

I ain sealed his ship's hatch behind him and turned to face the tiny cargo and passenger space. Dim, familiar. It was a plain commnet ship—fast, but not intended to carry much cargo or more than one passenger. The ship's air hissed from the vents, still hot from the warm-up cycle. The passenger pod gleamed in the dimness, empty, its status lights neutral blue.

Forward, in the pilot's compartment, Iain checked the status board. Everything appeared to be optimal, as the Master had promised. Quickly he stripped off the soiled guard uniform, stuffed it into the cycler, and slid into the piloting pod. No time to clean himself, no time to prepare, but he did not intend to jump far.

The pod closed around him with a sigh, and Iain felt the familiar cold tickle of neural leads slipping into place. He overrode the automatic process. No need for waste tubes or food, not this jump.

It did not matter. All he needed now was—
This.

The universe burst into being around him. The bulk of Dock loomed close and dark beside him. He had to get away from it, out into clear space.

He flexed a thought and felt the fuel lines and power lines snick loose from the ship—from him. Another, and with a metallic *tunk-tunk-tunk* the docking grips let go. Iain released a puff from the attitude jets and held his breath as the ship drifted slowly away from the station. This was the moment when he might be detected, when Dock's defenses could still disable his ship.

But they did not. The vast, dark station lay silent. No word on the comm channels, no demands for clearance.

Another puff of jets, and the ship turned away from Dock; a final tap stabilized it in its new orientation. Any course would do, for this jump, but he might as well appear to be jumping for one of the core worlds. It was logical— he could lose himself most easily among tens of millions of people on one of those worlds. His mind sought the natural vector for a jump to Terranova.

Then he touched the engines to pulsing life. He was still closer to Dock than regulations allowed, closer than he should be for bringing up the ion engines—but he was already a criminal. He took a breath, and the ship leaped away.

Acceleration pressed him firmly back in the padding of his pod. He must still be barely in range of the Dock-based sensors when he jumped. Let them think he had made a mistake in his hurry. No one could track a ship through otherspace, but one could extrapolate much from the insertion vector.

Again he oriented himself toward Terranova. Then he cleared his mind, caught his breath, and *flexed*.

At first, as always, he saw nothing, felt nothing—he was cut off as completely as any passenger would be. No senses at all. He waited, letting his training flow back into his mind, tamping down panic. Nothing that had been done to him could change his ability—the way *would* open for him. . . . He waited.

A flicker. A whisper.

A flash of purple.

Warmth rippled along one arm.

Cold liquid trickled down his back for an instant, there, gone—

Otherspace bloomed all around him. He caught his breath again to keep from weeping. Light that was more than light, that was a caress, a lover's breath, a burst of the scent of oranges. Mutterings of sound that formed shifting patterns, music then not music, always beautiful—sound the color of black roses, maroon velvet sliding along his skin, flickers of indigo fire. He cried out, though he could not hear himself. *Beauty, beauty—*

Enough. He dropped back into realspace. Otherspace was there, it waited for him. He would have it for many days when he made his real jump.

The pod released him and he floated free of it, brushing tears from his eyes. The drops glittered, scattering in free fall. He had to prepare.

He had to think.

He washed himself quickly but carefully, and that was luxury unimaginable, even in a ship's tiny refresher closet. His stiff tangled hair yielded to soaps and oils and hard combing. As soon as he was clean he dressed in one of the pilot tunic-and-trouser sets he kept in the ship. Before, he would not have bothered to dress, but, after so long naked, to be clothed was comfort and pleasure—though the tunic was too loose for his bony shoulders.

He made himself a meal from the ship's stores—cheese and spiced meat, dried fruit, and a bulb of cool apple-tasting wine. He found he had to stop between bites to absorb the experience.

Time. He slid his arm into the ship's diagnostic unit and waited as it chirred, considered, then prescribed and delivered, with a prickle along his arm, nutritional supplements and antibiotics.

Now he was well enough, considering. He was safe here, far beyond tracking or tracing. Even a ship that knew his insertion vector would not know where, in all the vastness, he had dropped out of the jump.

He should sleep. But time—

He straightened, taking careful, calming breaths. The Master had been right. Rafael, at least, would know where Iain *had* to go. Even now, even too late, he had to try.

When he spoke, when he told his truth, he would need proof. And Linnea knew where that proof could be found. So she was the starting point.

No. Iain went still. The truth—the truth was . . . She was *his* starting point. His center.

The moment he delayed now might be the moment when she was found, the moment she was caught, infested, killed.

He would go now, and quickly. He might still be in time. The nanobot infection passed slowly among people, at first; it could pass only by touch, and so until many people had become infested, the risk was not great. If she discovered what was happening, hid herself—

Rafael would follow Iain, and no doubt others of Fridric's men. But Iain was young, and skilled—he might arrive days before they did, if he jumped with near-maximum efficiency, found the optimum hyperdesic.

If I jump now, I'll find her.

He would see her, and ask her forgiveness. He would take her away with him, and help her heal. Together they would—together they could do anything.

He stripped off the tunic and trousers, letting them float free, and settled into the piloting pod. This was right. Contented, like an arrow to its homing, he jumped for Freija.

R afael threw back his head and screamed.
   Emptiness gave back no echoes.

He did not know how he had come here. The 'weave. The 'weave had brought him outside the climate shield, under the red furnace glare of the setting sun, his lungs burning in the cold, sulfurous air. No breath mask. Perhaps he had dropped it. But how had he climbed this cliff, without clean air to fuel him?

He rose from his knees and stood unsteadily on the icy black shelf of stone. The cliff below dropped steeply away, harsh jagged stones with hard edges of blue shadow. Rafael could not imagine how he had climbed so far in the 'weave. Sometimes in the 'weave he dreamed of flight. Perhaps, in the 'weave, he flew. He would not remember it if he had.

Memory had fangs. But pleasure could dull those fangs,

even kill the memory entirely. He had built his life on that knowledge.

Shaking in the ebbing tide of spiderweave, he dropped again to his knees, nearly falling headlong from the shelf. Oh, he had come too far.

or not far enough

He pressed his palms to his burning eyes. In time he would trigger his summoner implant, and help would come. But not yet. They must not see him like this. He had promised his father months ago, promised him there would be no more 'weave. And in exchange Fridric had promised him wealth, position, power—a political sinecure to step into, once he made his last piloting voyage.

Well, so they had both lied. His father, his *father* was sending him away. Sending him into danger.

After half a year of being the chosen, the one, the sole heir of David sen Elkander's two sons, Rafael sen Fridric lived and breathed and moved in the heart of emptiness— in the echoing blankness that other men filled with truth, and honor, and all their smug blind certainties. That blankness had always been his home. But he was alone there. Now, when Fridric appeared to believe that Rafael had yielded to him, would give him a grandson, loyal service, become his true heir—even now his father rarely spoke to him. Fridric wanted the truth buried, had done terrible things to accomplish that burial. Now the grave lay between him and his only son. A cairn of stones with a stench beneath, and foul fluids seeping from its base.

And now—memory returned in a demanding rush. Thanks to an old fool's confession, his father knew that Rafael had disobeyed him. Had sent the woman—Iain's lover—not home to her miserable world, but to Freija. To die.

And his plan that this would mean death for Iain— failed, for that same old fool had helped Iain to escape. Iain had gone beyond their reach. . . .

Rafael groaned. Too long since last night's 'weave. Memory again—spiky, demanding: his father pale with rage. *You cost us the woman who was to be our hold on him, and he has gone to seek her. Sen Kaleb told me.*

He remembered laughing, then his father striking him. *What have you done?*

Sent her to the Cold Minds, to horror and death . . . and now Iain had followed. All very neat. . . .

Go after him, Fridric had said. *I will not admit you to my sight until you bring him to me alive.*

And so he must go—he should have gone already. Time was very short; death was coming to Freija. Iain might still escape it—unless Rafael was there to help.

The sun had gone, and in the first frigid breeze of evening Rafael realized he was naked. Naked, bruised, scraped. When they came for him, the dull and dutiful servants, he would refuse to explain, and another tale would be told of him.

But one night in the 'weave would soften the memory, and another would set him free of it. Free of it, as he longed to be free of everything. His father and his father's tedious dreams for him. Politics! Power! To become an old man muttering plans in the shadows, brooding over treasures in an empty house. No. He would die first, die young. All their honors meant nothing; their honor meant nothing. He was not one of them. The Line—words. All their earnestness, the words, the words—

He leaned over the edge and vomited acid sweetness—
some feast he had forgotten. Some words they had said to
him. Words his father said . . . He slumped down, trembling, and spat slime. The feast—three nights ago? Ten
nights ago? Before Fridric's discovery of his little trick . . .
At the feast they had given him another woman to make
pregnant, because the first one had so displeased him. And
they all, those old men—even the young ones were old—
they looked at him so seriously, as if this disgusting ab-
surdity were the greatest act he could perform. As if two
bodies could create anything but slime.

As if to create another life had any meaning in this
weary, doomed world.

Retching racked him. What had he done with the
woman? Had he done what they asked of him—given her
what she was paid for? Or—

He had killed a man once, a servant whose dark beauty
obsessed him and who had betrayed him with another. He
did not think his father knew of it. But the woman—he saw
a memory-shape, a pale face, yellow curls . . . they thought
he would want a son as pale as himself, like some blind
thing grown in a cave—

He wiped his mouth on the back of his arm and stared
out at the fading crimson slash over the horizon. He should
not continue. They should not continue, their whole dis-
eased line—his father, himself, Iain—

He would not touch the woman again, or any woman.
He would leave no door open for lies like the one that had
engendered his father.

Let the Line die. He did not care. But more than that.
Dark certainty filled him, as darkness filled night. He
stared up at the black between the stars.

Let *all* lines die. No hope, no hearth, no fire to warm them; no music, no voice of welcome at the door. The Cold Minds had come and would swallow them all, obliterate all human pretensions. Nothing remained but a little pleasure before the end.

He rose to his feet, a pale shadow against dark stone, and pressed the code implant in his palm against the side of his neck—summoning the servants who would save him from the death he did not fear.

Let them all die. Iain, and the woman he loved. No doubt the nanobots had already taken her.

Iain—he would kill Iain himself.

And then, he promised himself, there would be darkness—the 'weave, more and more and more. He would drive himself down into forgetfulness that would last forever.

He would bring them death in open hands; he would bring them the truth that was the absence of truth; the fire that was no fire, but pain; the fear that mirrored and extinguished hope. He had begun that half a year ago, with the woman Iain loved.

Now he would finish it, with Iain himself.

Adan sen Kaleb had forgotten he was ever the master of anything. Pain had mastered him.

He lay in darkness, waiting for death. The truth he had not had time to speak burned in his heart. That he would never know what would happen to Iain choked him with bitterness. That it might all have been for nothing—

That Fridric might win.

The hours of pain had done something to his heart. He

felt dizzy even here, lying on the floor. He knew the room was cold, but he could no longer feel it.

He was old. That was a good thing; Fridric could do nothing more to him without killing him.

Adan had betrayed Iain, as he knew he would; Fridric knew where Iain had gone, and why.

But the boy was fast . . . the boy was strong. There was still hope, even if Fridric sent that mad wolf of a son of his in pursuit.

Adan had too little breath to speak. But the words formed in his mind.

Paolo, brother, I am sorry.

I tried.

At that moment he felt as if he were rising, being lifted, though he knew he still lay in the dark, on the hard floor, in the locked room. But he was rising, rising. Light all around like the pale blue light before dawn.

A face, a dear face smiling at him. Paolo, friend and comrade and lover of so many years. . . . Adan smiled, stretched out his hand.

His heart stopped.

EIGHTEEN

Linnea walked on through a night without end, in the dim golden light of the planet overhead. Sweat prickled her neck and back. Twice now she had drunk from the river, gambling that the water was safe. The thick heat, the air rich with smells of dirt and lush vegetation drained her strength too fast. An alien world.

Now and then she passed a lane winding up into the trees, into the low hills to her right. But from the road, which ran along the valley floor next to the stony course of a small river, she could not see the farmhouses that must be at the end of the lanes. Small, neatly painted signs marked each lane: PATSON. TAGUCHI. SMIT. Soon, she was sure, the sun would come up and people begin to stir about.

She was gazing up at the huge world in the sky and wondering why it never seemed to rise or set, when she heard the rumble of an engine coming down the road, behind her. Heading to the city, then—maybe someone who could give her a ride. At least, she could ask directions to the skyport—

Then a wave of unreasoning fear washed over her, and without further thought she slipped into a clump of brush beside the road. Better to be careful, to be safe. She didn't know these people or their ways.

It came into view around a curve up the road, like a small flatloader that only a couple of people could ride in, with an open box behind the cab. It moved slowly and gave off the smell of burned oil. She could see the faint outlines of two people through the dust-clouded glass of the cab. As it passed she shrank down in the blue shadow of the brush. When she saw into the box at the back, she gasped.

Piled in the box were human bodies, sprawled and dirty, rag-clad. A couple of men, a woman, and—her heart shrank—two or three children. She could not see what had killed them, but she knew they were dead from the way a stiff foot here, a rigid arm there bounced with the truck's motion. Horror froze her.

Something evil was happening here.

Linnea crouched in the deep shadow of trees, at the edge of a farmyard. The night still continued, the planet overhead had not moved—this world must keep the same face always toward the big planet, so a "day" here must last as long as the little world's orbit did, many days, maybe even weeks. There would be no dawn today. But she had been on this world long enough that people should surely be up and about—if there were people. The farm, a tidily square arrangement of red-painted wood and sheet-metal buildings, lay dark and silent.

She'd been here at least an hour and seen no movement. Her belly ached. The postjump hunger had set in hard; she had to find something to eat or else faint. And she had to look for some clue to where she was, what was happening, how she could escape.

And a way to travel. Her blistered feet stung in her sweat-damp cloth shoes.

She rose and ran toward the nearest shed, intending to stop in its shadow. But as she came nearer a stench caught her, a death-smell so strong her empty stomach heaved. Keeping her distance she walked around the shed to the side facing the farmhouse. Inside the screened doorway, mounded against the wire as if they had died struggling to escape, lay a mass of limp white birds. She knew them from books. Chickens. These were long dead. Abandoned to die of thirst? Black clicking insects swarmed over the carcasses.

No one could still be living here. No one would leave living creatures locked up to die.

She walked more boldly toward the house, which looked prosperous, a two-storied metal cube with plenty of windows. Halfway there she caught the putrid stink again, and she stopped. A small wire-fenced, wire-topped enclosure to her right—something dead lay inside there, too, in a ruffle of black fur. A dog? She remembered the howl she had heard after she landed. Perhaps many animals had been abandoned—why?

The door of the house opened to her at a touch. Inside she smelled only mold and vinegar. A lot of abandoned food had spoiled here. Some papers lay on a counter. She paged through them in the dim light near the window. A list of food to buy, a child's arithmetic paper, an advertisement for wire fencing—a note, written hastily. *Smit's north pasture. Bring supplies. Tonight.* Then a page, a printout from the local commnet: CRISIS AT AN END. The date meant nothing to her. The article said people were to return to their homes and remain calm, and help would be sent to them from the city. It did not name the crisis.

She looked back at the door that had opened so easily for her. Even in the dimness she could see, now, that the lock was broken. And over there in the corner of the kitchen was a shattered window, the glass shards leaning crazily outward, as if someone had burst out that way.

The silence pressed in on her. Death and emptiness— With a surge of fright she knew, she *knew* that this place was a trap. She turned to the door again, and screamed.

A tall, thin woman stood between her and the door. In the filthy remnants of a long sleeveless tunic, her head bound under a stained gray cloth, she regarded Linnea with hard eyes. She held a kitchen knife in one strong-looking hand. "Speak," she said.

"I—I—" Linnea stammered. "Who are you? What is this place? What's happening?"

The hand on the knife relaxed. "Questions. So you are still one of us, ah? What is that accent of yours?"

"I'm from Santandru," Linnea said.

"I never heard of such a place," the woman said. "But we must hurry. Soon they will come here, and us they must not find, or we are both ended. You will help me, ah? And then we will see what to do with you. . . . There is some jarred food inside that cabinet. Take this bag." She moved to the doors she had indicated, opened them, began loading glass jars into her own cloth sack.

"What's happening?" Linnea asked again. "Who is coming here?"

"Those *things*. They are cleaning the farms where they raided, taking the dead things away—trying to protect the bodies they use from disease. Because they need the farms, ah? They need food. For now . . . And so do we. Be silent. Work quickly."

Linnea set cloudy jars of vegetables into the bag, matching the older woman's haste. She had to ask another question. "What world is this?"

The woman stopped and stared at her, one hand on the handle of the knife stuck in her belt. "What world? Is your mind clear?"

"I just arrived here," Linnea said. "I was dumped, dropped off by a pilot. I thought I was going home, but—"

"Dropped here? There is an embargo. No one comes in, no one goes out, ah?" Her hand tightened on the knife. "The Pilot Masters—they are leaving us to this. All of us left to die, left alone with that horror."

Cold rippled up Linnea's spine. "What do you mean?"

The woman smiled now, and Linnea saw the mad gleam in her eyes. "The Cold Minds have Freija," she said. "Didn't you know?"

M any hours later, at the end of a hot, sweaty climb through a dusty forest bare of undergrowth, Linnea and her guide reached the bottom of a steeply sloping meadow, vivid green in the yellow light. At the center loomed a jumble of big pale rocks, an outcropping of the hillside. The woman led her to its shadow. "Sit and wait," she said. She looked along the slope toward the trees. "Don't move, ah? Because my good friend Ishak is watching you, and a fine shot he is." She left, carrying both bags of food.

Linnea sank down onto the dusty grass. She knew she should take the rags of her shoes off her feet, but they had stuck to her skin, glued by blood and broken blisters, and she was afraid to touch them. Her head swam with weariness, another powerful aftereffect of the jump. In spite of the pain in her feet and her empty, cramping belly, she fell asleep.

She woke as rough hands pulled her to her feet. Two men held her. Facing her was an old woman, small and wiry, dressed neatly enough in a long black tunic, her head covered with a black scarf. She looked Linnea up and down. "It's true?" she said in a harsh voice. "You were on the ship that touched down in Eshfe Valley?"

"I don't know what the place was called," Linnea said. She felt dizzy with hunger and pointed with an unsteady hand. "Back there. I was on that ship."

"And why would they leave you here?" the woman demanded. "Why do they want to feed you to the Cold Minds?"

Linnea clenched her jaw against nausea. "An enemy," she managed at last. "He's forbidden to kill me, but he wants me to die."

"A Pilot Master?"

"Yes."

"If those are your enemies, then you will do," the old woman said. "You can work?"

"Kwela, she needs food and rest," the woman who had found her said. "Then work."

"A little food, a little rest. Then good hard work. If she can do it, she stays. If not—" The old woman—Kwela—eyed Linnea again. "If not, she will be easy to kill." She smiled coldly and walked away.

L innea had never worked as hard, even on Santandru, as she did over the next few weeks and months. Seventeen survivors of the Cold Minds' attack had found refuge in a deep cave high in the hills, sheltered from thermal surveillance. They moved out to forage and hunt only during the five standard days of relative darkness, and huddled out of sight in the chill blackness of the cave for the five days of daylight. Sometimes vehicles came up the road from the city, to gather food, everyone said. None of them seemed to be trying to get in any of the crops standing ready in the fields. "Still stupid, those things," Kwela said once, dismissively. "It will take them time to grow enough brains to see past one day."

They had lost everything, these few people who had escaped. All had lived on farms in this valley. Linnea pieced together the story: a strange silence from the city, odd stories on the local commnet. Then a mother or a husband traveling to the city on errands who never returned. Those who went after them, to find them, never returned either. A few days later came the raids, wiping out entire families. "They keep alive only the people whose bodies they need," Kwela told Linnea. "Strong ones, young ones that can work. They are building something near the center of the city, some kind of nest where they can live and grow and build machines to carry themselves. Then they will let the human bodies die."

"So that's why they aren't farming," Linnea said. "They don't care if there won't be any food next year."

"But we do, ah? And so to work, Lin. Both of us."

Linnea fit with these people. They had the dogged determination to survive that she knew so well from home. They never talked of any plan for the future; at first, she gathered, they had expected rescue or intervention by the Pilot Masters, but that hope had long since died. They lived moment to moment, each day's hard work spent to gather the food to live one more day.

She fit with them in more ways than that. She had thought she'd saved her people. But now—Fridric had lied to her, saying he was sending her home; maybe all the rest was a lie as well. Maybe even now Marra was struggling with the knowledge that her children would starve, later or sooner, but certainly.

Or maybe all was well. Linnea would never know. There would be no ship to take her home. In time, it was certain, the Cold Minds would find this last refuge of free humans; and then everything would end.

During the days of hiding, she sat huddled with the others around fires in the center of the cave. Sheets of water trickled, glistening, down all the walls and columns, patiently building the ripples and folds of pale stone that had been growing there for thousands of years. They would go on growing long after the last human died, on this world, on all worlds.

The fire held them all in a close circle, but people rarely spoke. Linnea knew why: too much lost, too many dead;

no one here had even one family member still living—or free. There was no hope, no need even to pretend hope.

On a day when the sun had sunk low in the west, the confinement in the cave near to an end, Linnea sat on a straw mat near the mouth of the cave, soaking up sun-warmth streaming in from the rim of the next ridge. Her bones ached from the days of cold. During this time when no one could work to gather food, they all rested; there was so little to eat, nothing to spare. She was trying to remember the amount of cracked grain left in the last basket when the quick double slam of a ship passing high overhead made her start.

She knew that sound from hearing it in Middlehaven, once or twice; she'd thought never to hear it again. She jumped to her feet. "Come quick!" she called. "Come and see! Kwela!"

As some of the others ran out to join her, a bright blue-white point of light came into view—moving slowly against the sky but brightening every second. Clearly it would land in this valley—but farther south, toward the city, Fjellheim. As its landing spot became more certain, her heart went cold.

Rafael.

In her mind the dark place shook with the beating of her heart.

Omoi, the woman who had brought Linnea to this place, spoke. "That's not far off your spot, Lin. Where you came to ground."

"No one could be looking for me," Linnea said. "I'm where they want me to be." She looked away from Omoi's questioning gaze. "M-Maybe the pilots are trying to find survivors. To help us."

Omoi smiled grimly. "Changed their minds, ah? And come down to offer us all a ride to glory." The man next to her laughed, a bleak sound.

The ship's light vanished behind a hilltop. It had landed. Sickness crowded her throat. *Rafael.* It must be. Who else was left? Who else would come for her?

"Lin," Omoi said quietly, "is it that you know this one who is coming?"

"Not—for certain," Linnea said.

"You're all fear, you are." Omoi set her hands on Linnea's shoulders. "Is it just that it's one of *them*? Or do you know why this ship has come?"

"I don't," she said, and shivered.

"But you guess," Kwela's voice said from the mouth of the cave.

"It—it may be . . ." She found she could not speak his name. "A man who wishes me dead."

"Then he will be disappointed," Kwela said. "Though you will meet. Atuel, Ishak, and Naman will take the truck. Ishak, the good rifle. Now, quickly. You must get to that ship before those others do, and take the man."

"You don't know," Linnea said. "He's dangerous."

"So is Atuel," Kwela said. "So is Naman. We will take him, and use him to bargain with. Those men in their ships in orbit—to keep this one alive, they will agree to help us."

Linnea looked away from the hope in the eyes of the men and women around her. *The Pilot Masters will not save you*, she wanted to say. *They will never let you leave this world.* "I should go along," she said. "I know him. I can tell you if it's the one I fear."

"When they return, you will see him," Kwela said.

"You should kill him, you know," Linnea said, distantly.

"We will keep you safe from him," Omoi said. "Never have any fear, Lin."

"Kill him," Linnea said again. Her clenched fists ached, and she fought to keep from shuddering.

Omoi looked at her with troubled eyes.

NINETEEN

I ain made himself spend a day in far orbit around Freija, his ship on minimal power, its running beacon silenced. He should be undetectable by the blockading ships in their patrol orbits. It was to his advantage that his fellow pilots, orbiting in their ships, were all focused on the surface of the little world, watching for any vessel that might try to take off. None of them would expect someone to deliberately land on that doomed world, now only days from destruction. The asteroids could not be seen from the surface, even as the faint sparks of light that they were at this point; all three were approaching from behind the huge primary, Odin. At the end, slingshot orbits would bring them swiftly around Odin, to smash into Freija in close succession, with immense force.

Iain used the day to listen tensely to the pilots' private channels. He heard no word of the ship that had landed Linnea, though it must have been detected, at least when it left; but then, that pilot had been in Fridric's pay, and the blockading ships had no doubt been ordered to ignore his passage.

Only Fjellheim, the skyport city, still had power: Clearly the Cold Minds were concentrating there. Elsewhere the power grid had gone, and some isolated towns had burned. The commnet down there was silent. Transmissions by the Cold Minds were fragmentary, deeply encoded—bursts of shrill noise, useless.

Near the center of Fjellheim an area almost a kilometer across apparently had been deliberately set on fire. And when the flames died down, heavy equipment had moved in. They were building their hive, just as the stories from Old Earth described it: digging down into the ground, down where they would be safe, where the minerals they needed for manufacturing could be found. This mountain city was perfect for their purposes.

They could not know, yet, how soon they would all be destroyed. Iain took comfort in that. Then thought with despair of Linnea down there, lost and alone. How could he hope to find her? He knew only that he must.

After a few orbital passes he had found the faint ion trace marking the landing site where Linnea had been dropped—months ago. The pilots in the blockading ships did not seem to know of the oncoming asteroids, or did not discuss them on comm channels. And Iain's ship could not detect anything as small as an asteroid beyond cisplanetary range. The fact was that he did not know how long he had—the strike could come ten days from now, or in a matter of hours.

He plotted his landing orbit carefully, reckless of fuel;

he needed only enough to take off again and make his jump from low orbit.

With Linnea. He would find her. He did not let himself imagine not finding her.

When he found her, he could breathe again. He could think again. He would find her and they would escape and they would be free, together.

The change of orbit and the landing were punishingly hard, high acceleration slamming him against his piloting shell, but it was the only way to be sure that the blockading ships could not intercept him. They had no weapons that would reach him on the ground—or at least, that had always been true before. He could only hope that there had been no new developments.

Iain landed near the place where Linnea had been set down, on the western slope of a narrow valley that ran down into Fjellheim. He lowered his ship carefully into a clump of trees, bending and snapping their branches, scorching their trunks. This was a moment of danger; the landing would certainly have been seen from the ground. The Cold Minds' human puppets would come to investigate. The only question was how near they were. He had to get away from here, to be free to find Linnea.

He looked up as he climbed out of the hatch. The branches of the trees nearly met overhead. That might be enough to hide the ship from a cursory air search, but not from a determined one. But there was nothing he could do. He picked up his pack, heavy with food and a medkit, and started down into the valley.

It was the end of the local "day." Freija's sun had already sunk below the ridge behind him, though red sunset light still washed the upper eastern slopes of the valley.

The huge planet Odin stood as always at the zenith, the sunward half of its disk brilliant, the rest dim. The atmosphere of Freija softened the wide swirling bands of red-brown and yellow and white.

Iain stood looking down at a road, a small farm compound just across it. The field in front of him should have been harvested long ago. The dry wheat lay in flattened, untidy swaths. Below, the farm buildings showed broken windows, wildly overgrown plantings. He saw no movement, no sign of human life.

He looked north toward Fjellheim, the skyport city. Linnea would have walked in that direction, at first. And if nothing had turned her aside, if she had reached the city, then she was already dead. There was no sense in looking for her there.

No, if she was still alive, it was because she had turned aside. Hidden. Gone another way.

If she had gone or been taken any distance from here, he would never find her. He had no chance of tracking her, weeks and months afterward. He could only hope that by some chance she was nearby, had seen his landing.

He knew, bleakly, that it was not much hope to hold to.

Iain went down to the farmhouse first; Linnea would have seen it, too, might have gone there and left some sign. But he found nothing: a looted kitchen, broken windows, rain-damaged floors and furnishings. Muddy footprints were everywhere, booted feet and bare feet. Across half the floor of one room was a black, sticky-looking stain. Old blood. Iain kept carefully away from it. That was how the bots passed from man to man—in blood, in fluids. So the old stories said.

Nothing here but death. For one moment it occurred to

him to wonder whether that blood was hers—then he forced his mind back to discipline.

He made his way to the open doorway again, blinking as the sunlight struck his eyes. Then went still. A distant whine of engines. Vehicles coming up the road, fast.

The Cold Minds. People they controlled. They might be coming to investigate his landing—or to this house—

They must not take him.

Iain flung himself out the door, pelted down the path behind the house, his pack slamming against his back. A wide patch of shrubs bordered the deep grass of the yard. From there he could watch the house, see what they did, see if they found his ship. Behind the shrubs was forest; in the shadows there he could escape unseen, once he knew what they intended.

The sound of engines was louder now: many vehicles, still out of sight through trees, around the curve of the road. Iain plunged into the deep shade of the bushes.

The world exploded into pain and he fell into blackness.

He woke lying on a pile of filthy cloth sacks in the dark, stuffy cargo box of a truck of some kind. He heard the engine laboring. They were climbing.

When he turned his head, pain split it, made him gasp. He raised a shaking hand and felt a crusted lump on the side of his head.

Behind him a man said, "Your feet are bound."

Iain went still. He did not dare turn his head again, yet; he was afraid the pain would make him vomit.

"Wise, it would be, to lie still," the voice continued. "You are little use to us dead, but if you proved inconvenient, we should not hesitate. I have a hunting rifle, and it is aimed at you."

Iain struggled to think. This man did not speak like someone inhumanly possessed. "The Cold Minds," he rasped.

"Oh, those. A little thing, ah? So you Pilot Masters seem to believe. Leave us to them, you say. It would be inconvenient, no doubt, to do a thing but stand away and watch. Is it not so?"

Iain turned his head, slowly, fighting down the nausea rising in his throat. A man sat against the far wall, legs stretched out—a man with a shock of disordered white hair and old eyes. Across his lap he held a weapon, a projectile thrower of ancient design that would be lethal at this range.

"Some of us want to help," Iain said.

"Cheering words," the old man said. "Ships, then, you have brought us? To evacuate the survivors, in your grand old Pilot Master tradition? The saviors of humanity—I believe that is what we were all taught in school?"

"I—" He fought to think. Of course there would be no evacuation. The contamination had spread so widely. But he could not tell this man that; to stay alive, Iain had to appear to be of some use as a hostage. "I am alone here," he said. "Looking for someone who was marooned here eighty-seven standard days ago."

He saw with interest that the old man's eyes narrowed at these words, almost imperceptibly. But his voice did not change. "And what is it you want with this man? If you find him?"

"To save her," Iain said roughly.

"A woman, so." The man shrugged. "And your ship—we found it, I saw it. Very small." He waited.

"Yes," Iain said. "A commnet ship."

"But with room for this woman," the man said.

"Just enough," Iain said. "I cannot take more."

"Your friends can," the old man said comfortably. "And we will make a few little arrangements with them, ah? Because they won't wish to see you shot dead."

Iain considered, looking at him. The men in orbit would join together to kill him if they could, outlaw and fugitive as he was. But there was no reason to admit that.

"This woman," the man said abruptly. "She is worth such trouble?"

"She is," Iain said on a wave of anger.

"As all of us are, ah?" the man said calmly, and settled back, clearly done talking. Iain closed his eyes and fought the pain.

H ours later. The truck stood in a narrow clearing, well off the road. Two men worked to cover the battered old vehicle with brush, while the older man, Ishak, kept the rifle on Iain. From the amount of dry brush lying about already cut, Iain deduced that the truck had been hidden here before. His head ached less now. "Hurry," Ishak said to the others. "We know the day will come when they will learn to follow us. It might be today." Carefully he untied the rope from Iain's ankles, coiled it, and put it into the pocket of his trousers. "Walk silently."

There followed more than an hour of climbing on slippery pinelike duff, up steep slopes and along a rocky trail that hugged the ridgetop. At first they traveled in separate pairs, Iain with Ishak, who no longer carried the hunting rifle. A reasonable precaution, Iain decided, against Iain's taking the weapon. And if he ran, where would he go? There was no other place. And anyway—

If Linnea was alive, she would be with these people.

If she was not with them, she was dead.

Iain put his head down, put one foot in front of the other. His pilot's boots, cut for style and show, chafed at his heels. Sweat soaked his black tunic in the rich, humid warmth.

She could not be dead.

If she were dead, he would know it. If he was never again to see her dark, serious face, hear her soft voice— touch her— He would know. And the world would be a place of stone and ice.

No. She was alive.

He began to turn his mind to how he would save them both.

I ain limped the last bit of the way down a steep, stony cliffside trail and under an overhang, to a rocky shelf that narrowed at the rear into a dark cave mouth. His captors stopped him at the edge of the shelf. A pale, stolid-looking young woman rose from her seat on a rock near the cave mouth and went inside.

Orange sunlight spilled into the cleft. The sun was lop-sided, distorted by the heavy, damp air, setting with surreal slowness behind the ridge across the valley. Iain shifted his shoulders, trying to relieve the itch from his sweat-soaked pilot's tunic.

"Hah!" A woman's voice, throaty and satisfied. "It *is* a pilot we have!" She stepped forward into the light, a small, lean, aged figure dressed in black, her head covered with a black cloth. "I was in fear that you would not be in time, Atuel."

The small dark man who had driven the truck shook his head. "Too fast we went, down and up again. There's no being sure the old truck will manage it again."

"Were you seen?"

"No," Atuel said. "They stopped to look for his ship, ah? A machine, you see—much more interesting."

The woman turned to Iain. The authority in her old eyes—a woman's eyes—was strange to him, but he recognized its presence. "I am Kwela," she said. "And you I have heard of."

Iain's breath caught.

"I should kill you," she said calmly. "Our families lie dead on our farms, all we have ever had is taken from us, and your people . . . watched."

There was nothing he could say to that.

She sighed. "But instead we will get some use out of you. Those few of us who survive—you will tell your friends that we are to have passage offworld, ah? Or we will kill you." She looked past him at Atuel. "We have a comm unit that can reach orbit. You know their codes. They are your people. You will tell them."

An odd certainty came over Iain, that it would be a mistake to lie to this woman. "I can tell them nothing," Iain said. "I am an exile. An escaped prisoner. They *want* me dead."

"Is it so? It would be convenient for you if I could believe that." She shook her head. "We will try our plan, tomorrow when darkness falls. But until then, Ishak will keep charge of you, and keep you bound and safe. And if you do anything not to his liking, he will shoot you in the knee. Very painful that would be. And we have no doctor here. No medicine."

He could no longer make himself wait. "Is there a woman here? One who came from offworld, not long ago?"

Kwela's expression did not alter. "Questions are not yours to ask, Pilot. This place—it is the only safety left, and we have the only food you will find in all these mountains. Outside this place is only death for you." She looked past Iain. "Atuel."

Strong hands bound his wrists behind his back, hobbled his ankles. He stood steady, keeping his gaze on Kwela.

"And last," she said, "the bag, Atuel."

There was no way for Iain to resist. A heavy bag of coarse black cloth covered his head, blinding him. It smelled of dirt.

"Put him to bed, Ishak," Kwela's voice said. "And watch him well."

TWENTY

Linnea did not see the pilot arrive at the cave. Omoi and the others seemed to wish to keep her safely away from him—they were older; they wanted to protect her. They thought they could. She had heard that he was tied, hobbled, blindfolded— Not enough. Her dread of seeing Rafael again was a sick ache in her belly.

All night, in the side passage of the cave where she and several of the other women slept, she lay awake. The fire died down slowly to embers. Far above, winged creatures chittered and shifted, clinging to the roof of the cave. Her blankets, of damp wool, kept her warm enough, but she could not close her eyes. Knowing that Rafael lay somewhere near, in the same dark, breathing the same air.

She was not to be allowed to die here, exiled and hopeless. No, he must follow to haunt even her death.

She wondered what Rafael would say when he saw her tomorrow—what poison he would spit. Because of course she must see him. Seeing him, she knew, would make her sick, as she had been sick in those three days in his power. She felt sure that the fragments of memory she had been able to bury, push out into the dark corners of her mind, would crawl together and form themselves again, into shapes that her mind could not bear.

She should get up now and go out to the main cave. She should see him first, from the shadows. She would not speak. She would not let him learn, yet, that he had found her.

But she could not—

She sat up quietly. Nothing to be done but what must be done. So Ma had used to say, long ago. So she had said when she was dying.

Linnea got quietly to her feet, tugged the gray dress straight, rubbed her cold, trembling hands to warm them. When the time came, she would face him with what she had of strength, what she had of dignity. It might not last long.

She walked carefully along the steep, slippery passage from the sleeping hall to the largest chamber of the cave, where a fire always burned, where meals were cooked.

It was later than she had thought—already morning. She smelled smoke, and porridge cooking; heard men's voices speaking in low tones.

Her heart caught and stammered. In another moment she would see him: Rafael, here to make sure of her. Eerie peace washed over her. *All finished. Now I can rest.*

She came around the last pillar of stone and into the firelight, and the ring of men around the fire all turned and looked at her.

She saw him, across the fire. They had freed his hands

to let him eat, pulled off the sack that had hidden his face.
But her mind had room for only one thought: This was not
Rafael. *Not Rafael.* This man wore black Pilot clothes, as
Rafael would on a voyage, but he was darker.

The stranger, silent, unmoving, looked at her. Firelight
gleamed on his smooth black hair above the braid. He
was—the *way* he was looking at her . . .

Linnea's throat closed tight.

Not a stranger.

Iain sen Paolo. Iain, her lover once, long ago. Iain . . .
not dead.

He looked at her, his eyes dark as ash, unsmiling. But in
his stillness she saw his gladness, the depth of his relief.

It could not be Iain. He could not be alive, and here.

"This is the one we caught for you, Lin," Naman said,
scooping the last of his porridge from the bowl. "He's
pretty enough. Did we do well?"

She could say nothing. She could only look at Iain. He
looked unhurt. But his face, oh, his face—changed, tired.
Watchful.

As the men around the fire were watchful. Naman, a
tall, heavy, brown-skinned man, looked sharply from Linnea to Iain. "You told us there was a woman you wished to
find. Is this the one?"

Iain nodded slowly, his eyes meeting Linnea's. He did
not seem able to speak.

"And so, Lin—this is your enemy," Naman said. "The
one you warned us to kill, ah?"

"No," she said in a small voice.

"No?" Kwela came in from a side chamber. "Is this not
the man you told us had come?"

She fought to keep her voice steady. "No. I made a mistake. This man is not my enemy."

"You said you were no friend of the Pilot Masters." Naman's face darkened. "This is one of them. So that was a lie, then?"

Iain leaned forward and set his empty bowl on the stones by the fire. "As I told you, I am no longer a Pilot Master," he said, his voice low and even. "Linnea did not lie." He looked up at Kwela. "I wish to speak to her." Linnea heard the assurance in his voice—the expectation that his wish would be heard as an order, even in this place.

Kwela's old, hooded eyes considered him. "Speak with Lin if you like," she said. "Here and now. And we will all listen."

"And we will all watch," Naman growled. "Lin is our friend."

"Tie him again," Kwela said.

"No," Linnea said. "I know that he won't harm me."

Kwela lifted an eyebrow. "You are sure, then? Very well. But Ishak, the rifle."

She did not know where to go, where to look. Iain got up stiffly and came around the fire, behind the other men. She knew she should step forward to meet him, but she was paralyzed. He came to within a meter of her, where she stood by the pillar, not touching its wet surface, and he stopped.

He stretched out his hands to her. "Linnea," he said. His voice shook a little—

—his hands, long-fingered, fine in proportion, palms up, waiting—

She wondered how she could ever have thought she'd forgotten him. "Iain," she said, in a strange high voice not hers. Her hands floated up and touched his, all on their own, not her will. . . .

His touch drained her of breath. The bond—it was still there, under the scars, under the pain, under the dirt she'd shoveled on its grave to dull her grief.

She'd mourned for him. For *this* man. His living fingers stirred and tightened around hers.

No. All over now. Rafael had put an end to it, even if they both stood alive.

She let Iain's hand fall. "Why are you here?"

His face went still. "To save you."

"You can't." Her voice trembled. "*He* told me you were dead." No need to name Rafael between them.

Iain's expression tightened. "I know what happened. He—came to me in prison, told me what he did to you. I tried to kill him."

Her heart leaped. But his look—

"I failed." He shook his head slightly. "I'm sorry."

"He didn't kill you, either." Then the blackness washed in all around her like a tide. Only Iain's face stayed in her vision, small and distant and clear. Rage leaped up. "He knew you were alive. But he told me—"

"I know." His voice was quiet. "He told me the same, about you. To divide us, to hurt us." He stood now with his hands at his sides, as if he knew not to try to touch her. Beyond him the men watched silently. Omoi stood there, too, now, her eyes wide.

Linnea shivered, cold and empty as a dead shell.

"Don't be afraid," Iain said gently. "It's over now. I'm here. I'll take you away from here. My ship is waiting."

Bitterness was her strength now. "I thought you weren't a pilot anymore."

He must have heard the danger in her voice, because he looked away. Then he took a breath, and his shoulders straightened. "I must fight against Fridric, and the Cold Minds. My father died, my teacher offered his life, so that I would be free to fight. It would help me if—if you were safe. Linnea, please."

Anger rose in her. Here he was, like some high prince in a story, stretching out his hand to the beggar girl—so certain of how it would end. She looked away.

He set his hand on her arm.

Again his touch shocked her, took away her breath. Like the pain she'd heard men felt in limbs long cut off.

A ghost of the hunger for him that she'd long forgotten. A flicker, an instant of memory, *real* memory. Iain's arms strong around her, his body hard against hers, joy filling her eyes with tears, warmth and darkness and his breath mingling with hers as they strove and strove and strove—

That was over. She looked at the fire wavering through a curtain of unshed tears. Then back at Iain.

"I will not leave without you," he said steadily.

"You will." She was shivering now. "Leave me here with my friends. They saved my life. I can't go back to—back to where *he* might—" She broke off.

She saw an unspoken message in his eyes then. One she could not decode. "You must come," he said. "I need you."

"I am not your servant any more," she said quietly.

"Come with me. Help me hunt Rafael," he said.

She went cold, looking into his cool, remote eyes. Darkness there, in his eyes, behind them. She knew that darkness. She lived in it. Rafael, dead—if Rafael were dead, she would be free. . . .

Nothing else he could offer her meant anything.

Except—"We must take these people with us," she said.

She saw him shake his head slightly, another message she could not read clearly. "My ship can carry only one passenger," he said. "I am sorry."

"Pilot!" Omoi stepped forward, planted her fists on her hips. "Ahead of yourself, are you not? We have an arrangement to make with those others up there. There will be ships for us." She nodded her head sharply.

"There will be no ships," Iain said. Linnea heard the regret in his voice. "They will give no ransom for me. If they knew I was here, they would be glad. They have cast me out. They want me to die. And even if"—his voice shook—"even if they wished to help you, they could not. Can you not understand? The contamination *must* not spread from this world." He looked pale. "No matter the cost."

"Yet *you* will leave," Atuel said coldly.

"I know that I have not been contaminated," Iain said.

"And we know the same!" Omoi shouted. "They have touched none of us. Their blood has touched none of us. We are not the ones who fought—those were taken or killed—we were the ones who ran, who hid. . . ." Angrily, she scrubbed the tears from her face. "We can still be saved!"

Linnea went to her and silently took her hand.

"The Pilot Masters will save no one," Iain said. "When they see me launch, they will intercept and destroy my ship if they can. I am sorry. It is over."

"Then we will all die together—all of us, and you," Naman said.

Iain stopped and looked into the fire for a moment. Then seemed to gather himself. "There is one small hope," he said finally. "Not for you, but for other worlds. Linnea and I—we are that hope. If we die here, it ends."

Linnea looked at him and frowned. What kind of game was this?

"Tell us," Kwela said, her eyes hard, doubting. Beside her Ishak stood, the rifle aimed steadily at Iain.

Linnea saw the tension in Iain's shoulders, knew that he dreaded what he was about to do.

He spoke. "The Pilot Masters—" His voice was tight, controlled. "It is not true that only they can pilot jump-ships. There are others—outside the Line."

The others looked at each other. Atuel got to his feet. "Where?" he asked scornfully. "Show me these pilots who are not Pilot Masters."

Iain spread his hands. "Here," he said. "Before you."

There was a disbelieving silence. "But you come from Nexus," Omoi said at last, gesturing toward Iain's black tunic and trousers. "You wear the braid. You talk like them, ah? All proud and exact."

"But I am not," Iain said, "one of them." He looked at them all around the fire. "My grandfather came from San-tandru. Like Linnea."

Linnea stared at him in shock. So this was what it had meant, the thing she had tried to sell to him. . . . All his grand pride, nothing? In truth, he was no more than she?

"If you are not one of them, how is it they let you become a pilot?" Omoi asked, puzzlement plain in her voice.

"It was well hidden," Iain said. "My father knew, but I did not. Until this year."

Iain was not a Pilot Master. He never had been. Linnea could see in the line of his shoulders, in his dark eyes, how

thin his control had become. There was not so much of
Santandru in him, after all. One grandfather . . .

But as she watched him, he mastered himself. "You see
what this means," he said. "We *can* have enough pilots to
protect us all from the Cold Minds. There must be men
with the piloting skill on all of the Hidden Worlds. We can
keep them all safe, in time."

Linnea's breath caught. Hope, of a kind. But she was so
tired.

"In time?" Kwela said. "Alas, no. You are not in time to
save us."

"I am sorry," Iain said. "If this had been known
sooner—"

"For this miracle of yours to be accomplished," Kwela
said, "the power of the Pilot Masters must be broken. You
will do this?" Linnea heard the doubt, the disdain in the old
woman's voice.

"I don't know if it can be done," Iain said. "But someone must try."

"You say you believed yourself one of the Pilot Masters," Kwela said. "Until this very year, you say. You would
really do such harm to your own people?"

"I must," Iain said. "Two men I love died so that I would
be free to act. To spread the truth, to train new pilots—"

"To destroy everything you were brought up to honor,"
Kwela said. "And we should trust you to do this, if you are
freed? Or rather, will you mend matters with your former
brothers and return to your comfortable home?"

Iain met her hard gaze. Then held up his right hand,
the old scar plain across the palm. "I swear by the—" He
stopped. Linnea knew he had been about to say, "by the
Tree," the repository of a Pilot Master's binding word; but

it seemed that was closed to him now. He shook his head. "I can only give my word as a man, that I will do what I have said." He turned his head and looked into Linnea's eyes. "Linnea will vouch for me."

Kwela looked at Linnea. "I think we will not ask her to do that yet," she said, her dark eyes reassessing. "Perhaps not ever. For there is the question, do you see? Either both of you can be trusted, or—" She shook her head firmly. "No. It is a fine tale. It may even be true. But we will test the matter, tonight. We will transmit to the Pilot Masters, ah? And if they show you for a liar, then we have won, have we not? We will be saved. And if they say they wish you dead, well, it may be that we will believe you, then, at last."

"There is so little time," Iain said. Linnea heard the plea in his voice. "Please. Let us go. If the Cold Minds find us—"

"I have listened. I have decided," Kwela said. "You will stay until I am satisfied that your word is true."

Iain looked down, his eyes wide and afraid. Linnea found herself wondering what it was that he feared—what it was that he could not tell these people.

"And," Kwela said, "I think we will keep a good watch on our friend Lin as well. Just until tonight."

Linnea met her eyes, then looked down.

That afternoon the last of the sun sank out of sight. Winter was coming, Omoi had told Linnea, and in the new coolness of the day of evening, a thick layer of clouds rolled in, lashed along by the wind. Rain began to fall outside the cave. The trickle of fresh water that ran through the main cave grew to a gush.

Kwela ordered that the evening meal be a good one—a sign of hope that they would all be gone from here soon. Omoi and Linnea between them contrived a kind of stew, with two whole cans of chicken meat, fresh-gathered greens, and three double handfuls of barley. Linnea had not spoken with Iain again; she had nothing left to say that she wanted these people to hear. She did not know what she would say to him, in any case. She sat beside him when she could, trying to show them that he was not to be feared; but it did not matter. They would have to wait as Kwela had ordered, until tonight, when the darkness would be deep enough that the comm could be carried safely into the woods, a kilometer or more away for safety. And contact would be made.

And these people she had come to care for—their hope would end.

Linnea was crumbling salt into the stew when a man's bubbling scream brought her bolt upright. The cry came from the mouth of the cave. She looked sharply at Iain, who had been sitting near the cooking fire but now stood as she did, looking toward the passage from the cave mouth.

A young man she did not recognize appeared at the end of the passage. He wore filthy stained clothing, and his hair hung in oily ropes. He carried a rifle that she recognized: Ishak's. Ishak had been on watch—with leaden certainty she knew that Ishak was dead.

The young man's eyes were empty, his face slack.

"They must have tracked us," Iain said numbly.

In one movement Omoi took up the iron stewpot in her bare hands and flung it at the man in the passage.

He did not scream as the boiling liquid struck his face. He raised clumsy hands to scrape it away from his skin, now red and blistering. A pale blue light flickered behind the pupils of his eyes.

"Run!" Omoi shrieked. "Hide! They are—" The rifle went off, deafening in the confines of the cave, and she fell, her chest a wet mass of red.

More men had come in now, men with the same slack faces. Linnea caught Iain's wrist and turned to run, through the back passage of the cave. They could hide in the parts she didn't know, hope to find their way out through some new passage; it was a better chance than—

Two more of them stood in the passage, blocking it. Without thinking she started toward them, but Iain caught her. "No!" he was shouting. "No! Don't touch them!"

The two—things turned and faced each other. Their eyes flickered blue, briefly. Then they raised their hands, and Linnea saw the long, dark cylinders they held. "Stun-rods," Iain groaned. "I'm sorry—Linnea, I'm sorry—" He sobbed.

Without thought she wrapped her arms around him, and they clung together as the men moved closer. She buried her face in his shoulder and held her breath. She would remember this; she would remember being alive and free— even if they made her not human, she would remember—

Darkness.

TWENTY-ONE

B y the time the line of trucks reached the city, Linnea
was shivering helplessly. The five survivors huddled
together in an open cage in the rear of the third truck,
lashed by rain, numb with sorrow and cold. Linnea held on
to Iain, who used his hand to shelter her face from the
worst of the rain. Sometimes she wept—for Omoi, for
everyone.

The city streets they traveled seemed dark and dead, il-
luminated only here and there by streetlamps. The trucks
rattled down empty avenues, past dark windows of shops
and houses—then out into a vast open space of rutted mud.
In the weak yellowish light that shone through the clouds,
Linnea saw dark, glistening mounds of rubble burned
black by fire. Here and there smoke still curled up from a
pit or a pile. It did not seem possible that they had a desti-
nation in all this desolation. She burrowed closer to Iain's
warmth.

"The hive," Iain muttered once, but she was too cold to ask him to explain. She could hear his heart though, beating fast. So he was afraid, too.

The trucks lurched to a stop. Three of the infested men came around to open the cage. They stood well back as Naman, then Atuel climbed out. Naman resisted briefly, but two of the infested closed in on him, and he subsided at once. Of course he would fear their touch. The two living men helped Kwela and Linnea get stiffly down. Kwela seemed barely able to stand. Linnea's rag-shod feet sank into frigid mud the consistency of mush.

Iain came last, looking around, his face blank. She knew what he must have hoped for this moment, but there was no opportunity for escape. All the infested had to do to get them to move was raise a hand, or take a step closer, and they shied off, herded in the direction chosen for them: onward toward blackness, toward the distant rumble of heavy machinery, and light flickering blue on the low, heavy bellies of the clouds.

The heart of the city was gone. This was a stinking desolation, smelling of wet scorched wood and putrid mud and dead things half-burned and half-buried. The light from the clouds gave it all a sickly fungal glow, yellowed and spoiled, glistening with rain. Where in this waste a human would go to find safety, or food, Linnea did not know. They walked as they were meant to walk, toward the end that had been chosen for them. Kwela, Linnea, Iain, Naman, Atuel.

Kwela had lost her head scarf but did not seem to know or care. Her long gray hair hung loose, muddy and tangled. Once or twice she turned her head and Linnea heard her whispering, whispering. Prayers maybe. There didn't seem much use to that.

Linnea wished she could walk beside Iain, that they could touch. It would be some comfort. Once she turned to look at him, but beyond him were the half-dead, with their glowing eyes and slack mouths, and she could not bear it.

At last they came to the blackness: huge heaps of raw earth, meters tall. They toiled up a slippery, winding path between two piles. When they reached the crest, wind drove the rain into their faces again. In the uncertain light it was hard to see, but Linnea could sense the drop-off. The trail they were being forced along turned left along the rim of a vast pit, its muddy lip treacherous and slick. The grind and clatter of machinery echoed from far below, louder than the cold whistle of the wind. Linnea took a breath to warn Kwela to walk carefully—

And Kwela stopped, turned, looked into Linnea's eyes. "Never forget us," she rasped—

And leaped.

Her body plunged silently into the hollow dark and vanished. "No!" Linnea cried out in horror. "Kwela—" Hands seized her arms from behind, pulled her back, off balance. Iain's hands. "Don't go, don't go," he said, his voice tight, his arms wrapped tightly around her. The infested ones had moved in around them, moved between them and the edge. Then, silently as ever, urged them along again. Linnea walked, head down, blind with tears, moving under Iain's hand without thought. She heard Naman whispering now—more prayers, prayers for Kwela maybe, or for them all—

The trail climbed back from the edge now, farther and farther. The rain fell harder. A black gap opened ahead of them between two metal walls and they passed between. Into a small, cold space—she could hear how small it was—and behind them the gap closed with a grind of sliding metal, the unmistakable rattle of a chain lock.

Linnea fell to her knees on icy metal. A little light came down through a grate at one end of the space. Naman reached up and tried to shake it loose, but it was solid.

"They'll hold us here a bit," a voice said, teeth chattering, and she barely knew it for Atuel's. "A bit, until they need us."

"Until they kill us," Iain said. She heard the weariness in his voice.

"They killed everyone when they first came," Atuel said. He stood huddled into himself, his face twisted with grief and terror. "So they can't kill *us*. They need more bodies for their work. They killed too many—it was too easy."

"So they can miscalculate," Linnea said.

"It doesn't matter if they do," Atuel said. He took a shaking breath, and she saw that he had been crying for a long time. "We can't stop them, we can't help even ourselves. Except Kwela's way."

"I know," Linnea said, shivering. Those things could not mean to leave them in this cold box for long; all four of them would die, and what would be the use of that?

"They will come for us soon," Atuel said. "It takes them a little time, you see, a few hours, to grow enough bots in their bodies to pass to us. . . . I saw them do it once, to two other men. I was—" He stopped, screwed up his face and went on, "I was hiding. Up above in the loft, a barn it was . . . And they came in with two men, one of our farmhands and—and my brother—"

"Be quiet," Linnea said, weary beyond patience. "It does no good."

But he had to finish his confession, sure as any dying man back home. "I was hiding," he said again. Tears ran openly down his face. "The way they do it, they open their mouths and it's all black in there, full of the bots, and they reach in with their fingers and scoop some out and put them into the other man's mouth. They hold their mouths shut, make them swallow—"

"Be quiet," Linnea said again. "You aren't helping the rest of us."

"I hid!" Atuel screamed. "I watched them do that to my brother! To Amal! He was younger, I should have protected him. I should have saved him. I deserve this—"

Naman took him by the shoulders and flung him back against the cold metal of the box wall. Atuel slid to the floor and slumped there, weeping.

"We all hid," Naman said to him coldly. "Even Kwela. We all deserve this end." He looked at Linnea. "Except you. You and your pilot, you wanted to fight these things. Maybe you would have done it. Too bad, the way it's come to end."

"We would have done the same as you," she said, numb.

"No," Naman said. "Let us believe you would not. That you would have turned and fought. That is the bad dream of this. You would have turned and fought and died."

Perhaps an hour later the door of the box opened.

The four of them were huddled together at the end of the box farthest from the grate, Linnea between Iain and Naman. When the lock rattled they all got to their feet. She kept hold of Iain's hand. When they did it, would she be conscious? What would it feel like, what would those things *taste* like . . . how much longer, afterward, would she still be human and aware?

But they did not come in. One of them set a battered pot on the floor just inside the door, flickered a blue glance at them, and withdrew. The door grated shut, and Linnea heard the lock close.

The pot sat on the floor, steam rising from it. Linnea smelled some kind of meat broth. Naman and Atuel made no move toward it.

"Could—" Linnea swallowed hard. "Could there be bots in that?"

"Too hot," Naman said curtly. "But—" He broke off.

"We should eat," Iain said tentatively. "It doesn't make sense to starve ourselves. We might need to move suddenly."

"No," Naman said. "You don't know." Linnea saw sweat gleaming on his face despite the cold. He looked sick. "They put—in their soup, they put any flesh that comes to hand. Any flesh at all." He stopped and swallowed hard. "It's logical—they are logical, these things."

Linnea pressed her fingers to her mouth. Shivering with cold and dread had already made her queasy, and this—

Iain put an arm around her. He looked sick. "And they expect that we will eat this?"

"We might have," Atuel said, "if we didn't know their ways—if we hadn't been watching them."

He fell silent. The rain roared on the metal roof of the box.

"We should sleep," Linnea said shakily. "If you can't eat, that's next best."

"If you can sleep, Lin," Naman said, his deep voice gentle, "then you should. The pilot, too. I will keep watch."

Atuel groaned. "Against what? What can you do?"

The big man looked down at him. "What I must," he said softly. "When they come again, Atuel—we will pull them into the box."

"Pull them in?" Atuel shook his head. "Why?"

Naman smiled at him. "You and I—we will kill them, ah? And Lin and the pilot will run."

"No," Linnea said. "No! If you kill them, their blood will touch you, and—"

"It will be no different from what would happen anyway," Naman said. "But if you get out—if you get out!" His eyes blazed. "You can fight these things. You can raise up people to fight them! To protect other worlds. So this cannot happen again, the way it happened to us. So no one else loses what we have lost."

"We can't," Linnea said. "We can't accept that—your lives for ours."

Iain set his hand on her shoulder. "We can," he said, his voice cold. "And we will."

In the end Linnea did sleep, off and on, curled up against Iain's shoulder. The rain drummed, drummed on the walls and roof of the box. A pool of water stood under the grating at the far end, and as cold air ruffled the water's surface, ripples of yellowish light danced on the ceiling.

The lock rattled.

At once they were all four on their feet. Iain held Linnea back as Naman and Atuel moved silently to flank the door. She wanted to speak to them, thank them, say her good-byes—but it was too late. The door was already grinding open.

Atuel waited, his back flat to the wall beside the door, the soup pot in his hand. Naman crouched ready across the opening.

A head appeared in the gap, flickering eyes scanning around. Naman seized the thing by the neck, dragged it into the box, twisted. Linnea heard the snap of the neck breaking, but the thing did not die. It struggled, more clumsily than before, as two more appeared in the gap. Atuel swung the loaded pot by its handle and crushed the head of the first, which fell—swung again and missed the second, which gripped him and pulled him close. The pot clattered to the metal floor and spilled. Atuel screamed and twisted his face away from the open mouth of the thing that held him, an open mouth gleaming black, drooling black spittle.

Iain pulled Linnea forward, over the struggling bodies, out the door. Rain pounded them as they ran. She could hardly see where she was going—rain, tears— Iain's hand pulled her.

The only way out was to skirt the pit, and she followed Iain—sick with certainty that it was far too late for Atuel and Naman. And she had discovered that she did want to live, for now—live to kill these things.

They picked their way along the edge of the vast cylindrical gulf, lit only by weak blue lights here and there on the walls, lights crawling slowly up or down. Shapes moved at the bottom, heavy equipment or something else—"What is this?" she whispered.

"Their hive," Iain whispered. "They must be down there

now, the Minds that came in their ship, that control all this."

"But why? What are they doing?"

"If I were to guess," Iain said bleakly, "they intend to build a ship. A jumpship with life support, and enough room to carry infested humans to another world. And I—I was to pilot it."

"You could still pilot, infested with those things? Machines can pilot?"

"They must," Iain said. "These things are here. Or—or perhaps they use people who are still human for that, keeping them alive. . . ." He still looked sick. "Come. They use this path. We have to get off it."

Now they were climbing up the vast rim of earth left from the excavation of the pit, and they scrambled and slid in the soft, sodden, untrampled dirt. After a long gasping struggle they reached the top of the pile and began a deliberate slide down the slope on the other side.

Running again. She stumbled as she ran, with his hand gripping her wrist inescapably. She wept as she ran. Through the warren of equipment sheds, lightless—they needed so little light, these things, just for the human eyes while they still had them. . . .

A corpse, stiffened in its last convulsion. Dead of neglect? Broken and abandoned? They ran wide around it, weaved between high piles of scrap metal, burned and twisted, spider shapes against the glowing clouds where lightning flickered and snapped.

They slowed to a walk when they reached the unburned part of the city. Linnea's feet were numb. She knew that was the only thing sparing her pain. They moved silently from shadow to shadow, listening for the sound of engines.

The road straightened; the houses thinned out. "I have to rest," Linnea gasped.

"We can't rest yet." Iain's voice was cold, stern. "When they know we have escaped, they will put a heavy guard on my ship. We must try to reach it before that happens."

"There may already be a guard," she said.

"Perhaps so," he said evenly. "We will see. I think they won't be willing to risk shooting me, so you must keep very close to me."

Now and then they found a bubble car or a truck standing abandoned in the street, and Iain would hastily check whether it still contained fuel, or batteries; but always the fuel had been drained, the batteries taken. "They took it all for their work, for the pit," Iain said. "If we find one they overlooked—"

But they did not. Hours, miles. They were climbing now, southward into the valley where Iain had landed.

They stopped to drink from the river. Linnea felt sure she would never stand up again, never take another step. She shivered. "Iain—"

"Yes?" He was already on his feet again, peering back down the road, watchful.

"When they took us," she said shakily, "they stunned us. Iain, what if they—what if, while we were unconscious, they—"

"They didn't stun me," Iain said calmly. "And I know they did not touch you. I carried you to the trucks myself. You are not infested."

Relief only weakened her more. "If they ever touch me—"

"I know," he said.

"Swear," she said thinly. "Swear you'll kill me. It's the only good you could do me."

"I know," he said again, no trace of feeling in his voice. "Linnea, it's time to move on."

"I—" She shivered. "I don't know if I can. I'm so cold, I—"

"Up." He lifted her to her feet, and his cold eyes looked into hers. "Do you want it to mean nothing, what those two men did for us?"

"I didn't think you noticed," she said, bitterness twisting her voice.

"Think what you like," he said. "Let's go."

Climbing, climbing—she knew none of this country, recognized nothing in the strange weak light, the slashing rain. But Iain knew, as if guided by a homing sense she could not understand. Now they were climbing westward away from the road, under the shadow of trees. Their sodden canopies gave no shelter after hours or days of rain; heavy drops pattered down all around them, and the pine duff was slippery.

"We must move very quietly now," Iain whispered. He had picked up a heavy knotted branch and gripped it tight, ready. "They will be watching the ship. When I attack them, stay back. I'll try to keep clear of them."

They found the first dead guard shortly after that, the body sprawled half-under a bush. One of the infested, a woman—ragged and filthy as they all were. There was something strange about the corpse. Iain picked up a stick and poked at it. The matted hair fell away from the skull.

"Burned," Iain said.

The corpse's mouth was open, as if it were still straining to scream. Its eyelids lay slack over burst eyeballs, and fluid, half-cooked to whitish gobbets, gleamed on the gray cheeks. Clear fluid and clotted blood had run down the sides of its face from the nose.

"What did this?" she whispered.

"A neural fuser," Iain said. "A jump pilot's weapon. It can kill without punching holes through the skin of a ship."

"It's foul," she said, anguished.

"It's efficient," Iain said shortly. "Also highly restricted."

"Why would these things carry neural fusers?" She had read about them, back home—a snubbed gun that cooked human brain tissue to a curdled mass. "Nobody they killed that way would be any use to them."

"I know," Iain said, his brow wrinkled. "And why they would use them against—" He broke off, tugged her back to her feet. "Silently now."

Another body, of a man killed the same way. They moved deeper into the trees.

A dark shape hulked ahead of them, in a hollow inside a ring of trees. She wondered why Iain's tension did not ease. This was his ship. They had made it. Food, shelter, rest, escape . . . She started forward with new strength.

And Iain caught her, pulled her back into the shadow of the trees. "Wait here," he whispered. "Something is wrong. The dead guards—"

Iain moved silently to the ship's hatch, set his palm on it. The hatch irised open. She heard him take a sharp breath, shock. She could see that the inner lock was open as well. Brilliant light spilled out over the scorched ground.

A shadow moved into the doorway. A tall, elegant figure—orange hair—

"No," she whispered, and saw Iain sag against the rim of the door.

Rafael smiled down at Iain. "Little cousin," he said. "Welcome home."

TWENTY-TWO

Rafael stood at ease in the hatchway of his cousin's ship, refreshed by the cold rain, by the slash of the wind. By the fear in Iain's eyes—his cousin stood soaked and filthy, staring in shock, a crude stick dropping from one limp hand. Rafael looked down at him, masking the inward tremor of triumph. At last, death for Iain. *Savor this.*

Rafael flexed his fingers, so strong and sure now, and felt a ghost of pleasure. To prepare for this moment, he had brought no 'weave on this voyage, and there would be none to be found on this world. But now that the worst withdrawal was over, he did feel stronger, heavier, more present. More visible. No longer could he turn sideways and vanish, whirl away into the ripped chaos of storm-sky. He was anchored to life again, for a little while: for these final moments with Iain. The hunger still burned; every minute was still an acid eternity of longing. Though killing those inhuman *things* guarding Iain's ship had eased him, a little.

"Come in, cousin," Rafael said gently. "Come out of the rain."

Iain's eyes flicked sideways for an instant. Rafael noted it with pleasure. So there was someone else—maybe the woman? Or some other stray. Let her shiver outside, for now. Rafael stepped back as Iain dragged himself up and into the ship, on into the cargo compartment.

Rafael watched with pleasure as Iain saw what he had been busying himself with, during this long wait. The passenger shell lay askew, half-ripped from the bulkhead on which it had hung. Its delicate connections to the ship had been torn loose, its control circuitry smashed, leaking clear gel. The shell was useless—beyond repair, anywhere short of a major skyport or Nexus itself.

Iain let out a sharp breath, half a cry, then looked away, clearly fighting for control.

"You won't need it anyway." Rafael smiled.

"You—you are—" Iain broke off, but Rafael read rage in the tight line of the younger man's shoulders, his still hands. Rafael slipped a hand into his own shirt and found the smooth heavy silky grip of the neural fuser. Iain might snap, might attack him. He hoped so. The fuser was a bad death. And now he'd had practice—knew how it was best done.

"I barely had time to begin with the piloting compartment," Rafael said. "But now that you are here, there's no need of that."

Iain stared at him. "Why are you here?"

"I was sent," Rafael said calmly. "Your noble uncle is so concerned for your welfare! He sent me here to find you and rescue you. To bring you safely back to your proper home." Rafael smiled fondly down at him. "It's terribly sad that I won't in fact manage it. That you'll be obliterated with everyone else on this planet, in just a matter of hours."

He saw the blood drain from Iain's face. "Hours!"

"Only Fridric had the correct information," Rafael said comfortably. "Old Master sen Kaleb was most distressed, before the end, to find that he had sent you off with such a very narrow margin of safety."

"Then he is dead," Iain said in a voice without color.

"Alas, yes." Rafael smiled. "And while we are inquiring about mutual friends—that woman of yours? Is she here as well?"

"She's dead," Iain said.

That slight note of defiance betrayed him, of course; coddled as he had been, Iain had never learned proper subtlety. He had never had to learn it. "You're lying," Rafael said. "Badly. In fact you still hope to save her. And yet—I feel certain that she is listening—"

He swung around into the little air-lock space. But if she had been there, listening from outside the hatch, she had moved out of sight very quickly. He had hoped to drag her into the ship, put the two of them together, use them against each other—

The rain came down in sheets. But over there to the left—movement in the shadows, under that tree. He leaned out to see better.

Something hard and knobbed took him in the back of the head, and he fell from the hatch onto slippery burned needles from the trees. Pain split his skull, and his vision swam. He rubbed at his ear, and his hand came away bloody.

Enraged, he fought to his knees, rain pelting his face. He saw the woman raise the stick again and caught her wrist, squeezed with knowledgeable fingers. She screamed in agony and dropped the stick.

Then she flung her full weight onto him, knocking him flat onto his back in the mud. She screamed again, words this time. "Iain! Iain, go!"

This would not do. Because Iain just might go. Rafael rolled hard to the left and pinned her under him. "Yes, do leave," he called. "I'll take her away on *my* ship. Back to Nexus."

And, predictably, there was Iain. Like so many men, he could always be led around by his honor—by his loyalties. He was a good toy. It was a shame that he had to die.

Rafael pressed the neural fuser against the woman's cheek and looked up at Iain, who spread his hands in a gesture of surrender. Rafael rolled smoothly to his feet. "I see no reason to continue this in the cold," he said. "You, inside." With one hand he pushed the woman toward the hatch. Iain watched silently—as he must, with the black mouth of Rafael's neural fuser now pressed against his skull.

Rafael's hand tensed. He should simply finish it now. Time really was short. If he was to return to his own ship, make orbit before the first strike, he had very few minutes to spare for this. He had already waited almost too long for these two to appear.

But no. Now that it came to it, it would not be so satisfying to end Iain's life all in a moment. It was worth a little expenditure of time.

•　　•　　•

Linnea stood against the bulkhead at the rear of the passenger compartment, at the foot of the ruined shell that meant her death. She watched, sick with rage, as Rafael guided Iain into the ship, then shoved him hard, off-balance, to fall at her feet. Iain struggled upright as Rafael covered them both with the neural fuser.

"You *are* a bastard," Linnea said.

Rafael's eyes widened. The dim light shone on his peculiar orange hair, his high, pale forehead damp with rain, his cheeks faintly flushed with cold. "I should kill you for that," he said, his teeth showing white. "Remember. My *father* is the bastard. Now give me that silly club you're hiding." Rafael's blue eyes glinted, pellucid as ice. She tensed to strike. He moved as fast as before, and the club was in his hand. He flicked a glance at it and tossed it contemptuously out through the hatch. Linnea pressed her stinging hand against her side.

"Now," he said, facing them both squarely. Light glinted on the snub, silver shape of the neural fuser. The opening at its tip looked like the round sucker-mouth of an eel, the kind that swarmed over dead things under the sea.

Death opened beneath her. She only had to fall. Memories long buried crowded in on her. She could leap at him, and it would be over—she would be dead.

Or, stubborn as always, she could still hope. Bide. Try to help Iain.

Rafael's eyes on her were steady, the irises dilated so far they almost looked black. "I could simply keep us all here," he said in a remote voice. "We could all die together. An hour—two hours at most—and we could rest, all of us."

She had heard him earlier, telling Iain about obliteration, but she had not understood those words. Or these. She looked at Iain. "He's mad."

But she saw in Iain's eyes, astonishingly, confirmation.

"This world is ending," Rafael said. "It's all ending, you see. Those things, the Cold Minds, they've come to end us all. They won't succeed here, because this world is about to be destroyed."

Lost, she turned again to Iain. "It's true," he said quietly. "Asteroid bombardment. Soon."

"Futile," Rafael said. "One nest wiped out. But out there, out in the Hidden Worlds—we can't fight them. We can't even find them."

"My da couldn't fight the sea," Linnea said in a low voice. "But he tried."

Rafael smiled at her. "Why?"

"To make a life," she said. "To have hope, for a time."

"Hope!" His smile widened. "I'll make you clean of that at least. Once and for all."

"We *can* fight them, Rafael," Iain said. "You want to live. I know it. Free us, and perhaps you will."

"But I don't," Rafael said, "want to live, you see." He shrugged. "I really can't understand why you are so attached to life, cousin. Orphaned son of a bastard, penniless, exiled . . ."

Rage shook Linnea. She took a steadying breath and focused her anger inside herself, like compressing a coal to a diamond pinpoint of white heat. She clenched her fists and stared into Rafael's face, and as she did a wave of memory swept over and around and through her: Rafael's face over hers, the textures, smells, colors of pain and shame he had taught her. Grief filled her belly and chest, choking her. What he'd done to her. What he'd *really* done, the unhealed wound, made her believe she was nothing, her life was worth nothing. Made her ready to believe she might as well die here and now.

She felt her face twist into an animal snarl. Then she flung herself onto Rafael, reckless of the neural fuser. He staggered backward, locked in her hold. They both fell.

Something crackled close to her skull; she felt heat, heard Iain scream her name. But it missed her, it missed her, and Rafael went down on the ruins of the passenger shell. The neural fuser flew free of his hand, skittered forward into the piloting compartment. Under her Rafael strained, strained, his blue eyes wide, his mouth wide open as if to scream, but no sound came. He had stopped struggling against her. She felt heat, wetness against her chest, pulled back—only then saw it. The tip of a sharp shard of split metal from the shattered box, pushing up from his blood-soaked shirt.

Iain stood in the hatchway between the two compartments. "Roll him out," he said, weariness heavy in his voice. "We must leave at once. It may already be too late."

Between the two of them they dragged Rafael off the metal shard that had stabbed through his belly. "He's still alive," she said in revulsion.

"Not for long," Iain said. Together they carried him to the hatch, shoved him out, and Iain hit a control with his fist. The hatch irised shut. For the first time in hours, days, the rain, the wind fell silent. "We must prepare for launch," Iain said over his shoulder, moving into the piloting compartment.

"How?" Linnea looked at the ruins of the cargo compartment. "The passenger shell isn't useable. Can we find Rafael's ship?"

"No time," Iain said. He had opened the pilot's shell, was studying it, his hands moving surely to check connections, wires, controls. "His ship isn't keyed to me in any case—it would take days to adapt it well enough that I could pilot it in a jump. And we don't have days."

"I can't survive a jump with no shell."

"No. Even this takeoff might kill you." Iain closed the pilot's shell. "There is an auxiliary—makeshift, not meant for a long jump, but it will have to do. It is not so comfortable as the passenger shell. But it will keep you alive during the jump. Come now, quickly."

He was already kneeling against a bulkhead. His palm pressed against it and it swung open. "It's just a mat," Iain said, "with minimal connections." He laid it out on the floor, clamped it in place. "Meant for an instructor, or a student, on a short training run." Flaps of black cloth lay open on either side. "I'll close it over you when you are connected. Get ready. Hurry."

She moved to undress. Iain was already standing by the pilot's shell, stripping off his ragged tunic and trousers, then starting to connect himself to the ship. Linnea recognized the waste tubes, the food tubes, from her previous voyages. But there were other links as well—wires to Iain's wrists, his temples. They seemed to stick without anything holding them, snaking smoothly into Iain's flesh. The sight of them made Linnea feel queasy.

"I will connect you in the same way," Iain said. "Then you can see what I see before the jump, and we can communicate even in otherspace. And you will hear the ship."

"But I'll see nothing there," she said.

"Of course," Iain said. "No one without the gift can perceive anything in otherspace. But the link to your brain will let me speak to you." He looked seriously at her. "There is some risk. Your brain is unaccustomed. And I don't know how a passenger, an outsider, will manage a long jump with only a voice link. But we have no choice."

Linnea lay down on the mat, lay still as Iain prepared her. The tubes were much the same, but there was no blinding full-face mask, just a small oxygen cup over her nose and mouth. He gave her an injection: "For nausea. We will be in free fall for a time before the jump."

Iain reached out to the collection of tubes that had just attached themselves to the inside of her elbow, selected one, and tugged it loose, then twisted the fitting where it had been attached. "I've disconnected the medication tube."

She frowned up at him. "Why?"

"If the ship senses you've panicked, it will medicate you. That will cut you off from our connection. I don't know what it might do to your mind, to be cut off like that for any length of time. Some people die."

"I'll be all right," Linnea said.

Iain shook his head. "You don't understand about otherspace. We don't usually brief passengers completely. It only frightens them. The fact is, your senses can't function there."

"But on the other flights I've taken—"

"You believed you could feel your body, you believed you heard sounds, smelled the air supply, sensed heat and cold. That kept you oriented. But it was just a simspace recording."

Linnea took a steadying breath. "Then what is it like? Really?"

His eyes were stern. "You feel *nothing*. No sensory

input of any kind. You're lost—nothing to grasp, nothing to
orient yourself to. Not even your own body. Most people
panic. Some become psychotic—that's what the interface
is for, so that no one spends more than a few moments
without input. But this mat has no interface—it is meant
for pilots, or at least students with the gift. Who can sense
otherspace."

She swallowed hard.

Iain reached down and touched her hand. "Be strong,"
he said. He folded the cloth sides of the mat over her body,
sealed them shut. They shrank against her body, holding
her tightly. He snugged a strap over her head that held it
rigid, cradled in foam.

Then he bent over her again, and something that felt wet
and cold touched her right temple. Icy cold bloomed in her
flesh; something thin and icy slithered *inside* her head. She
fought to keep her panicked breathing under control.

"Close your eyes," Iain said, his voice calm, abstracted.
"Do you see a pattern?"

"I see something," she said. "A silver cube, spinning."

"Good. Do you hear it?"

She listened. *Whoop whoop whoop*, low and hollow as
the cube spun. "Yes," she said.

"Good," Iain said again, and the cube vanished. "Acceleration will be hard. Your mat is meant for training runs de-
parting from Dock, already in orbit. That is far less rough
than a launch from a planetary surface. And we must accel-
erate at the limit of safety if we are to evade the block-
aders. Though they should be pulling away into higher
orbits by now."

A heavy blow struck the outside of the ship's entrance
hatch. Another. Not Rafael; it could not be Rafael—Linnea

tried to turn her head to look, but could not. "Hold on," Iain said desperately, and vanished into his shell, which closed around him.

She felt the engines leap to life. The blows on the hatch continued, one, two, three more, until the sound of the engines rose to a thin shriek.

Something pressed her down, down into the soft padding, until she felt the hard floor beneath it. She was drowning, crushed by the pressure, and she could not draw breath to scream. The padding was rock-hard under her. She couldn't breathe. It was like her old bad dreams. Da's last moments in the storm-darkness, in the icy waves. Losing the line, choking on salt water, plunging down. Each time a longer struggle, stiff-limbed and numb, to the surface again. Each time a briefer rise into storm-roar, into air that was half blown spray, cold waves slapping him down, filling his nose and mouth. No line, no ship, no help. In the nightmare she had felt the moment when her father could not rise again. She had felt him drifting down and down. She had known, along with him, that the next breath—the next breath he could not keep from taking—would fill his burning lungs with water. And below him was only darkness, and the slow cold current drawing him offshore, forever.

Rafael heard the launch from a strange, strange distance. His pain, so white, so shrill, had eased. Someone was touching him, cradling him, carrying him—he could not see, the rain half blinded him, but there went the spark of Iain's ship, brilliant through the trees, fading. He could not care. He was dying. He was sure he was dying. He cried out for his ship, for the refuge of his piloting shell. His ship could heal him. But they must hurry, hurry. . . .

"Hurry," he gasped, but the people—the things carrying him—only slowed. A face hovered over his, eyes a pale shimmer of light, mouth drooling black. A thick, slow voice spoke. "Why?"

He told them.

TWENTY-THREE

Iain's strained voice spoke in Linnea's ear. "We're away. It will be rough for a while. If you want to see where we are, close your eyes."

Linnea had already noticed that her vision was oddly blurred, moving shapes she could not interpret. She closed her eyes and gasped. She was in midair, rising, rising, below them trees dwindling to a rough carpet, over there the city they had escaped—she could see in any direction to which she turned her thoughts. The ship—the ship must be making these images in her brain.

Clouds flicked past, one layer, two, and still they rose through fog glowing the color of sulfur. Then out into the clear. Sinking away below, behind, the heaped clouds burned amber and gold; above, stars lay scattered along the arch of the deepening blue sky. Directly above at first, then gradually slipping away to one side, was the immense face of the gas giant Odin, its brown and yellow and white bands sharply detailed.

Still held flat by the acceleration, she felt no fear, but looked all around her while she could. The shipmind had marked two of the stars low above the horizon with flashing red circles; as she watched, a third appeared. "Those marked stars are the asteroids," Iain's voice said. "The red means they are on a collision course."

"With us?"

"We are not yet at escape velocity," Iain said. "To the shipmind, we're still part of Freija."

More lights, green this time, appeared between her and the stars. These seemed to be crawling along the sky. "Blockade ships," Iain said. "They cannot reach us in time."

Linnea thought it sounded more like a prayer than a promise. "What can they do to us?"

"Missiles," Iain said. "Interceptors. At a programmed range they explode. The EM pulse will de-spin the jump engines, scramble them beyond repair. Then they come and collect us."

Now she saw the broad curve of Freija, cutting a brilliant arc against the complete black of space. The stars looked oddly uniform, and little tags floated next to them. She decided the ship must be putting them there.

She was getting more air now—perhaps the acceleration was less, perhaps the ship was helping her breathe. Freija continued to fall away below. For a moment the whorls of rain clouds looked like the inside of a bowl, hollowed away from her; then with a strange mental *pop* she saw that it was a sphere, a globe. A world. Dwindling as she watched. The three asteroid markers faded from red to orange, yellow, green. No more threat. No more threat to this ship.

And as she watched, the first asteroid struck. Just past the broad curve of the horizon. A black-shielded flash. "Oh!" she cried.

"Too bright," Iain's voice said. "The shipmind blocked it. It would have burned out our optic nerves."

Then she saw it, rising above the limb of Freija: a fireball, white fading to gold, to orange. Its silence, its eerie slowness mesmerized her.

"That was not far from the populated lands," Iain's voice said flatly. "They are all dead."

"And two more to come," she said. Her heart was numb. Those she had come to know had been dead, or worse than dead, before the strike; but this had killed everything, the trees, the rivers, the seas—when it was done, there would be nothing down there but a roiling cloud of dust and vapor that would hang in the air for centuries.

It was over.

Rafael—this at least she could hold to—Rafael was dead.

At that moment the weight lifted away from her chest, and she was floating, floating—falling— She whimpered. The cloth cocoon that held her against the mat was not enough to make her feel safe.

"Breathe evenly," Iain said. She sensed his distraction, preparing for the jump. "Trust the drug. It will stop any nausea. Then in the jump you will no longer feel free fall."

Not a perfect drug. Her mouth flooded with saliva. She didn't dare speak.

"Hold on," Iain said again. "We're about to jump."

Now she had to speak. "Jump. For Santandru?"

His voice sounded flat in her mind. "No. We need repairs that can't be done there. We're headed for Prairie—it's remote from Nexus, but there's a decent skyport."

"Santandru next, then," she said.

He did not answer.

F ree fall. The darkness of space embraced Iain. Darkness soothed his eyes like cool water. His ship held him, a tender brother, a familiar silence. He willed his hands to stop trembling, willed himself to look back at Freija one more time through the ship's eyes. At that instant he saw another impact, on the side facing him this time, flicker of a black shield and then stark blue-white, white, yellow, hot orange, at the center of a tight rippled bull's-eye of shock waves. If he looked closely he could almost see that they were moving, even from this distance.

No time for that now. He forced himself to follow the flow of projection and prediction the shipmind streamed at him. Optimum insertion for one Prairie hyperdesic after another approached, peaked, waned.

Now that it came to it, he was afraid. Rafael had defiled Iain's ship, broken it—

Rafael was dead.

Darkness called to Iain.

He jumped.

L innea felt the jump, felt the moment when her senses vanished. One moment she was herself, Linnea, a woman, bruised and tired—hungry, thirsty, the catheter aching. Her hair prickled her neck, and she felt the cold tracks that tears of fright had made down the sides of her head. Then with a flash and a jerk she was nothing. *Iain*, she called, but she could not hear herself, could not feel herself speak.

Iain did not answer.

I ain felt safe in that darkness. No one could find him. No one could follow him. This was *his* darkness, *his* silence. Here he was alone. Here, still, he was master.

He rested, waiting for the smooth blackness to shift, coalesce, take nameless and unnameable shape. Waiting for the silence to lift away, waiting for the complex shimmer of sound that was not music, not voice, that was the sound of the uncreated. His father felt very near. As if he were waiting. Calling.

Blackness, blackness, calling him down. Iain twisted in his shell. Something was wrong. . . .

F or Linnea, time was like crystal, and she was caught in it, like the Old Earth butterfly in a plastic weight that Father Haveloe treasured.

She called out to Iain again, and still he did not answer. She felt cold. "Ship—is this jump on course?"

"No hyperdesic has yet been confirmed," the shipmind said, in its calm, old man's voice.

"What does Iain say?" she demanded.

"The Pilot's interface is not at optimum function. Tampering may have occurred." The voice sounded unruffled. "The Pilot's physical readings indicate that he is agitated. He may be in pain."

Iain, in pain. Her mind moved slowly. The only effect of fear she could still feel. "Can't you stop us?"

"This system does not control," the shipmind said.

"Can't you get us back into normal space? It doesn't matter where."

"This system does not control," it said again. Then, almost sounding reluctant, "This system has no data. There is no hyperdesic. There are no jump parameters."

"We're lost," she said. And this time, the shipmind said nothing.

Linnea fought for calm. Iain had said there would be a link between them. Well, then she had to use it. Try to reach him.

But how?

The shipmind spoke calmly in her ear. "You are agitated. Please breathe normally. Please lie still. You are being sedated. You will feel calmer soon. You will sleep soon."

"Be quiet," she said angrily.

"Please lie still. Your dosage is being increased."

She could not tell if she was lying still. Her body was gone.

Darkness. No breath, no body, no voice, no sound. She was alone.

I ain found himself swimming in otherspace. Wrongness still twisted his mind. Time had fallen away from him, drifted away. Memories drifted away. He was gathering them up, one by one, and tossing them off into bright chaos. Sometimes chaos coalesced into an image from one of the memories, and he would weep a little, or laugh a little, and gather up the image and toss it away again.

It was all the wrong shape, all wrong. His ship was not his ship; this was not his place, his otherspace. It had a scent he knew, and hated.

He could not grasp the pattern. He could not control. It did not matter. Death would come, and free him. Like his father. Here their drifting patterns might meet, mesh, know each other. Then Iain could say, *I'm sorry for what I said the last time I saw you—I understand now. I know why you died. . . .*

Far distant, the shipmind was saying something, over and over. Part of it was "—lock in a hyperdesic—"

No matter. Iain closed the doors of his mind, and flew onward through not-darkness, alone.

L innea did not, could not know how much time had passed. Always she strained to sense something, anything—some faint contact with Iain.

Nothing.

Maybe this was death. Without senses, without even breath and heartbeat, maybe a human mind could sense no time—maybe a second, the last second of life, would never end, and she would float here for all time. . . .

No. She pushed the fear away firmly. Jump pilots faced this nothingness. They chose to face it. They found their way through it. Maybe they did have some magical inborn ability she didn't have; but they were human beings, they had brains like hers. What they could do so easily, she could at least try.

Here she could not calm herself with breathing as Iain

had taught her, all those months ago on Nexus. But she could pray, and count the prayers, and imagine watching the beads slip through Ma's fingers, as she'd done when she was little. By the last bead her mind was quiet, her heart at peace. Now she could listen properly.

It began as a feeling of flowing. Like a river flowing past her. She was an island, a stone in the night river. No sound, no light, but motion. She could have pointed in the direction it was coming from, if she'd had hands. She could not touch it or change it, but it was there.

The feeling grew and changed. She almost saw something now. Lights, dull lights glowing through fog, only she knew they could not be lights.

She sensed masses, forms—shapes—the bigger they were, the farther away they were— No. There wasn't any rule to it. And the sound, it wasn't like the wind at all, or like music, except that it was the size of the wind, strong and vast.

She tried again to call out for Iain. But she still had no voice.

Lay yourself open, she told herself. *Listen.*

She thought about Iain. Not the man she had lost. The man she was seeking, here in this madness. She thought about Iain in her arms, broken by grief for his father. She knew that grief, she had tasted it then, and now it was as if she felt it—

She *did* feel it.

He was there—he was out there, afraid and lost and running away. He thought he was alone. She stretched out again.

Something was wrong. She was losing him. She could feel his fear, his shame. But it was fading.

She fought desperately to think of something that might pull him back, toward life, toward her. The ship could not keep their bodies alive forever.

Iain's wounded mind revolved on itself. The memories kept coming back, and back again. Paolo, again—Paolo at the height of his powers, Paolo the honored teacher and father. But that only made it worse. The lie, the lie, like a blade turning in a wound, like heat on burned flesh.

He remembered Mekael, lost Mekael, his generous spirit gone.

He remembered—with black salt revulsion he remembered Rafael, that perfect face shadowed, darkly smiling, the fine hand clawed, cupped, to touch—to take—

Rafael just now, limp, mouth hanging slack, blue eyes half-lidded, staring blankly in death—

He forced that memory back, but another he could not. His uncle Fridric. Fridric's hand cradling the wine cup as he toasted his brother's death.

Iain should have killed him then. With the last of his strength, he should have killed him. Crushed his skull, or ground his neck around until his spine snapped. It would have been worth it, to die doing that. But he had failed there as well, and now it was too late. Always too late.

He could amend none of it, pay for none of it.

He coursed onward alone, toward emptiness.

Linnea felt weak, unfocused. Perhaps the tubes no longer fed her, their supply of food and fluids gone.

Without food, without water she might well be weak.
Maybe unconscious soon. Time was running out.

She forced herself to think about Iain. He was young,
like her. He'd lost his da, like her. But unlike her, he had
nothing left that he cared about. His proud promises on
Freija—she had known even then that his heart was not in
them, not yet.

She had Marra and the children to fight for. He had no
one.

Except her.

Patiently, she reached out again.

I ain could not quiet his mind. Memory kept returning—
memory held him back from the last step of his escape.
It was as if someone else were there with him in otherspace, pursuing him, calling to him. But that was impossible. No other jump pilot was here. And Paolo, if Paolo
were here, would not be calling Iain back. Paolo would be
ahead of him, calling him on.

Now he was seeing *her* again, Linnea, the one whose
life he had destroyed. Was destroying. He had known her
for so short a time.

And yet . . .

The memories deepened, strengthened, grew more detailed. Just flashes at first. Linnea's rare slow smile uncon-
sciously lighting her face. Linnea standing in his garden,
upright in a plain white dress, her dark eyes taking in the
light of the flowers all around her.

Linnea in the stormlight that one morning, her face still
as she turned to look at him. He had wanted her to smile,
but she had not. That was the morning after he had turned

to her in his own need, and used her. Now the memory came, striding, demanding, and he could not turn it away. Linnea . . .

Linnea in Iain's bed, astride him, a gleam of sweat on her body in the warm light of the candles as she moved, his hands slippery with sweat where they gripped her hips. Her hands pressed to the bed near his shoulders, not touching him. Her face looking aside, looking away, closed, a gleam of dark eyes half-closed, a gleam of tears.

He had not known her. He had used her. She had come to him, even at the risk of her life, because of a promise. Words bound her, and she didn't seem to care whether they bound anyone else. She came to him. She had trusted him.

He could not betray her.

Linnea gasped as light and pain and pressure burst in against her, cold metal against her body, against her cheek, wetness under her, and where the tubes had pulled loose, pain, pain, *pain*. Her heartbeat thundered in her ears, her breath roared in her throat. Iain's shell, still closed, loomed beside her, above her. She tried to move. She tried to speak.

PAIN.

She fainted.

Iain emerged from his shell dizzy and disoriented, with a headache that throbbed with his heartbeat. Unsteady in the weak grip of the pseudograv field, he staggered to the emergency case, held the inhaler to his face, and pressed the code for a drug that would ease his pain and clear his head. Two breaths, three, and the pain receded. His vision cleared. He set down the inhaler and turned around. The light was dim, as always, and his piloting shell blocked his view of the instructor's mat where Linnea lay. She might be asleep, but he could start disconnecting—

Then his heart froze, heavy in his chest. Something lay on the floor beyond his shell, just visible in faint bluish light. Something that could not be there. A naked foot, ashen, cold-looking.

Linnea lay twisted on the floor, mostly in shadow. He ordered the lights up, went to her, and knelt stiffly beside her. Her skin was drained of color, her lips cracked, blue. She had a sunken, quiet look. Gone.

He bowed his head, almost welcoming the half-dulled pain that surged with the motion. Near the source of Linnea's nutrient and water supply, a red light flashed steadily. Empty. How long? Had she had a seizure in otherspace? Died there, lost and afraid— He touched her cheek with a shaking hand.

Then pressed his palm hard against her flesh.

It wasn't cold—it was burning hot.

And he felt something, the barest whisper of breath against his wrist. He touched the side of her neck. A fluttering there. She was still alive. Somehow. For now.

She'd be half-starved. On the edge of hypoxia. In shock. With unsteady hands he connected a drug-and-nutrient line from the pilot shell to the inside of Linnea's wrist, and watched with relief as it began to supply her weakened body with water, glucose, drugs for pain and fever. Then he spread out a clean robe and moved her gently onto it, covering her with another.

Her fever was beginning to drop. How far to a port? He

went to his panel. They had been twenty-five subjective days in otherspace. His initial normal-space vector meant they were somewhere in the direction of Prairie. But how far?

The ship showed him, and his shoulders sagged in relief. They'd overshot, but not badly.

Iain ate some soup and took another drug for the headache. He had to run diagnostics on the interface in his shell. Rafael had done something—perhaps he had simply begun to make the changes that would make it compatible with himself. Perhaps that was Rafael's, the insanity that had taken Iain—the interface forcing his mind into Rafael's pattern.

What he had done—what he had almost done . . . He sat beside Linnea on the floor, leaning against the bulkhead, and watched her sleep. She still looked gray-skinned and haggard. But he had learned by now to see more in that face. Her determination, her honesty, the unflagging hopefulness that had once been hers. Gone now, ruined. . . .

Weary, he slept.

Linnea woke slowly. She was warm, and the pain in her head was gone. Her body was real again. Small aches and pains gave proof of reality. And there was her shaken and unsteady soul, too real, too painful to be part of any dream.

Then someone touched her hair lightly and spoke. "You're awake."

Iain. She blinked up at him, wondering if it had been a nightmare. The ship lost, out of control, herself lost in some other place— No. It had been real. She *had* been in otherspace.

She coughed, tasting rust. "Found you," she croaked.

"Found—me?" He looked perplexed.

"Called you back," she said. "In otherspace."

"Your voice, through the interface." He smiled down at her. "It saved us."

"I *saw* you," she said stubbornly. "Felt you."

"You couldn't have," he said. "It was a dream. Remember, we were in otherspace."

"I saw so many lights," she said dreamily. "And sounds. And—you. You were running away. Your father. You were thinking about your father."

He sat very still. "You can't know that. You could not have sensed it, or linked to me in that way. That is a jump pilot's skill. You were dreaming."

"I saw you," she said stubbornly. She felt dizzy, sick.

"You're a woman," Iain said. He had taken her hand, was rubbing it soothingly. "You cannot have the piloting gift. And even a man who did—without training, he could not have done what you say."

She only looked at him.

He frowned. Then, reluctantly—"What did you . . . see?"

"Everything." She could not keep from smiling, though her eyes had filled with tears. "There is no place more beautiful."

"No place," he echoed. And she saw belief dawning in his eyes. "You—*you* have the gift." He set his hand on her forehead, his face strange with astonishment and—loss? "You are a pilot."

TWENTY-FOUR

Iain did not make the final short jump for Prairie for more than a day—not until he was sure that his piloting shell was clean of Rafael's changes and that Linnea had recovered completely. On the jump, he tried to sense her presence, but in those few subjective hours he could find no trace of her. "Don't be troubled," he told her as he set up his approach to Prairie's orbital dock. "It takes time and practice to reach out with intention and find otherspace. You'll learn."

She looked away. He felt another flash of annoyance at her lack of interest in the world that was now open to her. It couldn't be her illness, as he had thought at first. Her strength seemed to have returned. During the approach she had showered in his ship's small refresher closet. Now she wore some of his spare clothing, plain trousers and a loose shirt, ship's wear. Her own clothing, a gray prison dress from Nexus, had been beyond salvage.

"We'll begin your training on the next jump," Iain said. "After the repairs."

She looked at him with something like surprise in her eyes. "Training?"

Didn't she understand? If he could face this, could accept her as a potential pilot, why couldn't she? "You have the piloting gift," he said. "You must be taught to use it." Now, after all, she could be so much more than she had ever been before, so much more than she would ever have imagined becoming.

More than *he* had ever thought she could become.

He glanced at his status board. "Best strap down for docking," he said. She did not ask to be connected to the ship so she could see the procedure—odd, but perhaps she was still becoming accustomed to the whole idea. Her whole future, changed. He should be more patient with her. She was not like Iain; she had not dreamed all her life of being chosen as a pilot, worked unceasingly to develop her talent.

Yet surely she must understand what a wonder it was. He would help her understand it.

Prairie's main skyport, an orbital dock, looked nothing like its counterpart above Nexus. This was a typical public commercial port, a small city contained in an orbital habitat: a huge cylinder surrounded by centuries of irregular attachments, ramifications, fueling stations, tethered living quarters, waste dumps, heat dumps. . . .

Though no word could have come yet from Freija—his, after all, was the first ship to jump here from there after the destruction—there had been ample time for news of his escape from Nexus to reach Prairie. Iain felt a twinge of nervousness as he submitted his ship's call sign and registration number to Docking Control.

Control said nothing in response, and directed him to the jumpship berthing area, well apart from the docks for the planetary shuttles and the spidery, powerful barges that served the orbital factories. As Iain guided his ship into place, he noted with relief that only two other jumpships were in at the moment. He would have fewer old acquaintances to avoid.

Not that their paths would cross. He would stay well away from the Pilot Masters' transit facilities here, and he knew from long experience—from his own experience—that men of the Line would have little interest in mingling with nonpilots in the public sections of the station. "We'll stay at this port for the moment," he told Linnea, as the docking clamps clanked into place. "We'll be close to the ship in case we need to leave quickly. And this is where the repair facilities are." He itched to get on with things—to make his ship whole again, and clean.

But the hatch stayed stubbornly sealed, even after the station's air-lock tube had attached itself and checked out as safe.

"Control," Iain said, "what's going on?"

"Remain there," the voice—a woman's—told him. "Inspection is required."

"Of a Line jumpship!" He did not have to work to put outrage into his voice.

There was no answer.

Linnea had unstrapped as soon as the port's pseudograv cut in, and she stood, looking a little uncertain, in the doorway to the cargo compartment. "They know who you are," she said.

"I can see that," Iain said. "The question is, who told them—Fridric, or Master sen Kaleb?"

"If you don't have credit through Nexus, how are you going to pay for the repairs?" she asked.

He concentrated on the control board, locking it down, placing it under palm seal. "I have some resources," he said, conscious of his own reluctance to admit that the jewels and other portable treasures in his ship's vault were not his own—had been a gift, a last gift, from Master sen Kaleb. "We have enough to pay for repairs and fuel, and to keep us for some time beyond that."

She only nodded. He wondered again at her remoteness.

The inspector kept them waiting. When he finally arrived—thin, balding, precisely uniformed in deep blue, a little too brightly embellished with braid—he eyed Iain's documents with suspicion and spoke coldly. When Linnea told him her papers had been lost, he looked disgusted. "Perhaps at home on—Sintedru?—slapdash is sufficient," he said. "But this, I will remind you, is *Prairie*. We take pride in good order on Prairie."

Linnea lifted an eyebrow. "And manners? Do you value manners on Prairie?"

Iain looked away, wincing. And as he expected, the inspection that followed was as exhaustive, officious, and slow as the man could make it. The damaged passenger shell, though cleaned of all traces of blood, still drew the inspector's strong disapproval. "I can't permit you to depart with a passenger aboard until that is in good order."

"Excellent," Iain said tightly. "That's why we're here. All pilots know about the superb quality of your repair facilities."

It still was not enough, in the end, to get them the freedom of the port. "I'm to escort you to the portmaster," the inspector said with obvious pleasure. "Bring your documents. The woman is to stay aboard, under seal."

Iain went, as he must, though he sensed, and shared, Linnea's unease. The portmaster was a cool-eyed, silver-haired woman, whose small but tidy office overlooked the shuttle refueling facility. She briefly slid the crystal containing Iain's credentials into her hand viewer, then pulled it out and handed it back. "I don't even know what to call you," she said. "Mr. sen Paolo, I suppose." Her glance took in Iain's simple but impeccable civilian clothing, his loose dark hair. Her voice sharpened. "And your—companion, Miss Kiaho. A woman from Santandru, I believe? Whose papers have been lost. You'll be taking her home, I imagine?"

"That has not been decided," Iain said.

The portmaster regarded him searchingly. "Mr. sen Paolo, I'm sorry to tell you that all ports have been alerted that we must not honor your credit. The repairs you have requested cannot be made without full payment in advance, in cash."

"I will pay it," Iain said.

"It's a considerable sum—"

"I will pay it," he said again, his hands tight on the arms of his chair. "I must ask. Have you received any communication from Dockmaster Adan sen Kaleb? He was—a family friend."

The portmaster's expression did not alter. "I was grieved, several months ago, to receive a bulletin from Nexus, saying that the Dockmaster had died. Of old age, I believe. He was a worthy colleague, and most helpful to our efforts to improve our facility here."

"Dockmaster sen Kaleb did not die of old age," Iain said. Even now he could not keep his voice steady. "He was murdered."

For the first time her expression changed, to a slight frown. "Murdered? Who would do such a thing? And on Nexus!"

He realized that he could not explain that in any way she would accept. She would know in a matter of days what was at stake; he had promised to reveal the truth, which meant a widecast commnet message, and it would have to come from here. "Events on Nexus are—in flux," he finally said.

"'In flux,'" she said. "Interesting." Her eyes narrowed. "I should tell you that in the same bulletin, I received notice of your dismissal from the Line, and your escape from custody."

"Not everything is quite as it appears," Iain said.

"I would never claim that it was," she said in a dry voice. "But the bulletin made clear that you are unstable, and that you have been making paranoid accusations against the Line Council and others."

"Do I seem paranoid?" Iain folded his hands calmly. "Master sen Kaleb told me to greet you personally, Portmaster. He said I could trust you."

"Master sen Kaleb knew that I am in no position to trust, where it endangers the port I manage," she said. "The Pilot Masters could do great harm to this facility, and to the flow of trade revenue, if they wished. Dockmaster sen Kaleb would not ask me to take such a risk in order to do him a personal favor."

"He would in this case," Iain said. "His message must have at least hinted that this is an important matter. Not just to me, or to him, but to all of the Hidden Worlds. To Prairie as well."

She looked down at her hands but did not reply.

"All I ask is the repairs, for which I will pay," Iain said. "As well as a chance to rest here while they are carried out. Then we'll be on our way."

She studied him for a long time, then nodded slightly. "I did receive a message from the Dockmaster, sent before his death," she said. "He gave me your name, and your ship's code, and he urged me to help you to the extent that I find prudent."

Iain waited.

After a moment she nodded again. "I believe I can allow the repairs. They'll proceed as soon as payment is confirmed. However, I cannot permit either of you to leave this facility to go planetside."

"All we want," Iain said, "is rest."

"The Highview Hostel, starside level eight, is clean and cheap," she said. "You'll draw little attention there."

I ain had never stayed in a place like the hostel: cramped, plain, lacking the simplest comforts. The Pilot Masters kept lavish private transit accommodations in ports such as these, and in his occasional forays into sightseeing or pleasure travel on the various worlds, there had never been any need to forgo the same level of luxury.

Yet their small windowless room was clean, as promised, and the one bed comfortable enough in the half-standard pseudograv. When Iain returned from the brief, tepid shower allowed once a day with the room, Linnea was already deeply asleep, curled with her back to his side of the bed. He sealed the room's door, then climbed wearily into the bed and fell asleep at once.

He woke, disoriented, sometime in the night—the time numbers glowing softly red in the ceiling conveyed nothing to him. The bed beside him was empty. Perhaps Linnea had needed the toilet, three doors down the passageway. But no, the door of the room was still sealed from the inside.

In the dimness he almost missed seeing her. She lay huddled on the thinly carpeted deck beside the bed, her arms and legs pulled close to herself. She had fallen out. Or— He sighed and pulled the coverlet off the bed, settled it softly around her. Under its warmth she uncurled a little, and her sleeping expression softened.

He did not know how he could convey to her the strange slow change that had come over his heart since he found her on Freija—the certainty that he was bound to her, and that in that binding was the first real freedom he had ever known. And it seemed unlikely that he would ever be able to tell her. Not when she shrank from him, was afraid of his touch. It would not be fair to burden her.

He wondered bleakly if she would ever feel safe again. Would ever trust him, or anyone, again.

He did not sleep again that night, but sat up thinking, and keeping watch. He wished they were safe in his ship, sealed in beyond anyone's reach with quick escape at hand. As soon as the repairs were complete, he resolved, they would move back aboard. The ship could offer only cramped quarters, but they would be safe there.

All around, the life of the skyport continued: the heavy vibration of a barge unloading a couple of levels down, a man and a woman laughing as they passed along the corridor outside the room, the hiss and rattle of water pipes.

Outside their ship, places like this would now be their only refuge, their only rest. At this moment it seemed a grim future.

I ain went out before Linnea woke and bought bread, smoked fish, and two bulbs of what passed for coffee on the station. When he returned she was fully dressed, perched tensely on the edge of the bed, the only place to sit. He handed her one of the bulbs, opened the bag of food, and set it beside her. "Did you sleep well?"

She glanced up at him nervously. "Later on I did." She looked away. "Iain—last night—"

"Don't worry," he said. "I won't touch you unless you wish it."

"I can't," she said, her knuckles white around the bulb of coffee. "I can't, yet. It's too soon, and—what happened, what he did was so—" She broke off.

He waited for her to go on, then said, "It's all right, Linnea."

She blinked hard, as if to keep back tears. "And what if I can never let you touch me—what if it never happens again?"

His heart ached for her. "Then it never happens," he said. "Eat. It's best if we think only about today. Tomorrow will keep."

She tore off a piece of the brown bread, set a piece of smoked fish on it, then sat holding it. "I keep dreaming about—about home."

"Naturally." Iain sat down beside her and took a piece of bread for himself. "You miss your family."

"I keep dreaming about those *things*, coming to Santandru," she said, her voice low and trembling. "Coming to my sister's house. Touching them. Touching the children."

"We'll fight them," Iain said. "We won't let your home be hurt."

She sat rigid, staring down at her bread and fish. "How do we know they aren't on Santandru already?"

Iain sighed. There was no answer to that. "We'll fight them," he said again. "Once you're a trained pilot yourself, we—"

"Stop," she said, and he heard desperation in her voice. "Stop talking about that."

"It's what we must do," he said.

"I know it is," she said unsteadily. "I saw more than you, of what they did to Freija. To the people there. But—" Tears stood in her eyes. "Iain, I want to go home. I want to see Marra, see that she's safe. I'm afraid to trust to—this dream of yours when all the time those *things* could be spreading on my world. My home."

Just as he'd expected. Iain shook his head. "I'm sorry," he said. "But we can't do anything about that now. Santandru is months from anywhere. We don't dare take that much time just to take you home—to go so far. It doesn't serve our purpose. There aren't enough people on Santandru for us to be sure of finding new pilots, and there's no orbital port for training runs."

"I know that," she said. "But don't you see? What I know doesn't change how I feel. I'm not a pilot yet. I may never be, not a real one. It won't hurt your plans, to take me home first. A few months' travel." He heard the stubborn certainty in her voice.

He stood up, walked to the door, set his hand on it. "If you go to Santandru, you will walk into Fridric's hands," he said. "That is where his men are waiting for us. I'm certain of it. That's where they know you most want to go. Think, Linnea! Fridric had you for so long. Do you think your keepers don't know every dream you had in that time? Do you think they don't know what you want most right now?"

"So you will not take me home." Her voice shook.

"I need you with me," he said. "You are Fridric's best weapon against me. If he recaptures you—"

"If he does, there's no reason you should care," she said. "He's wrong about me. I'm no use to you."

"It's not a matter of use," he began.

But she went on as if he had not spoken. "If you take me home, I'll ask Asper Cogorth to give you the proof of your ancestry, and you can use *that* as a weapon against your uncle. More use than me. And once that's off Santandru, my family will be safe. We can live in peace."

Iain's hand clenched into a fist against the closed door. "None of us will live in peace," he said. "Not for a long time. You saw it yourself! On Freija, you saw what we are fighting. You know how desperately we need pilots. Don't you understand what it means that *you* are a pilot?"

She was shaking her head stubbornly.

"You do know," he said. "It means that you have a duty to more than your sister, Linnea!"

Her eyes flashed. "You have no right to define my duty."

"You have no right to deny your duty," he said. "I know you were not brought up with any idea of obligation, of honor—"

She leaped to her feet. "You dare to say that!"

"—because if you had been, you would be able to understand me!"

Her face was dark with rage. "So my family, my people are so much lower than yours? We don't have your noble ideals? Well, we don't lie to ourselves, either, not the way you do. The way your father did. You are no better than anyone born to Santandru. You are one of *us*, Pilot Master sen Paolo!"

He turned away from her, opened the door with a blow from his fist, and left her there.

Around midmorning, when it was clear that Iain would not return, Linnea took a little of the money he had left on the table by the bed and went exploring. It kept her from wondering whether Iain had simply taken his ship and left her here. Whether the money she had would be enough for passage home, if it had to be.

It kept her from wondering why the thought that she would never see him again ached in her chest.

She found a transit lounge that had a viewport overlooking the world called Prairie: a green-and-brown globe ribboned with shallow, silvery seas. Explanations of what she was seeing crawled past on a screen below the viewport. She watched as Prairie's big moon edged slowly out from behind the planet. It looked like pictures of Old Earth's moon, gray and peppered with craters.

Prairie looked warm, serene, safe. But she remembered the death of Freija.

No. She would not think of that. She had a promise to keep, a promise to her sister.

She turned from the viewport. If she was to find her own way home through these strange new worlds, she needed more than the clothes Iain had lent her.

At an autovend, she bought a skyport map, a plastic disk that showed the different levels of the station as she touched the control spot. Four levels down seemed to be the main shopping arcade. It turned out to be a couple of shops selling little pots and weavings and paper souvenir books from Prairie, and one place where she could buy clothing. She bought trousers that fit properly, two tunics, a pair of soft boots, ship slippers. The prices stunned her, but the shop's attendant appeared genuinely shocked when Linnea tried to bargain. She paid without further question. There wasn't enough for a fare home even to begin with. She would have to find work.

And then there was nothing to do but go back to the room in the hostel. There was still a chance he would return, after all; she could ask him to lend her the fare. Or—or they could talk, at least. They could try again to understand each other. His people had cast him out; she shouldn't be surprised that he couldn't understand about family, about promises to family.

Though there was more at stake than family. Other people, other faces—Omoi, Naman, Kwela . . . Uneasily, she pushed the thought of them away.

She was eating a bowl of noodle soup for supper, in the hostel's tiny dining room, when Iain returned. The other two diners, a couple huddled at the end of the table, who had been whispering the whole time they ate, broke off and stared at the room's doorway.

She turned, and stared, too. Iain stood there, but not the Iain she had thought to see. His hair gleamed, pulled back into a tight braid once more, and he wore the severe black of a working Pilot Master.

It cut to her heart, to see him as she had first seen him. To see what he was once so proud to be.

She stood up slowly. He was looking at her seriously, soberly. "Linnea. Will you come with me?"

As the others watched in obvious horrified wonder, she left with him. He led her to their room.

As soon as the door was sealed behind them, he began to unbraid his hair. "Help me with this," he said. "Please." She heard the desperation in his voice.

She helped him as she once had, helped him out of the Pilot Master's clothing, into the plain serviceable civilian clothes he had worn this morning. "Are you all right?" She tried to keep her voice level, not let him guess how worried she had been—how glad she was now, to see him. And why was that, what was he to her? "Where were you?"

He sat down heavily on the end of the bed. "I had to make sure the ship's repairs and refueling were complete," he said. "And then I made a recording for the commnet."

So soon? Now? *Oh, Iain.* "You mean you've told them—"

"Everything," he said. "The Line. The Cold Minds. Fridric's plan. What was done to Freija and—why it had to be done."

"And who you are," she said.

"And who I am not." His face was lined with tiredness. "Did I do right, Linnea? I am not so sure as I was."

She folded her arms tightly across her chest. "I—didn't know it had to begin now," she said. "Here."

"You must see," he said, looking off at something far away, "that we have no time to waste. The sooner the word begins spreading, the less time my uncle will have to prepare. I outlined the truth of the threat of the Cold Minds, of my uncle's plan to abandon the smaller colonies, and—and the truth about his ancestry and mine. I sent it to every news organization on Prairie, to major organizations on every other world, to public discussion areas—everywhere I could think of. It is embedded in the traffic for every world."

Almost against her own will, she sat down beside him. "Won't the Council block it?"

"They cannot," he said. "Commnet ships are equipped to carry traffic, not to manipulate it. It's isolated under seal in transit; we cannot access it ourselves. We are under oath not to tamper with it."

"That wouldn't stop Fridric."

"Fridric is on Nexus," Iain said. "By the time the message propagates that far, by the time my—my brothers understand what I've done, the news will be everywhere. They will never be able to block it or suppress it."

She sat for a while, thinking. "What will people do?"

"Panic, I think." He rubbed his eyes. "They will demand answers. Demand their rights."

"And get them?"

He looked at her, sadness clear in his eyes. "Not without a fight."

"And there can't be a fight when only the Pilot Masters have power," she said bleakly.

"We will correct that," he said. "You and I."

She looked away. "At least—it's done."

"Yes," Iain said. "I've completed my father's dishonor."

Slowly, almost reluctantly, she took his hand. There was nothing she could say, nothing else she could do.

"And now," Iain said, "we must leave." She felt his gaze on her. "Linnea. Please. Come with me."

She looked up at him, tried to speak, could not.

"Please come," he said again. "The Hidden Worlds need you. And we must go tonight."

"Tonight?"

"Now," he said. "You know what will happen, now that this message is public on Prairie."

"People will be angry," she said slowly.

"If there are riots," he said, "I could be arrested for inciting them. Held for months. We must go."

She tightened her hold on his hand. "Please. Let's go to Santandru. Let this—let the word spread. I need to know that Marra is all right."

"No." He looked at her, his eyes dark with distress. "Linnea, I promise you, I will take you there. Someday. But not first. Not when the risk is so great, and before we have even begun our work." His gaze at her was steady. "The message I published will not be enough. It may bring a few others of the Line to our side, and that will help, but—we have to find new pilots. We have to teach them the Line's secrets. And there are so few who can do this work. Who will be willing to do it."

"I know," she whispered.

His voice strengthened. "So will you come?" For the first time it seemed to Linnea that he was genuinely asking: asking without certainty of her answer. "Please, Linnea. Come with me. Not just to learn piloting, but because—because—"

"Why?"

"Because I need you," he said simply.

She let go of his hand and stood up. She was shaking. "You need me," she said flatly, looking away. "Because I'm a pilot, you need me. For your plan."

"I do," he said, his voice harsh with strain. "It's true. But it's much more than that." He took a steadying breath. "*I* need you."

She would not look at him, at his face. "Don't say that. I won't help you pretend anything, not for all the people in the Hidden Worlds. Not even if it's for my sake."

He swung to his feet, faced her, gripped her arms. "I'm not pretending anything."

"I am a pilot," she said slowly. "You need me for this work of yours. You think it's some kind of miracle, that I have this mysterious gift, the only gift your people care about. Well, it's just as much a miracle that you have it, don't you see? You don't need *me* to show that people outside the Line can pilot. You're proof of that yourself."

His expression fierce, he shook his head. "How can I make you understand? Yes, we have work to do, and we need every pilot, everyone who has the gift and can be trained. But—" His hands tightened on her arms. "But even if you were not a pilot at all, I would still need you. You are my hope. I will not leave you. Not ever."

She looked up into his dark, serious face, and she went still.

Far inside, far below the darkness that scarred her mind, she felt her heart shift—change. . . .

She said cautiously, "That is what you really want? To be with me? Even though I can't—I may never be—what I was to you?"

"I do," he said. "You're why I can dare to do this. We can dare it together." He touched her cheek. "It will be dangerous at best. But we will face the danger together. And at worst—we'll be together when it ends."

Her breath caught. *Together.*

It was enough, for now. She looked up at him, not with joy, but with a somber acceptance. Gently he bent down to kiss her. And she did not turn away.

TWENTY-FIVE

Late at night, in his private chambers on Nexus, Fridric faced his son for the first time since his return from Freija. The boy looked better: stronger than before, despite the wound from which he appeared to have recovered so quickly. Perhaps it was true that he had given up the spiderweave. But even so—"You failed," Fridric said softly. "They escaped. Their ship was seen, its initial vector tracked—"

"I know, Father," Rafael said. He looked steadily into Fridric's eyes, as he had never done before, never in years. His blue eyes were beautifully clear, the pupils very black.

"Injured or not, you should have pursued them," Fridric said. "With the help you could call to yourself, you would have tracked them down in time, and taken them."

"I was wounded," Rafael said. "The search can be done at any time, by others. It was more important that I come here."

Fridric snorted. "To report your failure?"

"If you command it of me, of course, I will go after them now," Rafael said. "But my wish is to be here on Nexus." He looked earnestly at Fridric. "To be at your side, Father. To serve you."

Fridric shook his head slightly, studying the boy. Always before he had been restless during their talks, in haste to get on with his own plans and pleasures, shifting in his chair. Now he sat perfectly still, an outward model of courteous patience. "You have changed," Fridric said, marveling.

The blue eyes did not waver. "Yes. I have changed."

The wound, perhaps. Pain had done this, brought the boy out of his selfishness—just in time. Fridric looked away, frowned, finally said, "Very well. Stay here with me. These are dangerous times. I need someone whom I can trust absolutely."

"I know," Rafael said, and smiled.

"If word should escape about the threat of the Cold Minds—if that boy talks—"

Rafael was still smiling. "I understand perfectly. I will help you to discredit those stories. And to prevent their spread, of course."

"Of course," Fridric echoed. How strange this was. And yet, had he not always been certain that in time Rafael would see reason? Would see where the profit truly lay? Had he not always hoped for this moment?

"Very well, then," Fridric said, and reached across the desk to grip his son's cool hand.

How glad he was, now, that his son had returned alive from Freija.

What a gift it would be, in the struggle to come, to have at his side a man he could trust with anything.

TWENTY-SIX

I n her dream, Linnea flew. She flew beside Iain, their arms outstretched, their hands clasped. They flew through water, or air—she could not tell. The jewel-colored fish were winged and sang like the birds in stories; the bright trees swayed with the grace of seaweed. And she and Iain flew so fast, so fast, hand in hand through depths of blue clarity. In the dream the sky and the water were the same; she knew that this was important, a truth she had been seeking all her life.

She woke in the embrace of otherspace, and felt again its eerie, shifting beauty, rejoiced again in the freedom she felt there. She was learning to understand it now, to use it; she was beginning to be able to sense the ship as clearly as she sensed Iain's mind, there with her. They did not need to speak, now. She felt him there, over and around and below her. She felt his strength and knowledge, guiding her as she learned. She trusted his judgment—trusted *him*.

Riots had broken out on Prairie, as Iain had feared;
they'd heard the news as they were breaking orbit, just
ahead of the portmaster's angry order for their arrest. The
message Iain had made would travel ahead of them everywhere, propagating with every jumpship voyage. By the
time Iain and Linnea reached their next port, Terranova,
everyone there would have seen it. People would be waiting for them. Some to blame them, or arrest them, or attack
them; some to help them, and to learn.

Linnea stretched out with her mind, saw otherspace
swirl and coil around her thought, felt Iain's pleasure at her
progress.

She could not hide her fear for her home, her longing
for her family, from Iain. Despite all his warnings, she
knew that she must return there, and soon. Marra might not
understand what Linnea was now, what she must now become; but Linnea would keep her promise. Danger might
wait on Santandru. But there was danger everywhere.

For this moment, though—she had much to learn, much
to do. Much, soon, to teach, side by side with Iain: her
hope, and, for now, her home. They flew on, enfolded,
toward the new world they would build together.